Come Back *Tomorrow*

Embrace Tomorrow
Duet – Book 1

AMY ARGENT

Turning Tree
Press

ISBN (paperback): 978-1-7369405-0-1
ISBN (e-book): 978-1-7369405-1-8

Cover design by Jada D'Lee Designs
Illustrations and Turning Tree Press logo by Jared Pace
Edited by Susan Atlas

Turning Tree Press
First Edition

For Jared, my partner on every journey
and
For everyone who's battled cancer and didn't get
the happy ending they deserved

BOOKS BY AMY ARGENT

The Embrace Tomorrow Duet

Come Back Tomorrow

Whatever Tomorrow Brings

Sometimes the bad things that happen in our lives put us directly on the path to the best things that will ever happen to us.

— *NICOLE REED*

CHAPTER I

The door has barely closed on my last patient when I hear a quiet tapping. I've already switched into chart-annotating mode, so I don't even look up as I call, "Come in." The door swings open, and I glance up to find Jenny, one of my best friends and a nurse on the oncology floor, leaning against the doorway.

I grin up at her but then continue with the notation I'm making. I don't want to forget the exact words my last patient said regarding finally coming to terms with his wife's death. "What's up, Jenny?"

"Hey, Tori, I have some work for you."

"On your floor?"

"Yes."

Sighing, I pause in my notation. I love my job at the hospital. I've been a practicing psychologist here for six years, and I get a great deal of satisfaction from working with my patients, particularly when I'm able to help families through the grieving process after losing a loved one. But I have another job, mostly in my off-hours. About two years ago, I overheard a few of the nurses talking about a terminal patient on the oncology floor who had no family coming to see him, and I knew I had to meet him. Over the next few weeks, we formed a friendship, and I was able to help him find some happiness in the last days of his life. After that, I made it a point to ask the nurses to tell me when they had a patient like that who got no visitors, and the rest, as they say, is history. I am now the go-to psychologist when a terminal patient with no family is discovered, and I've made it my mission to offer them friendship and comfort at a time when they are most in need. It's work I feel compelled to do, but I'm not taking any new patients at the moment.

"Jenny . . ."

"I know! You're taking a break for a while, but this one I just couldn't let go."

Over the last year, I befriended and supported four elderly patients as they made ready to leave this world. The last died just three months ago, at about the time I broke up with Peter, my boyfriend of four years. I really thought he was the one, but we had . . . irreconcilable differences. In the weeks that followed, I was very depressed. Hell, sometimes I think I still am. My therapist told me to take a break for a while, to take some time for myself to heal from both the break-up and the amount of time I've spent face-to-face with death.

I rub my temple, trying to ease the ache that's formed there.

"What have you got for me?"

"William Everson, twenty-nine, Angioimmunoblastic T-cell Lymphoma, stage four B."

My gaze snaps to her. "*Twenty*-nine?"

Jenny just nods, her hands clasped together in front of her. Jenny has been working on the oncology floor for five years now, and I swear she's seen everything. This one has her rattled. My curiosity is piqued.

"He was brought in for a secondary infection a week ago. He was delirious at the time due to fever, but he begged us not to treat him. He has a DNR in place, but that only applies to intubation, not antibiotic treatment. Even after he was back in his right mind, he still asked us not to treat him, but that would violate the hospital's ethics code. No one has come to visit him the entire time he's been here. He wants to die, and quickly. He's completely given up." She finishes, and there are tears in her eyes.

"*Should* he have given up?" I ask softly.

"You need to see him."

After finishing my notes on the day's patients, I head up to the oncology floor. Jenny is still working, so I check in with her at the nurses' station.

"He's in room four-twelve. He was having some pain today, so he's had morphine, but I think you should still be able to talk to him."

Nodding, I head down the hall, stopping outside the door and steeling myself. Jenny's reaction to this guy has me on edge.

Not wanting to invade his privacy, I knock softly but hear no response. I don't want to knock hard enough to wake him if he's sleeping, so I open the door just a bit and peek in. If he's asleep, I'll come back another day.

Angling my head around the door, I draw in a sharp breath. Even as sick as he is, William Everson is stunning. His hair is a mass of brown, wavy locks strewn with brassy red highlights, made even brighter by the fluorescent hospital lighting. It's relatively short on the sides but long on the top and hangs down onto his forehead. He has bushy eyebrows that match his hair and a chiseled jaw that squares strongly in the front. His shoulders are broad, and although his hollowed cheeks tell me he's underweight, clearly he has a muscular build. *Oh, wow.*

Completely lost in my ogling, I push the door open a little farther, and it squeaks loudly. He whips his head up, and the greenest eyes I've ever seen meet mine. I start breathing again with a gasp and shake my head. I smile at him tentatively, and what happens next blows me away.

His gorgeous face breaks into an absolutely incredible smile. His eyes seem to turn an even deeper green, and small laugh lines appear at the corners as his cheeks pucker into a boyish grin. His full pink lips narrow to reveal perfectly straight, white teeth, and the spread of his cheeks fills in the hollows so that if not for the circles under his eyes, I don't think I'd even be able to tell he's sick.

The smile stays there as he looks me over. *He's waiting for me to say something.*

I shake my head again and take a few more steps into the room. "Hello, Mr. Everson."

"Hi there," he responds lazily, his head rolling a little to one side.

Looking closer, I notice the glassiness of his eyes. *Exactly how much morphine has he had today?* "My name is Tori. Would you mind some company?"

"If by company, you mean you, I wouldn't mind at *all*." His eyes rake over me in a way that makes certain parts tingle.

I clear my throat and sit in the chair at his bedside. "How are you feeling today, Mr. Everson?"

He grins at me again, his tongue poking out between his lips to moisten them. "Please, call me Will." Then his brow furrows adorably. "What did you ask me?"

I can't help but chuckle as I realize what kind of conversation this is going to be. He's seriously high from the morphine. "I asked how you were feeling today."

"Right . . . sorry. Well, I think I was having a crappy day, but then the nurses gave me this." He holds up the button of the infusion pump for the morphine. "And then you came by. So at the moment, I'm feeling pretty good," he says with a grin.

I can't help but grin back at him, and I also can't bring myself to ask him any serious questions. He's in too good a mood, and I don't think I would get any straight answers anyway. "I'm glad to hear that."

"You're . . . Never mind," he murmurs, blushing to the roots of his hair and looking away.

"What were you going to say?"

"I was going to say . . . you're pretty, but it didn't seem like a good idea for some reason," he answers, looking perplexed.

"That's okay. You can tell me I'm pretty."

He closes his eyes, then opens them again slowly.

"Hey, I think you're getting a little tired. Why don't you rest now, and I'll come back and see you tomorrow," I suggest, moving as if to stand up.

He grasps my hand, surprising me. His fingers are warm and soft, and my skin tingles underneath his fingertips.

I look into those impossibly green eyes, now tinged with sadness.

"Will you stay? At least for a few minutes? You're the first visitor I've had," he says softly, and I remember why I'm here. *Oh, damn.*

"Of course. You close your eyes and rest, and I'll stay right here."

"Thank you," he whispers as his eyes fall closed, finally succumbing to the pull of the morphine.

I sit there for a while, just watching him sleep. He's gorgeous. *Jesus Christ, Tori—he's dying. You're not supposed to notice how good-looking he is!* But I can't help it. He's one of the most handsome men I've ever seen despite the obvious signs of his illness.

And I have so many questions, questions that don't even come to mind for elderly patients. How did he end up in this place, seemingly at the end of his life, at such a young age? Where are his family and friends? Is he keeping them away somehow, or is there truly no one who cares about him? I find the latter *very* hard to believe. Hell, I've known him for all of five minutes, and I can already see why Jenny is taken with him. I can feel his pull on me, too, even though we just met.

He seems pretty easygoing. Maybe it won't be too hard to get to know him and find out where the people who care about him are. But God, he's so young. This is so . . . different from anything I've ever done before. I've never befriended a terminal patient who wasn't elderly. *Can I really do this?* I already suspect this will be the hardest "terminal" friendship I've ever made, but as I watch him sleep, I know I can't turn my back on him now. I already told him I'd come back tomorrow.

CHAPTER 2

I arrive at Will's room around the same time as yesterday, and this time when I knock, I hear a muffled "Come in" from the other side. I take a deep breath and brace myself for the sight of him, but even knowing how attractive he is, he still takes my breath away. Again, bright green eyes meet mine, but today they're sharp and clear, and the creases at the corners that appeared as laugh lines yesterday are now more firmly etched. His skin is pale, almost gray, making the hollows of his cheeks and the circles under his eyes even more noticeable. It's clear just to look at him that he's very unwell. What a difference a day makes.

His lips curve into a faint smile, but it doesn't reach his eyes, and there's a slight wrinkle in his brow.

"Hello again," I say brightly, but I stop as the wrinkle deepens. "I'm going to guess by the look on your face that you don't remember talking to me yesterday."

His eyes narrow. "That was you?"

I nod. "I'm Tori."

He closes his eyes, huffing out a breath. "I was in a lot of pain . . . yesterday . . . so they pumped me full of morphine." He doesn't seem to be able to breathe deeply enough to speak a full sentence. "I didn't realize . . . you were real. I thought . . ."

"You thought . . . ?"

"I thought you were an angel." His cheeks color as he looks away. But his gaze soon returns to mine, and this time it holds suspicion. "Why are you here?"

"I wanted to see how you were doing. I came to see you yesterday, but as you said, you were a bit out of it, so I told you I would come back today."

"But . . . why?" He repeats his question, the smile fading from his face. "Do you work . . . in the hospital?"

"Yes, I do," I reply, holding firmly to his gaze because I know what's going to happen next. "I'm a clinical psychologist—"

"Oh God!" he exclaims, shaking his head. "This is because I tried . . . to refuse treatment . . . isn't it? Now the doctors think I'm . . . not right in the head. I have the right to decide . . . how I want to spend . . . what remains of my life! No one . . . can take that . . . away . . . from me!"

He tries to take a few deep breaths, but he just can't do it. His face scrunches in pain as his arm flattens the sheet to clutch over his now visibly distended abdomen. "Fuck!" he swears, as a pained grunt escapes him.

His reaction and the pain it's causing him hit me like a bucket of cold water, and I freeze, wide-eyed. Rattled by his inability to catch his breath, I move toward him. "Do you need me to—"

"I'm . . . all right." He pants, raising a hand to stop me as he cradles his belly.

Oh my God. How did this go so horribly wrong? "Mr. Everson, I'm not here because of anything you did, and I'm not here to interrogate you! Please, try to calm down. No one is going to take anything away from you." I take a few more tentative steps toward his bedside, my hands raised in supplication.

"I didn't mean to upset you. Please, just let me finish."

His eyes remain closed, but his breathing slows, and he makes no move to object.

"I'm a clinical psychologist here at the hospital, but I'm not here in an official capacity. Someone brought your situation to my attention, so I came to see if you might want a little company."

"My . . . *situation*?"

"Yes. Your cancer is terminal, and you've been here for a week and have had no visitors."

"Is that a crime?" His green eyes pin me, daring me to answer.

"No, but no one should have to die alone."

"Everyone dies alone."

"Yes, in the strictest sense, we do. But until that last moment, no one *has to* be alone, and I don't really think anyone should be."

"So that's why you're here? Pity? Or am I some sort of . . . psychology project?"

I sigh. "No, Mr. Everson, you're not a project, and I'm not here to pity you."

I decide to come clean. Most patients never really ask why I show up. They're just grateful to have me, but Will obviously needs a thorough explanation. "One of your nurses, Jenny, is a friend of mine, and she's concerned about you. The nurses know me, and they know I've befriended certain patients and been there for them when they really needed someone. Jenny asked me to come and meet you."

"What if I *want* to die alone?" he asks, but the fire is gone from his eyes. He closes them wearily, and it occurs to me that maybe he's had as much as he can take today. In all honestly, so have I.

"I can see that you're tired, and I've upset you. I'm not going to ask you any questions, but with your permission, I'd like to come back to see you again. I'm not asking anything of you other than to tolerate my company, if you're up to it. Can I come back tomorrow?"

He tries to draw a deep breath, but it catches before he's able to fill his lungs, and even though he isn't focused on me, I see desperation and despair in his eyes. He's going to say no, and there's no way I can let him. I can't let him choose to die alone.

"Please?" I whisper, allowing my clinical façade to drop and tears to well up in my eyes.

He closes his eyes and gently nods his head, and I turn on my heel and leave the room before my tears can fall.

As I walk down the hall, though, I start to fall apart. *Jesus Christ, what the hell just happened in there?* I can't lose my professional detachment regarding Will. Not now—not before the work is done. I always lose it in these relationships, but usually it happens on the day the patient dies or very close to it. Why, then, am I standing here crying on the first day I've really talked to him?

Maybe it's because Will is different; the other patients I've befriended have been older and at least somewhat accepting of what was happening to them. The young man I just left is unprepared and terrified. And unlike the others who had no friends or family left, Will is *choosing* to be alone.

The memories fly through my mind unbidden, and regret slides up the back of my throat like bile, to choke me. I thought it had been long enough, that all this was behind me. *Oh God, can I really handle this?*

I give myself a good shake and wrestle the memories back into the vault where I keep them. I can't let my own issues interfere with helping Will. My father always told me that anything truly worth having requires a lot of effort to get, and anything worth doing is never easy. Getting this man to trust me and to change his mind about being alone may be one of the most difficult things I'll ever do, but I know I have to try—for his sake as well as mine.

CHAPTER 3

As I push through the double doors to the oncology ward the next afternoon, Jenny's face lights up.

"So," she says eagerly, "how are things going with Will?"

"Well, he told me I could come back today, so at least that's something."

"That bad, huh?"

I nod. "We didn't get off on the right foot yesterday. He's going to be difficult. I can already tell."

"You can't give up on him. He's—"

I hold up a hand. "Don't tell me anything about him, Jenny."

Her jaw drops, so I hurry to explain.

"It's important that he tell me what *he* wants me to know, so I can see it from his perspective. I need to understand why he's given up and how he's gotten himself backed into this corner, all alone. I'm sure he has family and friends who would help him, but he's distanced himself from them. I need to understand why, and the only way to do that is to see it as he does. Does that make sense?"

She nods, biting her lip. "How do you know he has anyone? What if he's an orphan, or he has no close friends?"

"I'm sure he has friends or family or both because of the way he reacted when I pointed out he's had no visitors. He got so defensive, he might as well have screamed, 'I'm alone because I want to be!' He's chosen this for himself, so he needs to be the one to tell me why."

"I just . . . He needs someone so badly, Tori. I wish I could do more for him, but I don't know how."

"And that's why you came to me."

I walk around the desk and put my arm around her. "Don't worry; I'll do everything I can to be there for him. And I promise if I need any information, I'll come to you. I'm eager to learn about him, but it has to be this way."

"I understand." Suddenly, she narrows her eyes. "Are you okay doing this? It reminds me a lot of—"

"Don't, Jenny," I say, tensing. "It's fine. I can handle it."

"Are you sure? It's only been—"

"Yes, I'm sure. He needs my help, and I can't let him down. I can't fail him."

She scrutinizes me, so I do my best to look calm and collected, to convince her of something I'm not even sure of—that I can, in fact, handle this. She frowns but lets it go. "Just keep me in the loop, okay?"

"Absolutely," I tell her, giving her a squeeze before I head down the hall.

The mask of calm I'm projecting begins to crack as I approach Will's door, and nerves flutter in my stomach.

Will is obviously very ill and very afraid, and I need to gain his trust as quickly as possible. But it's more than that. Those few minutes in his room yesterday profoundly affected me in a way no other encounter with a terminal patient ever has. I was literally shaking as I left the hospital, and it wasn't just because he'd scared me half to death when he couldn't breathe. It was the depth of emotion in his eyes as he'd prepared himself to tell me I couldn't come back. It hit me like a lightning bolt, and I knew in that moment I would do anything and everything to make things easier for him.

I know I can't get involved emotionally. It's not good for either of us, and it won't help him make peace with his life. I slipped up yesterday, breaking down like that, and I have to make sure I keep my distance so it doesn't happen again.

As it had been the previous two days, Will's door is closed. I knock and hear his call to come in, and as I slowly open the door, I catch his look of surprise. *He didn't really believe I would come back today despite what I said.*

Today, he's sitting up in his bed straighter although he's still allowing the mattress to support him completely. The lines around his eyes are fainter, and his cheeks hold a little more color.

"Hello, Mr. Everson. May I call you Will?"

"Um, sure," he answers, clearly caught off guard.

I smile at him. "How are you feeling today?"

"I'm fine."

Bullshit. I stare back, knowing he's lying through his teeth.

His cheeks begin to color as he looks down. "Well, better than yesterday and the day before anyway. The pain isn't as bad, and it's a little easier to breathe."

"I'm glad to hear that."

He looks up at me sheepishly. "I'm . . . sorry for snapping at you yesterday. I jumped all over you before you could explain, and it was rude of me. It's not a good excuse, but I've been feeling really awful since I got here, and it's got me snapping at everyone."

"It's all right. It's hard to be nice when you're not feeling well, and you seemed to be having a really bad day yesterday. I didn't take it personally."

"Thank you. But that being said, I don't think it's a good idea for you to stay," he tells me, his eyes meeting mine for a few seconds, then darting away.

"Would you mind telling me why?"

"Because I have nothing to say to you."

"Okay, you don't need to say anything."

That one catches him by surprise. "What do you mean?"

"I mean if you don't want to talk, you don't have to. I came here to keep you company—I can talk to you, or if you'd prefer, we can just sit here in silence. The point is for you not to be alone all day, not what happens while I'm here."

"I still don't think it's a good idea. Why would you want to be here? If I'm not going to talk to you—"

"You let me worry about that. Look at it this way. You're going to be here for a while, aren't you?"

He swallows thickly and nods.

"So what's the harm in spending some time with me? Have you got something more pressing to do?"

"No—"

"So if you've got nothing better to do, and I'm not asking anything of you, then what's the problem? Do you find me that distasteful?"

"No, of course not," he says in a rush, blushing fiercely. "I just . . . I want to be left alone."

His statement breaks my heart, but I know I almost have him. I hate myself for what I'm about to do, but it's necessary. "Well, you've pretty much gotten your wish since no one has come to visit you."

He flinches, and my heart breaks a little more, but driving my point home is my best chance to get him to see where he's put himself and to realize he needs me.

"Just give it a try today, please? Let me hang around for a while. I promise I won't ask you any questions, and if I bore you to tears, you can tell me not to come back, okay?"

"Suit yourself," he responds, resting his head back and closing his eyes.

I sit, gathering myself for the next phase of my plan, and my gaze strays to Will. Since his eyes are closed, I take a moment to really look at him. I was tempted to google his diagnosis last night, but I was afraid of what I'd find, and I want him to eventually tell me himself anyway. So for now, all I have to go on is what I see.

As I stare at him, my heart wants only to see the beauty there—the strong line of his jaw, the soft stubble dusting his cheeks, the amazing bronze and brown hair scattered in an unruly mop on his head—but instead, I force myself to see the signs of his disease.

He's obviously underweight—by at least thirty pounds. I note again the hollows in his cheeks and the thinness of his fingers as they lie on top of the blankets. The lymph nodes in his neck are swollen, and he swallows with an effort around their volume. Although clearly better than yesterday, his breathing is still rapid and shallow.

My eyes scan downward and land squarely on the obvious roundness of his belly. I hadn't noticed it at all the first day, and yesterday I only saw it when he clutched at his stomach, flattening the blanket against the bulge there. I wonder what the cause is.

Other than the IV in his right arm, he isn't hooked up to any equipment. I can tell he's very weak though. His every motion looks as if it costs him a large amount of effort, and I have yet to see him raise his head from the pillow supporting him.

Will winces as he reaches across his body to scratch his forearm, and his sleeve rides up to reveal a bright red rash covering his skin. He opens his eyes and follows my gaze, hastily grabbing the cuff of his pajama shirt and dragging it back down to his wrist. "Are you just going to stare at me?"

Shit. "I wasn't . . . No, I would much rather talk to you. Do you mind if I talk for a bit?"

"Whatever." He huffs and then closes his eyes again.

Time to get this show on the road.

"Well, since I'm hoping we'll be friends, I might as well tell you a bit about me. My name is Tori Somerset, and I'm thirty-two. I've worked here for six years as a clinical psychologist. I work with a variety of patients, but I specialize in helping people deal with difficult diagnoses and helping surviving family members cope with the loss of a loved one.

"I grew up in the suburbs of Seattle, living with my dad. I don't have any brothers or sisters.

"I was a good student in school, and when I was in college, I decided I was really interested in relationships and in how people respond to one another. A good friend turned me on to psychology, and it became my passion. I did my bachelor's at U Dub, and then I went to Berkeley and got my clinical doctorate. I love Washington, and Seattle in particular, so I decided to come back here to practice."

I prattle on a while longer, talking about what I do at the hospital but keeping the details to a minimum. I watch Will carefully, and I can tell he's relaxing a bit and getting used to the sound of my voice. He's following along, too. If I pause for more than a few moments, he opens his eyes and glances my way.

Eventually, his responses to my pauses become slower, and I know he's getting tired. I finish what I'm saying, and this time when he checks on me, I meet his gaze.

"Well, I think I've talked your ear off enough for one day. You seemed interested though. Can I come back and bore you with the really fascinating details, like how I met Jenny and how I managed to lose the state title game in basketball for my high school?"

He stares at me, betraying nothing.

"Come on, you know you want to know why the nurses all call me 'Tenacious Tori'."

He raises his eyebrows at that one, and the hint of a smile touches his lips.

"Can I come back, please?"

"I guess," he says grudgingly.

"Good. Then I'll see you at the same time tomorrow," I tell him, waiting until I've turned my back to let the smug grin spread across my face.

CHAPTER 4

The next afternoon, I arrive at the usual time, and when I open the door, I watch as Will's eyebrows disappear beneath the longish hair on his forehead.

"You're here," he stammers.

"Well, I said I'd come today, didn't I?"

"But, it's the weekend."

"So it is. Does that mean I shouldn't be here?"

"I just thought . . ."

"I told you I'm not here because you're my patient, but I'm getting the impression you don't quite believe me."

At least he has the decency to look sheepish as I say it, but I want to drive the point home even further.

"Do you get the weekend off from being sick?"

"No," he answers, the word filled with scorn.

"Well, then I don't get the weekend off from being your friend."

He shoots me a glance that is equal parts confusion and gratitude, but he says nothing.

"So, how was your day?" I ask, but before he can answer, I correct myself. "Oops, I said I wouldn't ask you any questions. My apologies."

A furrow appears in his brow, but he stays silent. I still want to play by the rules for now and make sure he knows I'm playing by the rules.

"My day was pretty boring. I did laundry this morning, cleaned up my apartment, then spent the afternoon on the couch in front of the TV. There is *nothing* worth watching on a Saturday afternoon, unless, of course, you're into reruns of the week's reality shows or movies from the fifties."

He smirks at me, and I get the idea he wants to comment, but he's not letting himself. So, I guess it's time to sing for my supper . . . again.

"Well, what shall I tell you about today? I know I mentioned something about high school, but who really wants to go back there after they've finished, right? I sure don't.

"So, how about if I tell you how I met Jenny—you know, the little, blonde-haired ray of sunshine who's one of your nurses? She's always been that way—hyperactive and perpetually cheerful.

"When I got to U Dub, I was this quiet, serious, introverted girl, and into my dorm room bounds this crazy extrovert who just wants to go out and party! She took one look at me and said, 'Oh, we have to get you loosened up!' You'd never know she was such a party girl to look at her now. She's toned it down a lot. Nowadays, it only seems like she's *drinking* Red Bull instead of injecting it."

Will chuckles softly, laying an arm across his swollen belly.

"She got me in so much trouble in college! She was forever trying to get me to go out, particularly on Thursday nights, and I always had tests on Fridays. I would go to the library to hide from her, but somehow she'd always manage to find me and drag me downtown with her. It's a wonder I passed any of my undergrad classes.

"She introduced me to all the typical college vices—cigarettes, alcohol, weed—"

Will's eyebrows rise.

Yes, I smoked weed—a good bit of it during college, in fact. Don't I look like the type to you?

"She even tried to get me to join a sorority. She made it in, and I didn't, but she stayed and lived with me anyway instead of moving into the sorority house. We partied our way through our first two years, but eventually, she got serious. She's really smart, so it didn't take much for her to ace a few classes and get accepted into the nursing program. We still went out a lot, but by junior year, she was studying more, too, and it helped us to become even closer friends.

"When we graduated, I went to Berkeley, and she went on to get a master's in nursing at U Dub; she worked at a few other hospitals in the area before coming here. We stayed in touch but just barely. In fact, I moved back to Seattle and started working here, and she didn't even know it until we ran into each other in the hallway!

"Our friendship seemed to pick up right where we left off, and we've stayed close ever since. She's always there when I need to talk, and we take care of each other."

I risk a glance at Will, and he's staring out the window with a wistful look in his eyes. He catches me watching and shifts his gaze downward, setting his jaw firmly. I didn't talk about Jenny as a way to get a reaction from him, but it seems to have done the job anyway. *Who is it he's longing for?*

"Well, enough about Jenny. What else can I tell you about me? My dad used to take me fishing as a kid, so I'm not one of those girly girls who's afraid of breaking a nail. While my middle school girlfriends were giving themselves manicures, I was putting worms on hooks and cleaning my dad's catches. On the weekends, we'd go out on his boat on Lake Washington, but my favorite part was the end of the day when he was cleaning his fishing gear. I used to love to go lie on the boat dock and watch the little waves on the lake. If I was really lucky, it'd be sunny, and I'd watch the sun glint off the water. It was just so beautiful and peaceful."

I stare off into space for a few moments, living in the memories, and when I come back to myself, I find Will watching me with a peculiar look in his eyes. It's a look of . . . understanding. He gets it. He has a special place or thing that makes him feel the way I'm feeling right now. Somehow, he looks surprised I've shared this. Maybe we have more in common than he thought. I grin at him, and he looks away awkwardly. It seems we're both learning a lot about each other today even if only one of us is speaking.

I continue on, telling him how I like to read spy novels and that my guilty pleasure in my spare time is knitting even though it makes me seem like a grandma. He listens thoughtfully as I tell him all about me, but he never says a word.

When it's almost time for me to go, I find myself telling him about my other guilty pleasure: football.

"I love the Seahawks. Like most men in Washington, my father's a rabid Seahawks fan, and trying to be a daddy's girl, I used to watch the games with him. When I was finally out on my own, I tried to convince myself I didn't care about the team, but dammit if I didn't manage to find a way to watch all their games anyway. When I admitted to my dad that I was a Seahawks fan in my own right, I don't think I'd ever seen him look prouder. He told me that my love of the Seahawks was the best thing he'd passed on to me, hands down."

Will chuckles, but he stops quickly and draws in a sharp breath, wrapping an arm around his distended belly. He holds his breath until the pain subsides, letting it out slowly as his muscles relax. His voice is raspy as he breaks the silence he's been keeping all afternoon. "They say laughter is the best medicine, but that really fucking hurt!"

"Why does it hurt so much?"

He looks at me pointedly as if to let me know he's on to what I'm doing, but he's going to allow it. "My liver and spleen are enlarged, and I have too much fluid in my belly. It's caused by the cancer; it's pretty painful and can make it hard to breathe. Don't you already know all this?"

"No. Why would I?"

"Because you work here. I'm sure the first thing you did was go over my chart."

"Not at all." I meet his gaze so he'll see the truth in my eyes. "I keep telling you, I'm not here in an official capacity. I don't know anything about you—well, Jenny told me your name, age, and diagnosis, but that's all."

"Even if you're not here officially, I'm sure Jenny would have given you my chart."

"No. Since you're not my patient, she can't do that. But even if she could or would have given it to me, I wouldn't want it."

"Why?" he asks, looking truly confused.

"Because I don't want to take away your choice in the matter. I came here to be your friend, and a friend would only know what you choose to tell them."

The look he gives me is unreadable, but I can see the wheels turning behind his eyes. Suddenly, he looks away, staring at the floor on the other side of the bed.

"I should get going. It's getting late, and you must be getting tired. Can I come back tomorrow?"

His gaze meets mine, and his teeth latch on to his bottom lip for a moment, but he releases it quickly.

"Yes."

CHAPTER 5

"Hello, Will," I say cheerfully as I walk into his room. Even though it's Sunday, he doesn't look surprised to see me. I guess he believed me yesterday about not having days off from spending time with him.

He looks at me but quickly bows his head. "Hi, Tori."

"What's the matter?"

"I think I owe you another apology," he says, staring down at the white blanket that covers him, his fingers playing idly over the lattice pattern of the cotton. "I don't know why you keep coming back. I'm still snapping at you and assuming you have an ulterior motive for being here, and yet all you've been is kind to me, and you've shown nothing but respect for my feelings. I don't know what to make of you."

His complete honesty takes me by surprise, and I have to bite my lip to keep the smile off my face. "Well, couldn't it just be that I'm a nice person? That I'm here with no strings attached?"

He shrugs his shoulders but winces as he does so. I wonder if there is any movement that doesn't cause him pain.

"So, what shall we talk about today?" Although the question is rhetorical, he surprises me again by actually answering.

"What happened to your mother?"

"Will," I say, unable to keep the smile off my face this time. "Did you just ask me a question?"

He grins wryly as the realization dawns on him. My answer is going to cost him something.

He seems to think about it for a moment, then sighs in defeat. "Yes, I guess I did."

"Well, in that case, I'll make you a deal. I'll answer your question if you'll answer one of mine."

He narrows his eyes, so I hurry to clarify. "I won't ask one that I think you won't want to answer. I'll ask one that gives me a little more information about you, the kind of question a friend would ask. Fair enough?"

He starts to chuckle but stops abruptly as he winces, nodding instead. "Okay, you first."

"All right. My mother left us when I was six years old. She wasn't exactly cut out to be a parent, and it pushed my folks' relationship to the breaking point."

"Did you ever see her again?"

"Sometimes." I close my eyes to block out the picture of her in my head —the last time I did see her.

"I'm sorry," he murmurs, his gaze turning soft and warm.

"It was a long time ago," I say, shaking my head. "Dad was more than enough to make up for losing her. So, is it my turn now?"

"I suppose." He concedes, but I can tell he's nervous.

I intend to keep my promise, though, and not ask any of the things I really want to know. That will have to come later. "How did you end up here?"

He blanches at the question. *Shit. That didn't come out right.*

"That's not a question I'm going to answer," he responds shortly.

"What I mean is, when were you diagnosed, and will you tell me exactly what's wrong with you?"

"That's two questions."

Damned if he isn't going to make this as difficult as possible.

"All right, so it *is* two questions, but you may well have told me when you were diagnosed if you answered the question about what's wrong with you. And honestly, I've told you my whole life story. Don't I deserve a little latitude here? It's not truly a personal question. If we were both inmates in a prison, and I asked, 'What are you in for?' would you consider that too personal?"

He can't hide the smirk on his face. "You're good at what you do; do you know that?"

"I just make rational arguments," I tell him, but inside, I'm beaming at the compliment.

"I can't argue that," he says, conceding. "Okay, then. I was diagnosed with stage two B Angioimmunoblastic T-cell Lymphoma a little over two years ago. I'd been having fevers and night sweats for weeks, and I was losing weight. Finally, when my lymph nodes swelled up, they did a biopsy and discovered the cancer.

"I had chemotherapy and went into remission, and that lasted a year. Then I started having symptoms again, and I was diagnosed with stage three B. I had chemo again, and the next remission lasted six months. Two months ago, I was diagnosed with stage four B since the cancer's now in my bone marrow, and I was given up to six months to live with no further treatment.

"I had been doing okay, but my immune system is shot, and I ended up getting an infection in my blood. I thought the fever was just one of those caused by the cancer, but it was really high. Then I started vomiting. I had decided to stay at home, but I must have called 9-1-1 when I was delirious because I ended up here.

"So now I'm on IV antibiotics for a month to try to clear up the infection. I don't know why they're bothering, really. If it's not this, it'll just be something else in a few weeks."

He tries to speak with no emotion, but there's a quaver in his voice as he gets to the end of his little speech. *Shit! Does he really have that little time left?* I've been treating this as a bit of a game, trying to get him to talk to me, trying to keep my distance, but suddenly, I realize this game is deadly serious, and the clock is running. I'm desperate to ask him where his family is and if anyone was with him through his chemo, but I know he's not ready to tell me. I try just one more question, so I can at least get an insight into his current state of mind.

"What symptoms do you have now?"

He narrows his eyes at me.

"Well, I can probably guess most of them from what you've already said, so what's the harm in telling me? In my mind, this still falls under 'What are you in for?'"

I hold my breath as I wait to see if he'll answer. Knowing what he's experiencing is key to figuring out why he's giving up and not fighting for every day he has left.

His lips twist into a sour-looking smile. "You're probably the only person on the planet who's interested in hearing this. I still get fevers and night sweats, and most of my lymph nodes are swollen and painful, particularly my neck, under my arms, and, um, down south," he says bashfully. "My spleen and liver are enlarged and painful, and I have a buildup of fluid in my belly. The cancer also causes joint pain and a rash that makes me itchy, pretty much all over. And I'm exhausted all the time. I think that's everything." He sounds as if he's just rattled off some sort of laundry list.

Oh God. I'm speechless for a moment, trying to get the barrage of emotions I'm feeling under control. I can't let him see me react to what he's said the way I feel like doing, the way I know I shouldn't feel like doing. I've dealt with this and worse many times before, but for some reason, the thought of Will going through this is making me nauseous.

"I'm sorry," I whisper, trying to fill my gaze with compassion and not pity.

I think he understands because he ducks his chin and mutters a quiet, "Thanks."

Because he asked about my mother, today I tell him the few stories I remember about her from before she left us. They're sweet memories, like her reading stories to me at bedtime and kissing boo-boos after I fell. The sentiment makes no sense in the face of the anger I feel because of everything that happened afterward, but we don't really get a say in what we remember.

After an hour, Will's eyes are drifting closed. "I think I should go. You're falling asleep."

He slowly turns his head toward me, barely opening his eyes. "Are you coming . . . back tomorrow?" he whispers, nearly asleep.

He doesn't see, but I smile so widely, I think my cheeks might split. This is the first time I didn't have to ask him if I *could* come back, and warmth flutters in my chest. "Yes, Will. I'll be back tomorrow."

"'Kay." He sighs, falling headlong into sleep.

CHAPTER 6

As I make my way out of my office, I find myself looking forward to spending time with Will. Yesterday, I didn't have to work so hard. I feel like I'm really starting to get somewhere with him, and I hope today will be even better.

When I knock on his door, there's no response, so I open it slowly, wondering if he's asleep. My mouth falls open the moment I lay eyes on him. He's lying there, eyes closed, shaking from head to toe.

"Will!"

His eyes pop open as he startles, but his gaze is dazed and vacant. He stares into space for a moment before he can focus on me.

"I'm all r-r-right," he manages to say as shivers wrack his frame. "J-just c-c-cold."

I take a deep breath as the panic recedes. I thought he was having a seizure! My chest tightens and tears sting my eyes as I hear his teeth chattering. "Here, let me get you another blanket," I say, already walking to the small cart on the other side of the room.

I pull out another woven, white blanket identical to the one that covers him, and as I turn around, I try to hide my shaking hands as I unfold it. These damn hospital blankets are horrible. I don't know how they keep anyone warm. I gently cover him, tucking it in closely around his legs and covering his arms as well. As I bring it up to his chin, my mothering instincts take over, and I put a hand to his forehead. "You're burning up!"

"It's n-nothing n-new," he explains, opening his fever-bright eyes. "The n-nurses know. It's a s-symptom of the c-c-cancer, l-l-like I told you. I'm f-feverish more often than n-not."

I've been coming here for almost a week, and I'm pretty sure he's been feverish at least two of those days, and I have no idea what's happening when I'm not here. The snapshot I'm getting in the hour or so I've been visiting each day doesn't even begin to give a complete picture of how things really are for him. I swallow thickly as my stomach does a nervous flip.

As I lift my hand, I can't help but smooth the hair back from his clammy forehead. I need to touch him. I need to do something to make him feel better. I know I shouldn't, but today? Today I honestly don't care. He leans into the touch, so I do it again. It's nothing intimate, I tell myself—just simple human comfort, and he needs it so badly right now.

"You d-d-don't have to do th-that." He stutters, pulling his chin away. He's still shivering violently, and I know it has to be causing him pain.

"I want to, if you'll let me. Maybe it will distract you," I say, continuing to run my fingers through his unruly locks.

He looks like he wants to argue, but he just doesn't have it in him. He closes his eyes and cocks his head to the side, relishing the touch.

I continue my ministrations, and after a few minutes, his shivers seem to become less violent. After a few more, they stop altogether, and his breathing evens out into sleep.

What the hell am I doing? I've touched patients before. Touch is one of the most powerful ways to offer comfort, and I have no problem with that. The problem is I think I'm comforting *me* as much as I'm comforting him. Why is everything so much more intense with Will? Is it because he's so young? Is it something else? I shake my head but make no effort to stop. His hair is so soft, like duck down. I wonder if he lost it all during his last round of chemo.

I sigh as I continue running my fingers through his hair. He was doing so well these last few days. He was still short of breath, but it seemed at least a little better, and I almost forgot how sick he is as I told him so many stories from my life. I think back to the elderly patients I've befriended and how they had good days and bad days toward the end, and I realize that before long, Will is going to come to that point if he isn't already there.

And it's a point of no return.

I close my eyes and vow to get him to answer another question for me tomorrow, so I can help him move a bit closer to being ready to let go.

CHAPTER 7

When I push Will's door open, I can immediately tell something is wrong. His eyes meet mine, and they no longer have the fever glassiness they held yesterday, but today he's wearing a nasal cannula and having a very hard time breathing.

Panic shoots down my spine as I hurry over to him. "Will, are you all right? Do you need me to call someone?"

He shakes his head slowly as he struggles to draw breath.

As I watch, it's as if he doesn't exhale at all. He only inhales in ridiculously short spurts. "What is it? Can you tell me?"

"The . . . fluid." He pants, changing his breaths to exhale each word separately. He places his hand on his distended belly; it's even more bloated than it was yesterday. "Needs . . . to . . . be . . . drained."

Oh God, this is an elective procedure. He can refuse it. With a stab of fear, I realize that this could be it right here. I haven't gotten far enough with him yet to get him to open up to me, and if he chooses to, he can suffocate right before my very eyes since he has a DNR in place. *No, dammit, no! I need more time!*

"Will, are they planning to drain it? Did you agree to the procedure?" I try to keep the panic out of my voice, but my words are rapid and high-pitched.

"Yes . . . don't . . . want . . . to . . . die . . . this . . . way." Fear shines in his eyes.

Oh, thank God! "Hang on; I'll be right back," I tell him as I whirl around and almost run from the room.

Jenny is standing at the nurses' station, and I yell to her as I fly down the hall. "Jenny! What's going on with Will? He's so short of breath, he's starting to panic!"

"Shit!" She swears as she picks up the phone, angrily punching numbers. "I've been waiting over an hour for the chief resident to get his ass up here to do the procedure! I asked Will to buzz me if it got any worse!"

"It's worse."

"Go keep him company until I get this sorted," she says, drumming her fingers on the counter as she waits for a response to her page.

I spin around and go back to Will's room and, thankfully, things are mostly as I left them, except his eyes look a little wider with panic. "Jenny and the doctor are coming. They're going to drain the fluid right away."

"Thank . . . you." He gasps as his hands ball into fists, and he fights for each breath.

I desperately want to touch him, to offer comfort in any way I can, but we just aren't at that point yet. I touched him yesterday to calm him, but I don't even know if he remembers, and now isn't exactly the right time to ask. So I stand there helplessly, watching him struggle as the minutes tick by.

After what feels like an eternity, Jenny and the chief resident finally walk in. When Jenny sees Will's panic-stricken eyes, she gasps, and the color drains from her face.

"Oh, Will, you should have called me sooner! I know I checked on you an hour ago, but this got bad really fast!"

The doctor goes right over to Will. "We need to do this procedure immediately, so I'm going to give you the brief explanation, okay?"

Will nods as his breathing becomes even more erratic.

"We're going to numb your skin and insert a large needle to draw out the fluid. You'll barely feel anything, but I'm going to need you to stay as still as possible. I know that's going to be difficult, but I need you to try. Will Miss . . . Somerset be staying?" he asks, glancing at my tag and nodding to me.

Will looks down at his swollen belly, then turns his eyes to me, and the full-blown panic I see there galvanizes me into action. "Will, you're terrified. I can see it in your eyes. I promise I won't look at you if you don't want me to. Just let me help you get through this, all right? Let me help you focus so the chief can do his job. *Please.*" *Please, please let me stay!*

He nods as his breathing turns into gasps, and I step forward and grasp his hand between both of mine. I don't even understand how he's still conscious because it doesn't sound as if he's taking in any air at all. I swallow hard, trying to regain some composure, and I do the only thing I *can* do. I talk to him.

"Will, look at me." He turns his terrified eyes to mine. "Everything is going to be all right. Just look at me, and listen to the sound of my voice. You're going to get through this. Stay as still as you can, and don't think about breathing. Think about whatever makes you happiest, and try to stay there for the next few minutes. I'll be right here. I've got you. Stay with me and everything will be okay."

For the rest of my life, I will never forget the look in his eyes as he hangs on my every word as if his very life depends on it, and it nearly does. Both of us are oblivious as Jenny preps him for the procedure. He winces as she delivers the local anesthetic, but he never looks away from my eyes. I continue soothing him softly until the doctor interrupts me.

"Right now, I need you to stay very still."

Will cries out and grips my hands even tighter as the doctor inserts the larger gauge needle, and both of us watch his fingers as he attaches a large syringe to the needle he just inserted. I nearly gasp as I look at how distended Will's belly is. He has always shielded it with the blankets that cover him, but with only the surgical drape over it, I can see the full extent of the problem that has caused this crisis. If he were a woman, I would have thought he was carrying twins. Looking angry and inflamed, the same bright red rash I saw on his arms also covers his torso. *Oh, Will.*

"I'm ... gonna ... be ... sick." He forces out the words.

I look around for a basin or something, but Jenny's shout brings me up short.

"He can't do that now!" She's unable to move from the other side of the bed because she's holding the ultrasound wand in place so the doctor can see where he's drawing the fluid from.

I grab Will's chin and raise it so he has to look at me. "No, you're not. You can't be sick right now, or it will mess up the procedure. Look at me, and breathe as slowly as you can. You can get through this. Don't look at what they're doing; look right here." I free one of my hands and bring it up to stroke his cheek. "Feel me touching you, and concentrate on that. Close your eyes if you need to, but just feel my touch on your skin, and don't think about anything else."

He closes his eyes as he swallows loudly. Over the next few minutes, I can tell he's making an effort to slow his breathing, and for the first time today, it's actually working. My own breathing starts to slow as well. I continue to stroke his cheekbone, but since his eyes are closed, I look over my shoulder to see how things are going. Will's belly is noticeably smaller. It has gone from a full-term pregnancy all the way down to a small potbelly, and I can easily see the reason. There are at least three liters of fluid in the vacuum bottle on the floor. I choke back the sob that threatens to escape.

As I look over at him, Will opens his eyes very slowly. He's beyond exhausted, but the panic is gone, and his breathing is slow and regular. I move my hand up to brush his hair back, and as he did the day before, he leans into my touch. He closes his eyes again wearily.

There's a flurry of motion at my side, and I realize the doctor is removing the needle and dressing the puncture wound. Jenny has shut down the ultrasound, and she's cleaning up the equipment from the procedure.

"You did it," I whisper. "The doctor is all done, and you can rest now."

His eyelids flutter, but he's so wiped out, he can't even lift them. He squeezes my hand gently, and as he surrenders to sleep, the sound of his deep, even breathing is music to my ears.

Taking a deep breath of my own, I slowly disentangle my shaking fingers from his and place his hand on the mattress. I need to leave this room *right now* before I fall apart.

I make it as far as the hallway outside his door before I have to lean up against the wall as my knees buckle. I slide down slowly until I'm curled in a ball, my knees hugged to my chest. I'm hyperventilating; all I can think about is how close I came to losing him today. I can't lose him. I just can't. Not like this, not before I can help him. *No!*

A few minutes later, or maybe it's a long time, Jenny pulls me into her arms.

"It's okay. You were fantastic. You really helped him through today."

"Jenny, I don't know if I can do this! I'm so . . . God, I don't know what I am, but it's totally different from any of the other times I've done this. I can't bear to watch him go through this! How do I help him when I feel like I need help myself?"

"Oh, honey, you care about him just like I do. You've lost your detachment, and you need support too," Jenny says, giving me a squeeze.

I turn my head to grin wryly at her. "Who's the psychologist here?"

She snorts a laugh, shaking her head. "You know I'm right."

"Yes, dammit, you're right, but how the hell did I get so attached in only a week? He hasn't even told me why he's alone yet, and already I feel more bound to him than I have to any of the other patients I've helped."

She shrugs. "Now you know why I came to see you. I don't know how he does it, but he did it to me too. There's something special about him, something that shouldn't be leaving this world so soon."

Her words send a chill down my spine. She's right, as usual. Will *is* special, and I'm sure I don't even know the half of it yet. But I have to find out. Soon.

CHAPTER 8

After the events of yesterday, I want to see Will first thing in the morning, but I resist the temptation. I make it until lunchtime, but by then, not knowing how his day is going is driving me insane, so I call Jenny to make sure he's okay. She can't give me any details about his condition because I'm not family, but she gives me a curt "yes" and tells me he was asking about me earlier. It's enough to hold me over until I can see him in person.

As I walk through Will's door at my usual time, he smiles at me. This is the first time seeing me has evoked that kind of response from him, with the exception of when he was high on morphine, and the satisfaction I feel blooms into an excited grin. He looks tired and weak but peaceful. His hands are resting on his belly, and I'm struck again by how much flatter it is. But the best thing of all is the even rise and fall of his chest as he breathes. Every time I've visited him, he's always had to struggle to breathe.

"Hi, Tori," he says, greeting me first.

I'm thrilled by the obvious change in our usual routine. "Hello, Will. How are you doing today?"

"Much better." He smiles again, and this time, it reaches his eyes, making their emerald depths sparkle. "I'm still tired from everything that happened yesterday, but this is the best I've felt since I got the blood infection. I'm in a lot less pain, and it feels amazing to be able to breathe again."

Suddenly, he looks down, focusing on his fingers as he runs them over the weave of the blanket, which I realize is a nervous habit. "Thank you —for what you did for me yesterday. I don't think I would have made it through the day without you."

His words are so honest and sincere that they melt my heart, and I have to swallow past the lump in my throat. I take my usual seat next to his bed. "You're welcome. It was no big thing. I'm just glad I could be there for you."

"No big thing, huh?" he says, cocking an eyebrow at me. "That's interesting because at the time, I seem to remember thinking you looked as terrified as I was."

I don't like being called out, but the fact that Will feels comfortable enough with me to do it is a major step in the right direction. "Okay, so I was as scared as you were. Is that important?"

"To me it is. The fact that it scared the shit out of you, and you still stayed with me means . . ." He pauses awkwardly.

"Means what?"

"Well, it means more to me," he says quietly, his cheeks turning crimson.

Oh my.

"I'm glad you let me do it," I tell him, looking into his eyes and covering his hand with my own.

Somehow, that's more than he can handle because he looks away from me, so I pull back my hand.

He stares out the window as if he's trying to make up his mind about something, so I sit and wait patiently.

After a few minutes, he looks at me again, somber and resigned.

"I think I owe you an answer to another question. A harder one this time."

"What makes you say that?"

"Well, I still don't understand why, but what you went through with me yesterday has made me believe that you really want to be here. You want to know about me, and I've got nothing to lose by telling you."

"Okay, Will."

He draws in a deep breath, bracing himself for me to ask the all-encompassing question: "Why are you alone?" But I know he's not ready to tell me. He's maneuvered himself into this space between a rock and a hard place. If I try to take all the walls away at once, he'll fall to pieces, and he'll never see what I need him to see, that the end of his life needs to be about what he needs, not about what he can spare other people from.

So I take aim at just a piece of the puzzle. "Was someone with you when you had your chemo?"

He releases the breath he was holding in a whoosh, and I know I made the right choice.

"Yes. I had some very close friends help me through my chemo after my diagnosis and then again after my first relapse. When I relapsed this time, I decided I couldn't burden them any longer. So . . . I pulled away from them all. A few of my closest friends know I've relapsed again, but I told them other friends were looking after me, when actually, no one was."

"Do you think they'd understand your decision?"

"No, probably none of them would. But this is my problem, and I just couldn't bear to watch them suffer with me. It's bad enough that I have to go through it, but watching people I care about suffer because they feel bad for me . . ."

"So you did this for them."

"Yes."

"But what about you?"

"What *about* me? I'm going to die either way, so if I can save everyone else the pain of having to go through it with me, then it seems to me I should. Like I told you before, everyone dies alone."

He's angry about what's happened to him, but it's buried deep and tightly controlled until something makes it rise to the surface. I stare at him impassively, trying to decide my next move. He's made this decision, and he's using his anger to fuel his resolve, but what will happen when the anger runs out?

He looks down at the blanket again, biting his lower lip and scratching absently at his arm. "You've already done so much for me, but . . . I was wondering if I could ask you for a favor."

Wow, now this is progress! "Of course you can, Will. Anything."

He glances over at me shyly. "If I gave you my keys, would you be willing to go to my apartment? I was brought here by ambulance two weeks ago, and I was delirious at the time. I don't even have my cell phone. There are some things I'd like to have here, and . . . I left a friend behind."

"A friend?"

"Yes. God, I hate asking you to do this," Will says, but he takes a deep breath and plunges ahead. "I have a cat named Sebastian. I took him in off the street as a kitten the week after I was diagnosed, so he's kind of been with me through everything. I knew I might . . . disappear, so I made an arrangement with this sweet old lady who lives down the hall from me. She would check in with me every few days, and if I was suddenly gone, she'd look after Sebastian. She has a key to my place, and I'm sure she's taking care of him, but I wanted to ask you if maybe . . . if I told you where to find it, you could leave some money for her for food and for taking care of him."

Will has a cat. And he's worried about who's taking care of it despite the fact that he's terminally ill, in the hospital, and he nearly died yesterday. It's the absolute sweetest thing I've ever heard. Warmth floods through my chest as I look at him, and I'm taken aback by the strength of it. I can do more than see that the old woman is compensated. Much more.

"Of course I can do that—all of it, but . . . would it make you feel any better if I took care of Sebastian for you? I had a cat when I was at Berkeley, but she died, and I haven't gotten around to adopting another one. Just until you're out of the hospital, of course. I'm sure your neighbor is looking in on him, but at least this way, Sebastian would have some company in the evenings while you're away from him."

"You would do that?" he asks, his eyes alight with hopefulness.

"Sure, why not?"

Suddenly, the light goes out. "I can't ask you to do that. It's too much," he says, shaking his head.

"Well, you didn't ask; I offered. I wouldn't mind the company in the evenings, and cats aren't much trouble to take care of."

"Maybe I *was* right that first day," he murmurs. "You just might be an angel."

I chuckle, and he gives me a brilliant smile.

"Is that a yes, then?"

"Yes. I'm sure you and Sebastian will get on famously," he answers, his gaze warming parts of me that it has no right to warm.

"Would you like me to go today? I have time this evening if you know everything you want."

"Sure, that'd be great. I'm thinking the easiest thing to do might be to have you call me once you get there. I'm not exactly sure what state things were in when I left, so I'll probably need to give you some direction," he says, looking down.

"Don't worry about that. You've been sick, and I'm not going to inspect the place. What things did you want me to get?"

"Well, my phone and charger, and I was going to ask you to grab some of my own pajamas—these damn hospital gowns irritate the hell out of my skin and are making me even itchier—and I'd like some of my art supplies."

"You're an artist?" I ask, my eyes widening.

He grins. "Yes. I think it'll be fairly obvious once you see my place. Mostly, I'm a painter, but since I can't really do that at the moment, I'd at least like to be able to draw when I'm feeling well enough."

He's a painter? I never would have guessed that, but then again, I never put much thought into what he did before he came here. "I think that sounds like a wonderful idea. Why don't I leave you now, and I'll stop by your place on my way home. I'll get your things and Sebastian and take them home with me tonight, and then I'll bring everything by in the morning, all right?"

"Tori, thank you," he says, covering my hand with his own. "This means a lot to me, and I really appreciate your doing it."

My stomach flutters as electricity shoots up my arm. He's touching me. Why am I reacting like a schoolgirl? *Get a grip, Tori!* I smile at him sweetly, and the warmth of my blush stings my cheeks. "Think nothing of it, Will. So I guess this means I get to come back tomorrow?"

He chuckles, and for the first time, he doesn't wince. "Yes, you can come back tomorrow although I still don't understand why you want to."

"That's my business to mind," I say teasingly. "Tell me where your keys are, and give me your address. I'll go grab my stuff and head there now."

Will gives me what I need, and I hurry down to my office to grab my things. Will has an apartment on the southwest side of the city in Pioneer Square, a historic neighborhood known for its many art galleries.

I find parking in a garage around the corner and walk quickly to the address Will gave me. He lives in a five-story building that spans the block with an art gallery and a few storefronts taking up the first floor. The building is red brick and has lots of evenly spaced windows, each with a sculpted terra cotta relief underneath. It's obviously very old—maybe even a historic landmark. *Wow.*

I glance up and grin at the twin griffins carved in the pediment over-head as I push through the outer doors. I love old buildings.

I make my way up to the fourth floor, eager to learn more about the still-mysterious young man I just left at the hospital. The apartment is a gorgeous loft with hardwood floors and red brick interior walls climbing to a ceiling at least twelve feet high, but what draws my eye and has me clutching at the doorframe is the absolutely stunning picture of the nighttime Seattle skyline that takes up most of the living room wall.

As I stare, a gray blur catches my eye as it flies down the hallway, breaking the trance I'm in. I push the door closed behind me, not taking my eyes off the picture, and slowly cross the room toward it. *Oh my, it's a painting.* The detail is so precise and so realistic, I was sure it was a photograph, but as I get closer, I can see the rich strokes of Will's brush on the sky and the trees surrounding the rooftops in the fore-ground. It's breathtaking. And enormous. The painting is at least six feet tall, mounted over a low leather couch.

Suddenly, my legs give out as I remember that the beautiful, artistic soul who painted this is dying in a hospital all alone, and I'm the only person he's currently allowing to care about him. I swallow past the lump in my throat as a few tears trickle down my cheeks. *Oh, Will.*

I sit there on the floor for a moment, taking in the other artwork that adorns the walls of Will's apartment while I try to compose myself. There's a smaller painting of the skyline of a city on the water hanging over the table in the dining area and paintings of other cities and architectural structures everywhere I look. I decide that I'd better take a walk through the place before I call him in case I react to anything else the way I did to the painting of Seattle.

The loft is small but cozy, despite the hardwood floors and high ceilings. Will has scattered area rugs about the space, and the furniture is a rich cherry, the couch and chairs overstuffed and comfortable-looking. The kitchen is a galley opposite a wall of windows, with range, dishwasher, fridge, and sink all falling in line, and there are dishes strewn across the countertops. The sight contrasts sharply with the impeccable neatness of the apartment, but then I remember Will was very sick when he left here.

I proceed down the hallway to his bedroom, and I'm stunned again. Over the simple double bed with no headboard hangs a painting of San Francisco that is at least as large as the one of Seattle in the living room. The view of the city is from across the strait, and the Golden Gate Bridge is angled in from the left, twinkling streetlights dotting the span. The city is lit up against a soft purple sky, and there's something . . . inviting about it. Will has never said where he comes from, but I wonder if San Francisco is home. His bedroom is decorated with two other smaller paintings of San Francisco—a closer view of a portion of the skyline and a row of brightly colored two-story houses on a swiftly sloping street. I think it's a good bet one of them is home.

As I return to the hallway, I'm confronted by a portrait of a gray tabby cat with hazel eyes, whom I think I might be getting acquainted with shortly. Finally, I turn to the second bedroom across the hall. Canvasses line the walls, finished and unfinished work alike, the skylines of at least a dozen more cities, storefronts, landscapes, a few castles in Europe, but the piece that draws my eye is the skyline of New York City that takes up the entire right-hand wall of the room. It's unfinished.

Will has gotten about two-thirds of the way across the large canvas. Then the buildings abruptly stop. I wonder when he was last able to work on it. It's the most detailed—and the most beautiful—of his paintings I've seen yet. As I stare at it, I can almost hear the cars honking in the distance and the gentle hum of white noise that pervades all large cities.

I suddenly realize I've been here almost twenty minutes already, and Will is probably wondering why I haven't called yet. I head back to the living room, dialing the phone as I go.

Will picks up on the first ring. "Tori," he says softly, and I hear relief in his voice.

"Hi, Will. I'm at your apartment."

"Did you have any trouble finding it?"

"Nope, none at all. The building is gorgeous, and your apartment is lovely."

"How bad is it?"

I glance around the immaculate living room, unable to hide my snicker. "Bad. You're a total neat freak. I don't think I can handle it."

He chuckles. "Funny. But seriously, is it a disaster?"

"No. There are some dishes lying around that I'm going to clean up, but other than that, the place looks fine."

"You don't have to do that," he says, and I can tell he's uncomfortable.

"Don't worry about it. I'm one of those weird people with the instinctual need to set things right. If I leave these dishes here, I'm going to know they're sitting out, and it's going to bother me. I'll have to come back and do them later, so I'd rather just do them now. I won't snoop; I promise."

He chuckles again.

"Have you seen Sebastian?"

"I think he flew down the hallway as I opened the door, but I haven't seen him since."

"Okay, he'll be hiding under my bed, then. That's where he goes when he's scared. If you look in the cupboard to the left of the sink, there are treats in there for him. That should be enough to lure him out, and there's a carrier in the closet in the hallway."

"I'm sure he and I will do just fine. Where are the rest of the things you wanted?"

"Well, I'm hoping you'll find my phone somewhere in my room."

I walk back down the hall to his bedroom and find his phone on the nightstand next to the bed. It's a wonder the paramedics didn't think to grab it. "I found it. It was sitting on the nightstand."

"Okay, good. You should find some pajamas in the top left drawer of the chest."

I follow his directions and find several neatly folded silk nightshirts. "Silk?"

"Yeah," he says nervously. "It's the only thing I've found that doesn't irritate my rash, and . . . I . . . had to get shirts because it hurts too much to wear pants."

I suddenly remember what he told me about his lymph nodes "down south" being swollen and painful, and I curse myself for accidentally delving into what is obviously a very delicate subject for him. "I'm sorry, Will, I didn't mean—"

"It's fine," he says hastily. "I didn't want you to think . . . Never mind."

Time to change the subject. "You also said you wanted some art supplies?"

"Yes. I do my work in the other bedroom."

"Okay, I'm heading over there."

"As soon as you walk in, you'll see a set of plastic drawers to your left. In the top drawer, you'll find a silver tin with charcoals and pencils in it. I usually use it if I'm drawing somewhere outside the apartment."

"Got it."

"In the drawer below that, there should be a few blank, hardbound sketchbooks. If you can grab a couple of those, that should be all I need."

I look into the drawer he indicated and pull out two blank sketchbooks, one red and one black. "Okay, I think I've got it all."

"Oh, you'll need things for Sebastian too. His litter box and food and water dishes are in the kitchen. You'll find his food with the cat treats, and I keep the litter in the closet around the corner from the kitchen."

Will proceeds to tell me where to find a pen and paper, dictates a note for Mrs. Howard, his neighbor, and tells me where he keeps some cash to leave on the counter for her. "I want you to take some, too, for taking care of him."

"No, I volunteered to take him, and I'm happy to have a friend for a while."

"Tori—"

"Will, I'm here and you're there. I'm going to win this argument."

"For now." He concedes, and I swear I can see the pouty look on his face even through the phone. "Oh, and there are some toys for Sebastian in the basket next to the couch."

Did he seriously just tell me where to find toys for his cat? I smirk and wonder if I'm going to be smothered by the cuteness. "Okay," I say quickly, trying to keep the smile out of my voice.

"What?"

"Nothing! You're just very . . . detail-oriented."

"I'm sorry! I know I'm asking too much of you."

"No, it's not that at all. It's . . . cute."

He actually laughs this time, and it's a beautiful sound, right up to the point when he hisses in pain. It's the first time I've ever heard him laugh, and I know I don't want it to be the last. I also realize we were having a normal conversation for the last few minutes. He sounded relaxed and even a bit . . . happy. For a moment, I forgot what I'm doing here and the reason we know each other. For a moment, we were something else, and as I hear him clear his throat, I feel the loss of it keenly.

"Thank you, Tori, for doing all this," he says, a quaver in his voice. "It really means a lot to me."

"You're welcome. I want to be your friend, and these are the kinds of things friends do."

"Yes . . . well . . ."

"Listen, I should go round up Sebastian and get him settled at my place, and it's past your bedtime. I'll bring your things by in the morning, all right?"

"That's great. Have a good evening."

"You too. I'll see you tomorrow."

Tears sting my eyes as I hang up the phone. I've learned so much about Will in such a short time today. He told me quite a few things, but coming here and seeing the life he leads and the things he cares about have shown me a dimension of Will that I never would have seen in the hospital, a dimension I've never known for any of the other terminal patients I've befriended. I'm grateful and heartbroken all at the same time.

I shake myself, looking up at the clock on the wall and realizing it's already almost eight, and I have a lot of work to do. There's no way I'm leaving Will's apartment as I found it for him to clean up if . . . when he returns.

By the time I'm finished and ready to tackle Sebastian, it's past nine o'clock. He's right where Will said he'd be, sitting like a sphinx directly under the center of the mattress.

"Hey, Sebastian, your buddy Will sent me to be your friend for a while. He wishes he could be here himself, but I'll take good care of you until he comes back, okay?" I place a treat on the carpet in front of me. Slowly, he shimmies toward me and ducks his head to sniff my offering. I offer my hand as well, and apparently, I pass inspection because he comes out from under the bed and sits down in front of me to eat his treat. I caress his downy head and scratch behind his ears.

He's as beautiful as the portrait in the hallway, his intelligent, hazel eyes sizing me up as I offer him affection. He's all smooth and sleek, gray fur with a darker gray pattern of tabby stripes with white socks on each of his paws, the color going a bit higher on the hind ones. As I continue to scratch, he rolls over and offers me his belly, purring deeply as he arches his back. Oh yes. Sebastian and I are going to get along just fine.

A few more moments and he allows me to pick him up and put him in the carrier, and then I gather everything up to head back to my car. Not for the first time, I think about Will sitting alone in his hospital room, and I hope what I've done today will make things a little easier for him.

CHAPTER 9

The next morning, I go straight to Will's room to drop off the things he asked for. I've also brought him a gift of sorts. After I saw him have chills with his fever the other day, I went through my afghan stash and picked one out for him. It's a beautiful basket weave, and the soft, forest green color reminds me of his eyes.

I slip into the room, figuring he'll still be asleep, and I'm proven right as I listen to his soft, even breathing. I put the afghan and his nightshirts down on my usual chair and lay the art supplies and his phone on top.

As I turn to leave, a soft, sleepy voice calls from behind me.

"Hey."

"I didn't mean to wake you," I say as I turn, grinning as I look at his sweet, smiling face. I know he has to lie on his back and can't move around very much because of the various parts of him that are swollen and painful, but somehow, he apparently still manages to have spectacular bedhead in the morning. His hair sticks out in every direction—not long enough to be truly curly, but far from straight. I can't help but chuckle.

"What?"

"You have a nice morning look."

His runs his hand self-consciously through his hair, and his blush is adorable. "That's it; pick on a guy the moment he wakes up."

I bite my lip so hard, I almost go clean through. Will is teasing me. Now that he's accepted I want to be here, he's willing to lower his guard with me—well, most of it anyway.

His brow furrows as he catches the vibe I must be sending. "What is it?"

"Nothing, I—I brought everything you asked for."

He looks at the pile I placed on the chair. "What's that on the bottom?"

"Oh, I brought an afghan for you that I made. Those damn hospital blankets are so thin, and I know you sometimes get chills when you're feverish. I thought it might help to keep you warm."

I hold it out to him, and he lays his hand on it, caressing it gently with his fingers. His teeth grab his bottom lip, and he swallows hard. When he finally looks at me, his eyes are soft and warm. His smile makes my heart skip a beat. "Thank you, Tori. This is beautiful. You made it?"

I smile and nod.

"I really appreciate it. It's cold in here sometimes even when I'm not having chills, so I know I'll get a lot of use out of it." He begins to unfold it, then looks at me again. "Would you?"

I take the afghan from his hands and spread it over his legs for him, pulling it up to just below his waist.

"It really is beautiful work. It's the nicest gift I've gotten in a long time."

My heart surges in both happiness and sorrow. It's criminal that he's not surrounded by people who are taking care of him like this, but I'm thrilled I've made him happy and that he's letting me do things for him. "You're welcome."

The moment stretches as we look at one another, but it becomes too intense, and he looks away.

"How's Sebastian?"

I smile as I think about the little furball who has already taken over my apartment, and I imagine Will petting him and smiling. He said he found Sebastian the week after he was diagnosed—I wonder how much hell that cat helped him get through.

"Tori?"

I startle, blushing as I realize I'm sitting here daydreaming about Will and his cat while I'm sitting in the same room with him.

"Sorry. I was just . . . Never mind."

He grins, and it's sweet and warm and reminds me of that first day I met him. *Is it hot in here?* I know it is because I'm blushing, and . . . my cheeks heat even more, and I clear my throat. *What the hell is going on?*

"He's doing just fine. I got him out from under your bed with a treat last night, and he warmed up to me pretty quickly and let me put him in the carrier."

"Wow, I knew he was a ladies' man, but that's quick even for him."

"He seems comfortable in my apartment too. He sniffed around for a while, but when I headed for the bedroom, he seemed to know it was time to settle down, and he curled up on the pillow beside me."

Will snorts. "Either you managed to charm him, or he's getting soft in his old age. It took him two weeks to get up the courage to join me on the bed after I took him in."

"You said you found him on the street?"

"Yeah. He was a few months old at the time, and I kept seeing him around the front steps near my building. When I first saw him, he looked as if someone had been taking care of him, but he got scruffier and thinner as the weeks went by, so I knew he'd been abandoned. And one day I just decided to take him up to the apartment with me."

"And that was right after you were first diagnosed?"

He looks at me from the corner of his eye. The ice is thin here; I need to tread carefully.

"Yes. I was still trying to come to terms with things, and I needed . . . a distraction. Sebastian gave me something to focus on besides myself, and I think it helped me."

"I'm sure it did. And you helped him too."

"Oh, he repaid me plenty for taking him in. He's very affectionate for a cat, and he'll actually come when I call him. I had lots of rotten days during my chemo when I was too tired or sick to do anything, and he would come and sit on the bed with me and let me pet him. I owe him."

"Well, I'll be sure to take extremely good care of him," I say, picking up his cell phone.

"I wasn't messing with your phone or anything, but I thought you might like to have this." I pull up the shot I took of Sebastian this morning and show it to him.

His smile lights up the room and fills me with so much happiness, I can barely contain it.

"Aww, there's my boy! Thank you so much for taking this!"

"You're welcome. I wish I could bring him to see you, but since I can't, I can at least send you pictures."

"Really, thank you," he says again, his green eyes capturing mine and holding them.

I swallow, my mouth suddenly dry. "Well, I should go for now, but I'll come back this afternoon after my last patient, all right?"

"Yeah, that sounds good."

When I return to his room around four o'clock, Will is wearing one of the nightshirts I brought. He looks like he's had a good day; there's a bit of color to his cheeks, and the midnight blue of his shirt seems to bring out the bronze highlights in his hair.

And he's drawing in the red sketchbook I brought for him. He has his table across his lap, but set high enough that it's not touching his belly, and the book is resting against his chest and leaning against the table so he can work at an angle, like he's using a drafting table or easel. He quickly closes it up, but it reminds me of the paintings in his apartment.

"Hi, Will."

"Hey."

"I see you're already using everything I brought."

"Yeah, I'm much more comfortable and a lot less bored," he answers, smirking as he rests his hand on the sketchbook. "So . . . can you stay for a while?"

"Of course I can. How is today different from any other day?"

"Well, I just thought . . . it's Friday night . . ."

"And?"

"And, well, you know, I thought you might have something . . . else to do."

I stare at him quizzically. *Something else to . . . Hold up! Did he just ask me if I have a boyfriend? It was kind of roundabout, but . . . No, he's dying of cancer. He's not thinking about me that way.* But I fully answer his question anyway.

"No, I don't have any plans tonight. I'm not dating anyone right now, and I don't go out that often. So you're stuck with me."

He blushes, and I think I see a gleam of satisfaction in his eye. *What the—*

"So my place was really okay last night?" he asks, and visions of Will's apartment flood my mind.

"Will, your paintings are absolutely fantastic!" I gush as I sit down in my usual chair.

The proud smile that spreads across his face and the ruddiness of his cheeks make my own smile grow even wider. "The amount of detail in them is just incredible, and they're so realistic!"

"Thanks," he says softly.

"I mean it; you're an incredibly talented artist. How did you learn to paint like that?"

"I didn't. I just . . . knew. Same as how one day you start walking and talking; I started drawing and painting. I didn't learn that much in art school. I went because I had to, but it was easy because I somehow just knew already."

"What you do is amazing."

Will blushes, shaking his head. "See, now I think what you do is amazing. You talk to people and help them sort out their lives, make them feel better. You have an impact on people, and they're better off for knowing you."

I gape at him, wide-eyed.

"What I do is selfish. I paint because of how it makes *me* feel."

"Oh, but Will, your work makes people happy! When I walked into your apartment, I loved that picture of Seattle, but when I got close enough to realize it was actually a painting, I was completely floored."

"Really?"

"Yes, it's breathtaking. And the fact that you're able to do that without even thinking about how it affects other people makes it even more amazing."

"I never really thought about it that way. I paint what makes me happy, and I guess I just hope there's someone else out there who sees what I see in it."

"And what is it you see when you paint a skyline like the one that hangs in your living room?" His brilliant green eyes pierce me as if he's trying to figure me out, and suddenly I'm unsure. "You don't have to tell me," I say quickly.

"No, I . . . You're the first person to ever ask that question. I wasn't expecting it." He takes a deep breath—because he can now—and his stare is unfocused, as if he's picturing the painting in his mind.

"I see . . . life. There's nothing more alive than a city. It teems with it. And there's an energy to it, an excitement. When I paint all the windows in those buildings, I imagine the events of life that are playing out behind them: family dinners, first kisses, birthday parties. It's like there's a whole world in each one, and they all just sit side by side, going on day after day.

"It also reminds me of home. I grew up in San Francisco, and when I look at my skyline paintings, I can hear the sounds of the city in my head."

I smile, remembering my own thoughts when I was in his apartment. "You seem to paint mostly nighttime skylines."

"Yes, I have a few reasons for that. Aesthetically, I think it's prettier to paint all the bright lights, but it goes back to what I said about energy. The feel of a city is different in the evening. People are home from work; some are going out. The evening is when most people truly live their lives. And I like the smell of the city in the evening. I have so many memories of being outside on summer nights—the smell of food grilling, seeing people out enjoying themselves—those are the places I go when I paint a skyline."

I stop breathing as he finishes his explanation. Will is as beautiful on the inside as he is on the outside. He's just so . . . deep. I can't believe he shared all that with me after all the time it took me to get him to answer a simple question. But I realize that the Will I saw before wasn't the real one—*this* is the real one. The *real* Will is much more open—he's as willing to wear his heart on his sleeve as he is to paint it onto a canvas. We just met under the wrong circumstances—in a situation where he felt he needed to protect himself and his decisions. My chest tightens and I swallow hard.

"Wow."

His gaze snaps back to me, and he blushes. "Well, you asked."

"Yes, I did, and now I understand so much more about your work. Thank you."

He smiles a bashful little smile and ducks his chin.

"I can't imagine doing what you do. I'm so right-brained; I don't have a creative bone in my body."

"Oh, I'm sure that's not true," he says with a disbelieving grin. "Everyone is creative in some way. Maybe you just don't know what it is yet, or you don't realize that something you're doing is creative." He pauses for a moment. "Your knitting is creative."

"Not *really*," I say, shaking my head. "It's just a bunch of yarn I weave together. Anyone can do that."

"But are you the one who picks out the colors of the yarn, and do you decide what pattern to use?"

"Yes—"

"You see? That's creative! You're making something no one ever has before and using your own ideas to do it. That's the definition of creativity."

Warmth fills my chest, and I blush. How in the hell did he take my knitting abilities and raise them up to the same level as his incredible artistic skills? On a rational level, I know it's complete bullshit, but on an emotional one? He just made me feel talented and special.

57

"I still think you're a hell of a lot more creative than I am. Have you been to all the places you've painted?"

"Most of them. There are one or two skylines I've done from pictures, but I don't think they're as good as the ones of places I've been. Every city has a distinct feel to it, and I try to capture that when I paint. And the only way to get that feel is by going there and feeling it for yourself."

I think back to the paintings in his studio; not all of the cities were in the US. "What about the paintings of Paris, and the castles?"

"Actually, most of those were painted on location," he admits, and I gasp.

"Really? Wow! When were you in Europe?"

He hesitates, pursing his lips, and a shadow of pain crosses his face.

"I'm sorry. I didn't mean to make you uncomfortable. We can talk about something else."

"No," he says firmly. "I feel like I should tell you . . ."

"You don't have to tell me because you feel like you owe me something. You don't owe me anything, Will."

"No, it's more than that. I want to tell you. I don't have a lot of choices left to me, and if telling you about my life will make you happy, then I want to. And . . . I want you to know me. You've given of yourself every day you've come here, and I want to give to you too."

I'm . . . stunned. He really *has* been doing a lot of thinking. We're not all the way there, but I'll take it.

I reach over and cover his hand with mine, and this time, he doesn't seem overwhelmed. His skin is warm underneath my fingers; he's probably running a low-grade fever, but at least it doesn't seem to be bothering him. I rub my fingers over his knuckles and feel the softness of the skin there. "Thank you, Will. I do want to get to know you."

"So, you asked about Europe . . ."

I nod, and although I stop rubbing my fingers over his, I leave my hand there.

He looks down at our hands, then turns his upward underneath mine and laces our fingers together so he's now holding my hand. He glances up at me, asking "Is this okay?" with his eyes, and I nod as I smile at him. He squeezes my fingers, and my chest tightens.

"I stayed in San Francisco after high school and went to the California College of the Arts for my art degree. While I was there, I made a lot of good friends, and after graduation, a bunch of us decided to go bum around Europe before we really started on our careers.

"It was fantastic. Paris, Milan, Venice, Florence, Rome, Madrid—we went wherever the wind blew and saw all there was to see. We went to the Louvre, the Musée d'Orsay, the Uffizi Gallery, the Prado. And when we were done, we settled in France to paint. My friend, Jason, and I rented a house and stayed there for almost a year. His specialty is painting landscapes, so he had plenty to work with, and I traveled around and painted the castles. It wasn't until later that I discovered my true passion was cities. Toward the end of our time there, I painted Paris, Milan, Madrid, and Vienna, but I know so much more now. I'd give anything to go back and paint London, Frankfurt, and Rotterdam."

I hear the longing in his voice, and I bite my lip, knowing he's never going to get there. He'll never see those places, and they'll never flow from his brush onto a crisp, white canvas. *Fuck.* "Where did you go after Europe?"

Will closes his eyes for a moment before he answers, and I wonder if he's thinking the same thing I was or if we're approaching whatever he doesn't want to tell me.

"Jason and I came here, to Seattle. That was . . . six years ago now? I can't believe it's been that long."

"Is Jason still here?" I ask, latching on to this guy's name because he seems to be the key to Will's current discomfort.

"Yes, he's still here. But he's pretty pissed at me about now, I'd wager."

I hadn't mentioned it to Will, but when I'd used his phone to take the picture of Sebastian, I'd noticed several missed calls from Jason.

"Is he the one who helped you during your chemo?" I probe gently.

Will looks over at me with sorrow in his eyes. He purses his lips, and I can see the exact second when he decides to tell me everything. "Yes, he was. The first time, I had a lot of help. When Jay and I moved here, we met so many great people in the art community. We had lots of friends, and we went to parties all the time. Everyone was really supportive and encouraging of one another. When I was first diagnosed, they rallied around me. They all took turns driving me to appointments and staying with me when I was too sick to take care of myself. I felt very loved, and I got better."

"What about the second time?"

Will looks down, his fingers tracing the weave on his afghan. "The second time was different. Everyone was just . . . busy. Some of them helped, but I could tell they were put out that I was sick again. I don't blame them. Hell, I was pretty put out that I was sick again, and I knew how much effort it took to take care of me. Jay stayed with me, though. He took me to almost all of my appointments, and he even lived with me for the last month or so of my treatment. I couldn't have gotten through it without him."

He stares at his fingers as they trace the squares in the basket weave over and over again until his eyes become unfocused, lost in memory or regret; I'm not sure which.

"Will," I call softly, and he slowly raises his eyes to mine.

"I . . . I can't talk about this right now. I'm having a good day today, and—"

"It's all right. I understand."

"No, you don't. I do *want* to tell you, and I will; I just don't want to get upset today. I feel like I need to pretend things are normal for a bit while I'm feeling well. Does that make sense?"

"Yes, of course it does," I tell him, squeezing the fingers of our joined hands gently. I know I should push him now that he's gotten this far, but as I stare into his warm green eyes, I can't make myself do it. "What else can we talk about?"

"Well," he says hesitantly, ducking his chin. "I was thinking maybe we could . . . do something tomorrow night?"

"Do something?"

"Yeah. There's this cart-thing with a flat screen and a DVD player that the patients can borrow. I was wondering if you wanted to watch a movie with me tomorrow night."

I almost laugh out loud because he's trying so hard to do something normal in this completely abnormal situation, but I bite my lip to hold it back, afraid of offending him. His smile is tentative, but oh so hopeful, and I swear it's the sweetest thing I've ever seen. The words are out of my mouth before I can even think. "Of course I do! That sounds like fun!"

He beams at me, and that warmth fills my chest again.

"Good! I'll ask Jenny about it when she brings my dinner in tonight." Suddenly, he stares down at his afghan. "Um . . . can you bring a movie for us to watch?"

I chuckle, and he chuckles right along with me. "Of course I can."

"And . . . will you bring popcorn?"

Now I just laugh and shake my head at him. "Can you even *have* popcorn?"

"Sure. I have no dietary restrictions. And I could certainly stand to put on a little weight."

"Well, if I really *can* bring you anything you want to eat, is there anything else you'd like to have?"

He ducks his head, but his smile is mischievous as he looks up at me through his eyelashes. "Raisinets? I kind of have a sweet tooth, and it's been more than three weeks since I've had any chocolate."

"A *guy* with a sweet tooth? I thought it was only women who crave chocolate."

"Are you saying I'm a girl?"

"No—"

"Because I eat my Raisinets in a very manly way. By the handful! No pinkies involved!"

I double over laughing as I picture him gobbling handfuls of candy.

"Seriously! I always keep a bag of them in the studio when I paint. Or sometimes Hershey's Kisses. They're great energy boosters, and chocolate just makes me happy."

God knows I'd do just about anything to see him happy. "Yes, I'll bring you candy so you can get your fix. And I'll bring popcorn and a movie. It's a date—"

My eyes widen as I realize an instant too late what I've said. If he wasn't thinking that way, he'd continue on with the conversation. But he doesn't. He looks away, and suddenly his cheeks are flaming red. If I wasn't thinking that way, I'd laugh it off and keep talking. But I don't. I swallow thickly and look up at him, knowing my cheeks are a mirror of his own.

He can't date, Tori. He's dying. He knows it. You know it. The only thing this will do is hurt you both and interfere with your helping him.

"So, you'll be back tomorrow, then?" he asks, recovering first from the awkward moment.

"Yes," I answer, finding my voice. "I'll be here with bells on."

I go home and try not to let myself think about those last few moments in Will's room, but I'm failing miserably. After heating up some leftovers, I curl up in my bed to watch some TV, but I'm really not paying any attention.

Sebastian leaps up next to me, giving me an accusing glare. "What?" I ask, reaching a hand out to stroke him. He stares back at me, stone-faced. "All right, all right! Yes, I'm thinking about him. Are you staring at me because I shouldn't be thinking about him or because I should be?"

Sebastian cocks his head to the side and cuddles up against me, purring softly as I continue to pet him. Disgruntled feline notwithstanding, I *am* thinking about Will and what happened tonight. I'm definitely attracted to him. I've known that since the first moment I laid eyes on him, and there's nothing wrong with that. Hormones make no distinction if someone is dying, so I can't fault myself for that one.

I also care about him. Watching him go through what he has to with his cancer is hitting me very hard. Is it because he's so young or because I care about him more than I have about any other patient I've helped? I don't have the answer to that, but it doesn't matter. I already care deeply for him, and I'll do anything I can to help him.

But the part that's scaring me is how my caring about him is changing. I want to help him get to the point where he's ready to face what's coming, and that means he'll need to contact his friends and family or at least make peace within himself with not contacting them. But I find myself wanting to *be* someone he cares about.

I sigh in frustration. I shouldn't be thinking this way. My focus should be on him and what he needs, not what I need or feel. *Fuck.* Somehow I've managed to complicate this for myself, but I can't let it interfere with helping him. What we're doing tomorrow night is *not* a date.

I pound my fist on the bed hard enough that Sebastian jumps. I have to stop this. It doesn't matter. He's dying. Even if he cared about me the way I do about him, soon he won't be here, and the closer we get, the more it's going to hurt us both when we reach the end. I swipe angrily at the tears streaming down my face and cry myself into a restless sleep.

CHAPTER 10

Despite my pep talk last night, I find myself looking forward to movie night with Will—in completely inappropriate ways. I can't help it. I'm excited he's doing so well this week and that he's happy. About lunchtime, it occurs to me that since it's the weekend, I don't have to wait until four o'clock to go see him. In fact, if we're going to watch a movie, it would probably be better if I went earlier because Will is usually pretty tired by the time I leave around six.

So I pick three movies from my collection, grab some microwave popcorn, and stop by the grocery store to buy him his Raisinets. I buy a big bag instead of the usual movie box, and since he mentioned them, I pick up a bag of Hershey's Kisses too. *Shut up*, little voice in my head. *They're on sale.*

I arrive at Will's room around two o'clock and peek in the door as I usually do. He's sleeping. *God, he's beautiful.* I stand in the doorway, staring at him and feeling all the things I told myself last night I shouldn't and wouldn't feel. He looks so at peace when he's sleeping. The lines of pain disappear, and I can see the man he was before he got sick. I wish I'd met him then.

He shifts on the bed and raises his hand to scratch at his chest. *The poor guy. He's so itchy, he's even scratching in his sleep.*

My thoughts are interrupted by soft green eyes and a sleepy smile. He's wearing a forest green nightshirt today that matches his eyes precisely and intensifies their brilliance. *Damn.*

"Tori," he greets me softly; then his brow furrows. "Is it four o'clock already? Did I really sleep that long?"

"No, it's just two. Since it's Saturday, and we were planning to watch a movie, I thought I'd come early."

His grin is spectacular. "Really?"

"Here I am," I say, spreading my arms. "But I can come back later if you still want to rest."

He shakes his head and winces. "I'm fine. I've kind of gotten into a routine of resting after lunch until around three, and then I usually draw until you get here. But I feel like I sleep all the time; don't worry about it."

"Okay, if you're sure."

"I'm positive."

He cocks his head and cranes his neck toward me. "Whatcha got there?"

I chuckle. *God, he can be cute when he puts his mind to it.* "I brought your drug of choice along with popcorn and a few movies," I tell him as I set the bag down next to him.

He starts rummaging and pulls out the Raisinets and the Hershey's Kisses. "Oh, you're spoiling me," he says, ripping open the Raisinets and shoveling a handful into his mouth.

"Mmm," he moans appreciatively, and I feel it between my legs and on my cheeks too.

"Why don't you have a look at the movies I brought, and I'll go see about the TV and the popcorn."

"Okay," he agrees, completely oblivious to the effect he's having on me, and I'm able to make my escape.

I head down the hallway and find Jenny at the nurses' station. "I thought you didn't work on Saturdays."

"I traded shifts with someone who really needed the day off. I thought *you* didn't visit patients on Saturdays."

I grin guiltily, and I know I'm blushing. "This is different, Jenny, and you know it."

"Uh huh. What's up?"

"I came to see about getting the loaner TV and DVD player for Will's room. We're going to watch a movie."

Jenny giggles. "I know. He told me yesterday."

"So you made me ask because . . .?"

"Because I love the color your face turns when you're nervous!" she exclaims, laughing. "But seriously, what's up with you and Will?"

"Nothing's up! He just wants to do something normal since he's feeling better this week." I do my best to keep my voice even, but she raises an eyebrow at me. "And I can't seem to tell him no."

"He *is* a sweetheart, once you get to know him. Have you made any progress with him?"

"Some. Because I stayed with him when he had the fluid drained from his belly, he decided that I'm here because I want to be, and he started opening up to me a bit. I still don't know where his family and friends are, but at least he's telling me things about himself."

"I hope he lets you help him. I don't want to see him go through this alone."

"He won't be alone even if I don't manage to convince him to contact his friends and family. I'm going to stay with him until . . ." I trail off because I can't seem to get the words out.

Jenny looks at me thoughtfully, but she doesn't say anything more. "Go on back down with Will. I'll bring the cart in a few minutes."

"Actually, can I sneak into the nurses' lounge?" I ask, holding up my package of popcorn.

Jenny giggles and nods.

I just roll my eyes at her and walk away.

By the time I get back to Will's room, Jenny has already dropped off the cart and disappeared. Will is waiting for me, a smile on his face and a few Raisinets in his hand. He inhales appreciatively as I walk into the room.

"Mmm, that smells amazing. I haven't had popcorn in months. Thank you *so* much for bringing it!"

Chuckling, I set the open bag next to him. Making him happy is making *me* happier than I've been in months; I can't help but notice. But you know what? I'm going to have a nice afternoon with him, and I'm not going to have another thought about what I should and shouldn't be feeling. He's happy; I'm happy. How can this possibly be a bad thing?

"So what movie are we going to watch?"

"Your selection of movies was a bit . . . surprising. This is really stuff you like to watch?"

"Well, I figured you wouldn't thank me if I delved into my chick flick vault, but yes, I like action movies and suspense thrillers too."

"Well, we're definitely going to have to watch *The Avengers*, then. I'm a pretty big comic book fan."

I raise my eyebrows at him.

"There are some amazing graphic artists who work in comics. I always liked to draw and paint, but comics drew me in and got me really thinking about art as a career. I would have gone into comic book art, but I'm much better with a brush than I am with a pencil, and I like to put more time into my work than you can afford to if you're drawing under a deadline."

The thought of Will painting, or drawing for that matter, does funny things to my stomach; there's something so . . . intimate about watching him create as I picture it in my head. I wonder what he'd say if I asked him to draw something for me. I file that one away for later as I stand up with the movie in my hand.

"I hate that you have to sit in that uncomfortable-looking chair while I get to lie here and relax. I wish we could both sit on the couch."

"Is that a possibility?"

"I don't think so," he replies, looking crestfallen. "I'm hooked up to a few things that don't make me very portable, and I don't think I could sit at that angle because of my lymph node problems.

"But you could . . ."

"Could what?"

"Well, you could sit over here next to me if I slide over," he says bashfully. "There's enough room, and you'd be more comfortable and able to see better."

He won't meet my eyes, and I think it's because he doesn't want to admit that he just wants to be close to me. I wonder when he last had a girlfriend because he seems rather starved for a woman's touch. Every time I've touched him since he decided to trust me, he's leaned into it, and I can tell he likes holding my hand. I could easily see him being a cuddler—maybe even a Momma's boy when he was younger. I wonder where his mother is and when he last saw her.

"But you don't have to . . ."

I jump, startled out of my thoughts. There *does* seem to be enough room, and try as I might, I can't smother the voice in the back of my head that's cheering at the thought of being that close to him.

"Sorry. No, I'll sit next to you if it won't hurt you too much to move over."

He grins at me, surprised. "Well, I can't promise it won't hurt me, but it won't do any permanent damage."

He plants his hands on either side of his hips and uses his arms to slide himself over carefully. The whole process is punctuated by a series of hisses and pained grunts, and the only reason I don't insist he stop is that I think I'll offend him.

When he gets to a position that seems to give me enough room, he stops and lies there for a moment with his eyes closed, breathing heavily. Once he's collected himself, he looks over at me and smiles.

"There," he says as he pats the spot on the bed next to him.

"Let me get the movie going first," I tell him, going around to the DVD player and putting the disc in. Once it's started and I've handed the remote to him, I go back around the bed and gently position myself next to him. He winces as my weight depresses the bed, but he doesn't make another sound as I get comfortable. Once I'm still, he starts the movie.

We share popcorn and Raisinets as we watch, and I find myself watching *him* way more than what's on the screen.

I watch him eat popcorn. I watch as he smirks and laughs at what's on the screen. I watch and I have to remind myself that he's dying, because right now, he looks like a guy I could be out on a date with. A guy I wish I *were* out on a date with.

I'm acutely aware of the second his shoulder comes into contact with mine, and I glance down and see he's sliding his hand across his thigh toward me. I wait, but as soon as his hand brushes over mine, I entwine my fingers with his.

A grin spreads across his face, but he never looks away from the screen, and my heart feels like it's going to explode out of my chest. God, nothing in the world feels as good as making him happy. I could become addicted to this feeling, easily.

I'm relaxed and comfortable, and without realizing it, I lay my head on his shoulder. The grin is back—I can feel it radiating off him rather than see it—and a few moments later, he leans his head against the top of mine.

I wake with a start and look over to find Will's sleepy green eyes staring back at me, just as confused as I am. The TV is displaying the menu for the movie, and the door to Will's room is closing slowly.

Will is smiling at me, looking as if he doesn't have a care in the world. "I think we fell asleep," he says, his voice warm and gravelly. *Damn, if that isn't the sexiest sound I've ever heard!*

"We did." I agree, grinning right back.

He glances at the clock over the door. "Wow, it's six o'clock already. I bet that was Jenny bringing my dinner."

"Probably. Why don't I go chase her down, and you can get yourself settled again?"

"Sounds like a plan," he says as I slide myself carefully off the bed.

I'm not even halfway to the nurses' station when I hear Jenny's excited squeal.

"You guys looked *so* cute, I didn't have the heart to disturb you."

"Yeah, we must have fallen asleep watching the movie."

"You were awfully cozy," she says, giving me the hairy eyeball.

"You know it's not like that."

"Maybe it isn't for you, but I'm not so sure about him. I think he naps in the afternoon so he can be awake when you come in the evening. It's the high point of his day now."

I blush as she says it, an increasingly vocal part of me hoping it's true. But to her, I offer a noncommittal shrug. "There's nothing to it, Jenny. I care about him . . . a lot, but it's not anything more than that. It *can't* be anything more than that. He just needs comfort. If I can give that to him, and it makes him happy, then I'm going to do it."

"Good. He needs someone to make him happy. And I get the feeling it's making you happy too."

She's got my number, but I'm not ready to admit it yet, so I roll my eyes. "Were you bringing Will's dinner down?"

"I was just going to check on him, but food services is already on the floor. Let me go grab his tray, and you can take it to him."

She flits off down the hall and returns a few minutes later with Will's dinner. Tonight, he's having chicken parmesan with penne pasta, green beans, and apple pie for dessert. It doesn't look half bad.

Brilliant green eyes and a bright smile greet me as I enter the room, and I see he's managed to move himself back to the center of the bed.

"Wow, dinner *and* a movie. Lucky me," he teases as I move the TV away from his bed and position his rolling table so it's over his thighs.

I retrieve his tray from where I left it on my chair, and after I set it down, I remove the cover with a flourish and say "Bon appétit!" in my best French accent.

He chuckles at me and shakes his head, but then his expression turns serious. "Do you, um, need to go?"

"Well, I should get going pretty soon," I reply, but I'm brought up short as I see his face fall. He doesn't want this day to end, and if I'm being honest with myself, neither do I. "But I can stay for a while yet."

His eyes light up again as he grins, and my stomach flutters giddily.

"Are you hungry? Because I can share what I have—"

"No, that's okay. I wouldn't want to deprive you of that most excellent-looking mystery meat parmesan," I say in my best deadpan.

"Hey! It's most definitely identifiable as chicken, and it's not half bad," he says defensively, but I can see the twinkle in his eye.

"I know. It does actually look decent. But, honestly, I'm not that hungry yet anyway. We had popcorn and candy this afternoon, remember? And you need to eat it more than I do."

"Yeah," he agrees, looking a little offended. "I know I'm way too skinny."

Shit. "I didn't mean that," I say quickly. "I just meant I'm sure the night nurses don't do room service if you get the munchies in the middle of the night."

"Oh," he answers, looking at me thoughtfully.

Nice save, Tori!

"Well, I'm too thin anyway."

Damn, I must have really hit a nerve if he's not dropping this. "Will, that's not your fault. The cancer causes weight loss; there's nothing you can do. *I* think you're beautiful."

His eyebrows disappear into his hairline, and I blush furiously. *Where the hell did that come from?* I duck my head and try to change the subject. "Hey, since you're not on a special diet or anything, that means I could bring dinner in for you, doesn't it?"

His eyes widen. "Why, yes, I think it does." I swear I can almost see the wheels turning in his head.

"Would you like that? We can pick a night, and if you tell me where to go, I'll bring you whatever you're hungry for."

"You'd really do that?"

I laugh. "Of course I would! I wouldn't have made the suggestion otherwise."

"That would be awesome! But I have one condition," he says, and suddenly, I'm drowning in a sea of green as he fixes me with his stare, a persuasive smirk on his face.

"What?"

"You have to eat with me."

Oh my. What I wouldn't give to read his mind for just ten seconds. But we're teasing now, not being serious, so I put aside the realization that this is the second time this week he's sort of asked me out on a date.

"Well, I wasn't planning to sit and watch you eat, but I'll warn you now, if I don't like the place you choose, you'll just have to eat by yourself."

"You know something? You're a bit sassy once you get to know you."

Smirking, I raise an eyebrow at him.

"Not that there's anything wrong with that," he says, raising his hands defensively.

I laugh and shake my head. "So you pick the night, and I'll bring us dinner. You've got my cell phone number. You can call me at lunchtime and put your order in, and I'll go pick it up before I come to your room that night. Deal?"

"Deal."

"Now, eat your roadkill parmesan before it gets cold."

He laughs so hard he ends up having to curl an arm over his belly, but he's still grinning despite his discomfort.

He eats quietly for a few moments, and I peruse his menu for tomorrow to try to disguise the fact that I can't stop staring at him. He's just so damn happy today, so different from the man I met almost two weeks ago. That Will was brooding and moody, but now that I understand why, it makes sense. But this is definitely who he really is. He's soft-spoken and open, playful and sweet. He's perfect.

Will moves his plate away and zeroes in on dessert, and I'm happy to see he ate most of what he was given. He pulls the slice of apple pie to him, fork-cutting the first bite and offering it to me.

"You *have* to sample dessert," he says enticingly.

I close my eyes and try to think about seeing my dad naked because if I let what just popped into my head go any further, I'm going to have a serious problem. *Yuck! The dad thing worked. Okay, now answer him, Tori, before he notices you're clenching your thighs.*

"Oh, that's okay . . ."

"Come on, Tori! I've never met a girl who didn't like dessert."

Oh God, Will. You have no idea.

I realize the quickest way out of this is just to eat the damn pie, so I open my mouth and allow him to feed me. It tastes pretty good, and it puts me in mind of grandmothers rather than having Will for dessert, so it turned out to be a good solution after all.

"Mmm, that's actually good!"

"I told you this stuff is not only edible but also recognizable as food."

"Well, I'm glad they're feeding you decently, then."

He leans back and closes his eyes, and I can tell he's fading. *Dammit.* I can't imagine what it would be like to be that tired all the time. Sadness slices through me as I realize our lovely day is about to end.

"I should go. It's getting late, and you're tired. Besides, Sebastian is waiting for me. He's going to think I abandoned him," I add, to take the emphasis away from his condition being the reason I'm leaving.

"I guess," he murmurs, looking down at his lap.

I stand up and raise his chin with my hand. "Hey, it's okay. I'll—"

"No," he says, cutting me off. "Let me this time. Tori, would you please come back tomorrow?" he asks in that velvety voice of his, his eyes soft and serious.

I get weak in the knees, but I take the hand that was under his chin and lightly run my fingers through his hair. "Of course I will," I whisper.

He leans into my touch and mumbles, "You could do that again."

I smile, but he doesn't see because his eyes are closed, enjoying the feel of my fingers in his hair and already drifting toward sleep. I continue to stroke his hair until I hear his breathing become heavy and even.

Goodnight, sweetheart.

CHAPTER 11

I float through my evening and the next morning, not allowing myself to think too hard about my feelings for Will. We had a great day together yesterday, and I'm grateful for it. There are still things I need to do to help him, but sometimes, I need to remind myself to just stop and smell the flowers, or in this case, appreciate the gorgeous man who's smiling only for me.

Thank you, sir. May I have another? I think to myself as I walk into his room at two in the afternoon on Sunday, ready for another movie-watching day and awesome visit with Will.

I push the door open, but I grab it before it gets to the squeak point so I can have a look at him before he notices me.

Something's wrong. His eyes are closed, and even though he's lying still, I can tell every muscle and nerve in his body is tense. He looks pale, almost . . . gray and worn out. The skin around his eyes is tight, and his jaw is set firmly. He's in pain, and a lot of it, unless I'm completely off base. *Shit.*

As I let the door make its customary squeak, he opens his eyes and smiles weakly at me. "Hey, Tori."

I walk over to the bed and cover his hand with mine, but he flinches, so I quickly pull back. "What is it?"

He closes his eyes for a moment, and his breathing is all wrong. He doesn't seem to be having trouble breathing, but he's huffing out his breaths as if he can't relax.

He opens his eyes again, and he looks so incredibly tired. "I'm not having a good day today," he admits softly.

What in the holy hell happened since yesterday? How can he go from happy and almost carefree to this in less than twenty-four hours? "What happened? You were feeling so good yesterday."

"I was, but I woke up this morning in a lot of pain, and it seems to be getting worse as the day goes on."

"Where does it hurt?" I ask, reaching up to cup his cheek.

His sigh is pure frustration. "Where doesn't it hurt? My joints feel like they're on fire." He winces as he raises his hand to show me his swollen knuckles.

I wince myself as I stare at his fingers. They even *look* painful. "Does the cancer do this?"

He nods, grunting out a breath. "Yeah, the cancer causes inflammation in my joints that's like arthritis. It always hurts, but it can flare up and cause severe pain like this sometimes."

"Is it only your hands?"

"No, but they seem to be the worst. I can feel it just about everywhere today—feet, ankles, knees, wrists, elbows. Fuck," he mutters as he closes his eyes again.

"Have they given you any pain meds?"

"Yeah, they're giving me anti-inflammatories and codeine for the pain, but it's not even making a dent."

"What about something stronger, like morphine?"

"Jenny would give it to me, but I don't like taking morphine. I get sick to my stomach, and I feel out of control. I have to be hurting pretty badly before I'll ask for it."

"And *this* doesn't qualify as pretty badly?"

His lips turn up in a lopsided grin, and despite the situation, I'm happy I can get him to smile a little bit.

"Yes, it does, but I'm hoping I can outlast the pain. Actually, the last time I had any morphine was the day you first came to see me. That shit makes me high, and I don't remember half of what I'm saying and doing. No, if I can live without it, I plan to."

I smile as I recall that first day, but from his point of view, I'm sure it's not nearly as memorable. *God, he looks tired.*

"We can watch our movie another day. Do you want me to leave so you can rest?"

"Please don't," he says, sounding a little desperate. "There isn't a chance I could sleep right now, and I could really use something to take my mind off the pain. I couldn't even draw today to keep myself distracted," he says, glaring down at his swollen fingers. "Can we watch our movie like we planned? Please?"

"Of course we can. I don't want to leave, but I would if you needed me to. I'll do anything I can to make this easier for you."

He gives me a sweet smile. "Thanks, Tori. Just your being here makes it easier."

Warmth flows through my chest, and I know I'm blushing . . . *again.* How is it he can make me go from zero to full blush in like, five seconds?

"Thank you, Will. I *want* to be here. Now, why don't I go see about our TV and DVD player? Will you be okay until I get back?"

"Of course," he says, smirking. "I'm certainly not going anywhere."

I grin at him, not allowing myself to think about the implications of his words, and go in search of Jenny. I find her at the nurses' station, typing away at the computer.

"Hey, Tori. Are you and Will watching another movie today?"

"That's the plan. Is the TV available?"

"Yes, I can bring it down for you guys. Hey, what's the matter?" she asks, and I wonder what she sees on my face.

"Isn't there anything else you can do for him? He's really miserable."

Jenny frowns. "Yes, I know he's in a lot of pain. He won't let me give him morphine, although I can't say I blame him because he got really sick from it last time. I'll check what we're giving him and see if I can up the dosage. He can also put heat or cold on his joints for some relief. Did he say what was bothering him the most?"

"His hands," I tell her, wincing as I remember how bad they look.

"Why don't I give you a few cold packs for him, and he can see if that helps. I would have offered them to him sooner, but he's so quiet, and he never complains—he needs to learn to speak up so I can be of more help."

"I'll see what I can do about that. Thanks, Jenny," I say as she hands me four cold packs.

"Don't let him ice anything for more than fifteen minutes at a time. It can actually make it worse if he overdoes it."

"Okay, I'll keep an eye on him," I call over my shoulder.

I return to his room and find him just as I left him—eyes closed with his head resting back against the pillow, pain etched all over his face.

"Jenny is going to bring the TV down, but in the meantime, she gave me these," I tell him, holding up the cold packs. "She says the cold might give you some relief."

He looks skeptical, but he nods slowly. "Okay, it can't make it worse, right?"

"No, I don't think so," I say as I squeeze the pack to make it cold. I put it on my own hand until it feels noticeably colder, and then I move closer to him.

He watches me with trepidation, and I see his arm tense as I get close, but the minute I lay the pack over his knuckles he moans in obvious relief.

"Oh, wow. That definitely helps tone the fire down. I didn't think it would make that much of a difference."

I smile as I go around the bed and place a second pack on his other hand. "I've got two more. Where do you want them?"

"Damn, that's a tough question," he mutters, shifting on the bed and wincing.

"Well, Jenny said to only do fifteen minutes at a time in any one spot, so we can move them around."

"Um . . ." He hesitates, looking distinctly uncomfortable.

"What is it? I'll do whatever you need me to."

"Well, I'd really like to put them on my knees."

Now I see the problem. He doesn't want to uncover his legs in front of me.

He starts to slide his hand out from under the ice pack, cringing as he does so.

"Will, sweetheart, stay still. It's all right; I understand. What if I just uncover your knees from the sides and put the ice on that way? I won't uncover your legs at all."

He's looking at me strangely, and I have no idea why. *Am I wrong about this?*

"Thanks, Tori. I'm sorry; I —"

"Hey, you don't need to explain. I get it. But let me help you, okay?"

"Okay."

He watches as I lift his blanket and sheet gently over his knee in a triangular fold and place the point between his legs. A bright red rash covers his thighs and calves, but I do my best not to look as I drape the ice pack over his poor knee. Like his hands, he's got some swelling there, too. *Damn cancer.*

I do the same to his other side, and he sighs softly. He looks a little more relaxed, and his breathing isn't quite as uneven.

"There. Why don't we watch our movie now?" I suggest, trying to get us back to something normal and away from the problems of Will's day.

"Well, we—" He stops as Jenny pushes the TV cart through the door.

"Sorry it took me so long," she says, grinning at us. "I got called away by another patient, and it took a while. Are the cold packs helping, Will?"

"Yes. Thank you."

She narrows her eyes at him. "You know, if you told me half as much as you tell Tori, I'd be able to make you a lot more comfortable."

He grins at her sheepishly. "I'm sorry, Jenny. I'm just not a natural complainer. Tori either pulls things out of me, or she comes to her own conclusions about what I need and then comes and talks to you. I'll try to do better, though, because I really could have used these sooner today."

My chest tightens at his words. I wonder what else Will has missed out on or suffered through because of his quiet nature and the fact he has no one to advocate for him. It's not Jenny's fault. The nurses are busy, and I'm sure it takes them most of their day just to meet the basic needs of their patients and deal with people's requests. There's not a lot of time to sit and think about what a less assertive patient might need.

I know I have no legal power to advocate for Will, but I promise myself I'll be more observant. Maybe I'll start coming by in the morning, too, just to see how his night went and if he needs anything.

Jenny smiles at us as she leaves the room, and I walk around Will's bed to set up the DVD player. When I'm finished, I come back to my chair, and he looks at me sadly.

"I wish you could sit with me today, but I really don't think I can slide over without making myself cry."

"Oh, no, I wasn't even thinking about that. I would hurt you every time I moved even the littlest bit. You need your space today."

"Yeah." He agrees, but he sounds dejected.

"Another day. We can watch movies again next weekend, if you want, and I'll sit next to you then."

"Deal," he says, brightening.

"Are you hungry? I brought more popcorn although I realize you're not exactly up to feeding yourself today. I'd be happy to stuff both our faces," I say, grinning.

He smiles at me, and I detect the hint of a chuckle. I'm amazed I'm getting even that much from him right now.

"No, I'm not hungry. And to be honest, I don't know if I could keep anything down anyway, hurting this much. But you can make some for yourself."

"No, that's okay. We'll save it for next week." I'm not about to torture him by sitting here and eating popcorn in front of him since I know from yesterday how much he likes it.

Continuing with our action theme, today we watch *Star Trek Into Darkness*. I watch the clock, and every fifteen minutes, I pause the movie and move the ice packs around for him. By the time we're near the end, I've managed to ice all his major joints twice, and he seems more relaxed than when I first got here.

Unlike yesterday when he was chatting and cracking jokes, he's been silent through the entire movie. He's been closing his eyes a lot, but just when I think he's asleep, he opens them again and stares at the screen.

I feel utterly helpless as I sit here, watching him.

When the movie finishes, Will's eyes are closed, and I'm fervently hoping he's managed to fall asleep. I take out the disc and shut everything down as quietly as I can, but when I turn around, I find him watching me.

"Dammit, I had hoped you were asleep. You really look like you need it."

He shakes his head, grunting. "I wish I could because I'm really fucking tired, but there's no way until this lets up. Do you need to head out?"

His voice is neutral as he asks, but his eyes tell me he wants me to stay. On a normal day, I can't deny him anymore, but today, I'd do absolutely anything he asks if it'll help him even the slightest bit.

"No. Can I stay for a while?"

"Of course you can. I'm sorry I'm not much company."

My jaw drops. "Seriously? You're apologizing to me for *this*? Damn, Will, you need to cut yourself some slack. You're not here to entertain me."

He smiles faintly. "I know. I just meant that we had such a nice day yesterday—well, I know I did. I'd been hoping today was going to be the same."

"I had a nice day yesterday too. I wish today was exactly like it, but I guess we can't win them all."

"No," he murmurs, looking entirely too lost in his thoughts for my liking.

"Well, if you're happy for me to stay, do you want to watch another movie? Did that help distract you at all?"

"Yeah, it did. A bit. That's fine."

I pop in the first Abrams' *Star Trek* movie and continue to ice his joints for him. He spends most of the two hours with his eyes closed, and I spend most of them watching him, wishing there was something I could do to ease his suffering. I wonder how many times this has happened in the three months since his relapse and how many more times it will happen before the end.

I try to throw myself into the movie for a while, but I finally glance over and find Will staring at the ceiling. He closes his eyes, and a tear escapes down his cheek.

"Will, what can I do?" I ask, unable to keep the pain out of my voice.

He doesn't open his eyes, and his quiet admission breaks my heart. "I'm sorry. I'm just miserable right now. I don't think there's anything anyone can do."

"Why don't you let Jenny give you some morphine? It can't be worse than this, can it?"

"It was pretty bad last time. I couldn't tell you how many times I threw up, and it went on for hours. That's certainly not going to help me get any sleep, and I don't think I could handle it on top of everything else today."

Damn. I wouldn't be eager to have that experience again either. I can't resist the urge to touch him anymore, so I stand up and run my fingers into his hair.

He opens his eyes and shakes his head. "As much as I normally like that, I can't enjoy it today. I'm too on edge."

I nod as I withdraw my hand. There really *isn't* anything I can do for him.

"Why don't you go home, Tori? It's getting late, and you have work tomorrow. You need to get some sleep."

The thought of going home and curling up in my warm, comfortable bed while he lies here suffering is more than I can take. Tears sting my eyes. "I don't want to leave you."

"I'll be all right. I'll feel better knowing you're home and sleeping, and there's really nothing you can do for me anyway, other than listen to me complain. And you'll be here tomorrow, right?"

"Yes, of course I'll be here tomorrow."

"Then go," he says, giving me a small smile. "With any luck, this will let up soon, and I'll get some rest, okay?"

He's the one taking care of me right now, and I hate that I'm letting him, but watching him like this has really gotten to me today. I'm sure he can see it on my face. But he's right. There's nothing I can do, and sitting here feeling bad for him is just making *him* feel worse about the whole thing. I shake my head. This is the kind of shit that happens when I let my emotions get involved. I should be trying to take away his problems, not adding to them.

"Okay, I'll go home. But I'm going to tell the night nurse to come down and see you, so you make sure to tell her how bad this is. Maybe she'll have something else for you to try."

"Okay, I promise I'll talk to her."

"Thank you. I'll come and see you first thing tomorrow, okay?"

"Yeah," he says, closing his eyes again.

I beat a hasty retreat before I can change my mind. I get the night nurse to up his pain medication and promise to check on him at least every half hour through the night since he's in such bad shape.

Then I go home and cry myself to sleep, wrapped around a gray tabby ball of fur.

CHAPTER 12

My first stop this morning is Will's room, but Jenny intercepts me before I can get to his door.

"I wouldn't even go in this morning. He was up most of the night, and he's only been asleep for a few hours. The last thing you want to do right now is to wake him."

Damn. I want to question Jenny about his night, but I know she's not legally allowed to tell me.

"Thank God he's finally getting some sleep. No, I certainly don't want to wake him. I'll come back at four to see if I can talk to him then."

Jenny smiles and pats my shoulder, then continues on her way.

Will's face lights up when I open his door later that afternoon. His green eyes are glassy and sparkling. He looks so relaxed. *This is good!*

I draw in a rapid breath. *This isn't good.* This means he's had morphine today. *Fuck.* The pain must have gotten bad enough that he finally asked for it. But that thought floats away as he gives me a goofy grin. I haven't seen that look since the first day I met him, and I can't help but grin back.

"Tori," he says, drawing out my name as if he's savoring the sound of it.

"Hi, Will. When did they give you morphine?"

"That obvious, huh? Do I look as drunk as I feel?"

"You seem . . . relaxed. And yes, you do look a little toasted."

He chuckles. "Great. I'm lit but I don't get to enjoy the drinks or the good time." He shakes his head lazily. "Um . . . you asked me something . . ."

"Yes," I answer, trying hard not to laugh. "I asked when you started taking morphine."

"Right! I asked for it about five this morning. I didn't sleep last night. The pain kept getting more intense until I couldn't take it anymore."

"You must be tired, then."

He scratches at his chest as he answers me. "Not really. I slept all day . . . I think. Well, most of it anyway. I also tried to get all the vomiting out of the way before you got here, but I can't promise."

I raise my eyebrows at him.

"I told you this stuff really messes me up. Today hasn't been as bad as before though. I got sick this morning when they first gave it to me, but they changed the dosage somehow, and it's been better. I still feel pretty queasy though."

As if he doesn't have enough problems. "Do you want me to go so you can rest? I can just see you tomorrow—"

"Tori." He interrupts me, slurring my name slightly. "I've been waiting *all day* for you to get here. There's not a chance I'm going to let you leave."

I smirk at him. I gave him an out to keep his dignity, and he threw it back at me as if it were on fire. *Yep, this is going to be an interesting visit.* "You've been waiting for me?"

"Yes, of course I have," he replies matter-of-factly. "Seeing you is the best part of my day."

"Really? I didn't realize I'd become the highlight of your day."

Bright green eyes sparkle at me. "Are you kidding me? A visit every day from a beautiful woman like you? How could anything else in my day possibly top that?"

I chuckle, and his brow furrows adorably.

"Why are you laughing?"

"A beautiful woman like me, huh?"

"Did I say that? I *did* say that, didn't I? Well, I was wrong. You're not beautiful; you're fucking gorgeous. How did I get lucky enough to have someone like you decide to be my friend?"

Whoa. Well, I think I might have an answer to my question about whether Will finds me attractive. *Just maybe.*

"I'm the lucky one. I've gotten to see your amazing artwork and to make friends with Sebastian and, most of all, to spend time with you."

"You really like spending time with me? It's not an obligation or something you're doing out of pity?"

I thought we'd put this whole thing to rest, but the fact that it's coming up again when he's high and has no filter tells me it's still a worry of his.

"Yes, I really like spending time with you. You're sweet and funny, and I know underneath everything that's going on, you're a very open and loving person."

He frowns. "I'm sorry about that. I wanted to be nicer to you when you first came to see me, but I really *was* afraid you were here to examine me. And I had . . . other things to protect." He raises his hand and rubs his forehead. "I really shouldn't be talking about this. My head isn't clear, and I know there's a reason I didn't want to talk about it. I just don't remember what it is right now."

Well, filter not entirely missing, then. "It's all right, Will. You don't have to talk about it. I don't want you to tell me anything you'll regret later on."

"But I *want* to tell you everything. Right now, I really don't understand why I haven't," he says, looking up at me as if I might have the answer.

"Will, sweetheart, let it go for today, okay? You're in no condition to change your mind about any of your decisions. If you still want to tell me everything once you're not on morphine anymore, I'll be happy to hear all about it. I don't want you to do anything you're going to be upset about tomorrow. I would never take advantage of you that way."

He smiles at me as he reaches across his body to scratch his arm. "Thanks, Tori. You've been taking such good care of me. It really means a lot to me."

"You're welcome. That's what friends are for."

"Is that what we are? Friends?"

"I'd like to think so. I think of you as my friend, at least."

"You called me 'sweetheart' just now. You did it yesterday too. I liked that."

My eyes widen. *Oh. I guess I did.* I bet that's why he was looking at me funny yesterday. I've been thinking of him that way in my head for a while now, and obviously, he's been thinking things about us too. The question there was not *if* we're friends as much as if we're *more* than friends. *Oh my.*

"Tori, how come . . ." He stops and closes his eyes. "Never mind."

"What? You can ask me anything, Will. It's okay."

He opens his eyes slowly and smirks at me. "Well, I was going to ask you why you don't have a boyfriend, but that seemed too abrupt, so I was trying to think of a smoother way to ask."

I bite my lip to keep from laughing. *Wow, morphine is like truth serum for him.*

I consider deflecting his question, but he's probably not going to remember what I tell him anyway.

"I did have a boyfriend, but I broke up with him about three months ago. We'd been together for four years. I met him through some friends, and we really hit it off, so we started dating, and within a few months, we were living together. He's good-looking and a lawyer, so everyone seemed to think he was perfect for me—even me—but he wasn't. He wasn't interested in who I really am; he just wanted a trophy wife to accompany him to social functions and take care of him. He thought once we got married, I'd quit all this silly psychology stuff, stay home, and raise his babies. I broke up with him the night he asked me to marry him."

"Oh, Tori. I'm sorry! I think you made the right choice though. You should be with someone because they're your soul mate, not because it's easy or convenient."

I stare at him for a moment because he's managed to sum up in a sentence what it took me months to figure out. "Thanks. I think I made the right choice, too, although at the time, it really hurt me to do it."

"That guy was stupid. He should have talked to you about what you wanted instead of telling you how it was going to be. I would never treat you like that."

Um, is he sitting here thinking about how he would treat me if we were dating? Did I hear that right? "What about you? Did you ever find your soul mate?"

"No," he answers softly. "I was dating someone when I first got sick, but it was casual, and she didn't stick around when things got tough. Not that I blame her really. I dated before that, but nothing too serious. And I haven't dated anyone since."

Okay, exactly why the hell did I ask that question? He's sitting here alone, so the only two possible answers to my question were: a) no, he's never found his soul mate; or b) he found her, but he lost her somehow. And now we're both sitting here thinking about how he'll never find his soul mate because he's dying. *Brilliant, Tori. Just brilliant.*

"I'm sorry, Will."

He shrugs and scratches at his arm again, harder this time. "You seem to be scratching a lot today."

"Yeah, itchiness is a side effect of the damn morphine. As if I wasn't already itchy enough," he mumbles.

Fuck, pain relief shouldn't cost you this much!

"Tori, I'm so glad you come here every day. I don't really want to be alone, and now that you're here, I don't have to be. And you're sssoooo pretty," he says, slurring drunkenly. "Your eyes are just *so* brown. Like chocolate and honey all mixed together. Did you know that?"

Don't laugh. Don't laugh! Oh God, but it's so hard not to when he's being this cute, and he has no idea what he's telling me about himself when he's saying these things. "No. I didn't, Will. So you like the color brown they are?"

"Hell, yeah. I get lost there all the time."

I can't help it this time, and I chuckle softly.

"What?"

"You're just so damn cute," I say without thinking.

I panic for a second. Then I remember he's not going to remember any of this anyway, and the smile that lights up his face would have been worth it even if he did.

"You think I'm cute?" he asks, smirking at me.

"Yes, I think you're cute."

"How cute?" I laugh again.

"As cute as they come," I tell him, reaching up to ruffle his hair. I start to move my hand away, but he grabs it and entwines my fingers with his.

"Cute enough to let me do this?" he asks as his eyes drift closed.

"Yes, cute enough to let you do that." *And a whole hell of a lot more . . . but not today.*

"Sweetheart, you're sleepy. I know morphine knocks you out, plus you probably still need rest after being up all night. Why don't I go, and I'll come back first thing in the morning to check on you."

"I guess," Will says, pouting. "But tomorrow, I'll probably be back to 'boring' Will. I think I'm much more fun when I'm high on painkillers, don't you?"

"I admit you are . . . entertaining, but I'm happier when you're not in pain, and I like when we both get to remember what we talked about."

"Yeah, I guess there's that. But I like me better this way. I'm more like I was before I got sick."

I bite my lip, thinking about a completely unaltered Will flirting with me this way, and it nearly takes my breath away.

"Get some sleep, sweetheart. I'll see you tomorrow," I tell him, and I just can't resist the urge to lean in and kiss his forehead before I go. He grins up at me lazily, his lips still curled in a smile long after his eyes close.

CHAPTER 13

As I walk out of the elevator, Jenny glances up from the nurses' station and comes around to waylay me as I walk down the hall. "You need to prepare yourself. Will is having a really bad day today."

My heart clenches in my chest. *Jesus Christ, what have the* last *two days been?* "What's wrong?"

"His fever has been hovering around one-oh-four all day, and he's delirious and confused. We had to put him in restraints because he tried to get out of bed this morning and fell, and he's tried to pull his IV out twice already. He's in and out of consciousness, and when he's awake, he's unpredictable. I've got one of the nurses sitting in there with him as much as possible, but I can't keep someone in there all the time."

"Oh, shit! Why didn't you call me? I would have come up and sat with him!"

Jenny's eyes widen. "Oh, I . . . I didn't realize. You and I haven't really talked in a few days, and I didn't know . . ."

"Yes, I would have dropped what I was doing and come. Please, let me know when he needs *anything*."

"Of course," she says, as one corner of her mouth turns up.

"We'll have to talk later, Jenny. I really need to see him now," I tell her as I give her arm a squeeze.

I hurry down the hall, taking a deep breath before I push the door open. My peripheral vision registers the nurse sitting in the chair, but my gaze zeroes in on Will.

His eyes are closed, his brow furrowed as he rolls his head from side to side. His cheeks are flushed, his cheekbones tinged a ruddy pink, and there's a sheen of sweat on his forehead. As I get closer, I see his shirt is soaked through under his arms as well.

I bite my lip and finally glance at the nurse sitting next to him.

She smiles at me kindly. "He's been out for a while now, but he's very restless."

"I'll stay with him if you have other things to do."

"Buzz if you need anything," she says, patting my arm lightly as she walks from the room.

I start to walk over to Will but change my mind halfway there, going into his bathroom instead. There's a stack of washcloths on a shelf next to the sink, and I quickly wet one with cold water, wringing it out and folding it into a compress. Then I go to him and gently press the cool cloth to his forehead, wiping away the sweat that's gathered there, then refold it and press it to each of his cheeks.

He huffs out a breath as I run my fingers through his hair, still holding the compress to the side of his face. He opens his eyes and stares at me for a full minute before whispering, "Tori?"

"Hello, Will. How are you feeling?" I ask, smiling to cover how upset I am.

"So . . . hot . . ."

"I'm sorry, sweetheart. You have a really high fever today; that's why you're so hot. Do you remember?"

"No . . ." He licks his dry, chapped lips.

"Would you like some water?"

"Yes."

I walk around to the other side of the bed and retrieve his cup.

He drinks thirstily, grunting as he shifts position on the bed. When he's done, he releases the straw, wetting his lips again. "I need to go to class today. I have to finish my painting for Mr. Warner."

He opens his eyes again and looks down at himself, pulling against the restraints and wincing.

"Will, you can't go anywhere. You're sick and you can't get out of bed."

"Sure I can," he says, moving again and crying out in pain this time.

"No, sweetheart, you can't. Please, just lie still, okay? Then it won't hurt so much; I promise."

"O-okay," he says weakly.

I press the cloth to his forehead again, and he leans into the touch.

"That feels . . . so good."

Tears sting my eyes as I smile at him, but his own eyes are already closed. I stand next to him for a while, holding the cloth to his forehead and running my fingers through his hair until he begins to move again in his sleep. I don't want to wake him by trying to keep the compress on his forehead, so I sit down, holding my head in my hands.

Holy shit, how much worse can things get for him? I had thought the last two days were bad enough, and now this? Well, there's no way I'm going to leave him like this, so I settle into my chair and pull out my Kindle.

Will is neither still nor quiet in his fevered sleep. He's in almost constant motion, moaning and whimpering from the pain it's causing him. I watch over him, feeling completely helpless. At this moment, there is absolutely nothing I can do to ease his suffering, and that's getting to be an all-too-familiar feeling. I want to talk to him and spend time with him so much, but his illness is becoming a physical barrier between us. He's there, on the other side, and I know he wants to be with me, but he can't get past the ever-increasing failings of his body, and I can't do anything but watch him drift further away.

Tears are streaming down my face, but thinking this way isn't going to help either of us, so I bury myself in my book again until I hear the door open behind me.

Jenny peeks around it, but her usual smile falters as her gaze falls on Will. She walks over to him, laying a hand on his forehead, then pressing her fingers to his wrist and staring at the clock over the door as she takes his pulse. When she's finished, she turns to me. "Well, he doesn't seem any worse off than the last time I checked on him. Has he been awake at all?"

"When I first came in, I put a compress on his forehead, and he woke up, but he didn't stay with me long. He's so restless that I gave up on the idea because I didn't want to keep waking him."

"It's a good idea for when he's awake, but you're right. When he's sleeping, you should probably let him be. His body needs all the help it can get to fight off the fever."

"What happened this morning? When did this all start?"

"Sometime during the night. When I got here at seven, he was already feverish. His temperature was around one-oh-two then, but it spiked around nine in between checks. He must have woken up and been completely confused, because he tried to get out of bed. I found him on the floor with his IV partially ripped out.

"We got him re-situated in bed, restarted his IV, and tried to use a chest band to restrain him, but it was too painful for him, and he yanked the IV out of position again, so we ended up having to use the arm restraints."

"Damn. He knew who I was when he talked to me, but he told me he needed to go to school today to finish some project."

"Yeah, that sounds about right," Jenny says, nodding. "A high fever makes you lose your grip on the present and often on reality. Hopefully, his fever will break soon though. Low- and medium-grade fevers are fairly common for his cancer, but high ones like this aren't."

"Do you think something else is wrong?"

"No, I don't think so. He doesn't have any new symptoms, and so far, his labs are clear. His body just has to work through it. Are you heading out soon? It's almost seven."

I shake my head. "No, I can't leave him like this. I don't want him to be all alone this way, and I know the nurses are too busy to sit with him. I'm gonna stay."

Jenny looks at me—I mean, *really* looks—then shakes her head as if she's decided something. "Listen, why don't I get one of the nurses to sit with him for a while, and you can run out with me and grab some dinner? You have to be starving, and you may have a long night ahead of you."

Hmm . . . she's probably right. "Thanks, Jenny, I guess I should have some dinner, and we haven't really talked in a while."

"Great! I'll send one of the nurses down, and I'll clock out and get my stuff."

I glance over at Will, and he's shivering, so I get him another blanket, then lay the afghan I gave him on top and bring it all the way up to his chin. He never wakes, but after a few minutes, his shivers become a little less violent. I want to touch him, but I'm afraid of waking him, so I just blow him a kiss as I turn to meet Jenny at the door.

Since I don't want to be gone too long, I suggest the Subway right across the street from the hospital.

"You look like hell," Jenny tells me, taking a bite of her sandwich.

I snort. "Tell it like it is, Jenny. Don't hold anything back."

She grins at me. "That's what I'm here for! They don't call me 'honest Jenny' for nothing."

"I always thought they called you 'annoying Jenny,'" I grumble, and I'm rewarded with a shot in the arm.

"Is it Will?"

"Yes." I respond without hesitation. "He was doing so well, and then everything just went to hell in a handbasket on Sunday. I wish there was more I could do for him."

"You're doing a lot for him already—more than you usually do for patients in his situation."

"Yes, Will is totally different from all the other patients I've befriended. It's not that I didn't care about the others, but with Will, it's on a whole different level."

"Is it because he's so young?"

"I'm sure that's part of it. It's heartbreaking to see someone so young with a terminal disease, and I never knew lymphomas could have such nasty symptoms. It's . . . more than that though."

"Have you figured out yet why he's alone and where his family and friends are?"

"No, not yet. He's telling me things about himself now, which is better than before when he wasn't even really interacting with me, but I can't get near the topic of his family without him freezing up. He did talk to me a bit about his friends, however, and I know he has a friend named Jason who took care of him when he was sick before."

"Where is Jason now?"

"I don't know. Something bad happened between them because he told me Jason is pissed at him right now. When we got to the point of why, he stopped because he didn't want to get that upset when he was having a good day. He promised he *would* tell me, so at least we're heading in the right direction."

"That's good!" Jenny says.

"I feel kind of bad though. He's in denial, and I need to get him to see that he needs these people, but he'd been feeling so good since last week's procedure that I didn't have the heart to try to push ahead to the hard topics. And he can be *so* persuasive and cute when he wants to be."

"You seem to make him happy."

I blush because I'm surprised she's noticed, but then again, she's with him every day.

"Do you find him attractive?"

I raise an eyebrow at her. "Is it possible to be breathing and female and *not* find him attractive?"

She giggles. "No, I guess not. He kills me with those green eyes."

I smile, thinking of those eyes paired with his gorgeous smile until Jenny's chuckle invades my daydream.

"You seem . . . different with him. *Really* different. If I didn't know better—"

"No, Jenny."

"I can see how much you both care about each other, and you're both attracted to each other—"

"But what does it matter? The reality is he's dying. I can't help but care about him, and I'll do anything I can for him, but it has to end there because anything more is just going to cause us both more pain in the end."

"But what if he weren't dying?"

I raise my eyes to stare at her. "What does *that* matter? He *is* dying, and I can't afford to let myself think about if he weren't."

"Just humor me. Would things be different if he weren't dying?"

I take a deep breath and make the admission to myself as well as to her. "Yes, things would be very different if he weren't dying. He's perfect, Jenny. Making him happy makes me happier than I've ever been, and he's so . . . deep and affectionate and sweet. Did you know he's an artist?"

"No!" She gasps, her eyes widening.

"Yes. When I went to his apartment to get his things for him, I saw some of his work. It's so incredibly beautiful. I can't believe how talented he is. And the things he's told me about what he sees and feels when he paints—"

Jenny has gotten up and put her arms around me, and I realize tears are streaming down my face. "Oh God, Jenny, I already don't have any idea how I'm going to survive watching him die. If I let myself feel anything else for him, when he dies, it really *will* destroy me."

Shaking my head, I swipe at my tears. "Dammit, this isn't supposed to be about me! This is why you don't get emotionally involved with patients, because if you do, your needs and feelings start to come into play when what you really should be worrying about are their needs and feelings. That's exactly what's happened to me with Will, and I need to put a stop to it. I have to focus on helping him make peace with his life and getting back the people he needs rather than trying to *become* one of the people he needs. It's too—selfish a thing for me to do. Fuck!"

"I'm sorry, Tori," Jenny says, her arm still around me. "I didn't mean to upset you. I just see something happening between the two of you, and I don't know that ignoring it is the right answer. I don't know that it's good for either of you."

"I don't think anything about this whole situation is good for either of us. And now these last few days have been so bad for him . . ."

"Are you sure you don't want to take him on as a patient?" she asks, not meeting my eyes.

I laugh. "I can't do that. I'm way over the doctor-patient line right now. I'm glad I never did take him on. Otherwise, I'd have to stop this or risk being fired."

"Right."

"Why did you ask that?"

"It would . . . make certain things easier. You could see his chart, and I wouldn't have to watch what I say around you."

"Is there something I need to know, Jenny?" I ask her point blank. I know I shouldn't, but if it's something that might help Will . . .

She just looks at me, a sad smile on her face.

"I'm sorry. That wasn't fair. I'm just . . . more than a little involved right now."

"It's all right. But you should think very carefully about your feelings for him. Knowing how much you care for him might not make things easier for him, but it still might be something he'd want to know."

"I'll think about it. Listen, I'd better get back to him. I know you can't keep a nurse in there all the time, and I really don't want him to be alone today."

"Okay, hon. I hope I don't find you there in the morning when I come back on."

"I hope I'm not there either," I tell her, gathering my belongings.

When I return to his room, Will is alone, but he looks as if he's okay. His shivering has stopped, and sweat is beading on his forehead, so I pull the afghan down so it's only covering his feet. He's relatively still at the moment—sleeping more peacefully than he has all day.

I sit down with my Kindle and settle in to keep watch over him until his fever breaks.

About an hour later, Will lets out a pained grunt, and I immediately raise my eyes from my book. His face is screwed up in pain, and he's tugging hard against the restraints and whimpering. He thrashes his head from side to side, eyes closed. I don't think he's even really awake. I jump up and grasp his chin, caressing the side of his face.

"Shh . . . Will, it's all right. Don't fight the restraints."

His eyes snap open, and I don't know if he recognizes me or not, but he glares at me. "So . . . itchy." He grinds the words out and tries to reach toward the center of his body with his hands. They've put softly lined leather cuffs on his wrists, and they're fastened to the rails of the bed, so there's no way he can scratch anything.

For a moment, I think about letting him out, but I have no idea if I can control him, and if he does anything to his IV, the nurses will kill me.

Keeping hold of his chin, I use my other hand to stroke his hair. "Will, it's Tori. Do you understand me? Stop fighting, please. I'll help you, but you have to stop struggling, or you're going to hurt yourself."

He stops moving and looks at me again, and recognition flickers in his eyes. "Tori?"

"Yes, I'm here," I say soothingly, continuing to stroke his hair.

He closes his eyes and rolls his head from side to side on the pillow. "Why can't I move? I'm so itchy, but I can't . . . reach . . ."

He jerks his arms against the restraints again, wincing as he strains his already sore joints.

"Sweetheart, you're in restraints because you tried to pull your IV out. You have a very high fever, and I can't take them off because you've been delirious, and we don't know what you're going to do. But I can help you. Tell me where it itches, and I'll scratch it for you, okay?"

His eyes open, but they're dull and vacant as he stares at me. "I'm sorry . . . Tori . . ."

"There's nothing to be sorry for. Just tell me where you're itchy, and I'll take care of it for you, okay?"

"My . . . arms," he whispers.

I take his hand in mine and run my fingernails back and forth over the skin of his arm, pressing firmly but not too hard. He moans appreciatively, so I keep going. I start scratching further up toward his elbow, and he winces.

"Hurts . . ." he murmurs, so I catch the sleeve of his nightshirt and unbutton the cuff, tugging it up toward his elbow.

I swallow thickly at the sight of the inflamed rash that covers his arm, but when I get to his elbow, I gasp in shock. The delicate skin on the inside is scabbed over and cracked, and the spot where I scratched is now bleeding a little. *Holy shit!*

"Will, your skin is all broken here!"

He furrows his brow. "Too itchy . . . can't help it . . ."

Damn. Just fucking damn. I close my eyes and shake my head. *No wonder he's so careful not to let me see him—he's a mess!*

I open my eyes to find him watching me, and I continue gliding my fingernails gently over his skin. "Do you want me to do the other arm?"

"Yes," he answers, closing his eyes and humming as I do what I can for him.

After a few moments, he shifts his shoulders on the bed and winces. "Tori, can you . . . do that on my chest, too?"

"Of course I can." I put my hand on the buttons of his nightshirt, but he tenses.

"Don't want you . . . to see," he mumbles.

"Shh . . . I'm not really looking; I promise. I just need to see where your skin is already broken so I don't hurt you again, all right?"

"'Kay."

I pull down the blankets and slowly unbutton his nightshirt, bracing myself for what I'm about to see. The rash on his chest is bright red and angry, like his arms, and there are several spots with broken and scabbed-over skin. I avoid those as I scratch over his pecs, and he sighs. As I move toward his shoulder, he winces, so I pull his shirt back to see what I've managed to irritate. There's a large lump on the side of his chest, almost under his arm, and I realize this must be one of the swollen lymph nodes he's told me about. It looks extremely tender, so I'm careful not to come anywhere near it again. *Dear God, no wonder Will winces every time he moves!*

I bite my lip, trying to hold back my tears. I can't believe it's this bad, and I didn't know. *He's just so damn accepting of everything!* He never complains, but now I can see he has a ton of things he could complain about if he chose to. My admiration for Will's strength of character just went up by an order of magnitude. I know I couldn't take this all in stride and not get frustrated and pissed . . . and depressed. Hell, almost nobody could. I don't think he has any idea how unique he is in this regard. Most people in his position would be leaning heavily on family and on a therapist too. The others I've befriended who had no family came to lean on me pretty quickly, but Will hasn't. Every inroad I've made with him has been a struggle, and he's only really asked me for things when he's had no other options. Although it's not good for him to be alone, I marvel at his ability to do it, and I wonder if he could make it all the way through to the end by himself. I have no intention of letting him, but I think he's strong enough to.

Will shifts under my hand, and I startle. He seems to be moving upward, trying to get my fingers to move lower. Pausing, I unbutton another button or two on his nightshirt, being careful to keep the blankets low to preserve his modesty. His belly is becoming rounder again. I can see a definite difference in the week since he had it drained. The space is slowly filling with fluid, and eventually it's going to make it hard for him to breathe. This cancer just never fucking quits.

I start to run my nails over his belly, but he draws in a sharp breath, and I immediately pull my hand away.

"Softer," he whispers, his eyes still closed.

I'm barely touching him now, but it seems to be enough because he relaxes and takes a slow, heavy breath. I keep going, but he's already dropped off to sleep.

After a few minutes more, I stop and carefully button up his shirt, pulling the blankets back up to his chest. He seems to be resting more comfortably now, but there are still beads of sweat on his forehead, and I know from touching him that his temp is still very high.

Hours go by as I'm lost in my book, and though he doesn't wake again, Will's restlessness steadily increases. The nurses go in and out, checking his temperature and pulse, but nothing seems to really change.

Around one in the morning, I decide I can't read anymore and shift my gaze to Will. He's rolling his head from side to side again, making the beads of sweat slide down his face.

I get up from my chair, stretching as I stand, and go into his bathroom to make another compress for him. When I come back, I gently clean his face, then re-fold the cloth and press it to his cheeks and forehead just as I did earlier.

He stirs, opening weary eyes to look at me. "Mom?"

Oh, shit. He's obviously delirious, but not having any idea what happened between him and his mother, I have no idea how to handle this. *Do I pretend to be her?* Earlier in the day, he told me he had to finish a painting for class. He seems to be reaching backward in his mind, so I decide to take the gamble and assume he's doing the same now, and that he'd actually want to see his mother.

"Yes, honey. I'm right here," I whisper back, and his lips turn up in a small smile.

"I've missed you," he says, trying to reach for my hand, but the restraint stops him.

I lift his hand and entwine our fingers, and his grin gets a little wider.

Suddenly, his brow wrinkles. "Oh God, Mom. I'm so sorry! I just couldn't take it anymore! I had to . . ."

He trails off, and I have to bite my tongue to keep from asking him what he had to do. I want to dig so badly, but there are too many ways it could go wrong. And I want him to trust me. I don't want to put myself in a position where I'm lying about what I know and don't know, nor do I want to try to keep straight what he's told me when he's in his right mind versus what he's told me when he's not.

"It's okay. Don't worry about it."

"Oh, Mom, this is so fucking hard. I just want it to be over. There's nothing left for me. I need the pain to stop. There's just so much, and I can't . . ."

He chokes out a sob, and my heart shatters. This is the Will I never see, the one who's struggling and clawing and fighting under that calm exterior, not to keep living, but to endure until the end.

I stroke his face, his hair. I whisper words of love and comfort, and even though they taste of bile, I tell him it will be over soon. I lose myself in comforting him until his tears finally cease, and he begins shivering again. I reach down, pull the afghan over him, and fall wearily into my chair.

He needs his mother. I don't know where she is now and why they're not in touch, but he needs to make peace with her, and he needs her comfort. He's strong, but he's not invincible. This is tearing him up inside; he just refuses to let anyone see it. Even me.

But now I know why he isn't fighting to stay alive. He thinks there's nothing left for him, so he wants it all to end as soon as possible. He's cut all his ties, for better or worse, and he thinks there's nothing left for him but the ending. *Oh, Will.*

I can't let him go on like this any longer. I have to convince him to tell me about Jason and his mother and to contact them if that's what's best. My gut tells me he needs them both, and if I let him get to the end of this without fixing things, he's going to regret it until his last breath, and I'm going to regret it a lot longer than that.

And I have to convince him that he still has things to live for. This is it; this is all the time he has, and he needs to enjoy every moment because there are no do-overs. I can't bear for him to get to his last day and realize he's wasted any of the ones before. Even though he's been having a good time with me, he obviously still wants this to end as soon as possible, and I need to find a way to change that. Maybe his mom or Jason will have the key, something he's willing to fight for.

I startle as someone touches my shoulder, lifting my face from the white blanket before me.

"His fever's broken," the nurse whispers.

I focus my bleary eyes on Will. He seems to be resting comfortably now. The sweat on his forehead is drying, and when I touch his cheek, it's noticeably cooler. His breathing is slow and even. It's over, for now.

The nurse removes the restraints from his wrists and smiles kindly at me.

"What time is it?"

"It's nearly three. You should go on home if you're planning to. I'm pretty sure he's going to sleep peacefully through the rest of the night."

He *does* look at peace. I hope tomorrow will be a much better day for him. I rise from my chair, leaning in and kissing Will's forehead before I go.

"I'll be back tomorrow," I whisper, taking comfort in our routine.

Chapter 14

Seven a.m. comes much too soon, and since I don't have any appointments this morning, I decide to sleep in for another hour. When I finally drag myself out of bed, I shower and dress in a fog and drink two cups of coffee before I leave for the hospital. I'm going to need an IV drip of caffeine to get through this day.

My first stop is the fourth floor, and Jenny catches sight of me as I'm heading for Will's door.

"Jesus, Tori, did you sleep last night?"

"Um, a few hours. I didn't leave here until after three, when Will's fever finally broke. How is he this morning?"

"I've checked on him twice so far, and he's still sleeping."

"Well, I won't disturb him, but can I just—"

"Sure, go peek in at him," she says with a grin, squeezing my shoulder as she heads for another patient's room.

I open his door but not far enough to make it squeak. When I'm satisfied it won't make any noise, I look up at the man who seems to have become the center of my universe over the last two weeks. My breath catches as I gaze at him. He's stunning, even in sleep, even when worn out by fever and pain. The circles under his eyes are heavy today, but the skin around them is relaxed. His auburn hair is a spectacular, unruly mass, sticking out in every direction—more so than usual for the morning since he was so restless yesterday. I miss the bright green eyes, but the soft stubble on his cheeks makes me want to fly across the room so I can feel it—caress it with my fingers and watch as he leans into my touch. I can't help but smile as I back out of the room and head down to the second floor to start my day.

With the help of a chocolate bar and two cups of coffee in the afternoon, I manage to stay awake through today's staff meeting and my afternoon appointments. After I finally finish with my last patient, I scurry up to the fourth floor, hoping Will is awake, and I can start making some progress on helping him.

Jenny is in her usual spot at the desk. "Hi, Jenny. How's Will this afternoon?"

"He's pretty much been out all day," she says, shrugging. "I woke him at lunchtime to coax some food into him, but he could barely keep his eyes open. That fever took a lot out of him, and he's going to need a few days to recover."

Shit. I don't want to believe he's that weak from his illness, and it must show on my face because Jenny squeezes my shoulder.

"Hey. He'll be fine once he gets a little more rest."

I smile half-heartedly and nod, but the feeling that I may be running out of time weighs heavily on me as I trudge down the hall.

When I open his door, he's completely still, and his eyes are closed. Sighing, I'm already letting the door slowly close when I hear a soft call of "Tori?" from the bed. I push it open again, and the green eyes I've missed so much meet mine, but today they're . . . haunted. He looks desperately tired and weak, and his movements are deliberate and frail-looking.

My first instinct is to rush over to him, but as I look him in the eyes, I see things there I rarely see: anger and frustration. I take a deep breath.

"Hi, Will. How are you feeling today?"

He closes his eyes and flinches at the question. "I'm . . . better than I have been. The fever is gone and so is the pain I was in on Sunday and Monday."

"That's good," I say as I take my seat.

Will snorts derisively. "I wouldn't say that." He closes his eyes with a sigh. "Tori, I'm not in the best of moods today. I don't know if you should be here. I'm really not in any shape for company."

Shit. He's really upset.

"Do you want me to go?" I ask, knowing my eyes are begging him to let me stay.

"Yes." He huffs out a breath. "No . . . fuck, I don't know," he replies, frustration and confusion coloring his voice. He raises a hand to his forehead. "I'm just in a bad place today."

"I'm sorry, Will. Do you want to talk about it?"

"No." Then he laughs, and it's an ugly sound. "There's nothing for me to really talk *about*—the past few days are a blur. The last day I remember with any kind of clarity was when we watched the two *Star Trek* movies, and I was in so much pain. I remember bits and pieces after that, but it's kind of like a dream, a nightmare, really. I have no control over anything anymore."

My heart aches for him. I wish I had something other than words to offer or that I could tell him what he's saying isn't true. "Hey, it's all right—"

"No, it's not fucking *all right*!" He snaps at me, glaring. "I just lost three days of what little time I have left, and I don't even understand *why* I'm upset about that because I want this to be over with as soon as possible!"

He stares down at the blanket and picks at the weave with little flicks of his fingers—his nervous habit with a twist of agitation. "If I were strong enough to leave here on my own, I'd check myself out AMA and let this infection kill me."

"No! Will, don't even say that!"

"Why not? It's only a matter of time anyway," he says, his eyes daring me to claim otherwise.

I bite my tongue so hard I taste blood to keep myself from blurting out all the answers that he needs to find for himself, that the time is the key, and what he does with it is of the utmost importance, that he could have so much more right now if he would only look to his own needs instead of the needs of everyone else. But I stay quiet. Yelling at him isn't going to fix anything, and I have to keep my feelings out of this and listen to him.

"That may be true, but you don't want to die like that—suffering and with no one around you."

"You know what? Maybe I do. Don't old dogs just go off in the woods to die alone? I think they might have the right idea."

I count to ten because he has no idea what his line of reasoning is doing to me—on so many levels. "No, Will. That's not the way it's supposed to be." My voice quavers as I say the words, and I squeeze my eyes shut to keep my thoughts in the present. *This isn't the same. It's different—it has to be!* Not for the first time, I wonder, *Can I really handle this?*

He closes his eyes and shakes his head. "I'm tired of all of this. And I *hate* being upset this way. I just . . . need to get a grip, but today, I can't seem to *do* it."

"It's just a bad day, that's all. You'll feel better about everything tomorrow; I'm sure of it," I tell him, hoping he'll drop this for today because we're both too upset.

He gives that ugly laugh again, then winces. "I *won't* feel better about it tomorrow, Tori. And even if I do, does it matter?"

"Of course it matters! Why wouldn't it matter?"

"Because I'm dying, Tori! Nothing matters!" he yells, closing his eyes and breathing heavily.

Count to ten. Count to twenty. Keep your cool! You're both frustrated, and he's barely holding it together. If you blow up at him, he's going to push you away. But my need to help him is growing even more urgent; he's so far from ready for his life to end. When my breathing slows, I say evenly, "Yes, it does matter. You may be dying, but you're not dead yet."

"Is there a difference?"

Oh, fuck me! That's it! "Yes, god*dam*mit, there is!" I yell, and he jumps at the anger in my voice. "You have time! Maybe not a lot of time but enough to *enjoy* things if you want to! Enough to fix things if there are things in your life that need to be fixed!"

He takes a few seconds to recover from my outburst, and then he shakes his head. "No. There's not enough time for that."

"How do you know? How do you know until you try?"

"Because some things can't be fixed," he says ominously.

"Okay, let's let that go for now. What about enjoying things? I know you're stuck in this hospital, and there's not a whole lot you can do, but we had fun watching a movie on Saturday, didn't we? We've talked and laughed about so many things, and you can still draw; I just wish you'd look at the positives a little bit. You're so intent on focusing on how the glass is half-empty; if you're not careful, it's going to be completely empty, and you'll have missed all you could have had when it was still half-full. I'm sorry this is all there is, Will. I would give anything to make it different for you, but all I can do is help you try to get the most out of the time you have left."

"No! Doing things with my time now will just make the end that much worse! I can't do that to myself or to anyone else! I *can't!*"

"And what about Jason and your family? Would *they* understand that you can't do anything with the time you have left?"

He freezes, and as he draws in a deep breath, his eyes widen, then narrow. His anger is like an entity in the room, and now it's directed straight at me.

Oh, fuck, I've made a colossal mistake. I've shoved the two most sensitive topics—the issues we've been dancing around for weeks—right in his face. I let my anger get the better of me, and I let myself forget for a moment that he's in control here. He has the power to tell me not to come back, and I may have pushed him far enough that he's about to use it.

Oh God, it can't end for us like this, not because of something stupid I said! He can't die alone because I made the wrong choice! No, this can't be happening! I'm panicking now, my chest tight and my breath coming in gasps.

"Tori, I think you should—"

"Don't! Please, don't! Don't tell me not to come back! I'll stop. I won't ask you anything else; I won't do anything but be your friend. Just please, don't close yourself off from me. I can't stand the thought of you being all alone. I just . . . *can't!*" Tears are streaming down my face, and I know he doesn't understand, but I can't explain right now. I don't know if I can ever explain.

Either my outburst or my tears break through his anger because he closes his eyes and breathes deeply for a few moments while I try to get myself under control.

When he seeks my eyes again, his are deep green and sorrowful, but the blaze of anger is gone. "I'm sorry. I should never have let you stay today. I'm really depressed and angry, and I never wanted you to see me like this. I'm worn out, and I need to recover from this awful week. I didn't mean to make you cry."

And there it goes. As I watch him, he's burying his anger and frustration deep down, saving it only for himself and the moments he's alone. He'll never let me see it again if he can help it. I can see the resolve in his eyes.

"I'm sorry, too, Will. I never should have—"

"No, you shouldn't have." He snaps at me, his anger flaring. "And if you bring it up again, I *will* ask you to leave."

"I won't. I said I wouldn't, and I know that's what you want. I'm sorry," I tell him, knowing that eventually I'll have to break that promise, but it needs to be made right now, so he'll let me stay.

"It's all right. I know why you did it, but there's nothing more to be said."

Oh, Will, there's so much that needs to be said! I can't believe you're able to blind yourself so completely! But I can't force it on him. He's a gentle soul, but as they say, still waters run deep, and he's got a depth of stubbornness and strength I've rarely encountered before.

"Tori, I think I need some time alone if that's okay with you," he says softly, closing his eyes to dismiss me. He's going to break down the moment I leave, and there's not a damn thing I can do about it.

"Of course. I'll let you rest now, but I'll see you tomorrow." As I stand, I lean over and place my lips against his forehead without even thinking. I've done this for the last three days, but he startles at the contact, and as I back away and see him staring at me wide-eyed, I realize he doesn't remember a single one.

My cheeks heat as I stammer. "I'm sorry. I got in the habit of leaving this way the last few days, but I'm guessing you don't remember."

"No, I . . . Don't be sorry. You're right. I, uh, didn't know." And as he looks at me, his expression becomes so sad that he closes his eyes again to hide the pain there.

As I turn away, I hear a simple, quiet reply that I don't think was meant for my ears. "I don't mind though."

CHAPTER 15

As I walk into Will's room this morning, it's obvious that things have changed. He seems calm, but his guard is up—I can sense it, even from across the room. I did major damage yesterday. His earlier promise to tell me about Jason and his family is probably null and void now. *Dammit!*

He smiles at me, but it's muted and sad.

"Tori, I'm really sorry. I shouldn't have let you stay yesterday. I knew I was . . . volatile, and I should have just asked you to go. I didn't want you to see me that way."

"Will, it's okay to be upset about your situation—"

"No!" He cuts me off, but he takes a deep breath and starts again. "No, it's not. I'm done being upset about this. It's no use fretting over something I can't change, and I'm done with it. I was just tired yesterday and not myself after that high fever."

"Will—"

"Let it go. I said some things I shouldn't have yesterday, and I'm not going to talk about them. If I could take them back, I would."

"But everything that happened yesterday is perfectly normal—"

"Tori!" he says sharply, but the anger is gone as quickly as it came. "I'm not going to let you psychoanalyze me. If you're here to be my friend,

I'm happy to have your company, but if you're here to find out more about Jason and my family and to try to change how I'm approaching my death, then I'm going to have to ask you to leave."

I stare at him, and he stares back calmly. He's in complete control today, his defenses firmly in place.

He's not angry now—he's not saying these words to me in the heat of the moment. He's thought this through, and he's giving me an ultimatum. I draw a sharp breath as the pain of that realization cuts through my chest.

What I'm feeling must be showing in my eyes because his expression softens, and he grabs his lower lip with his teeth.

"Tori, I've just . . . I've made up my mind, and I'm not going to change it. I do want you to stay with me though—if you still want to."

"Of course I do," I tell him, covering his hand with mine.

I glance down at my watch, and it's already past eight; I have an appointment at eight-thirty. "I should get going for now, but I'll be back at four, okay?"

"Okay."

I return promptly at four o'clock, eager to talk to Will and get things headed back toward normal—or what's normal for us, anyway. But I'm brought up short when I see he's sleeping. Since I've been coming to see him, I've never found him asleep at this time unless . . . Oh *shit*! What the hell happened now? I turn on my heel, and I'm revving up to storm off in search of Jenny when I hear his voice behind me.

"Tori?"

I turn, and his eyes are open but just barely. He blinks slowly, then opens them a little wider as he focuses on me.

"What happened?" I ask as I walk quickly to his bedside and take his hand.

"Nothing. I'm ... fine." He sighs softly. "I just can't seem to keep my eyes open."

"Are you feeling all right?"

"Yes, I'm just exhausted. I've been like this all day. I napped on and off through the morning; I slept after lunch, and then I wanted to draw like I usually do, but I was too damn tired," he explains, frustration coloring his voice.

"Maybe you just need some extra rest today."

"It seems I don't have a choice."

Oh boy, tired and pissed off.

I reach up and run my fingers through his hair, and he leans into the touch as his eyes fall closed again. His lips turn up in a soft smile, but I know it's only because I'm touching him and not because he feels any better.

"Listen, I've been meaning to go by your place again to check on it, so why don't I go this afternoon?"

"No, I'm—"

"Will, you can't even keep your eyes open to talk to me for five minutes. Stop fighting it, and allow yourself the rest you need, okay? I'll go to your place tonight and come back in the morning. I'm sure you'll be caught up on sleep by tomorrow, and we'll be able to have a normal visit."

"You're not going to give me a choice, are you?" he asks, eyes still closed.

"Sweetheart, your eyelids aren't going to give you a choice, so what I would do doesn't even matter. I'll stay until you fall asleep, which from the looks of you is going to be in about ten seconds, and then I'll go check on your apartment. Is there anything you want me to bring back?"

He sighs in resignation. "Um, can you get the mail and grab me another sketchbook?"

"Of course. Now give up, you stubborn ass, and go back to sleep," I say, pointing a finger at him. Normally that would be more than enough to get a rise out of him, but he's too far gone to take the bait.

"'Kay," he mumbles as I begin running my fingers through his hair. He's out in under a minute.

I can't help but smile at him, but it makes me so incredibly sad at the same time. How does that expression go? The spirit is willing, but the flesh is weak? That's exactly what's going on here. But I try not to dwell on it. It's just one day, and although I really wanted to talk to him, I can't change the situation any more than he can. I go to my office and gather my things, then head over to his apartment.

The place looks exactly as I left it, so I quickly go and fetch his mail, retrieve the sketchbook from the studio, and place them on the table by the door so I don't forget them. And now I've decided I'm going to snoop a bit—not in his belongings, exactly, but in his artwork. He's told me about a lot of the paintings he's done, and I want to see some of the work he described for myself.

I head back to the studio and enter the room slowly, almost reverently. I've been in here before, but I've never stopped to think about what this place really is. This is Will's most sacred space. This is where he creates things—where he expresses his heart and soul on canvas. What happens in this room is magic. How he can take what he sees around him and reproduce it amazes me, but the truly astounding thing is that a part of *him* comes through in his work—his impression, his very essence. He is the lens through which everything he paints is seen, and that part of himself that shines through—how *he* interprets what he sees—is what sets his work apart from anything I've ever seen. There's just so much life, so much vibrancy to it.

I stop three steps into the room to take in what's around me. The painting of the New York skyline takes up the entire inner wall that's adjacent to his bedroom, and the wall opposite it has several rows of canvasses stacked against it. The far wall has two large windows, and in front of these sit two enormous wooden easels, one facing toward the windows and one away, so he has the option of painting in natural or artificial light. A table sits between the windows, and every inch of its surface is covered with art supplies: tubes and plastic bottles of paint of all colors, a large metal coffee can filled with brushes of every size and thickness, sticks of color that look like large, square crayons, a collection of what look like metal spatulas of various sizes and shapes, and– oh my—on the corner of the table lies a palette that is delicately smeared and dotted with at least a hundred different colors. It looks like a work of art in itself, and I cover my mouth with my hand as I imagine Will dotting and mixing all those colors as he works. The palette I'm looking at is the raw material for his creativity, and the image in my head of him holding it and painting in this room is so real even though I've never seen it. And I probably never *will* see it because I don't think Will is ever going to be coming back here. My knees buckle, and I fall to the floor with a soft thump, but my sobs are much more painful than my fall. The ache in my chest is so sharp, it takes my breath away. How can someone who creates such beauty, who has such beauty inside them, someone with so much to give, be so close to death?

In this room, Will's very soul is present, and the fact that soon this is all that will be left tears at my heart until I feel like it's in shreds. It's not *fair*. It's not his time; it's too soon. He's too beautiful to meet such a horrible fate. I cry until I have no more tears left. I cry for the brilliance and creativity that will be extinguished. I cry for myself because I will be destroyed when he takes his last breath. But mostly I cry for Will because such a perfect, tender soul deserves so much better than this.

He deserves a long, happy life so he can express all the beauty that's inside him. He deserves a loving wife who adores him and children playing at his feet. He deserves all life has to offer and more, and I would do anything—suffer anything—to be able to give it to him.

But I can't.

There's nothing I can do, and the emptiness of it consumes me. I've never felt so helpless. And lost. I've faced death many times before, but it's never been like this. I've never seen the life of a patient I've befriended this way. I've never sat in their apartment, taken care of their cat, and I've certainly never witnessed their inner beauty the way I have with Will.

But it's more than that. Will is different from all those that have come before him. He's young, and the light that shines from him is so bright I don't know how it will possibly be extinguished. And he's cute and sweet and endearing. He makes me feel important without even trying, and he just . . . God, I can't even define to myself what makes him so very special.

Or maybe it's that *I've* never been like this. My detachment went out the window long ago, and I'm trying to hold on to my heart because if I give it to him, it will only be broken in a short time. But is it already too late?

I wander across the room to the rows of paintings. The row closest to the window is all large canvasses—maybe five feet wide and four feet tall. The first picture is a study in blues—a city on the bank of a river at twilight—the blue of the water reflecting the yellow, green, and orange lights of the skyline and the deepening pink to blue of the sky punctuated by puffy clouds of soft cornflower and slate. The city is modern—tiered apartment buildings and parking garages in the foreground and taller office buildings in the back. The building at the center of the painting is the tallest, with a modern-looking, smooth spire reaching delicately toward the sky. The work is absolutely stunning. I wonder why Will hasn't sold this painting because I would buy it in a heartbeat, and I'm sure I'm not the only one. I don't recognize the city, though, so I lift the canvas and glance at the back to find "Vienna, fall 2006" in neat script on the top edge of the canvas back. I run my fingers over the words—I've never seen Will's handwriting before.

The painting behind that is of a bridge on the Seine at twilight . . . and it goes on and on. Cities I recognize and many I don't, Mont Saint-Michel and other castles, and scenes from city streets the world over. Will's brush captured them all, and I feel as if I'm seeing his life in pictures. At least he got to see some fantastic places and create some amazing work over the last few years.

This room is getting to me again. I feel as if I could stay here forever, in this place where I can live and breathe Will, but thoughts of the future keep creeping in like a slowly advancing tide, and if I stay here much longer, I'll be awash in a fresh sea of tears. A look at my watch tells me it's already past six, and I need to get home. Taking one more longing look around Will's studio, I force myself to leave the room.

I make a final check of the apartment, turning off lights as I go, and collect his things and my purse from the table. As I pull the door closed, my eyes fall on the stunning painting of Seattle on his living room wall, and I squeeze them shut tightly to try to stop the tears from coming. I'm so focused on my struggle that I don't even see the man standing in the hallway until I almost trip over him. I jump back with a squeak, covering my mouth with my hand as fear pulses up my spine.

"I'm sorry. I didn't mean to scare you," he says softly.

I look him over. He doesn't have a weapon, and his stance isn't threatening. He had been standing against the wall with his arms crossed, but now they're stretched toward me as if to keep me from falling. He's a few inches taller than I am with light blue eyes and blondish hair that falls to his chin.

"I'm not scared," I tell him, standing up straighter and looking him directly in the eye.

"Who are you?"

"I'm sorry, but who are *you*? You're the one ambushing people outside their apartments. I think you should tell me who *you* are first."

"That's *not* your apartment," he says quickly, and suddenly it clicks into place.

"Are you . . . Jason?"

He takes a step back. "Yes."

"My name is Tori. I'm a friend of Will's," I tell him, extending my hand.

He furrows his brow as he takes my hand, but he goes right back to his line of questioning as soon as courtesy will allow. "Where is Will now?"

"I think you really need to—"

"I've been trying to get ahold of him, but he won't return my calls! He's still here in Seattle, isn't he?"

"Yes." I respond without even thinking.

"Dammit!" Jason runs a hand through his hair, turning away from me. "I *knew* he was lying to me! What the hell does he think he's doing!"

I'm trying not to get angry with this guy because he's Will's friend, but after the emotional evening I've had, my patience is running very thin. And no matter what Will did, I'm suddenly feeling as if I need to defend him. "Calm down, Jason. He's in the hospital, and—"

Jason whips his head around, and all the color drains from his face. "What?"

"I said he's in the hospital. I've been checking on his place for him the last few weeks. Speaking of which, how did you know I was here tonight?"

"Is . . . is he all right?" Jason asks, all the anger gone from his voice. He looks at me as if we're in the desert, and I have the only water there is.

"He's hanging in there, but I really think you need to talk to him about it. You're putting me in a very awkward position."

He snorts and shakes his head. "I'm sorry. I didn't mean to give you the third degree. Will's my friend, and I'm concerned about him. I would like nothing better than to talk to him."

He's sincere, and I think he's truly looking at me for the first time. I can't help but feel bad for him.

"I know. I've been wishing he'd reach out to you, but he's stubborn."

"You've got that right!" He eyes me suspiciously. "How do you know Will anyway? I've been his friend for years, and I've never heard him mention you."

Oh shit, it's not my place to explain this, and I don't even know if I could do it if I tried.

"It's not my place to say. You really need to—"

"Talk to Will about this. I know!" He finishes my sentence, the sharp edge in his tone exposing his frustration.

"Should I ask him to call you?"

"Actually, please *tell* him to call me, and also tell him that if he doesn't, I'm just going to show up at the hospital tomorrow."

"Okay," I answer, drawing out the word. This is going to go over like a lead balloon with Will.

"I know he's not going to like it, and I'm sorry to have to ask you to be the messenger. I'll take it up with him tomorrow."

"You never did answer my question."

"Beg pardon?"

"About how you knew I was here tonight."

"Oh, I know Will's neighbor, Mrs. Howard. I checked in with her about two weeks ago, and she said Will had gone somewhere, and she'd been taking care of Sebastian, but then she got a note from him saying she didn't need to anymore. She also said that someone was coming by to check on the place about once a week, so I asked her to call me the next time she saw you."

Wow, having a nosy old lady for a neighbor has both pros and cons. Will also appears to have very determined friends.

"I'll see Will in the morning, so I'll give him your message then," I tell him, looking down at my hands awkwardly.

Jason looks at his shoes, then back up into my eyes. "Thank you, Tori. You must think I'm such an ass. I'm sorry. I'm just really angry with Will right now, but that's no excuse for being rude. I appreciate your passing the message along for me, and I hope I didn't scare you."

"It's all right. I'm happy to see Will has someone who cares about him enough to track him down. Just . . . take it easy on him tomorrow, okay? He's had a really rough couple of weeks."

Jason grimaces and huffs out a breath. He looks ill when he meets my eyes again. "Yeah. I'll keep that in mind."

"Well, good night, then," I tell him as I start to make my way down the hall.

"Good night, Tori," he murmurs, leaning against the wall and covering his face with his hands.

As I drive back to my apartment, I replay my conversation with Jason. He was obviously hurt by Will's lying to him, presumably about his whereabouts, but there's more to it than that.

I should be happy that half of what Will's been hiding is about to come to light, but somehow I'm not. Now I can focus on trying to find out where his mother is, but . . . this is one more step down the road I no longer want to travel, the road that forks in the not too distant future with Will going where I can't follow. *Dammit.*I should be doing everything I can to help him get there, but a growing part of me just wants to put the brakes on the whole thing. I don't know what I'm doing anymore. Everything was so clear-cut and straightforward at the beginning, but now it's a mess. Well, as Dad used to say, *"When you can't sort the forest, you need to focus on the trees."* Right now, I need to figure out what I'm going to tell Will in the morning, then do whatever I can to support him as he deals with Jason. I'm hoping and praying he has a good day tomorrow physically, because emotionally, he's going to be a wreck.

CHAPTER 16

Will's still sleeping when I peek around his door this morning. I tiptoe into the room so I can get a better look at him, being careful not to let the door squeak. He's very still, which is a good sign. When he's running a fever, even if it's not that high, he's still restless in his sleep. As I get closer, I can see he's not sweating at all, and his cheeks are a soft pink. I breathe a sigh of relief —I think today's going to be a good day.

I'm about to turn around and sneak out when Will shifts, wincing as he rolls his head to the side, and suddenly, I see a flash of bright green. As he slowly opens his eyes, he notices me, and a lazy smile spreads across his face.

"Good morning," he says, his voice deep and raspy from sleep.

It's as if the sun just came out. I can physically feel the warmth—*his* warmth—spreading across my chest, and I brim with happiness as I smile back at him. No other person in the world has ever made me that happy merely by smiling at me, and for a moment, I just stand there and *feel* it.

"Good morning, sweetheart," I say as I step closer and take his hand. His fingers are warm against mine, but not too warm, and I grin even wider. "How are you?"

He scratches at his forearm as he shifts position. "I'm hanging in there. I thought about asking for morphine during the night, but I stuck it out."

"Will, there's nothing wrong with taking morphine if you need it. There's no point in wearing yourself out by toughing out the pain."

"I know. I just . . . I like to actually remember talking to you."

I chuckle. "We have had some very memorable conversations when you've been on morphine."

"Memorable for *you*," he says, his tone grouchy. "For me, it's like I've been drunk. I only have these hazy memories of running off at the mouth in front of you, and I wake up the next morning wondering if I've said things I shouldn't have."

"Now, now, I've made a promise to morphine-high Will that I would never reveal the content of our discussions to unaltered Will or 'boring Will,' as you like to call your non-drugged self when you're high."

"Oh God!" He groans. "Well, you're still coming back here, so I guess whatever I'm doing isn't that bad."

"That's right; you just leave that to me and your alternate personality," I say with a smirk.

He grins back at me, and I feel a twinge of guilt because I know what I'm about to say is going to put him on the defensive. I hate to ruin his good mood.

"Will, we need to talk."

He tenses up and looks at me warily. "Okay. What do we need to talk about?"

"Jason."

"I told you I wasn't going to—"

"I saw him last night."

"*What?*"

"I saw Jason last night. He was waiting outside your apartment after I checked on it."

He runs his hand through his hair, hissing as he bends his elbow and shoulder. "Fuck! What did he say to you?"

"Well, he was pretty pissed."

"I'm sure he told you why that is." Will spits the words angrily.

"No, actually, he didn't."

He looks up, surprised.

"He wanted to know where you were, and he told me he was angry with you, but he didn't go into details. He also asked how I knew you and how you were doing."

"What did you tell him?"

"I told him he needed to ask you about those things, but he said you won't return his calls."

Will looks down, frowning. "Yeah, I was hoping he'd just give up."

Fat chance, Will. "He doesn't seem the type to give up."

"No, I suppose not."

"He, uh, wants you to call him," I tell him, staring down at his afghan.

"I'm sure he does."

"He said if you don't call him, he's coming here this afternoon."

Will sighs. "Well, there's no point calling him then. This conversation should take place in person anyway." Suddenly, he looks up, concern written all over his face. "Jason wasn't an ass to you, was he? He can be a little . . . intense when he's pissed."

"He wasn't an ass. Well, not a complete ass anyway. He's very concerned about you. You should have seen the look on his face when I told him you're in the hospital."

Will closes his eyes and takes a deep breath. "I know; he's probably worried sick. And he has every right to be angry with me, too. I did something I know he thinks is shitty, but I did it for both of us."

"Will, when did you last see him?"

He starts speaking immediately, seemingly not conscious of the fact that he's spilling one of the secrets he's been keeping since I first met him.

"He knows I relapsed again. I went to see him the day I found out. I was . . . wrecked. I couldn't deal with it, so I drank myself into oblivion, and he went right along with me. He said some things . . . I don't know if he even remembers. But I do. And I remember the look in his eyes when I told him. He was sad for me, but I saw that sinking feeling, too, and I knew he was thinking about having to help me again.

"So I made the decision to go it alone. I did pretty well until I started coming down with this damn infection. I called him and lied to him to keep him away, since I was hoping . . ."

My eyes widen as he trails off, remembering how he told me he had planned to stay home despite the infection and how Jenny told me he had begged them not to treat him when he was brought in. He'd intended to die from this infection, and the hospital messed up his plans. He'd hoped to just pass away with no one around him and not be a bother to anyone. *"Don't old dogs just go off in the woods to die alone?"* Oh, *Will.*

He glances over at me, and confusion and concern flash across his face, but they're quickly replaced by anger and defensiveness. "Don't look at me like that. You have no idea what this is like."

"But you were choosing to die—"

"I wasn't choosing to die! The cancer made that choice for me. I just want . . . control. If I have to die, I want to choose the time and circumstance and not by fighting and losing every battle until there's nothing left to lose. It can't win all the battles. I won't let it. That's the purpose of my DNR—I'm going to make the choice. Not some doctor or someone who cares about me. *Me.* I need to make the choice for myself."

His eyes pin me with their intensity, pleading for understanding. I stare back at him mutely. Those are two huge pieces to the puzzle that is Will, all in one morning. First, Jason, and now, why he's not fighting his cancer. But I don't agree with the second one. Not by a long shot.

"But, I don't understand how fighting takes away your control."

"Not fighting—fighting a battle you have no hope of winning. Or not enough hope to make it worth your effort. If I fight this every step of the way, I'm going to lose every step of the way, and I won't let the cancer have that kind of control. I can't win, but I can choose. The DNR gives me the power to choose, and it's very important to me."

All of a sudden, I can see it through his eyes and how it makes sense, at least to him. He doesn't see it as giving up; he sees it as taking the power away from the cancer and putting it in his own hands—his last and only choice to make. *Holy shit!* I should have known it wasn't as simple as it seemed. Will is anything but simple.

I close my eyes and feel the tears escape down my cheeks, and Will squeezes my hand. His anger is gone, and his soft green eyes beg for my understanding.

"I understand, Will."

He lets out the breath he was holding.

"I don't agree with how you see it, but I understand. If it were me, though, I would fight. If there was any possibility at all that I could win, I would fight. There's always hope, and there's always something worth fighting for."

For a brief second, Will's eyes pierce me with a depth and breadth of emotion I can't even define. He closes them quickly, and his teeth catch his lower lip.

When he looks up at me, his eyes are sad but determined. "I wish I could see it your way, Tori, but I can't. Sometimes, there's nothing left to hope for."

I want to reach out and run my fingers through his hair, to give him comfort in any way I can, but his body language is warning me away. His arm is tense as I hold his hand, and something in his eyes tells me to stay right where I am.

"Will, I . . . You could have ended this a few weeks ago when you couldn't breathe because of the fluid in your belly."

"Yes."

"But you didn't."

"No, I didn't." He sighs. "I should have, but I was afraid. I let my fear take over, and I couldn't make the decision I needed to. I don't intend to let that happen again."

My heart twists at his words, and the thought that I could have lost him right then without knowing how wonderful he is, is almost too much for me.

"I'm glad you didn't," I tell him, and now I do reach up and run my fingers into his hair.

He closes his eyes, and everything about him softens.

I cup his jaw, and warm green eyes stare into mine. "I'm glad I've gotten the chance to know you, and I hope to get to know you even better."

The emotions in his eyes are all over the place—anger, frustration, confusion, shock, wonder—but I gaze back at him patiently, trying to channel what I feel for him, trying to make him see that someone cares about him, and maybe that's worth fighting for. His expression settles on the warmer emotions, and a smile spreads across his handsome face. "Tori, I—"

We both jump as my cell phone starts ringing. I lean down and fish it out of my bag, but before I even swipe my finger across it, I see the time and swear. "Shit! I had an appointment at nine o'clock! I totally lost track of time!"

I don't even bother to answer it since I already know it's the clinic receptionist calling to find out where I am, but I text her a quick "on my way." I glance up at Will, and although he's still smiling, the moment is lost.

"I have to go," I tell him as I give his hand a quick squeeze and bend over to retrieve my bag.

"I know. I'm sorry I've made you late."

I chuckle. "You're just too interesting, Mr. Everson. I'll be back at four, all right?"

"I'll be waiting."

I lean in and give him a quick peck on the cheek, and I'm rewarded with a gasp of surprise and an adorable blush. That ought to give him something to think about today instead of worrying about Jason showing up.

Smirking at him, I turn on my heel and bolt for the door.

I'm late. I needed to finish my notes on today's patients, and it took longer than I expected, so it's now ten after four as I'm walking down the hall toward Will's room. The door is partially open, which is odd because Will likes it closed, and the nurses usually oblige him.

As I get closer, I can hear voices, so I stop just before the doorway and listen. The conversation is awkward, and I realize Will's talking to Jason, and it sounds like he just arrived.

"How are you doing?"

"I'm fine."

"I seriously doubt that. How long have you been here?"

"Four weeks."

"Jesus, Will. How bad is it?"

"Bad enough, I guess. I came here with a blood infection, and I just can't shake it. My doctor told me this morning that they're going to keep me for another two weeks of antibiotics."

"Damn. Not that that's not enough, but is that all? Have any of your other symptoms come back?"

"Um, pretty much all of them have. And most are worse than before."

"Fuck! This damn disease just doesn't quit, does it?"

"No, cancer plays to win," Will answers sarcastically.

They're both silent for a minute.

"You lied to me."

"Yes."

"Why the hell would you lie to me? You know I came *this close* to calling your parents, right?"

"Jesus, Jay—"

"Well, what choice did you leave me? I didn't know where the fuck you were, if you were okay . . . Did you really expect me to believe you'd go back there?"

"Well, I figured if you didn't believe it, you'd get the message that I wanted to be alone."

"Oh, I got the message. And I did leave you alone for a few weeks. But did you really intend for that to be goodbye?"

The silence is tense—and deafening—even out in the hallway.

"Well, did you?"

After a moment or two of quiet, I hear an exasperated sigh.

"Where's Sebastian?"

"With Tori."

"How do you know her anyway? I don't remember you ever mentioning her before."

"I didn't know her before. I met her while I've been here at the hospital."

"Seriously? So how come she gets to help you, and no one else does?"

"She doesn't get to, really. Other than Sebastian, I haven't needed anything."

"She gets to visit you, which is more than I'm allowed, apparently. Why is that?"

"Jason, I really don't think—"

"Well, I *do*. I wanna know why this girl you just met gets to spend more time with you than the friends you've had for years."

"That's exactly why she gets to be with me! *Because* she didn't know me before!"

"What the—"

"The pity, Jason! She doesn't look at me the way you do—the way all our friends do—because she doesn't know what I was like before! She doesn't know everything I've lost and how it's all changed, so she can't look at me that way. I couldn't take it anymore! I couldn't go through it for the *third fucking time*—the quiet conversations behind my back, the silence when I walk into a room, and, oh yeah, the people who are all supportive and volunteer to help, but then when things get tough, they vanish."

My heart starts to hammer against my chest. His words are so raw and painful and honest. God, what was he like before? What did this disease and his situation take away?

"Will—"

"I don't blame them, Jason. It's not their problem; it's mine. And I'm tired of burdening everyone else with my problems."

"You were never a burden to me."

Will laughs coldly. "Oh, yes, I most certainly was a burden to you."

"Why the hell would you think that? I've never said anything—"

"Yes, you did. I don't think you even remember, but *I* do."

"When?"

"The day I found out I relapsed again."

"When we were *drunk*? Jesus Christ, Will! I was completely wasted and so upset and worried about you! I have no idea what I said that night!"

"You told the *truth*! That happens when you're drunk! And the truth was that you couldn't go through this again. So that day, I decided I wouldn't ask you to."

"I may have said I couldn't go through it again, but that's because I was angry and in shock, just like you were! Hell, I'm pretty sure I said *you* couldn't go through it again either."

"Yes, but that's the difference! I *have to* go through it again. You don't."

"So that was it, then. That day *you* made the decision to do this on your own and not let anyone near you."

"Yes."

"Will, you are a selfish bastard."

I gasp and clap my hand over my mouth. *Damn.*

"*What?*"

"What about my feelings? Friendship is a two-way street, and you took away my choice in this. Again! Jesus Christ, after all we've been through, don't I deserve better than this? Shouldn't *I* get to choose if I get to see you before you die? Shouldn't *I* get the chance to offer to help you before you turn me down? Goddammit, Will, I'm so fucking pissed at you right now!"

"You're pissed? *You're* pissed? Well, you're not the one who's dying, jackass! I don't have a lot of choices left to make, but I *can* choose to spare the people I love from going through this shit with me!"

"And exactly who is going to help *you* get through this shit? Because in case you didn't know, that's what friends and family are for! *To help you get through shit!*"

The room is silent for several minutes except for the sound of heavy breathing.

Jason sighs. "Will, I don't want to upset you like this. I care about you, and I want to be here for you if you'll let me. Can I come see you? Just sit and talk? It's got to be pretty boring here alone all day."

"You've done enough, Jay. You've done more for me than anyone, and I don't want to cause you any more pain. It's hard enough to go through this myself without having to worry about—"

"Then *don't*. Don't worry about me and my feelings. I'm a big boy; I can take care of myself. You worry about beating this infection and getting stronger so you can get out of here."

"I don't know if that's going to happen," Will says quietly. "Things seem to be going downhill pretty rapidly. I don't think I'll be able to be on my own anymore."

I suspected as much, but I didn't think Will had really thought about it yet. I guess he has.

"It's been a month since I was up and around, and I'm so damn tired all the time."

"We'll figure something out. You get better first, and then we'll worry about the next step."

"I'm glad you came. And that you didn't give up on me. It means a lot to me—more than I thought it would. And I'm sorry I pushed you away. I'm just . . . this is . . . hard."

"I know it is. That's exactly why I don't want you to have to do it alone. Will you let me come see you? Please?"

Will sighs heavily. "I don't know, Jay. I don't think I can—"

"You say I've done enough. Well then, it's time you did something for me. And this is what I want you to do—I want you to let me come and sit with you. After all we've been through together, I think you owe me that much."

There's silence for a moment, and I hold my breath, waiting to see if Will gives in.

"Goddammit, Jay, you don't play fair." I hear Will grumbling, and I can't help but smile.

"I'll come by as often as I can, okay?" Jason says, and I can hear the happiness in his voice. "Is there a time of day that's good?"

"How about late morning? I usually rest after lunch, and Tori comes by at four every day, so my afternoon schedule is kinda busy."

Jason chuckles. "Sure, I can do that. Speaking of rest, you look like you could use some right now. Getting your ass handed to you by Jason Marks would wear anyone out."

I don't hear the rest of the conversation because I realize Jason is about to leave the room, and I don't want them to know I was eavesdropping. As I dash down the hall to the nurses' station, Jenny raises an eyebrow.

"Talk to me, and act like we've been talking for a few minutes," I tell her hurriedly.

She looks confused, but when she sees Jason walk out of Will's room, she jumps into the middle of a story about one of her patients.

I nod in all the right places as Jenny prattles on, and when I look up, Jason is staring at me as he approaches.

"Hi, Jason. I was just on my way down to see Will. Did you get to talk to him?"

"Yes, I did. Do you have a moment?"

"Of course." Jenny furrows her eyebrows at me, and I silence her with my eyes.

I follow Jason to the end of the hallway where he leans against the wall. "Thank you again for telling me where Will was. I'm sorry I was rude."

"It's all right. I know you were angry with Will, not me, and I know you care about him."

"Yes, I do," he says, and the intensity in his eyes is almost overwhelming. "How is he doing—really? He told me he can't shake this infection, but . . . he seems so much weaker and more tired than the last time I saw him. And it's worse than the last time he relapsed too."

I stare into Jason's concerned eyes and decide I trust him. He didn't abandon Will; Will lied to him to push him away. Jason needs to know what's going on, and I know from my eavesdropping that Will downplayed his condition.

"He's been really up and down over the last three weeks. His belly filled with so much fluid that he couldn't breathe, so they had to drain it. He's feverish more days than he's not, and last week, he had intense joint pain followed by a high fever that put him out of commission for most of the week. They've had to give him morphine a few times for pain, and he's tired all the time. I don't know how he handles it all as well as he does."

"Damn." Jason swears, swiping at his eyes. "Is there really nothing else they can do for him?"

"That's what he told me. He doesn't talk much about his illness though. He keeps the details very close."

"Yeah, that sounds like Will. Has anyone been here with him?"

"No. Other than me, you're the first visitor he's had. He's decided he doesn't want to inconvenience anyone else."

Jason groans in frustration. "Dammit, he's such a stubborn ass! What about *him*? Who's gonna help *him* get through this?"

"Well, I am. And now you can too. He needs to let people take care of him now, but we won't be able to convince him of that. He needs to figure it out for himself."

"How do you know?"

"Because I've been through this before," I tell him simply. "I think he'll figure it out. He's in denial now, but at some point, it's all going to fall apart, and we need to be here to help him when it does."

"You really do care about him, don't you?" Jason asks, his eyes searching mine.

"Yes. I've been here every day for almost a month now."

Jason looks down for a moment, chewing on his lip. "I'm glad. Thank you for taking care of him. It sounds like he really needed someone, but he was too stubborn to admit it."

"You don't need to thank me. Will's . . . very special. I'm glad I've been able to get to know him."

Jason smiles. "Yes, he certainly is. I'll see you around, Tori. I'm going to start coming to sit with him in the mornings to keep him company."

"That's great. I'm so happy the two of you were able to talk things out. And I'm glad he's willing to let you support him."

Jason nods and starts to walk away.

"Oh, Jason? Do you want to give me your phone number? If something . . . happens, I can call you."

He turns back and ducks his head. "Yeah, that would probably be a good idea. Can I have yours too?"

"Of course," I tell him as we both pull out our phones and enter each other's numbers.

"I'll see you soon," I say as he finally heads for the elevators.

Walking back up the hallway, I find Jenny leaning over the nurses' station, watching Jason as he walks away. "Who was *that*?"

"That was Jason. He's a friend of Will's who I met last night when I went to Will's apartment. I think you'll be seeing him around more."

"Well, he's welcome on my floor any time," she says, winking at me.

I chuckle as I turn to head for Will's room. "Oh, and he's an artist, just like Will," I call over my shoulder as I walk, and the loud and lustful groan that echoes behind me makes me laugh out loud.

Will's eyes are closed when I enter his room, and I stop for a moment to look at him. What Jason said about Will seeming weaker and more tired has stuck with me—can I see a difference in the few weeks I've known him? As I look him over, I'm forced to admit that I can.

The circles under his eyes are definitely darker, and I'm pretty sure he's gotten thinner. And he does seem to be more tired. Ever since he had that high fever, he's been sleeping a lot more, and I can see that having to cope with all this is wearing on him.

He's still beautiful though. He's so peaceful in sleep. All the lines of pain disappear from his face, and his lips gather into a little pout—just as they are right now. Warmth spreads through me as I watch him. I want to brush back the hair from his forehead and run my hand over the soft, reddish stubble on his jaw. I want to protect him from all the bad things, and I want the peace to stay with him when he wakes, but . . . it never does.

The mothering instinct in me says I should leave and let Will sleep, but I know he'll be pissed as hell if I don't wake him. And he's certainly had a rough enough ride today that I'm not going to contribute to it by letting him down.

I walk over and take his hand, holding it between both of mine and rubbing my palm gently over the back. "Will," I call softly.

He pulls in a deep breath and looks at me in confusion, squeezing his eyes shut as he shifts and winces. He opens them again, and a smile spreads across his face. "Tori. I must have dozed off while I was waiting for you. You're late," he says pointedly, fixing me with an accusing stare.

I glance up at the clock. It's a quarter to five, but Jason was here until four-thirty, so it's not like it's entirely my fault, but I play along anyway.

"*I* was here, Mr. Everson. *You* were entertaining other guests at my appointed time, so I was forced to wait."

He chuckles. "Touché, Miss Somerset. The first time I ever have a visitor other than you, and it manages to inconvenience you. My most humble apologies."

I smile at him. "Just don't let it happen again, or I might not wait around."

"I'll keep that in mind."

"So, how did things go with Jason?"

He shrugs, groaning and scrunching up his face in pain. "Um, as well as could be expected, I guess. He read me the riot act for lying to him and for trying to keep him away."

"He cares about you."

"Yes, he does. I knew that, but maybe I was wrong about his feelings about helping me. He could have given up when I told him I was leaving Seattle, but he didn't."

"So, will Jason be coming back?"

Will looks down and starts playing with the blanket weave. "Yes. He said he wants to come and sit with me, and I told him he could."

"But you're not happy about it."

"I'm . . . Yes and no," he says slowly. "I think I'll be glad for the company, but it's just going to make things harder for me. I have more trouble watching other people in pain than enduring my own. That's why I did what I did. Well, most of it was to spare Jason, but it was also to spare myself. Being alone was easier, but now I'm going to have to watch him react to watching me, you know?"

I squeeze his hand as warmth blooms in my chest over the beauty of the soul in front of me. "I know it's hard, Will, but this is how it's supposed to be. Let Jason do what he can for himself and for you. He's preparing to lose you just as you're preparing to . . ."

"Die?" he offers, dropping his chin to try to meet my eyes, which are now fixed on the afghan.

I can't look at him, and I can't go on, or I'm going to burst into tears. The warmth is still there in my chest, and it's so incompatible with the thought of him dying, it's more than I can take.

He wriggles his hand out of mine, breathes in sharply as he raises his arm, and cups my chin with his hand. "Hey," he whispers, warm and concerned green eyes meeting my watery brown ones.

I force a smile. I have to be strong so he can focus on himself and not me. "I'm okay," I tell him, raising my own hand to stroke the one he's placed on my chin.

"It's good that Jason's going to be coming to see you. He seems like a really great guy, and I'm so happy you have such a good friend."

"Yeah, I'm lucky to have Jay. It means a lot to me that he didn't give up even when I abandoned him. But let's talk about something else," he says, and I don't know if it's for my benefit or his.

Either way, I grip his hand and bring it down between mine again and tell him all about my day. He listens attentively, and I'm guessing he's glad to have the focus shifted away from him for a while.

"I'm concerned about my last patient today though. He lost his wife about six months ago. He'd been doing pretty well, but the last few weeks he seemed down, and today he was downright depressed. If this continues, I think I'm going to need to refer him to one of our psychiatrists so we can try meds in combination with therapy."

"I'm sorry, Tori," Will says, rubbing his fingers over my hand. "Hopefully, he was just having a bad day today, and things will look better in the morning."

"I hope so. I hate it when I feel as if I'm letting down a patient."

"Oh, you know it's not your fault, right? He's upset because his wife died, and you're doing all you can to help him. I'm sure he'll come around."

He smiles at me sweetly, and I can't help but smile in return.

"I don't know how you do it though."

"Do what?"

"Surround yourself with so much . . . sorrow. Most of your patients have either lost a loved one, or they've recently received a terminal diagnosis, right?"

"Yes," I answer, feeling myself tense.

"Why do you work with those patients in particular? Did you choose it?"

His gaze is soft and curious but not concerned, so I guess the shaking I'm doing inside isn't traveling to my hands that he's holding. For the first time since I made the choice, I want to tell someone the reason. To tell *him*. To lay myself bare before him and show him what I carry.

But I can't. He has enough to deal with without witnessing my sorrows because, in truth, they pale in comparison to what he's going through. And it will take us back to the issue of where his family is, and I know it's not time for us to go back there yet. This all sounds good until the little voice in the back of my head pipes up. *Isn't it just that you're not ready to talk about this yet?*

I smother the voice again with my reasoning as I try to figure out what to say to Will.

"Yes, I chose it," I answer, unable to hide the quaver in my voice. But I can't lie to him. Life is too short for bullshit—particularly his life.

"Why?" he asks, and that one word unleashes a storm of memories that I become lost in. I hear him calling me, and I gasp as I'm thrust back into the present. I'm clutching at his hand like a lifeline, and he's reaching awkwardly across his body with his IV arm, stroking my cheek.

He's breathing heavily from the exertion of holding himself up to comfort me, so I reach up and take his hand from my cheek. He slumps back against the bed, but his eyes never leave mine.

"There you are! You went away for a few minutes. Are you all right?"

"Y-yes," I stammer out, my heart pounding in my chest and my breathing still rapid and shallow.

"I'm sorry. I didn't mean to pry."

As I look into his eyes, I'm cocooned by support and concern, and I begin to calm down. "*I'm* sorry, Will. I just can't—"

"—talk about it." He finishes for me. "Believe me, I'm no stranger to that. Whatever it is, I'm sorry someone hurt you."

"Thank you." I feel like a horrible hypocrite because I'm going to be asking him to divulge more of his secrets, yet I'm keeping some of my own. But then again, I'm not dying. I have time to work through my issues, and he doesn't, and that's how we ended up here in the first place. I wish I could let him be there for me, but I can't add to the burdens he's already carrying.

"You're okay though?" he asks, still looking at me with concern.

"Yes, I'm fine. Thank you for calling me back."

"Anytime," he says, his tone casual, but his eyelids betray his weariness as they fall closed.

"It's time for me to go, Will."

His eyes open, and he's about to protest, but I put a gentle finger to his lips.

"You had an emotional day today with Jason coming by, and you're getting sleepy. You don't want to be all worn out tomorrow like you were yesterday, do you? Tomorrow we need to plan our weekend, and I need you awake for that."

He grins at me shyly. "Can we watch more movies together?"

"I think there's a good chance."

"And will you bring popcorn and candy?"

"You don't ask for much, do you?"

He ducks his head, and I reach over to lift his chin. He looks at me uncertainly, but I can't hold back my smile. "*Of course* I'll bring popcorn and candy, sweetheart."

I'm still holding his chin, but his eyes are holding *me*. I stare into their green depths, and I'm startled by the longing I see there. His breathing is shallow and uneven, and for a split second, I swear his gaze flicks down to my lips. *Does he want to—?*

We both jump as the door squeaks, and I release Will's chin. Jenny appears, carrying Will's dinner, but she stops at the threshold, staring at the both of us as we stare back at her.

She shakes her head and continues into the room. "Good evening, Will. Are you ready to eat?"

"Hi, Jenny. Sounds good," he tells her, but his eyes are fixed on me.

I'm still reeling from what just happened, but his gaze is steady and sure, and for the moment, it calms me. While Jenny sets his tray on his table and rolls it over, I step back in close to him.

"Can I come back tomorrow?"

"I'm counting on it," he whispers, and his eyes close as I lean in and press a kiss to his forehead. I stay there for a moment, feeling the heat of his skin against my lips, and I know it's not from fever. I pull back, and he's breathing unevenly again, but the moment we had before is lost, at least for now.

"I'll be here to wake you up," I tell him and head for the door as Jenny uncovers his dishes and asks how he's feeling.

I leave Will's room and head down the hall, but I'm so lost in my own thoughts, I almost run into one of the nurses as she's leaving another patient's room. I mumble an apology, but my brain snaps back to the events of a few minutes ago.

Jesus, did he really want to kiss me?

A thrill of pleasure ripples through me, but I shake my head sternly. I shouldn't be happy about this. I shouldn't, but deep down, I know I am. It takes two to tango, and I'm reasonably sure if Jenny hadn't opened that door right when she did, I'd be having a whole different internal monologue right now.

Oh God, does he really have feelings for me? We've flirted, and he's told me how pretty I am—granted, he was high on morphine at the time—but this is something different entirely. Or is it? Is it me for me, or me because I'm the one who's helping him?

Do I want to kiss him? I know the answer to that one almost before the thought makes its way from one side of my brain to the other. He's the most beautiful person I've ever known, inside and out, and I'm more attracted to him than I've ever been to anyone. I've already admitted to myself—and to Jenny—that if he weren't dying, things would be different, or at least I'd want them to be. I know this can't go anywhere, but if it gives him comfort, if it gives us *both* comfort, can it really be that bad?

Again, the warmth spreads through my chest, and I allow myself to think about what his soft lips would feel like sliding against mine. A shiver runs up my spine, and the warmth that was in my chest now pools between my legs, and I know I'm in way over my head. But I've been in over my head for a while now, and as long as I'm still helping him, it's okay. *Yup, this is okay.*

When I get home, I let Sebastian sit up on the kitchen table to eat with me, and I give him a treat after dinner. Somehow, spoiling Will's cat is cosmic repayment for how happy he made me today without even trying.

Chapter 17

I get ready in the morning with a spring in my step, eager to see Will today and make our plans for the weekend. I'm like a schoolgirl with a goddamn crush. The voice in my head saying this is a bad idea is still there, but today it's drowned out by the thud of my heart against my ribcage and the cheerful hum that seems to permeate my thoughts.

I enter the room quietly to find Will still asleep. He's not as peaceful as he was yesterday though. Today his brow is furrowed, and as I watch, he shifts and winces. He rolls his head to the side, away from me, but then he sighs and seems to settle. He doesn't look sweaty, but as I take his hand, he feels warmer than he should be. *Shit.*

"Will, sweetheart. It's morning," I say, squeezing his fingers.

He wrinkles his nose adorably, which is the only hint he might have heard me. I stroke my knuckles softly across his cheek.

"Hey, sleepyhead, I'm not going to take no for an answer. If I let you sleep through seeing me this morning, I know you're going to give me hell later. Let's save us both the trouble, okay?"

A smile spreads across his face, and I chuckle as it lights up the room. Sleepy green eyes greet me next as he squeezes the hand that's still holding his.

"Good morning," he says, his voice all rough and husky from sleep, and I swear it's the sexiest sound I've ever heard.

While I'm recovering my power of speech, my eyes roam over him; my hand shifts from his cheek to his forehead. "You're warm this morning."

"Yeah, I think I was a bit feverish through the night. I tossed and turned a lot and kicked the afghan down a few times. I'm all right though. It's not going to be a really bad day. At least, I don't think so." He finishes uncertainly.

My hand moves from his forehead to stroke my fingers through his hair, and he hums in contentment. "Do you want me to let you get some more rest? I could have just let you sleep—"

"No, I'm glad you woke me up. Even though I didn't sleep that well, I can catch a nap later. I like waking up this way."

My cheeks heat, and I know I'm blushing, and his shy smile causes my stomach to flip. "I'm happy to be of service, sir."

"Sweetheart," he says, smiling as he corrects me.

"Sir Sweetheart." I quip, and he laughs, but it ends abruptly in the usual pained grunt.

"I'm sorry."

"It's worth it," he declares, and I smile brilliantly at him. "Especially when you do that."

We're headed for another moment like last night, and although that makes my heart start racing again, now's not the time.

"I have to go. I have patients to see today, and you need to eat and then get some more sleep so you're ready for me to come back at four."

"I think Jason is coming by in a bit, but I'll make sure I'm ready and waiting for you." He smiles again, but I can tell it's forced.

"Hey, if you're not feeling well—"

"I'm okay, really," he says. Then he sighs. "You can always tell, can't you? I'm just off because of the fever. It's like this every time. I have to force myself to concentrate to keep up with the conversation, and it wears me out more quickly. But it's no big deal."

"Well, if you're still feeling that way later, I'll tell you boring stories you don't have to pay attention to because I refuse to be responsible for wearing you out."

"Tori, you can wear me out any time," he replies, but he freezes, and his eyes widen at the innuendo.

I laugh and shake my head, which relaxes him immediately. "On that note, I'm going to go. You have a good day, and feel better by the time I get back, okay?"

"I'll do my best," he says as I give his hand one final squeeze.

As I gather my things, he rolls his eyes and blushes in embarrassment, and I have to bite my lip to keep from giggling. It's going to be a very interesting weekend.

It's three fifty-five and I'm sitting in my office, holding my phone as tears slide down my cheeks. I can't go see Will this afternoon. I have nothing left to give. I need to go home, curl up in a ball, and cry myself to sleep. And, unfortunately, I need to let one more person down today.

I stare at my phone, but I just don't have it in me to call him. He'll make me explain, and I don't think I can go through it right now. And what if he's sleeping? He was feverish this morning, and I don't want to disturb him just to tell him I'm not coming. I'll text him; that way he'll know, and I won't have to explain.

Will, I can't come by this afternoon. Something happened at work, and I need to go home. I'll come by tomorrow.

I hit send, feeling like the total coward I am, and begin to gather my things. Not even a minute goes by before my phone is vibrating across the desk. *Dammit.*

I could choose not to answer it. Let him think I turned off my phone right after I sent the text. Hell, that's what I should have done. Then I wouldn't be standing here having this argument with myself. What if something's wrong? What if he really needs me, and he's calling to tell me so? *Oh, dammit all to hell!*

I swipe my phone angrily and say "Hello" in a pitiful, shaky voice.

"Tori, I got your text. I'm sorry to call, but I was really worried. Are you all right?" His voice is soft and gentle, and I can easily picture the look that goes with it.

"I'm fine . . . Oh, hell! No, I'm not. I just . . . I need to be alone."

"Now you're really scaring me. Won't you please tell me what happened? Did something happen to you, or is it something with a patient?"

"It's a patient," I say, as my tears begin anew.

"Tori, *please* come up. You sound like you really need a friend. Let me take care of *you*, for once. I'd come to you if I could"—he sighs—"but I can't."

I lean my head back against the wall and realize I don't really want to go home. I want to tell Will what happened and let him comfort me. He already knows about Mr. Matthews from yesterday; it's not as if I have to recount the whole story. And he sounds so eager for me to let him do something to help me. "Okay, I'll be up in a few minutes."

"Thank you. Today, it'll be my turn to listen. I'll see you soon," he answers, and I know I've made him happy. *That counts for something, doesn't it?*

I trudge into Will's room with my head down and fall wearily into my chair before I even look at him. When I finally do meet his eyes, he's looking at me with such tenderness and compassion that the dam breaks, and I burst into tears.

He can't really hold me because of his tender joints and lymph nodes, so I bury my head into the side of his thigh as I sob. His hand threads into my hair, and he strokes it away from my face soothingly.

"Oh, honey, it's gonna be okay. Dammit, I wish I could hold you right now," he murmurs, and I'm comforted by the fact that he wishes he could.

We stay that way until my tears are spent, and as I sniffle, I turn my head to look at him. His eyes are glassy, and I can't tell if it's from fever or unshed tears, and their warm green depths are filled with concern and sorrow.

"I'm sorry," I say, pulling myself together. "How are you feeling? Are you still feverish?"

I raise my hand to touch his face, but he stops me mid-motion and clutches my hand in his. "No. Not today," he tells me firmly.

"But—"

"Yes, I'm still feverish, but I'm all right. I'm more concerned about you right now." He glances downward. "Will you tell me what happened?"

I take his hand between mine and rub my thumbs over the back. He waits patiently, seeming to know that once I'm settled, I'll begin.

Finally, I force myself to look up. "Do you remember the patient I told you about yesterday? The one whose wife died six months ago, and he seemed depressed?"

"Yes."

"Well, he attempted suicide last night."

"Oh, fuck. I'm so sorry, Tori," Will says, his gaze warm and soft.

"Yeah, apparently he left his appointment with me, then went home and took a whole bottle of ibuprofen. He's very lucky to be alive."

"Did you see him today?"

"No. They have him sedated until the drug is out of his system. Then he's going to be transferred down to the psych ward, and one of the psychiatrists is going to start working with him."

"Will he be your patient again?"

"I don't know," I answer, trying not to get teary again. "I don't think he'll want to be, considering that I . . ." I look down at his afghan.

"Tori," Will says, his tone authoritative. "Please come sit up here." He pats the spot next to his thigh.

A little confused, I stand and turn around, sitting my backside on the edge of the bed next to him. When I turn to face him, he takes hold of my chin, and the look in his eyes captures me. His gaze is serious, fierce, and protective.

"This is not your fault. He made the choice, and you were doing everything you could for him. Don't blame yourself."

"But I didn't tell Dr. Weaver about him, and obviously I should have—"

"Hey, you made the best decision you could with what you knew, right? You did your best, and you *were* concerned about him; you mentioned him to me yesterday."

"But—"

"It's done, Tori," he says in a tone that brooks no argument. "Don't waste your time on regret. You did your best, and you can't change it, so learn what you can and move on." He caresses my cheek, and his voice softens. "Do you believe it's not your fault?"

"I guess—"

"No, you need to be sure. Say it for me."

"It's not my fault," I croak.

"Say it again. And believe it this time."

"It's not my fault," I say more strongly.

"That's better."

"Ugh, but I'm still frustrated, you know? I just don't understand making that choice," I say, shaking my head as I try to keep fresh tears at bay. "I've always had trouble with why people choose to die."

"Maybe he felt he had nothing left to live for," Will answers as I watch his gaze grow distant.

"Maybe, but I still can't see it that way. There's always something worth living for—worth fighting for."

Will looks down and away, and out of the corner of my eye, I catch the slight motion as he shifts his right wrist so it's flush against the blanket.

No. No fucking way.

I lunge across the bed, grabbing his arm and turning it so his wrist is facing me. He gasps in pain at the sudden, rough motion, but for once, I hardly notice. I'm too busy staring at the raised, slightly pink scar that runs atop the largest vein leading away from his wrist. Without thinking, I unbutton the cuff of his nightshirt and let it fall open. The scar is two inches long and runs in parallel with the vein, not perpendicular, and I can see other faint scars, the dots left by the stitches running on either side of it. Whenever he did this, he was serious about it.

I grasp his other wrist, but I can already see a similar scar before I even manage to turn his arm over. I can't believe I never noticed them because now they look so obvious, but he's always been so careful to keep me from seeing as much of his bare skin as possible.

Drawing in a sharp breath, I feel as if I've somehow been betrayed. It all makes sense now. This isn't the first time Will has felt he doesn't have anything to live for. Jesus Christ, I didn't know he had a psych history!

This changes everything! I curse myself for not taking him on as a patient so I could look at his chart, but maybe it's not even in there if it didn't happen here. Some small part of me knows I should feel sympathy for him, but anger is coursing through me instead. What the *hell* could have made the beautiful, incredibly talented man before me feel as if he had nothing to live for?

"When?" I force out between gritted teeth.

"It was a long time ago."

"Why?"

"No!" He snaps at me, his eyes suddenly brimming with anger. "And don't look at me like that! You didn't even know me then! Things were a lot different. *I* was a lot different!"

"I'm . . . sorry," I say tightly, and I force myself to dial it down a few notches. He's right; I didn't know him then. I don't know the circumstances, and I have no right to judge him.

He closes his eyes and takes a deep breath, and when he looks at me, the fire I saw there a moment ago is gone. The fire is still in *my* eyes, however, but he meets it with calmness and steadiness.

"It doesn't matter why. It was a long time ago, and it was a poor choice, but things are different now. *I'm* different now. It took me a long time to move past . . . that, but I did."

Cradling his right hand, I re-button the cuff of his nightshirt and gently place his arm back down on the bed. I take his left hand between both of mine. "I know you're not going to tell me, but whatever it is, I'm sorry someone hurt you," I whisper, echoing the words he said to me just yesterday as I turn his wrist and place my lips against the scar there.

Will tenses, surprised, but he doesn't pull away. His teeth latch onto his bottom lip, and he lowers his head for a moment, squeezing his eyes shut. Slowly, his brow relaxes, and he looks at me once more, but his eyes look glassy and tired. "Thank you, Tori. Dammit, I was supposed to be comforting you today, and somehow we ended up focused on me again. I'm sorry."

"Don't be sorry. You *have* comforted me today. I know it's not my fault, but I'm still sad about it. It's going to take me some time to put it into perspective."

"I hate that it has you down though. You're such a caring and thoughtful person, and you help so many people in your practice—hell, you even help people you don't have to help, like me. It makes me feel . . ."

I eye him curiously. "Makes you feel what?"

His eyes are riveted to his afghan, where his finger is tracing random boxes in the weave. "It makes me feel protective of you," he murmurs.

He feels *protective* of me? Here he is, dying of cancer, and his thoughts are of protecting me from things that make me feel bad at work. I don't think I've ever met a more selfless human being than the one before me. He has so many of his own worries, but all that seemingly goes out the window the minute I have a problem. For *me*.

I stare at him, and my eyes widen as I come to another realization—this is the first time he's admitted feeling anything for me. My surprise gives way to a warm smile, and he grins back at me, relieved. But suddenly, he rolls his head so he's lying flat against his pillow and closes his eyes.

"You're not really feeling that well today, are you?"

"No."

"Did Jason come this morning?"

"Yes. He came around ten and stayed until close to lunch."

"And did you put on a show for him too?"

He frowns and opens one eye to peer at me, but he doesn't deny it.

I place a hand on his forehead and feel at least as much heat there as I did this morning, if not more. "I think it's time you take care of yourself. It sounds like you've been taking care of other people all day today."

"I'm all right. I just feel . . . detached, like I'm one step behind every-thing that's going on. As I told you this morning, I always feel that way when I have a fever."

"Well, you need to stop wearing yourself out trying to keep up," I tell him, squeezing his hand gently. "We'll make our plans for tomorrow, and then I'm going to leave."

Will opens both eyes and begins to protest, but I cut him off.

"*And*, if you're not feeling well tomorrow, you're going to tell me. I'll still come, but I don't want you to feel like you have to stay awake for me. If you're still feverish tomorrow, we're going to take it easy, all right?"

"But tomorrow's movie day!" He's whining now, his face scrunched up in an adorable pout.

"Yes, it is, but if you're not feeling well, and it turns into a Tori-watches-a-movie-while-Will-sleeps-through-it day, then that's okay too."

He frowns as he ducks his chin, and I know he's disgusted with the situ-ation. I can't fathom what it must be like to have lost so much already. He doesn't want to give up the few pleasures he has left.

"Hey," I say, capturing his chin with my hand. "I'm just trying to take care of you. We've got two days for movies. Odds are you'll feel better one of the next two days, so if it's not tomorrow, then we still have Sunday, right?"

"I guess." He huffs but his eyes fall closed again; he's fading fast.

"So I'll come by around two tomorrow. I was thinking maybe we'd do a blast from the past this weekend. How do you feel about the Matrix movies?"

"There was only one, right?"

I frown at him in exasperation. "Okay, so the second and third were kind of a letdown, but it's still awesome when the machines finally get to Zion, and I cry every time when Trinity dies."

"Sure, we can watch them," he says, trying to stifle a yawn.

"Do you want me to tell Jenny to keep your dinner warm for later? You look like you're not going to make it until six."

"Would you? All of a sudden I'm exhausted . . . and a bit cold, too," he replies, shivering.

My chest tightens as I lift up the blankets for him so he can get his arms under the covers, and I pull them all the way up to his chin. "I'll tell her to let you rest for a while, and I'll stay with you until you fall asleep, okay?"

"Thanks, Tori," he mumbles, wincing as shivers wrack his frame.

I stroke his hair, and he sighs, seeming to settle. He's asleep in a few minutes, but I stay until his shivering stops.

As I'm leaving, I run into Jenny outside Will's door, his dinner tray in hand. "Hey, Jenny. Actually, could you keep that warm for him for a while? He's still feverish, and he fell asleep about fifteen minutes ago. I told him I would ask you to keep it for him until he got some more rest."

Jenny frowns at me. "Sure I'll keep it for him, but I need to at least go look in on him. Hey, are you okay?"

"Bad day at the office. I'll be all right though. Will managed to cheer me up," I tell her, smiling as I recall the last half hour.

"I'm glad. I popped in before you came, and he seemed really worried about you. He said you were on your way up, and you needed a friend."

My smile grows even wider.

"So, not only is he telling you things, he's also trying to do nice things for you?"

I nod, knowing where this is going but powerless to stop it.

"Uh huh," Jenny says smugly.

"What?" I demand, my voice a little sharper than I intend.

"He's more than just attracted to you. I can see it plain as day. He really cares about you, and as he's starting to open up to you, his feelings are getting stronger."

I blush because what she's saying is true, but I don't know what it means. I was so sure I should keep my own feelings out of this, but now that I'm seeing how he feels about me, I'm not so sure anymore. I feel as if I'm in the middle of the ocean, flailing around and unsure which direction will guide me to land. But I know now that whichever way I go, it's going to lead to his happiness and away from protecting myself because in my mind, his happiness has now become more important than anything else.

"I know, Jenny. I can see it, too, and I'm trying to figure out how I should handle it. He's so different from anyone else I've ever known."

"Do you want some advice?"

I raise an eyebrow at her, but I know that even if I say no, she'll continue anyway.

"Don't 'handle' it. Just let things happen without a plan, and let your feelings guide you. And I mean *your* feelings—Tori, the woman, not Tori, the psychologist."

I chuckle as I shake my head at her. "What's your degree in again? Because I seem to be having pro bono therapy sessions with you, and I think I'm going to need to see your references."

Jenny laughs. "I have a bachelor's degree in advanced friendship and a master's in trying to help two people who can't seem to help themselves. However, I accept payment in the form of wine and chocolate."

"I'll keep that in mind. Thanks, Jenny. You *are* a good friend, and I appreciate the advice."

"Of course," Jenny says, still grinning at me. "And are you coming tomorrow?"

"What else would I be doing?"

Her smile widens. "Have a good weekend with him. And call me if you want to talk."

"Thanks, Jenny," I say as I continue down the hallway.

As I drive home, I realize with a grin that I really *am* in a much better mood than I was in before I went to see Will.

CHAPTER 18

I spend a lazy Saturday morning, lying in bed, playing with Sebastian, and wondering what the day will bring. Jenny's words last night affirmed what I'd already been thinking—that I would kiss Will if the moment was right and then just see what happens next. God, he better not be feverish today—he desperately wants to have a nice day with me, and I hope the powers that be will give it to him.

Leaving my place around one, I make my pilgrimage to the grocery store for microwave popcorn, Raisinets, and Hershey's Kisses. While I'm there, I decide to branch out a bit and buy some Twizzlers—my favorite candy—and two bottles of Sprite.

I arrive at his room promptly at two, movie and junk food-laden, and crossing my fingers, toes, and every other appendage that Will is having a good day. Pushing the door open slowly, my heart stops when I see he's drawing. His brow is furrowed in concentration, and just the tip of his tongue is poking out of the side of his mouth as he focuses intently. My gaze travels downward, and I realize he's left-handed. I've never seen him hold a pencil before, and I'm mesmerized as I watch his hand moving over the page, pausing here and there as he ponders his next stroke. I wish to God I could get close enough to see what he's doing without his knowing, but I know I don't have a prayer.

As I'm mulling over the idea, his eyes meet mine and widen. He abruptly lifts his pencil from the page and snaps the book shut. He looks like he's been caught with his hand in the cookie jar. It's the black sketchbook this time. *Could he possibly have filled up the red one already?*

"Hi, Tori." He greets me, sounding nervous.

"Hey, Will. One of these days I'm going to catch you drawing and actually get to see what you're working on," I say, sidling over to him.

He pales and clears his throat. "Oh, uh, yeah, I guess."

"Would you let me?"

"Um . . . what?"

"Would you let me see what you're working on sometime or maybe even watch you draw?"

"You want to watch me?" he asks, a perplexed look on his face.

Oh, hell, yes! almost flies out of my mouth, but I stop myself just in time. "Well, sure, I'd love to watch you. And I know you draw every day you're able, so I'm guessing you have a few sketches finished?"

"I do," he admits cagily.

I chuckle. This is like pulling teeth; I've never seen Will so off-balance. Is he really that nervous about having someone watch him work or see what he's been working on? "Would you let me see some of your sketches?"

He seems to shake himself, as if he realizes he's making me suspicious. "Sure, I'll show you some of my sketches. Just . . . not today, okay? I want to get my stuff a little better organized first."

"That's fine," I tell him, eyeing the black sketchbook and wondering what he means by "organized." *Are there sketches he doesn't want me to see?*

"So how are you feeling today?"

"Actually, I'm having a really good day," he says, grinning at me.

I drop my bags on the chair and cross my arms in front of me, raising an eyebrow at him as I go over my checklist. He's sitting up farther today, and he's not sweating at all. He certainly seems happy, and he was obviously feeling well enough to draw, so he can't be that bad off, right?

Will fidgets under my scrutiny and fixes me with a pleading look. "Come on, Tori, I swear I'm telling the truth. I'm not warm at all. My joints aren't too sore; you saw I was drawing. My belly is a little tender, but I swear, that's it. I even went back to sleep this morning so I wouldn't be tired when you came. I'm having a good day, I swear to you."

My eyes still narrowed, I step over to him and place my hand on his forehead.

"Would you please believe me? It's bad enough I have so few good days —having to convince you this is one of them is like adding insult to injury."

Shit, I didn't want to make him angry. "I'm sorry, Will. I do believe you. I was mostly just playing with you. But, you can't blame me for being skeptical after what you did yesterday."

His irritation seems to vanish like smoke, and he smirks at me. "In my defense, I really wasn't feeling that bad yesterday, up until the very end there when I got the chills. Then I suddenly felt like shit, and it was good that you left. I slept for a while, and my fever broke later in the evening. I had a late dinner, and then this morning the nurses helped me get all cleaned up. I'm *so* ready for movie day!"

I laugh because when Will turns on the charm, he truly is adorable. "I'm glad," I tell him, finally taking his hand in mine. "I was really hoping you'd have a good day today. So, should I go get the movie cart and pop our popcorn?"

He eyes my grocery bag longingly as I scoop it up, preparing to take it with me. "Tori."

"Hopefully, we'll be able to get the cart today," I say, taking a step away from his bed. "Other people can use it, too, and one of these days, we might get unlucky, and someone else will have it checked out—"

"Tori!" he says more insistently, but I continue to babble on, trying to keep from laughing as I take another step toward the door.

"—and then what would we do? I think—"

"*Tori!*" He finally yells, wincing, and I feel bad for a moment until the irritated look returns to his face.

"What?" I respond, biting my lip to hold back my smile.

"Why are you taking the whole bag with you?"

"This bag?" I say innocently, holding it up.

"Yes, that bag," he answers, exasperated.

"Well, why not?"

"Aren't there . . . other things in there?"

"Oh, you think there's something in here for you? Something you don't want to wait until I get back to have?"

Now he catches on, shaking his head as he chuckles, curling an arm over his belly. My heart clenches, but I can't react to his pain; I promised myself we'd have as carefree a day as possible, so I have to pretend I didn't see that.

"You, Miss Somerset, are an evil, evil woman! Standing between a man and his chocolate is just criminal," he declares, shaking a finger at me.

I dissolve into laughter as he glares at me, and it turns into a fit of giggles as I keep picturing his exasperated look.

"It wasn't *that* funny." He huffs, his lips drawn into a sexy as hell pout.

I shake my head as my giggles subside. "Sweetheart, you know I brought you candy, and I would *never* stand between you and your chocolate. I was just teasing you. Won't you please forgive me? I offer Sprite and some of my Twizzlers as peace offerings," I say, walking back over to his bed and holding the bag out in front of me, my head bowed.

I drop the bag next to him, and he eagerly digs into it, pulling out the Raisinets first and tearing off the end of the box. As I head for the door, I hear a moan of pleasure so intense it makes me weak in the knees, and I grab the doorframe for support. *Dammit, he really is going to kill me one of these days.*

I come back to his room a few minutes later, popcorn in hand, and the nurse has already dropped off the movie cart. Will seems to have satisfied his initial chocolate craving as he's no longer guzzling Raisinets by the handful, but he still gives me a Christmas morning-like grin, his hand in the Hershey's Kisses bag.

"Are there any Raisinets left for me, or did you inhale the whole box while I was gone?" I ask as I circle around to put the movie into the DVD player.

He lowers his head guiltily, and I laugh, but he pulls the box out from under the blanket beside him and shakes it so I can hear it's not empty.

"You had me for a moment there." Will follows me with his eyes as I return to my usual chair, but before I can sit down, he reaches out and clasps my hand.

"Tori, would you please sit with me today?" he asks sweetly, and oh God, my heart melts on the spot.

"You seem to be already prepared for that," I say, noting that he's shifted all the way over to the far side of his bed. "Were you assuming I'd say yes?"

"Well, I know how much it bothers you to see me hurting, so I figured I'd get that part over with before you got here. And I was really hoping you'd say yes." He cocks his head as he finishes speaking and looks up at me through his ridiculously long eyelashes, turning the charm on full blast.

For a moment I'm stunned, lost in those fathomless green eyes until he blinks and breaks the spell. The familiar warmth blooms in my chest and spreads outward, making my fingers and toes tingle. "Of course I will," I tell him, and the smile I get in return would be worth walking through fire for.

I crawl up next to him and get comfortable as quickly as I can, trying hard to ignore that he's holding his breath and squeezing his eyes shut. Once I'm still, he relaxes, sinking back against the mattress. He looks over at me and smiles, brazenly grabbing my hand and entwining our fingers before I even manage to hit play.

Like the first time two weeks ago, we watch *The Matrix* as if we were on a date, and the sterile hospital surroundings fade away. It's obvious after the first few minutes that we've both seen this movie more than a few times, so we talk and laugh and tease each other back and forth as we watch. Will is animated and happy, and I can tell he's thinking only of this moment. It's so beautiful to see; a few times I have to struggle to keep the tears back.

We eat popcorn and candy, laughing as our hands end up in the popcorn bag at the same time.

"Ladies first," Will says gallantly. "Unless—" He pauses and then shakes his head.

"Unless what?" I capture his chin in my hand to raise his downcast eyes.

"—unless you would allow me to do the honors."

I furrow my brow for a moment, but a sly grin spreads across my face as I realize what he wants to do.

He's blushing already, but his cheeks flush even more when he sees my face.

"But of course, sir," I answer with equal formality, making him chuckle and shake his head.

He picks up a piece of popcorn with a shaking hand and brings it slowly to my lips.

I take it in my mouth, making sure to brush my lips against his fingers as I do, and he exhales heavily, his eyes never leaving mine.

He picks up another piece, looking at me expectantly.

I nod, all teasing aside. This has gone from cute and sweet to hot as hell in a heartbeat, and the movie is long forgotten. All I can hear is the sound of our breathing.

Will brings the next piece of popcorn to my lips, and this time as I take it, I suck the tips of his fingers into my mouth. He gasps and flicks his eyes upward from my lips to meet my gaze. The want I see there is so intense it takes my breath away. I've never wanted to kiss someone more than I do at this moment. The air is heavy around us—the way it feels on a summer night just before a thunderstorm, and time seems to be standing still.

"Will," I whisper, leaning slowly toward him, and his breathing becomes faster and more uneven. He does nothing to stop me, so I keep moving closer. I'm sure we're going to kiss, so I close my eyes, and the next thing I feel is the softness of his lips brushing against mine. We stay there for a long moment, and his kiss is feather-light, but he's shaking as our lips make contact.

I pull back and open my eyes, but Will's are still closed. I'm about to ask what's the matter when he swallows loudly.

"If you didn't want that to happen, please, just don't tell me," he says in a shaky voice. "When I open my eyes, we can go back to watching the movie and pretend it didn't happen, okay?"

"Will," I whisper.

Another hard swallow. "I'm serious, Tori. Please."

"Will," I say again, but he's frozen, expecting me to back away. But I have no intention of backing away.

I close the distance between us, and Will startles as my lips meet his, drawing in a sharp breath. I wonder if he's staring at me in shock, but I don't open my eyes to check. I just continue to move my lips softly against his until I feel him begin to respond.

With a needy whimper, he throws himself into the kiss, our lips moving against each other hungrily. I moan against his mouth as adrenaline shoots through me, fire spreading through my veins as wetness gathers between my legs.

I cock my head to the side so I can kiss him more deeply, and his tongue brushes against my teeth, begging for entry. He moans as I open to him, our tongues caressing one another as the moment becomes even more heated.

I'm desperate to touch him but not far gone enough to forget that I really can't without hurting him. So I raise both hands and run them into his hair just behind his ears, scraping my fingernails on his scalp as our tongues continue their dance.

He moans again and tries to pull me closer, forgetting where we are. His lips break from mine as he hisses in pain, and my eyes snap open. I'm about to pull back and ask what happened when his hand caresses my cheek, and he whispers "No" against my lips.

Closing my eyes again, I lose myself in the feel of his tongue caressing mine. Everything around us is gone—the movie, the bed, the hospital. All that's left is this beautiful man and what he's doing to me. My head has gone all fuzzy, and all I can think about is the warmth that's spreading from my center like a tidal wave.

I'm afraid to touch *him*, but there's no reason he can't touch me. I tense as his fingers gently stroke my shoulders and slide down my arms, leaving a trail of tingling fire in their wake. He winces against my lips from the movement, but he continues on as if it never happened. I do the same as his fingers retrace their path up my arms, and I moan softly at the feel of him touching me.

I'm intoxicated—drunk on the feel of Will as he ravishes my lips, on the knowledge that he wants this as much as I do. We kiss and caress each other until he finally pulls back, gasping for breath and laying his head against his pillow. We both pant heavily, trying to come back to ourselves as I rest my forehead against his.

"Tori," he whispers.

I shiver from the adrenaline that's still coursing through me, and in this moment, I'm blissfully happy. No one has ever made me feel this way before, and I'm afraid to speak, afraid to breathe—afraid to do anything that will shatter this moment because it's so utterly perfect.

Slowly, I pull back and open my eyes to find him watching me intently. We just stare at each other for a few moments, trying to figure out where we go from here. Suddenly, his gaze drops and he closes his eyes; wherever he's gone, it isn't good. I caress his cheek and pull his chin back up, but still, he won't look at me.

"Hey, where did you go?" I ask, stroking his cheek with my fingers.

"Tori, I don't think—"

"Exactly, Will. Don't think."

His brow furrows in confusion as he looks at me.

"Sweetheart, you're having a good day today. Don't think. Sometimes, you think too much. Live in this moment, not what comes after. Did you want to kiss me just now?"

"Yes."

"Good, because I wanted to kiss you too."

"You did?"

"Yes, Will, I did. So as far as I'm concerned, there's nothing else we need to know right now."

"So . . . it's okay? I mean, I didn't . . ."

"All you did was show me you're talented at more than painting," I say with a smirk.

He blushes a delicious shade of red as he smirks right back. And to my utter amazement, he lets it go. He settles against the mattress and turns his attention back to the movie.

I turn my head toward the window, squeezing my eyes shut as the biggest, cheesiest grin spreads across my face. *Oh my God, he kissed me! And it was fantastic!* Other than my smile, I show no outward sign of my racing heart or the blazing heat in the pit of my stomach.

After a moment, I look back at the screen, and as I do, I risk a glance at Will. His grin is at least as big as mine is, and my stomach does an elated flip.

Now that we've kissed, and I'm sitting this close to him, my need to be touching him is almost unbearable. I slowly stretch my hand out, and he startles as I place it on his thigh.

He takes my hand and entwines our fingers, and it seems to satisfy him but only for a moment. He raises our hands, his breath tickling me for a second before his warm lips brush against my skin. The electricity that shoots through me causes my stomach to clench.

But he doesn't stop there. He continues to kiss my hand, trailing down to my wrist where he squeezes his eyes shut and stops, pulling back a little. I'm about to ask him what's wrong when he places one more soft kiss on my now-heated skin and returns our hands to my lap.

He wants more; it's so plain, I can almost taste it. He wants more than he's able to do, and he's struggling not to dwell on that.

As the credits begin to roll, I glance over and Will's eyes are closed. We'd been quiet for a few minutes, but I hadn't realized he'd fallen asleep. I indulge myself in staring at his beautiful face, remembering the feel of his lips against mine. Today has been even better than I'd hoped, even with the few little hiccups in our happiness.

There's not a chance I can get off the bed without jostling him, and I certainly don't want him jolting awake in pain, so I opt instead to run my fingers through his hair. "Will, the movie's over," I whisper. He stirs, but his deep green eyes open wearily.

"I'm sorry, Tori. All of a sudden, I got really tired."

"Don't be sorry. I fall asleep during movies all the time," I tell him, and he brightens a bit as I shift the blame away from his illness.

I glance at him, trying to determine if he's too tired to continue, but in the end, I decide to leave that up to him. "Do you want to start the second movie?"

He gives me a sad little smile. "I would like nothing better, but I'm afraid I wouldn't make it past the first five minutes."

"Are you feeling all right?"

He sighs. "Yes, I'm fine. Well, as fine as I ever am these days. I'm just tired. I think the sugar high has worn off."

"That's okay. We can watch it tomorrow. And you were feverish yesterday. Maybe you need a little extra rest."

"Yeah, these last few times, it seems like I need a recovery day after a fever. I'm sorry," he tells me, squeezing my hand.

"Pfft, don't be sorry," I say, waving him off. "Actually, I'm kind of proud of you for admitting you've had enough before I had to tell you. In fact, I think this is the very first time you've done it."

He smirks at me and rolls his eyes, mumbling something about "overbearing mother hens."

I smile, reveling in the simple pleasure of our back-and-forth. But I have one more gift for Will up my sleeve today.

I stroke his chin as his deep green eyes re-ignite the fire in my belly. His look is questioning, but his eyes are begging me to come closer.

And I have every intention of doing so.

"I'm pretty sure you're going to say I can come back tomorrow, so I have a new question." I close the distance between us and brush my lips against his, then pull back to where I was. "Can I kiss you?"

His eyes seem to darken, and he can't contain the smile that spreads across his face. We both bask in it for a moment before I hear his husky "Please."

And suddenly, I'm in heaven again as our lips come together, his tongue plundering my mouth. This kiss is warm and sweet, but he's too tired to infuse it with the passion of our first kiss. But I don't mind. The tenderness of this kiss offers me just as much as the first one did, and I give him the same in return.

He pulls away all too soon and rests against his pillow, panting as he opens his eyes to grin at me like the cat that swallowed the canary.

"There, now you'll have good dreams."

"Of that there is no doubt."

"Well, shall I come again around two tomorrow?"

"Sure. Or you can even come earlier so we can try to get both movies in. Hopefully, I'll be less tired."

"Okay, I'll do that on one condition."

Will raises his eyebrow.

"As long as you promise me the same things you did today—that you'll tell me if it's a bad day, and you'll admit when it's time for you to rest."

Will strokes his chin as if this is a lot to consider, and I'm about to whack him in the arm before I think better of it. I think he sees it coming because he glances furtively at my hand before answering.

"Deal."

I move slowly and carefully off the bed, and the only sound beside me is one sharp intake of breath.

He lets it out as I turn around, his head back and eyes closed. "I had a really good day today," he mumbles, barely awake.

"I did too," I tell him as I reach over and stroke my fingers through his hair. A small smile plays across his lips as he drifts off to sleep, and that's the last thing I see as I leave his room.

CHAPTER 19

I float through Saturday evening and Sunday morning, my thoughts on the wonderful day I had with Will. I still have work to do with him, but convincing him to enjoy his good days is as much a part of that work as finding out about his family and helping him to come to terms with dying. And *I* need his good days too. They are a gift to both of us—for him to preserve who he is and for me to get to truly know that person. I'm greedy now for every moment I can get with him, and I want those moments to be as good as possible.

But I suspect today isn't going to start out well. It's obvious from everything Will's told me that he puts a lot of thought into his actions and decisions, and he's had almost twenty-four hours to think about what happened yesterday. I'm confident he wanted it to happen, but I'm reasonably sure he's going to tell me it shouldn't have happened.

Since we're going to try to watch two movies today, I head to the hospital around one. I bring nothing but myself since I left the movies and popcorn in his room, and there were Twizzlers and Hershey's Kisses left as well—unless, of course, he had a candy attack in the middle of the night and now there are none. I chuckle as I think about him waking up craving Hershey's Kisses and not being able to help himself. I've never seen a guy as in love with chocolate as Will is. It's incredibly cute.

As I walk into his room, he's finishing up his lunch, and he glances up and dazzles me with a brilliant smile. I know without even asking that he's having a good day, and I cast my eyes heavenward and thank the stars above for giving both of us a break.

"Hi, Tori," he says, the soft velvet of his voice sending shivers down my spine as it caresses my name. "Your timing is perfect. I was just finishing up."

"And what was on the menu today?"

"Today it was pizza and a fruit cup," he tells me as he puts down his spoon. "Not too bad, but I'd kill for some Domino's."

"Well, that's certainly something I could manage for you. We never did have our dinner together."

"You're right! How about maybe . . . tomorrow?"

"That sounds good to me. If tomorrow's a good day, you can call me in the afternoon and tell me where I'm going, and I'll bring us dinner."

"It's a deal," he says, grinning happily.

I take his hand and rub it between mine as he stares at me for a moment.

"Can you . . . sit for a minute before we start our movie?"

Here we go. "Of course."

He looks me in the eye, his own gaze clouded by conflict and sadness.

"I had a fantastic day with you yesterday, but . . . I don't think I should have kissed you."

"Why?"

He narrows his eyes at me. "You're not surprised. You knew this was coming, didn't you?"

"Well, I've been around you long enough that I'm starting to understand how you think," I admit sheepishly.

"That's . . . more than a little scary," he says, running his fingers through his hair. "*I* don't even understand how I think sometimes."

"You were about to tell me why we shouldn't have kissed?"

"I shouldn't have kissed you because it's not fair to you. I can't . . . There's no point in your feeling anything for me because I'm not going to be around long enough for it to be worth your while," he says in a rush, trying to keep his voice steady as he looks down and away.

My heart breaks at his words. He truly has no idea how incredibly important every moment I have with him is to me. "Isn't that my decision to make?"

"Well, yes, but—"

As I watch him struggling for the words to tell me something he really doesn't want to tell me in the first place, I realize I can't let him muddle through. It's too painful for both of us. I stand and lean on the edge of the bed, caressing his cheek with the back of my hand.

"Oh, sweetheart, stop for a moment, and let me talk, okay?"

He looks frustrated, but he closes his eyes and nods.

"Will, I'm a big girl, and I can make my own decisions. What happened yesterday was a choice we both made, and I don't regret it. I *wanted* to kiss you, and I know you wanted it just as much. We don't know what the future is going to bring for either of us, but right now, what I want most is for you to be happy. It was wonderful yesterday watching you let go and enjoy yourself. You don't know how many good days like that you're going to have, so when you have them, I want you to make the most of them. Does that make sense?"

Will nods, frowning and lost in thought. When he finally looks up at me, his eyes are a swirling storm of emotion. "I just . . . wish things were different."

I cup his cheek with my hand as I give him a watery smile. "I know you do. I wish they were too. More than anything." Our eyes lock, and they say silently what neither of us will utter aloud.

If I weren't dying, you would be mine.

If you weren't dying, I would be yours.

Suddenly, Will closes his eyes and drops his chin, struggling for control.

Oh my, how things are changing. A week ago he would never have been so honest with me, would never have let me see him struggle to hold himself together. I'm glad he's letting me in a little more, but the possible reasons for it frighten me. As much as he needs to change the way he's approaching the end of his life, I don't want to see him fall apart.

After a moment, he looks up. He's calmer now, but his eyes still reflect the turmoil he's holding in check. I need to get us to a place where he feels safe and comfortable.

"So what I'd really like to do today is to make you happy, and I'd like you to let me do that. Do you think you could?" I ask, cocking my head to the side.

He looks up at me and quickly glances away, snorting. "Wow, you need to put those puppy dog eyes on a leash—those suckers are powerful."

I laugh, and Will's eyes widen in delight at the sound as he laughs too. He wraps an arm around his belly and grimaces, but I give no sign that I've noticed.

"You haven't answered my question."

"So, exactly how do you plan to make me happy?"

"By doing whatever you want. All you have to do is ask, and we'll do it. We can watch our movies. I'll sit with you if you'd like. If there's anything you want, I'll run out and get it—anything."

As I'm talking, I notice the smirk slipping from Will's face. He looks at me intently, and his eyes soften to a warm, watery green.

"Thank you, Tori. I . . . It means a lot to me that you want to make me happy."

Oh, Will, you have no idea.

I grin at him as the familiar warmth fills my chest. "So, what would you like to do?"

He smiles, and excitement flutters through my chest.

"Well, I was all psyched up for movie day, so why don't we continue with that plan?"

"Okay, do you want popcorn?"

He raises both eyebrows at me as if I've said something ridiculous, and he looks so adorable that I can't contain my giggle.

I raise my hands to ward off his stare. "Okay, okay, stupid question. I'll go pop the popcorn and ask the nurse to bring the cart down."

He nods at me sharply, and I squeeze his hand before letting go and retrieving the microwave popcorn from the windowsill.

When I return to his room, Will's eyes are closed, and he's breathing heavily, one arm clutching his belly.

Panic shoots down my spine. "Will! What—"

"I'm fine!" He snaps at me, cutting me off as he opens his eyes. I think he realizes the harshness of his tone because his look is apologetic. "I'm okay, really. I moved over so you can sit with me, and doing that is fucking painful. It takes a few minutes to get myself settled again. I didn't mean to scare you."

My heart rate returns to normal, but my chest is still constricted at the thought of him in pain. "If it hurts that much, maybe you shouldn't do it."

He lowers his head and chews on his bottom lip. "I never thought I'd see the day when moving myself a foot to the right would be such a big production. Well, at least not until I was ninety or so."

Pain flares in my chest, but I can't think of anything to say that will comfort him.

He shakes his head and mutters, "Not today," as he raises his eyes to me. "You said we would do whatever I wanted today, and today I want you to sit with me."

"Well then, that's exactly what I'll do," I tell him, grinning.

He relaxes immediately, grinning back, and the tension in the air evaporates.

We both jump as a loud bang echoes around the room. Will's door opens to reveal one of the nurses pulling the movie cart. She must have accidentally bumped it into the door.

I hurry over and help her maneuver it into the room and give her a grateful smile once we have it positioned in front of Will's bed.

She gives him a wink and a smile as she turns. "Give me a holler if you need anything."

Will just nods and smiles.

I load up the movie and climb onto his bed with as much care as I can. He breathes in sharply and closes his eyes, but he opens them again almost immediately.

"You're getting better at that," he tells me, and I chuckle.

He turns to face me and brings his hand up to stroke my cheek with his thumb. "God, I love that sound."

He stares at me almost hungrily as his thumb pauses, and he draws his hand away. His eyes seem to be questioning me—asking for permission. Is it to touch me? I'm not sure what the question is, but I would give him anything, so I nod, still lost in his gaze.

He moves his hand forward again and traces my cheekbone with his index finger. His touch is feather-light and makes me want to shiver, but I hold it in, shaking only on the inside. He reaches up and traces my eyebrow with the same soft touch, and then he begins to gently explore my face.

I close my eyes as he traces my forehead and nose, my chin and jawline. Warmth spreads from every caress of his fingers, my face tingling from his touch and my breath coming faster. My eyes snap open at the sound of his voice, low and laden with emotion.

"I've wanted to do this for so long. You don't know how many times I've dra—dreamt of touching you like this."

He blushes, and I wonder if it's because of what he's said or because he tripped over the words.

"Tori . . ." Will pauses, looking down.

"Anything, Will," I whisper, and he raises his eyes, need burning in their green depths.

He starts to lean toward me, letting out a grunt, but I quickly take over so he doesn't have to stretch. I lean into him and brush my lips against his, warmth flaring in my chest. I pause for a second to make sure this is what he wanted, and he cocks his head for better access to my lips and deepens the kiss.

He runs his tongue along my bottom teeth, and I open my mouth eagerly, my stomach twinging giddily as he moans against my lips. Our tongues tangle and caress each other, and I taste the tangy sweetness of the fruit he ate for lunch. He raises his hand to my cheek, stroking it with the backs of his fingers as our mouths explore each other.

I kiss him until I feel my heart beginning to speed up, stopping before things become truly heated. We can't go any further than this, and in truth, I'm not sure if he wants to, so I lean my forehead against his.

His lips curve into an immediate smile even before he opens his eyes, and I chuckle as I pull back to look at him. He's smirking at me, as happy as I've ever seen him with or without morphine, and I giggle aloud as euphoria washes through me. He ducks his head and shrugs, causing a wince to mar his crooked smile, but even that isn't enough to wipe the smirk from his face.

"I think you liked that."

His smile grows even wider. "I did."

His voice is low and husky, and it takes everything I have not to assault his lips again. Instead, I run my finger over his bottom lip, my stomach fluttering as he closes his eyes and lets out a shaky breath. *Wait, wasn't I trying to slow things down?*

I pull my finger away slowly. "Why don't we start our movie?" *Before either one of us can get any other bright ideas that will lead us back to making out.*

Will snorts out a laugh and shakes his head. "Okay. I did say it was going to be movie day."

I lie back, mirroring his position, but before I start the movie, I retrieve the bag of popcorn from my chair and put it on his lap.

He tries to purse his lips to hide his grin, but he fails miserably and plunges his hand into the bag instead.

"You like that almost as much as chocolate, don't you?"

"Almost." He agrees around a mouthful of popcorn. He raises a finger while he swallows. "But not quite. This is good, but *nothing* is better than chocolate."

I laugh and shake my head, thinking again how adorable he is as I push play on the remote.

We watch in popcorn-munching silence for a while until the movie comes to the gathering in the cave. I draw in a sharp breath as I realize what's coming next. The scene is erotic—the crowd gyrating to the beat, interspersed with shots of Neo and Trinity having sex. It turns me on to watch even when I'm alone, so I can only imagine how it's going to affect me with Will mere inches from me. I swallow thickly as the music begins, and Will tenses. I think he's just figured it out too.

We watch in silence, but I can feel the electricity building in the room, my skin heating at the points where he's brushing against me—shoulder, hip, and thigh. The warmth is also building between my legs as I watch the sensuality play out on screen. I can feel Will looking at me, and I lick my lips as the desire to kiss him becomes almost unbearable. Why am I resisting exactly? If I had a reason, it's flown out the window right along with my resolve as I slowly turn to face him.

I only get a second to see the desperate need in his eyes before he crashes his lips to mine, plunging his hands into my hair and pulling me closer, until I'm almost on top of him. He grunts in pain because he can't help it, but he's paying no attention to the brokenness of his body as his lips and tongue devour me. I bury my fingers in his hair, pulling him even closer as he moans against my lips. I am instantly on fire—heat rolling in my belly and exploding into my chest. I lose myself in the raw passion emanating from him as his hand grips the back of my skull, our tongues and bodies still dancing to the sensual beat on the screen.

Now that my hand is holding him to me, his slips down from my hair and over the swell of my breast. He cups it in his hand, kneading gently, and I moan as his thumb circles my already peaked nipple. Suddenly, his hand stills, and he gasps against my lips, breaking the kiss. The sound is pained, not passionate, and I freeze as he tries to choke back a sob.

I pull back just enough so I can see him. His face is contorted into a grimace, his eyes squeezed tightly shut as he tries to hold back his tears, but as I watch, one slips down his cheek. I bring my hand down to cup his chin, but he resists when I try to get him to look at me, so I stroke his cheek while he struggles for composure.

"I'm sorry," he whispers, his words ragged and broken. "I shouldn't have . . . but I want . . . fuck!"

"Hey," I say softly as I nudge his chin upward again, and this time, he doesn't resist. His face is still twisted in sorrow, but he forces himself to open his eyes. They are a maelstrom of emotion, so tangled and desperate that I almost get lost there until I realize I'm the one who has to bring him safely back to shore.

"Don't think about what we can't have. Not now. Today, let's be happy for what we do have, okay? It's a good day, and I get to kiss you."

His lips turn up slightly, but his sorrow quickly overpowers his attempt to smile. "I'm sorry," he says again. "You're right. I . . . I wasn't expecting you to feel this way, and I'm a bit overwhelmed. What does it mean, Tori?" His question is childlike in its simplicity, but I can see the conflict and confusion still swirling in his eyes.

I wipe the tear from his cheek tenderly. "I think it means that we both want this. Beyond that, I don't know what it means. I think we need to take it one day at a time and live in this moment we've been given. I just want you to be happy, Will, and to know I'm the one who's making you feel that way."

He smiles, and I grin back at him. He glances down at his afghan, his fingers tracing squares in the weave as he takes a deep breath. When he finally speaks, his voice is soft and low. "You told me yesterday I think too much, and you're right. I'm trying not to, but it's a hard habit to break. I'm the kind of person who needs everything planned out, and with Jason coming back and now . . . this, I feel out of control, and I don't know how to deal with it on top of everything else.

"It's like every day, something is different. I wake up in the morning, and I never know if I'm going to be feverish or in pain or if some new goddamn thing is going to go wrong. I try to take it as it comes, but all of a sudden, it's getting to me. I thought I had it all under control, but now? Now, I just want to spend time with you, and it feels like so many things are trying to keep me from doing that, and there's nothing I can do about it."

I swallow thickly as I let his words sink in. He's reaching out because he feels like he's losing control of his situation, and he's dangerously close to falling apart. I never wanted to cause him any more pain or confusion, and I should have known Will couldn't just let this happen without overthinking it.

And I'm just the opposite; I don't want to think about where it's going or what it means because I know how it's going to end, and I'm not willing to acknowledge that yet. That's not the important part. The important part is right now—what we both think and feel *right now*.

I can't do anything about the weight of his illness on his shoulders or whatever he's feeling toward me. But I *can* take away any worry he has about my expectations.

"Sweetheart, I'm sorry this is so hard for you," I tell him as I pull him into my arms, his head coming to rest on my shoulder. "I want to try to make it easier in any way I can. I have no expectations of you. Truly, I don't. I want to spend time with you too and enjoy every minute we have together. I know we can't do any more than that, and I'm okay with it. And if you don't want things to change at all between us, if you want to go back to just being friends, I'm okay with that too. I care about you so much, Will, and I'll take whatever you feel you can give me— whether it's friendship or more than that. I'm here and I'm glad you're letting me be a part of your life and that you're sharing things with me. I need you to understand that this is making me happy too, and you don't have to feel you need to do more. I know you think this isn't fair to me, but it's simply not true. What would have been unfair is if I'd never gotten the chance to know you."

Will relaxes against me, and I can almost feel his relief. He rests against my shoulder, both of us just breathing and being. After a few minutes, he raises his head to look at me, and the emotion in his eyes is calm like a gentle sea.

"How is it you seem to know exactly what I need even when I don't know?" he asks, caressing my cheek. "I care about you, too, and I want this—whatever this is—to continue. You make me happier than I've been in a long time—maybe ever. I can't deny that anymore. A part of me—a very needy, insecure part—was still worried you were doing this just to please me, despite what you said earlier, and I didn't want that. I'm sorry for doubting you and for thinking too much."

I smile at him warmly. "Will, you wouldn't be you if you didn't think too much. Now, can we go back to the part where I spend the day making you happy instead of complicating your already over-complicated life?"

Will chuckles, swearing softly as he cradles his belly. I release him from my arms, and he grunts as he lies back against his pillow, eyes closed.

"Are you okay?" I ask, brushing the hair back from his forehead.

"Yeah, I think I am." He looks at peace now, and more than that, he looks happy.

I glance at the TV screen. "Well, we missed a good half hour of the movie at least. Should I run it back?"

"Nah, not unless *you* want to. I've seen it enough times that I can jump right back in."

"Me too." Aware of our surroundings again, I begin to carefully slide off the bed, but a warm hand lands on my forearm.

"Where are you going?"

"I think we need some chocolate," I say, gesturing toward the bag of Hershey's Kisses perched on the windowsill.

"I drive you to chocolate, eh? Is that like driving someone to drink?"

"No, I'm getting the chocolate for you. You drive me to Twizzlers, and luckily, we have some handy."

Will laughs as I snatch up the bags and return to his bed, handing him the bag of Kisses as I reposition myself. His moan of chocolate ecstasy catches me off guard, and the sound causes me to clench my thighs. I sigh in exasperation. Now that he's kissed me, it's time he knows what he's doing to me. "You *have* to stop doing that," I say, scolding him.

He furrows his brow, completely confused.

"Your response to chocolate is enough to make me need new underwear," I tell him, my eyes narrowing in mock aggravation.

He squints at me for a moment then raises his eyebrows in shock. "Oh. *Oh.*" He's trying to keep a straight face, but his self-satisfied smirk isn't containable. "So . . . this has happened before?"

"You realize that if it wouldn't hurt you, I'd be smacking you right now."

He covers his mouth with his hand to stifle his laughter, but I can tell because his other hand has crept over his belly.

I cross my arms and turn my attention to the screen. Out of the corner of my eye, I see he's still staring at me and smirking, but I don't give in. "Watch the damn movie," I order him, but that just sets him laughing again. Eventually, he turns his eyes to the screen, but a shit-eating grin is still plastered across his face.

After a few moments, I feel his eyes on me again. They're still sparkling with amusement, but now, he's at least trying to look contrite. He reaches over to my lap and picks up the bag of Twizzlers, taking one out and waving it in my direction.

"Can I buy back your affection? Are Twizzlers the way to your heart?" he asks with all the charm he can muster.

"No, but I don't think you have a chateau in France shoved in your back pocket, so they'll have to do," I answer, grabbing the licorice from him.

He chuckles and captures my hand, lacing his fingers through mine and squeezing, and all is right in my world.

We jump back into the movie, making jokes and chatting as we watch. I haven't seen him this content since that first Saturday we watched a movie together. Actually, he's even happier today, probably because he's no longer hiding so much from me.

The movie ends, and Will is still awake this time.

"Do you want to watch the last one?"

"Yeah, let's."

As I lean forward to get up, he captures my chin and pulls me toward him. I smile as heat blossoms in my belly, knowing he's about to kiss me again.

His lips meet mine softly, but I can feel his emotion behind them. It's not tentative or desperate this time, but comfortable and sure. He tilts his head and opens his mouth to deepen the kiss, and I oblige him, drinking him in. We explore each other as the heat builds slowly until he pulls away, panting as he leans his forehead against mine. He brushes his lips against mine one more time, then flashes me the most beautiful smile I've ever seen. I exhale in a whoosh as I stare at him, stunned.

"Okay, you can get up now," he says huskily.

I would if I could, but I don't think I'm capable of moving yet. I feel like prey caught in the thrall of the cobra, fascinated and unable to look away as an emotion I'm too afraid to name nearly obliterates me with its force. He laughs, and I shake my head, snapping out of it and getting up to put in the next movie.

The rest of the afternoon is fantastic. Will is relaxed and happy, and the conversation and teasing between us flows so naturally. It's unbelievable that I've only known him for a month. As I expected, when Trinity dies, tears are rolling down my cheeks, and the minute Will hears me sniffle, he reaches over and pulls my head onto his shoulder, squeezing my hand as he caresses it.

By the time the credits roll, I'm reasonably composed again, so I lift my head to gaze at Will. His eyes are closed, but his breathing tells me he isn't sleeping. As soon as my head leaves his shoulder, he slowly opens his eyes, and I reach up and run my fingers into his hair as he leans into my touch. "How are you, sweetheart? You look like you're finally getting tired."

Will smiles and ducks his head. "Yeah. I don't want our day to end though." His admission is soft as he glances back up at me.

I don't want our day to end either, even more than I didn't want yesterday to end. "Well, I'm going to need to go before too long, and I know you had pizza for lunch today, but do you want me to order us some Domino's for dinner? They deliver to the hospital, so all I'd have to do is call."

Will's eyes light up. "Really? Holy shit, why didn't we do this before? The hospital's food isn't bad, but I've been here for a month already. I truly would kill for something from the outside world."

I bite my lip, feeling bad I didn't do this for him sooner. He never asks for anything. I should have remembered my offer from a few weeks ago and followed up on it. Repeatedly.

"Hey, where did you go?" Will asks, stroking a curled finger under my chin. "You're not feeling bad because we didn't do this sooner, are you? Because that's not what I meant at all."

I frown at him, caught. "I should have asked you about it. I—"

Will runs his index finger down over my lips, silencing me and turning me on all at the same time. "It's fine. If I really wanted it that badly, I would have asked. I asked for my Raisinets, didn't I?"

I nod grudgingly as he starts to smile, knowing he's made a good point.

"Now, go order us some pizza so we can discuss the *real* food we're going to have for our date tomorrow night."

My eyes widen at the word "date," and suddenly, Will looks nervous. He swallows it back though, and his eyes lock with mine. "I can't take you out anywhere the way I'd like to, but I'm thinking we can have a nice dinner and conversation and pretend we're somewhere else. Would that be all right with you? Um, unless—"

I cover his lips with my finger before his nervous ramble really gets going. "Yes."

I'm stunned again by the amazing smile that lights up his face, and I leave the room in a daze to order our pizza. When I return, Will is lying in the center of his bed again, asleep. I decide not to wake him until the pizza gets here. He spent the day doing his damnedest to ignore the fact that he's sick, and I'm sure it took its toll on him. We had a fantastic day, but reality starts to creep back in as I stare at his angelic face.

No, I'm not going to do this. Not today. So instead of thinking ahead, I think back over our weekend, replaying all the memories in my mind and letting my happiness engulf me. I still can't believe we kissed yesterday and that he truly has feelings for me beyond simple friend-ship. And I really can't believe I ever thought getting this close to him wouldn't be worth it and that I should protect myself. How does that saying go? "'Tis better to have loved and lost than never to have loved at all"? I don't know how I'll feel when this is all over, but right now, I'm agreeing wholeheartedly. No matter how bad things get, I'll never regret my time with Will. But is what I feel . . . love? My feelings for him have grown so slowly and naturally that I'm not really sure, and every-thing has changed so much over the past few days that I haven't had time to think. And do I even really know what love is? I thought I was in love with Peter, but was it really him, or was I in love with the idea of being someone's wife and not being alone? I don't know the answer, but as I gaze at Will, I realize it doesn't matter. I'm where I'm meant to be.

Will stirs then, wincing as he pulls in a deep breath. He looks confused for a moment, but he smiles as he looks at me, blinking slowly.

"I'm sorry, Tori. I didn't mean to fall asleep."

I grin at him as his eyes drift closed again. "I know you didn't, sweet-heart, but I figured I'd let you rest until the pizza got here. It's probably good you're awake now, though, because it should be here soon."

Will is quiet for a few minutes, struggling to overcome his grogginess, but I can tell he's fighting exhaustion. I knew I should have left after the movie was over, but we both wanted . . . more. My thoughts are interrupted by the arrival of our pizza, and Will grins happily as I fetch paper towels from his bathroom to use as plates.

"Ooohhh," Will moans as he takes his first bite, and I squeeze my eyes shut as the sound seems to bounce off all the parts that make me a girl.

I snap my eyes open as he chuckles. "I did it again, didn't I?"

"Yes, you most certainly did," I answer shortly.

"I'm sorry," he says, giving me his best puppy dog eyes. "I'm just very . . . vocal."

My eyes widen as I feel my jaw drop. Oh my God, he's truly going to kill me. I thought the sound was bad? Well, that comment now has all my girl parts standing at attention and vibrating.

Will blushes to the roots of his hair. "Umm . . ." he starts to stammer, but I raise my hand to silence him.

"Stop. Stop right there. Anything you say is only going to make it worse."

He smirks at me, trying hard not to laugh.

"Just eat your pizza while I try to forget you said that."

Will ducks his head and chews quietly, but the smile never leaves his face. He seems to be living in the moment, but I'm struggling not to be pulled out. This is the kind of conversation we might be having if we were truly going to be dating, but the reality is pressing in on me. Even if we loved each other, and he got well enough to leave the hospital, I don't think we could ever be intimate because of his condition. But when I look into his eyes, it's so easy to forget everything around us and to say and do things I would normally do—with a man I was dating. The pain cuts like a knife in my chest, but I can't let him see. I've fought so hard to bring him to the point where he's enjoying himself. I can't bring him back down now.

Will's voice interrupts my thoughts, and I jump as his hand touches my arm. "Hey, are you all right?"

"I'm fine," I respond automatically, glancing up at him. His green eyes are warm and soft with concern. "I remembered something I need to do tomorrow when I get in, and I got distracted for a moment." I hate lying to him, but there's just no way I'm going to tell him what I was actually thinking.

He furrows his brow, but he remains quiet.

"So, what do you want to have for dinner tomorrow night?"

"I want Rigatoni Bolognese from Il Terrazzo Carmine. Have you ever eaten there?"

"No, but it sounds delicious. I'm thinking you won't be eating alone after all."

Will smirks at my smart-ass remark but doesn't comment. "It's this great Italian place in Pioneer Square. It's actually on the same street as my apartment but about three blocks down. Jason and I used to go there all the time, and I may have been singlehandedly keeping them in business these last few years with my takeout orders."

"All right. I'm sure they have a menu online. I'll have a look and then call in the order tomorrow afternoon for us and pick it up before I come see you."

"That sounds perfect," Will says, grinning, but it turns into a giant yawn.

"I think it's time for you to get some sleep," I tell him as I start to clean up our dinner.

"I guess." Will huffs, pouting even though he can barely keep his eyes open.

"Hey, we've had a wonderful day together. Don't let the last thing I remember be that pouty face you're sporting."

Will chuckles. "All right, I won't spoil our day by pouting. But I *am* sorry it has to end."

"Me too. But we have another fun afternoon planned for tomorrow, and I'll stay until you fall asleep, okay?"

"Yeah," he answers, staring into my eyes longingly. "Thank you, Tori. It's been an amazing weekend, and I'm so glad I got to spend it with you."

Warmth erupts in my chest, and happiness washes over me like a tidal wave. I stand up, gripping his chin gently with my fingers. "There's nowhere I'd rather be," I whisper, leaning in to kiss him.

Before I can back away, his hand is on the back of my head, and his kisses are warm and sweet. It's over far too soon, but I know he's given me all he has today. He lies back against his pillow, panting softly and eyes still closed.

"Go to sleep, sweetheart. I'll see you in the morning," I tell him as I begin running my fingers through his hair.

He leans into my touch, but he's asleep in seconds. I shouldn't have let him push himself so hard today, but I couldn't bring myself to tell him no.

He shifts and grunts in his sleep, and I realize I'm still stroking his hair. I reluctantly pull my hand back and resist the urge to kiss his forehead, afraid I might wake him.

I grin all the way home like a schoolgirl with a crush and turn in early so I can see Will again that much sooner.

CHAPTER 20

I wake up on Monday with a smile on my face and bounce through my morning routine. It's a rare sunny day in Seattle, and I feel as if it's just for me. I blast the radio on the way to the hospital, singing at the top of my lungs—I know I look silly, but I couldn't care less because I'm *happy*.

As I approach the nurses' station, Jenny's eyebrows rise as her jaw drops.

"Wow! What happened to *you*?"

"He kissed me."

Jenny squeals excitedly. "I just knew that would happen this weekend! Was it only once?"

"No, it was more than once."

"Okay, spill," she orders, grabbing my arm and shepherding me to the nurses' lounge. "I've been waiting weeks for this. I can't possibly wait until lunchtime."

I laugh at her eagerness, and to my surprise, I end up telling her everything as if we were in high school. She oohs and ahs in all the right places, and by the time I reach the end, she's grinning from ear to ear.

"I *told* you he had feelings for you!" she says, whacking me on the arm.

"Yes, you told me so. Are you happy now?"

"I'm completely happy, and *so* are *you!*" She gushes, almost knocking me over with a hug.

"Yes, I *am* happy. I don't know what the future holds, but I'm so glad I decided to just let things happen."

"I'm glad you did too. But I wasn't sure things would turn out this way even if you did make that decision. I thought there was a chance Will would pull away at the last minute. He's so set in his ways about certain things, and this wasn't part of his plan."

"Well, I did have to reassure him more than once that this was what I wanted too, and I encouraged him to let go and enjoy himself. And although I'm thrilled about it, his pulling me closer kind of worries me. He was so bound and determined not to. The change makes me nervous about his emotional stability. I don't want to be the reason he falls apart even though I think, in some ways, it might be good for him."

"I'm sure he'll be all right; he's tough," Jenny says, patting my arm. "Speaking of Will, shouldn't you be waking him up about now? It's almost eight-thirty."

"Jeez, you're right! I have a nine o'clock, so I need to get moving!"

I push Will's door open slowly, and I'm met with what's become my very favorite sight in the whole world: Will sleeping peacefully. He is utterly still this morning—a hopeful sign that he might have yet another good day. I walk right over to his bed, but I indulge myself in a few minutes of staring at his beautiful face and morning-wild hair before I finally reach up to push a few strands back from his forehead.

"Good morning, sweetheart," I whisper.

Will pulls his head away a little, scrunching up his face in a wince as his arm curls unconsciously over his belly. I scowl, hating that every move he makes causes him pain even in sleep. I don't know how he deals with it day in and day out, but short of keeping him on morphine around the clock, there's nothing to be done. I wonder if this is one of the things that's starting to get to him.

"Hey, I'm gonna let Jenny come in here and poke and prod you awake." I smile as I threaten him, take his hand in mine, and start massaging his fingers.

His eyes snap open as he draws a quick breath, but they fall closed almost as quickly. His brow furrows as he grunts.

"Do you want me to let you sleep?"

He opens his eyes slowly this time, and my stomach does its usual flip as he gazes at me. "Tori," he rasps, his voice thick with sleep. "No, I'm .. . I must have been dreaming or something. Sometimes, it's hard to sweep the cobwebs away."

He pulls his hand from mine to rub it over his face, and finally, the smile I've been waiting for appears. "Hmm . . . maybe I wasn't dreaming," he says huskily. "Did we have a fantastic weekend together that involved me kissing you?"

"Why, yes; yes, we did. You don't have to go back to sleep for that to be a reality."

"Wow, it's been a while since anything in this life has been better than my dreams."

My stomach does something funny when Will mentions his dreams, and warmth starts to spread through my chest. "Have you dreamed about me?"

Will ducks his head, then glances up at me. "Um . . . once or twice."

I smile as the warmth intensifies. "Once or twice, huh?"

"Well, maybe a bit more than that," he says, still looking bashful.

"I'm glad you think the real me is better." I raise my hand to his forehead and find it cool to the touch. "How are you feeling today?"

"All right. I'm not feverish, and other than my belly, nothing really hurts too much."

I glance down at the roundness of his middle, frowning.

"Hey, I can still breathe just fine, so it's not that bad. It's just tender when I move or laugh, and I tend to do both a fair bit when I'm with you," he says, grinning.

"Yes, you do." I grin right back at him. "Well, I'm glad it's going to be another good day because we have a date tonight."

"Yes," Will says seductively before winking at me. "I get more real food!"

I laugh as he blushes, and my gaze falls on the clock over his door. It's ten minutes to nine.

"I need to get going, but I'll order our food this afternoon and hopefully be back by five."

"That sounds fantastic," he says with a twinkle in his eye, and I feel my own happiness bubble up as I witness his.

"All right, I'll see you this afternoon, then," I tell him, turning to go.

"Hey, come here a minute," Will calls, curling a finger in my direction.

I turn around, and he grabs my chin, pulling me to him and gently kissing my lips. Fireworks explode in my chest, but he doesn't deepen the kiss; he just pulls back and gives me a brilliant smile.

"I'm not enough of an asshole to ask you to make out with me while I have morning breath, but I couldn't resist completely," he confesses.

I'm again struck dumb by how adorable he is, and all I can do is stand there and stare at him.

"You have to go," he reminds me.

"Oh, right," I stammer, shaking my head as he chuckles again. "Have a good day, and I'll see you later," I tell him as I finally make myself walk out the door.

I can still hear him chuckling as I step out into the hall.

My day flies by, and before I know it, it's a quarter to four, and I'm on the phone with Will's favorite restaurant. The hostess recommends the cannelloni fiorentina, so I order that along with Will's rigatoni bolognese. Unfortunately, they're backed up already due to a business dinner, so our food won't be ready until five. I'm upset about this at first until I realize I can see Will for a while before I leave.

As usual, I open the door slowly so I can peek at him without making any noise. I was worried he'd be resting, but he's awake and drawing. Again, I'm spellbound by the sight of him—the long fingers of his left hand curled around his charcoal pencil, his brow furrowed in concentration, and his tongue just poking out of his mouth.

My stomach twinges and flips as I watch him, and the experience is beyond intimate. Watching him create, knowing that he's sitting across the room from me, making something beautiful, is almost more than I can take. I breathe in sharply, and he glances up at the sound.

Today he doesn't look nervous at all, and a smile spreads across his sweet face. "You're early," he says, tipping his pencil away from the page. And to my utter amazement, he doesn't whip the book closed as he usually does.

I nod, a bit dazed that he hasn't put his work away. The book calls to me, lying open and propped against his chest, and my eyes never leave it as I cross the room.

Will glances down at it casually. "Do you want to see some of my sketches today?"

Do I? Is he serious? I would kill to see what's in that book even though what's in there is likely going to kill *me* to look at. But, *hell* yes, I want to see!

"Yes, if you're willing to show me," I answer, my voice shaking a little.

"Of course I'll show you." He's got the red book today. He sketches in this one often, but lately he's been working in the black book more. I'm dying to see what's in that one, too, but for today, I'll take what I can get.

As I cross the room, he pushes his table away and flips back to the beginning of the book. I gingerly sit on the side of his bed, and he offers it to me, gripping the top as he holds it open.

Oh my God. My jaw hits the floor as I stare in awe at the picture before me. It's a landscape, a scene of dense woods and fallen trees that looks like it could be from one of the forests surrounding Seattle. The detail is beyond incredible. It looks like a photograph. Hell, it looks like I could walk right into the picture, and I might actually believe I could if it was done in color instead of black and white. How the *hell* did Will do this with just a charcoal pencil?

"Have you ever been to Olympic National Forest?" he asks, smiling at me.

"My dad took me there once," I stammer, unable to take my eyes off the picture.

"Jay and I used to go there to paint. Well, he would paint, and I would sketch. But that picture is how I remember it."

"Will, this is incredible. And you say you're better with a paintbrush? I've never seen a drawing with this much detail before. It's breathtaking."

Will blushes and looks down. "It's not *that* good."

"Yes. Yes, it is! You're so incredibly talented. I can't believe you sat and drew this in a hospital bed."

He blushes even more, and his smile widens. "Thanks, Tori. I'm so glad you like it."

"Can I see more?"

He nods, staring at me with a peculiar look on his face, but I can't stop to ponder it with his sketchbook in my hot little hands. I turn the page, and I can't help but giggle. The next sketch is a picture of Sebastian. Will is a man whose main loves in life are chocolate and his cat.

Again, the picture is brilliantly detailed, and Sebastian looks so real that I reach out to touch him before stopping myself, not wanting to damage Will's work in any way.

The next one is another picture of Sebastian, but this one is a close up of his face as if he's looking outward from the page. I extend my trembling hand over the perfect image and realize that tears are streaming down my face.

Will grasps my hand, drawing my eyes up to his. "Are you all right?"

"Yeah, uh, fine." I stammer as my eyes burn, and my heart aches. The beauty of his work has affected me deeply, and I know I'm falling even further, but what's tearing me apart is knowing his life will end soon. All this talent, all the emotion he's able to evoke simply by moving a pencil over paper, all of it will leave this world forever when he draws his last breath. How can life be so cruel?

I'm dangerously close to breaking down, and I don't want to do that in front of him. I close my eyes, take a few deep breaths, and give him a watery smile, trying to convince us both I'm okay.

He still looks worried, but he doesn't press me.

The next sketches are of Jenny and Jason, and Will's captured them perfectly. "These are gorgeous," I tell him, and he gives me a little satisfied smile.

I flip to the next sketch, and we both draw in a sharp breath. The picture is a woman's face with long, wavy hair hanging down to her shoulders, her features immediately reminding me of Will.

I risk a glance up at him, but he's still staring at the picture, one hand curled into a fist and sadness etched on his face.

"Who is this?"

He looks up at me, the sorrow plain in his eyes. "That's . . . my mother," he whispers. "I forgot that one was in there."

"Will—"

"I'm happy you're here with me, but some of my decisions are already made. Even though things have changed between us, there are things I'm still not willing to explain or discuss." His words are hard, but his voice quavers as he says them.

His declaration stings, but I caress his hand gently, my words as soft as his were hard. "I was just going to say that she's beautiful, and I can see where you get your good looks."

"Oh," he says, blushing fiercely. "Fuck, I'm sorry, Tori. I didn't mean to jump on you like that. I'm an ass."

"No, you're not. You're doing the best you can, and I know that. And I promised you I wouldn't ask."

Will takes a deep breath, and his shoulders relax. "Well, I'm sorry anyway. You're entirely too understanding."

"Nah," I say, shrugging it off.

"Hey, what happened to our dinner plans?"

"Oh!" I exclaim, hurriedly glancing at the clock. "I called and placed our order, but they were running late, so they told me it wouldn't be ready until five. I need to run so our food doesn't end up cold!"

Will chuckles, shaking his head and wincing. "Well, hurry up, woman! Now you're standing between a man and his Italian food!"

"You know, sometimes you're entirely too cute," I tell him, kissing him on the nose.

He ducks his head and grins, an adorable blush creeping up his cheeks. Warmth flares in my chest, and I suddenly understand what people mean when they say they have warm fuzzies because that's exactly what I have right now.

Mercifully, there isn't much traffic on the way over, despite the time, and I make it to Il Terrazzo Carmine at exactly five o'clock.

The restaurant is upscale but not ridiculous, and as I glance around, I imagine Will and myself sitting at one of the white linen-covered tables, enjoying a quiet meal. What I wouldn't give to do that with him today. *Hmm . . . we can't do it here, but maybe we can still do it.*

Paying for our food hurriedly, I decide to make a flying trip to my place. I dash in and grab one of my white linen tablecloths, a pair of napkins, and place settings for two from my dinnerware and silver. I also grab two wine glasses, two bottles of water, and a bud vase, putting every-thing in a tote bag and wrapping the plates and glassware in the linens.

As I bustle about the apartment, Sebastian appears, stretching luxuri-ously and declaring it's time for dinner.

"I'm not here to stay, buddy," I tell him. "I need to go feed your favorite person dinner first." Sebastian just stares, meowing loudly at me.

"Are you this demanding with Will?" I ask as I open a can of cat food and deposit it into his dish.

"I'll be back later," I say as I scurry out the door, eager to get back to the hospital.

On the way up to Will's room, I stop at the flower vending machine in the lobby and buy a single red rose.

I arrive at Will's door at a quarter to six, amazed I was able to do all that in a little over an hour. Will's eyes are closed, but they fly open as the door squeaks, and I curse myself for forgetting about the damn thing.

A warm smile spreads across his face. "You're back," he says, his voice deep and husky from sleep.

"I am, and now I have some work to do," I tell him, setting my bags on my chair. "This probably would have worked out better if you were still sleeping, but . . . can you close your eyes?"

"What did you do?"

"Never you mind; you'll see in a minute. Now humor me and play along, okay?"

"All right," he says, closing his eyes, but the smile never leaves his face.

"Good. I'll tell you when you can open them."

I get to work quickly, moving Will's sketchbook and pencils from his table and spreading the white linen tablecloth over it. I set two place settings, intending to perch on his bed and sit facing him while we eat, and place the rose in the bud vase between them. The fit is tight, but I'm sure Will will get the idea. Next, I pour the water, then pull out the food, dishing it onto the plates. Thankfully, the restaurant packaged everything in foil containers, so it's still reasonably hot.

Will inhales deeply. "You're killing me here. Are you almost finished?"

I stand back, admiring my handiwork and making sure everything is in place.

"Okay, you can open your eyes."

He smiles in delight, and his eyes are watery as his gaze falls on me. "Tori, this is amazing. Thank you so much! You didn't have to do this!"

"Well, I know you were really wishing we could go out together, but since we can't do that, I figured I'd do everything I could to bring the restaurant to you."

I take his hand, and he quickly brings mine up to his lips, kissing the back as he stares at me adoringly. "Thank you again. This is fantastic, truly."

My heart flutters, and I grin from ear to ear. I carefully take my seat on the side of his bed as he beams at me. "Shall we eat?"

"Yes, please!" Will says, picking up his fork and spearing some of his rigatoni.

I watch in fascination as he brings the fork up to his nose, closing his eyes and inhaling deeply before popping the pasta into his mouth. He starts to moan as he exhales, and I reach over and squeeze his other hand. The sound cuts off immediately, and he gapes at me, surprised. Glaring at him, I shake my head, and he ducks his chin, grinning as his cheeks redden.

"You did that on purpose."

He stares at me in shock. "I would never!"

I raise one eyebrow in disbelief, and he crumbles.

"Okay, I would, but I didn't this time! It's just that fucking good!" he exclaims, and I laugh hysterically.

He laughs right along with me, but I have to release his hand so he can grip his midsection, grimacing in pain. He glides over the intrusion of his illness smoothly, taking a moment to breathe before looking over at me and smiling.

"Um, I'll just eat my pasta quietly now," he says, sounding properly chastised.

"I'm so glad you like it," I say, picking up my own fork and sampling my cannelloni. "Mmm," I hum, before I even realize what I'm doing.

"See?" Will declares triumphantly, stabbing his fork in my direction before he goes back to eating.

And that's the way things go all through our meal. Will is upbeat and happy, and we joke and laugh as we talk about movies and music, and I steer carefully away from any topic that would bring up his illness. We feed each other bites of our entrees and put down our forks to kiss more than once.

I stop to watch him as he's telling me a story about a drunken evening out with Jason and his friends, eating with one hand and gesturing with the other. Then it hits me. This is exactly what it would be like if we were out on a date. This is the real Will. I've seen glimpses of him before at different moments when he's been happy but never for this long and without the interruption of something to bring us back to reality. Joy and sorrow wash over me in equal measure as I realize how happy we could have been. But it doesn't matter. We're happy now; that's what matters.

I'm brought back to the present when I realize Will has stopped talking. He's staring down at his plate with a confused look on his face, his brow furrowed. He raises his hand absently to his neck, wincing as he touches the swollen lymph node there.

"What's the matter?"

He shakes his head. "Nothing. I'm sorry; I didn't mean to get distracted."

I smile to myself, knowing I was the one who should have been caught out for being distracted, and I take another bite of my cannelloni.

Will takes another bite of his pasta, but suddenly, his eyes go wide as a wheezing sound escapes him. He tries to cough, but he can't, so he makes the horrible wheezing sound again.

Oh my God, he's choking! Panic rips down my spine as I stand up and push the table out of the way. I reach across his lap and hit the call button for Jenny, but I know what to do, so I don't wait.

"Will, I'm going to sit you up more and pound your back between your shoulders," I tell him as I grip under his left arm. He can't acknowledge me, but at least he knows what I'm doing, and hopefully, my voice will calm him.

Will's still making strangled noises as he tries to cough, so he's at least getting some air. While I hold him up with my left arm, I pound between his shoulder blades with my right hand. He gasps, and then he's reaching for the napkin on his lap and coughing pasta into it, taking in a great lungful of air before each cough.

Jenny skids into the room, taking in the scene with alarm. "What the hell?"

"It's okay," I tell her, although I'm starting to shake. "Will was choking, but I think he's all right now."

Will is still gasping for breath, but at least he's stopped coughing. He's also still gripping my arm, and I know it's taking a lot of his strength to sit straight up, so I start to gently lower him toward the mattress.

He cries out, his right hand clutching his thigh so hard I can see the tendons in his forearm. He collapses back against the bed, still breathing heavily and grunting in pain.

I run my fingers into his hair and whisper words of comfort to soothe him even though inside, I'm still shaking like a leaf. After a few minutes, his arm relaxes, and his breathing slows.

"Are you all right, Will?" Jenny asks from behind me. I had forgotten she was there.

"Yeah," he whispers tiredly. "Tori stopped me from choking, but it hurt like hell to sit up like that."

"Dammit! I knew I had to be hurting you, but I didn't see any other way—"

"You did what you had to do, and you just saved my life. I'm fine," Will says, putting his hand on my arm. His words are reassuring, but there's still a touch of panic in his eyes.

Jenny stares at Will, her expression serious. "If you're sure you're okay, I'll come and check on you after Tori leaves, all right?"

Will looks over at her distractedly. "Sure, Jenny. Thanks."

Jenny turns on her heel and leaves without another word, and some of the tension in the room leaves with her.

My heart is finally starting to slow down as the adrenaline wears off. I take a deep breath. While it shocked me and scared the shit out of me for a moment, it wasn't *that* big a deal. Will was getting air the whole time, and I've choked on food like that before. "Are you sure you're all right?"

"Yeah. I'm just a little shaken up. That's all. I'm sorry for ruining our dinner."

"You didn't ruin anything! These things happen. I'm just glad it wasn't serious."

Will's presses his lips together tightly for a moment, lost in his own thoughts.

"Are you still hungry?" I ask, looking over toward the remains of our dinner.

"No, I . . . I think I'm done, but you should go ahead and finish yours. You were enjoying it so much," Will says, looking over to me. He gives me a small smile, but it doesn't reach his eyes. He's trying to steer things back to the way they were, but something is . . . off.

I pull the table back over and sit down again. After all that excitement, I don't have any enthusiasm for finishing my dinner either, but I take a few more bites for Will's sake.

"This really was a great idea. We'll have to do it again soon."

"Yeah," Will answers, staring down at his plate.

"Hey," I say, reaching out to cup his cheek in my hand. His eyes cut to mine as if I've pulled him out of deep thought, widening as he realizes he wasn't paying me the slightest bit of attention.

"Sweetheart, you're somewhere else, and I think you still need some time to calm down. Choking like that can be pretty scary. Why don't I pack up and go and let you rest?"

"Um, okay. Yeah, I . . . I guess I should," Will answers, his eyes roaming the room.

Now he's really making me nervous. I don't think I've ever seen him this unsettled. I stroke his cheek again, pulling him back to me. "Hey. Take a deep breath. Everything's going to be fine."

"I'm sorry. I guess that really did scare me. I can't seem to shake it. I'm sure I'll be okay after I sleep on it."

This time when his eyes meet mine, I feel like he's really here, and it calms me a bit. I stand and clean up our plates, smiling as I think back over what a lovely dinner it was. Will watches me for a few minutes, but by the time I finish, his eyes are closed.

He doesn't stir as I pack up the last few items even though I accidently clang the wine glasses together, and I wonder if he's already asleep. I can't resist the urge, though, so I lean down and kiss his forehead. He breathes in sharply as my lips touch him, but he doesn't open his eyes. I'm puzzled because he's never pretended to be asleep before, but I chalk it up to the scary ending to our evening.

I head home, clean up the dishes, and spend a few hours watching TV with Sebastian, but I turn in early. I'm eager to see Will in the morning, to wipe away the strange feeling that something wasn't right when I left him last night.

CHAPTER 21

I arrive on the fourth floor at eight a.m. on the dot, hoping a quick visit with Will can calm the unease I've been feeling since yesterday.

Jenny looks up as I approach, smiling at me, but somehow, it's not a happy smile.

"Hi, Jenny, how are you this morning?" I ask, smiling back and trying not to be paranoid.

"Hey, Tori. I'm fine. But it feels like a long morning already, and I've only been here an hour," she replies, sighing.

"I'm sorry to hear that. I hope your day gets better. Have you checked on Will yet today?"

"Actually, I have. He's feverish this morning, and Dr. Evans is in with him now."

A spark of fear runs through me, but I try to quench it. Will is a terminally ill patient; of course his doctor is going to come to see him. It doesn't mean anything new is wrong. But that nagging feeling I have just won't go away, so I do what I know I shouldn't.

"Is he okay, Jenny?"

Jenny purses her lips as she looks at me. "Dr. Evans stops by to see Will around nine-thirty almost every day; he's just here a little earlier today."

I release the breath I was holding as my anxiety level drops a few notches. "Okay, well, I guess I'll see him at four, then. Can you tell him I came by?"

"Of course," Jenny says, squeezing my shoulder before she walks away.

I stare after her, puzzled and a little disappointed. I was sure she was going to ask me about my dinner with Will last night, and I was looking forward to telling her. She must be really distracted and busy this morning. Shrugging, I turn and head back to the elevators.

My day passes quickly, and before I know it, I'm walking down the fourth floor hall toward Will's room. Jenny is sitting in front of the computer at the nurses' station, looking at least as frazzled as she did this morning, so I stop to check on her. "Hey, Jenny. Did your day get any better?"

"Hey," Jenny says, smiling at me tiredly. "Not really. Will's asleep. He's still feverish, so he's been in and out a lot today."

The smile slides off my face. *Damn.* After the fantastic three days we had, it's a rough wake-up call for me that he's having a bad day. I'm sure it's even worse for him. "I promise I won't stay long, but he'll be mad at me if I don't at least wake him and say hello," I tell her as I turn to walk away.

"Tori," Jenny says as she puts a hand on my arm.

I freeze, my eyes widening as the hair on the back of my neck begins to stand on end. "What is it, Jenny? Did something happen?"

"Tori, you're my best friend, so I'm going to be as honest with you as I can be. Will needs some time today. He has some things he needs to think about, and he asked me if I could intercept his visitors."

"Intercept his visitors? As in, he doesn't want to see me?"

"Yes," she answers shortly.

"And you agreed with this?"

"No, I didn't agree he shouldn't see you today; I agreed that he needed some time to sort things out in his head. He's the one who decided he needed to do it alone, and I took pity on him and agreed to help him do things his way."

I sigh in frustration, trying to contain my anxiety and fear.

"But he's okay right now, isn't he? I mean—"

"Yes. Other than running a fever, he's okay right now," she answers although her words seem to be carefully chosen.

"And you can't tell me what he needs to think about?"

"No, hon, I can't. You'll have to ask him about it, and I hope you do. You'll have a chance tomorrow. I told him I'd give him one day, but if he doesn't want visitors after today, he's going to have to explain that to you himself."

"But I'm sure he wouldn't mind if you—"

"Yes, he would," she says almost angrily. "He reminded me this morning what the law says, so he's definitely going to know if I step over the line."

"He what?" I ask, taken aback.

"He reminded me that I couldn't tell you anything about his condition."

"Why on earth would he do that?"

The look on Jenny's face is pained—she wants so badly to tell me what's going on, but she's bound by law to protect Will's privacy. My hands start to shake as my mind explodes with the possibilities of what Will might need to think about. None of them are good. I jump as Jenny puts an arm around my shoulder.

"Hey, it'll be okay. I'm sure he'll talk to you tomorrow. He was feeling overwhelmed today on top of being feverish, and he wanted some alone time. Don't freak out. He'll still be here when you come tomorrow."

I nod numbly, my mind still racing. Something is very wrong; I just know it. And now I have to wait until tomorrow to find out what. The silence between Jenny and me is strained. I think I understand now why she wasn't very talkative this morning. So, I tell her goodbye and head home.

I make myself dinner, but I can't seem to think about anything but Will. He reminded Jenny what she can't tell me, by law? What the hell is that about? *Something happened, and he doesn't want me to know.* Between that and his not wanting to see me today, I'm nearly panicked. What could possibly have happened? But I'll have to find out eventually, right? Unless he doesn't want me to know until it's too late to do anything about whatever it is.

I pound on the couch in frustration. This is getting me nowhere. I just have to wait until tomorrow and get him to talk to me. Oh God, but what is he going through right now—feverish and shouldering the burden of whatever this is—alone? Tears of anger and helplessness sting my eyes, and suddenly, I need to know he's all right.

I pick up my cell phone and stare at it. Six-thirty. Will might still be awake. I'm dying to call him, but I know it's not the right thing to do. He asked for space today, and I need to give it to him. But a text can't hurt. Just a little text to let him know I'm thinking about him? I type a message before I can change my mind.

Hi, Will. I'm not gonna call you because I know you needed some alone time today, but I wanted to tell you I stopped by and that I'm thinking about you.

I read it through and hit send, hoping he's awake and might respond. I put my phone down, but it vibrates almost immediately, and I dive on it, turning it over to see the message.

Thanks, Tori. I'll see you tomorrow.

Warmth spreads through my chest as I smile—I'm happy to have heard something from him even if it wasn't much. I go to bed early for the second night in a row, thinking tomorrow can't come soon enough.

———

I stop by to see Will first thing, but Jenny tells me his fever didn't break until four in the morning, and I should let him sleep. On a rational level, I agree with her, but on an emotional one, I'm dying to see him so I can figure out what the hell is going on.

The day drags horrendously, but finally, I find myself standing outside Will's door. Jenny is nowhere to be seen, and I wonder if it's on purpose. She's in a terrible position between Will and me, so maybe it's best that she lay low until he tells me what's going on.

I open the door slowly, hoping to find Will drawing, but he's not. He's lying listlessly on his bed, staring at the opposite wall as if he's not really seeing anything. His hair looks the way it does when I wake him up in the morning—sticking up in every direction as if he's run his fingers through it more times than he should've. His eyes look tired, the smudges under them dark and the skin around them tight. I stare at him for a moment, steeling myself for whatever may come today, before I push the door open enough to make it squeak.

Will startles, turning his head so his gaze falls on me, his dark green eyes seeming to brighten. He smiles at me tiredly as I cross the room and take his hand. "Hey, Tori," he says softly.

"Hello, sweetheart. I've missed you."

He gives me a small smile, but it doesn't reach his eyes. They still look sad, and the stress lines around them are deep. He looks like he's carrying the weight of the world on his shoulders.

"I've missed you, too," he answers, squeezing my hand.

"Are you all right? What happened yesterday? I was so worried."

He tenses, frowning, and seems to force his words out. "I'm fine. I was feverish yesterday, and it hit me pretty hard after the amazing weekend we had. I just needed to clear my head."

His voice quavers as he says the words, and I can't suppress the shiver that runs down my spine. Whatever really happened is serious, so much so that he's barely holding it together. But he's not going to tell me—at least not now, anyway. I swallow back the sickly feeling of hurt that bubbles in my chest and force myself to smile.

I stroke my fingers over his knuckles soothingly. "I'm here . . . whenever you're ready to tell me."

He flinches at my words but otherwise doesn't acknowledge them. God, he looks so broken right now. I want to gather him into my arms and tell him it'll be okay, but I don't because he's trying so hard to hold himself together, and I don't want to make it harder for him.

He swallows thickly, but he keeps his composure, sighing and resting his head back against his pillow. "I'm not feeling very well today. Yesterday's fever wore me out, and my belly is really tender. Can you just . . . tell me about your day?"

A tear runs down my cheek, but I wipe it away quickly so he doesn't see. "Of course I can, sweetheart."

I tell him what I can about what I did today, and he seems to relax a little, just listening to the sound of my voice. His eyes remain closed, but he responds in all the right places, so I know he's paying attention. I also tell him that Mr. Matthews has been removed from suicide watch and is responding well to medication.

"Wow, that's great," Will says, opening his eyes and smiling at me. It's the first bit of enthusiasm I've seen from him.

"Thanks. I actually talked to him yesterday, and he asked me if I'd be willing to resume sessions with him. He made it a point to tell me what he did was in no way my fault, and he hoped I didn't blame myself."

"See? I told you it wasn't your fault, but I'm glad he confirmed it for you. I know you were helping him, but . . . sometimes, it just isn't enough."

"Thank you again for that, by the way," I tell him, squeezing his hand. "You really did help me put things into perspective on Friday."

"You've helped me through lots of bad days. I'm glad I was able to return the favor," he says, looking pleased with himself.

I look at the clock, and I'm surprised. I've managed to entertain him with my stories for almost two hours. "Wow, it's after six already! I wonder where Jenny is with your dinner."

Will suddenly looks uncomfortable. "I'm sure she'll be here soon," he says, but he's not meeting my eyes.

I tense. Something's going on here, and whatever it is, it's related to why he's so upset. "Well, why don't I go see about it for you?" I ask as I stand and head for the door.

"Tori," he calls, and I stop and turn back toward him. "Don't bother. She's . . . not going to bring me dinner."

"Well, why the hell not?" Although I demand to know, dread floods the pit of my stomach.

He meets my eyes, letting the sorrow he's fought back all day finally reach them. "I . . . the lymph nodes in my neck are more swollen than they were before. I'm having trouble swallowing, and I can't eat anything."

I swallow instinctively. "How long has this been going on?"

He stares down at his afghan, slowly tracing squares. "Since . . . Monday."

"Monday?" I gasp and clap a hand over my mouth. "Our dinner! On Monday night, when you choked—you couldn't swallow, could you?"

Will shakes his head slowly without raising his eyes.

"Dammit, I knew something wasn't right!" But I'm relieved. If this is all that's wrong, it's fixable. "But hopefully, this is only temporary. In the meantime, they should be able to give you a feeding tube until the swelling goes back down."

Will closes his eyes tightly. "I'm not going to let them."

"You have to let them," I say automatically, but the dread I felt before starts to ooze down my spine again.

"No, I don't. Since I have a DNR in place, if I can't eat for myself, I don't have to let them do anything medically to help me."

"But if you don't let them, you'll starve."

"No, I'll dehydrate first, after they remove my IV. It'll take less than a week, and after the first few days, it'll be peaceful."

The dread turns into full-blown panic. "No, Will! You can't do that. It's not time!"

"I'm ready, Tori. Goddammit, I'm ready, and I want this to be over with!" Will huffs out a frustrated sigh as he runs his fingers through his hair. "I'm dying! If it's not this infection, it'll be the next one, and I'm just going to get weaker and sicker. I can't do this anymore! And I can't watch you go through this with me. I can't do this to either of us!" He drops his face into his hand and curls his other arm over his belly as his breathing accelerates.

I freeze as I realize this is the crisis that's going to unravel everything. The frustration and anger in his voice is killing me. He's not ready. He's nowhere near ready, and despite what he says, I can't let him do this. I have to tell him. He doesn't have any more time to figure it out for himself, and I can't bear to let him die this way.

"You aren't ready, Will," I say softly. "You think you are, but you're not. Not really."

His eyes flash, all his anger now directed at me. "And what the hell makes you think that?"

"Because I've done this more times than I can count! People who are ready, *truly* ready, make peace with themselves, and they make peace with their family and friends. They let go of the wrongs of the past, and they realize they're not alone and that they *have to* and *should* depend on the people who love them—to be there for them until the end.

"I hear what you're saying, and I know how hard this is, but I can't let you end your life like this. Not when I know you can die in peace if you listen to me. Please, Will, just listen to me!"

I try to keep my voice even, but inside, I'm panicking. It's true he's not ready, but I'm also battling the fact that I'm not ready. The thought of him being gone within a few days—wasting away before my very eyes —it's unthinkable. I would do anything to talk him out of it, and I'm about to play the highest card I have left.

I take his hand between mine, and although his eyes narrow, he doesn't pull away. "Will, where is your family?"

Now he does pull his hand away and closes it into a fist over his chest, turning his face away from me as he scrunches his eyes closed. "No. We're not going to talk about this."

"You miss your mother. You drew her in your sketchbook, and you thought I was her when you were delirious. I know whatever is between you isn't resolved. Please, don't let things end this way."

Suddenly, he crumbles and a sob tears from his chest. He covers his eyes with his hand as he shakes with the force of his emotion, his sobs filling the air and rending my heart in two.

"Will you tell me?" I whisper. "It's not too late. We can still contact her if you want to. I'll help you. I *want* to help you."

"Tori, I can't. I can't do this. I made my choice and I . . . I'm at peace with it. I can't go back," he says shakily, trying so hard to believe the words he's saying.

"Sweetheart, if you were at peace with it, it wouldn't be tearing you apart like this. You *can* do this, and I'll help you. Please, let me help you."

He's quiet for a long time, his face buried in his hand as I stroke his hair. His hand drops to the blanket, and he tilts his head toward me. The sorrow in his eyes makes my breath catch. "I have no brothers or sisters. I haven't spoken to my parents in four years."

I stare at him, knowing I'm missing something, and then I gasp. My chest tightens as the realization rolls over me. "They don't know you're sick . . ."

"No."

"Will, what happened?"

He scowls as he looks at the floor beside me, anger suddenly devouring his grief.

"I wasn't the son my father wanted. He was a college football player, and more than anything, he wanted his son to follow in his footsteps. I was never interested in sports—I was an artist from the day I could hold a crayon—and it infuriated him. He was embarrassed by me. Nothing I did was ever good enough, and when I decided to go to art school, he said he wouldn't help me.

"So I worked two jobs and put myself through school, but I still visited them through college and even afterward when I was starting to sell my work. It all blew up when I was twenty-five. I had gotten into pot and Ecstasy to boost my creativity when I was painting, and I found it made visits with my parents easier to handle too. I made a mistake and overdosed while I was visiting them, so they found out about my drug use.

"My *father*"—Will spits out the word as if it's an epithet—"told me I was nothing, and I disgusted him, and he never wanted to see me again. The last time I saw my parents was when I was still in the hospital after the overdose."

Holy shit! I'd guessed he'd had some sort of a falling out with his parents, but I never suspected it was the kind that's meant to last a lifetime. I bristle at the thought of someone talking to Will that way.

"Then what happened?"

He takes as deep a breath as he can and continues, staring down at his afghan and tracing squares forcefully. "I continued using for a while, but eventually I realized I was addicted and that the drugs were doing more harm than good. So I checked into rehab and got myself clean."

"Did you ever try to contact them?"

"No," he says, his voice quavering. "I know that what happened wasn't about the drugs; it was about who I am, and that's never going to change. I'll never be good enough for him even if my work sold for millions."

"Did you think about calling them after you got sick?"

"Yes, but I decided against it. I wasn't good enough then, and he didn't try to help me when I was addicted, so why should the fact that I'm dying make any difference to him?"

"Will," I say gently, "I don't know if you realize it, but throughout everything you've told me, you've only referred to your dad. '*He* was embarrassed by me.' '*He* wouldn't help me.' What about your mother?"

He runs a hand through his hair. "My mother . . . couldn't oppose my father. No one could. I can't really blame her for that. I know she loves me, and she might even be proud of my work if she saw it. I miss her," he whispers as a tear rolls down his cheek.

"Would you like to see her again?"

He closes his eyes wearily and nods, his lips forming a thin line.

"Why don't you call her, then? What do you have to lose? It sounds like from what you've told me that she does care about you, and I'm betting she would want to know what's happening to you. If you love her, give her the chance to make a different choice . . . before it's too late."

My heart races as I say the words, but now's not the time to think about myself. I look over at him, and his eyes are open, but he's looking down and away. Maybe he didn't hear the tremor in my voice.

"I'll think about it."

"Well, if you're going to think about it, then you need to let the doctor give you a feeding tube in the meantime. Otherwise, you're going to die."

"Tori, I'm . . . scared," he whispers. "I don't want to lose who I am piece by piece. I've lost so much already."

I bite my lip hard to keep the tears at bay. "Maybe the feeding tube won't be permanent, but allowing yourself to starve? That's permanent, and despite what you've heard, I doubt it's pleasant either. You're just . . . You're not ready. Trust me on this. Please."

Will huffs out a sigh. "All right. I'll allow the feeding tube. But I'm not happy about it."

After the stunt he just tried to pull, I don't quite trust him to follow through. "Well, if you haven't eaten anything since yesterday, I'm sure you must be hungry. Why don't I go tell Jenny now so she can get you taken care of."

He gives me an exasperated look, but he doesn't argue, so I turn on my heel and set off to find her. As I leave the room, I breathe a sigh of relief. I gambled and won . . . for now. With any luck, he's going to contact his mother and at least make peace with her, but what he tried to pull today proves I've made no progress in convincing him to fight for whatever time he has left. I'm frustrated, and some part of me hidden in a deep, dark corner is also . . . hurt. Despite everything that's happened over the last few days, he's ready to leave me so easily.

Jenny is at the nurses' station, typing away at the computer. She looks up as I approach.

"I convinced Will to let you give him a feeding tube."

She claps a hand over her heart. "Oh, thank *God*! I tried to talk to him about it, but he stonewalled me. And I wanted to tell you *so* badly! I convinced him not to have his IV removed until he saw you, hoping you'd be able to talk him out of it. How did you do it?"

"I played dirty. But I'm running out of tricks, so I hope nothing else comes up anytime soon. He's still unwilling to fight for the time he has left, and he's not ready to die. He still needs to come to terms with his fear, and there are things he needs to do."

"Well, one step at a time, right? At least now he's bought himself some more time," Jenny says. "Let me gather what I need, and I'll be down in a few minutes."

"Okay."

When I get back to Will's room, his eyes are closed, but I know he's still awake.

"Jenny will be here in a few minutes to insert the tube for you. I think it might be best if I go since I know you're not thrilled with this idea."

He opens one eye then closes it with a sigh.

"You're making the right choice, sweetheart. I know it doesn't feel that way now, but it will eventually; I promise you. Can I come back tomorrow?" I ask, hoping the return to our routine will help to ground him.

"Could I stop you?" he shoots back, not even bothering to open his eyes.

"Of—of course you could. I would never take away your choice in anything. I just want you to be at peace with the choices you make," I answer, trying to hide my hurt over his question and my fear that I've overstepped my bounds.

His eyes snap open, and although I can still see his pain, there's tenderness in his gaze too. "I'm sorry. Of course I want you to come back. I'm just ... tired."

I have a feeling he's referring to more than just this moment's exhaustion, but he's had enough for now.

"I'll see you in the morning, sweetheart," I tell him as I lean in to kiss him, thanking God for the gift of a little more time. His lips brush against mine, and although he doesn't open his eyes, I see the ghost of a smile as I pull away. He's still with me, and I pray that the day he isn't never comes.

Chapter 22

I stop by to see Will in the morning, but like yesterday, Dr. Evans is with him when I arrive, so I tell Jenny to let him know I'll see him at four.

In the afternoon when I walk through the door, Will is lying with his head turned toward the right, effectively hiding the tube in his nose as much as possible. He looks haggard today, even more so than yesterday. For the first time ever, he seems small and frail to me as he lies in his bed. He looks like a patient with a terminal illness.

I purse my lips and walk over to his right side, which I never do. The tube emerges from his right nostril and is taped along his cheek; it then goes over his ear and is clipped to his nightshirt.

I stand there until he casts a quick glance up at me, and then I lift his chin, forcing him to look at me. Sorrow and despair pool in his gaze, his eyes a watery green from unshed tears. "Hey, there's no shame in this. You're not giving up, and that's the important thing. You're doing what you need to do to stay alive."

He closes his eyes. "Then why do I feel ashamed . . . and embarrassed? I'm dying by inches, conceding a piece of myself at a time, which is exactly what I didn't want to do."

"Don't think of it that way. Please. And don't concede. You don't have to give this disease anything easily."

"Give?" Will says, his tone incredulous and bitter. "It's not about giving, Tori. It's about taking. This disease is taking whether I want to give or not, and very soon, it's going to kill me. I thought I understood that. I thought I was ready for it. I thought I could accept what was happening to me.

"Fuck!" Will swears, pounding the bed with his fist and wincing as pain ripples through him. "I thought I had everything under control, but . . . I'm scared, Tori. Jesus, I'm fucking terrified. This is really going to happen, and I don't have any control.

"I lied to myself. I convinced myself that by having the DNR, I'd have control over how my life ends, but it's a lie. The cancer has all the control here, and I'm an idiot for thinking any differently!" His hand is gripping his hair tightly, his eyes glazed with panic and fear.

My heart clenches in my chest. All the walls he's constructed are coming down at once, and I need to catch him lest he fall too far.

I reach up and remove his fingers from his hair, taking his hand between mine. "No, you're not an idiot. You're doing the best you can to deal with the hardest thing anyone ever has to deal with. And in a way, the DNR does give you control. You can't stop the cancer from killing you, but you can choose to end your life before you lose too much of yourself. I understand that now. And you can still have that power, that control. You just need to do a few things before you're ready to take that step.

"I know you're scared. It's normal to be scared; I would be too. Hell, I'm scared *for* you. But you're not alone. You've got Jason now, and I'm sure your mother will come if you call her, and I'm here too. I'm going to be here every day, and I'm going to help you get through this."

"So this is normal?"

"Yes, sweetheart, it is. Everyone I've ever known has hit the point where they have to confront their fear. But you can do this; I know you can."

Will bows his head, a sob escaping him as a tear rolls down his cheek. I reach over and put my arms around him, pulling his head onto my shoulder. He grunts, but he holds tightly to me, his cheek pressed into my shoulder.

"I don't know how to deal with this. I feel like I'm falling apart, and there's nothing left to hold on to," he whispers brokenly.

"Hold on to me, sweetheart." I choke out the words as my own tears begin to fall. "I'm right here, and I'll take care of you."

We sit that way for a long time, lost in our separate thoughts, until I realize Will's breathing is now soft and even. He's asleep on my shoulder. The last two days have been hell for him, and he probably hasn't gotten much rest, so I reach up and support his head as I lower him slowly to the mattress. He grimaces, but he doesn't wake, and as I stare at his angelic face, my emotions threaten to crush me.

In such a short time, things have gone from bad to worse, and I hope Will is as strong as he's always appeared—strong enough to fight through the fear and come out on the other side. I clasp his hand and say a silent prayer this won't be too bad for him—overcoming their fear has always been the hardest part for all the patients I've ever worked with.

It's bad. When I arrive the next morning, Jenny tells me Will didn't sleep most of the night, so I resist the urge to peek my head in, afraid I'll disturb him. My day passes in a haze of distraction, all my thoughts on Will and how *his* day is going.

At four o'clock, I'm in my usual spot, standing in his doorway. His eyes are closed, but I can't tell if he's sleeping or not. Even if he is, I still want to see him today, so I creep quietly to my chair, planning to sit beside him for a while even if he's not awake.

As soon as I sit down, he opens his eyes, and I feel the familiar twinge in my stomach that flash of bright green always brings. But today, the green is dull and haunted. He doesn't smile—he just stares at me for a moment before mumbling, "Hey, Tori."

"Hello, Will," I say, smiling and taking his hand.

He looks down, unable to meet my eyes. "I'm not in any shape for company today."

I rub my fingers over his knuckles tenderly. "You don't have to entertain me. I know how upset you are right now and that you have a lot to think about. Can I just sit here and keep you company? You don't have to talk. I can tell you about my day, or we can sit here quietly, but I want to be with you. Is that all right?"

A ghost of a smile crosses his face, and I'm relieved beyond words that he's not going to push me away. That was my biggest worry—that his fear would drive him to keep everyone away.

"Yeah. Thanks, Tori," he answers, and the sadness in his voice makes my heart ache.

We sit quietly, and Will's so lost in himself that he doesn't speak for the entire two hours I'm there. Most of the time his eyes are closed, and when they're open, he's staring off into space. I still hold his hand, though, running my fingers soothingly over his knuckles when he looks distressed, channeling support through my fingers.

At six o'clock, I give his hand a gentle squeeze. "I should go, but I'll be back tomorrow, okay?"

He nods absently, unable to look at me, and I just can't take the distance. I move to the edge of his bed and lean over, pressing my lips softly against his.

His response is immediate; his lips move hungrily against my own, almost desperate, and I whimper as a flame kindles in my chest. I try to deepen the kiss, but my nose brushes against the tube coming from his, and he pulls back as if he's been burned, his eyes snapping open.

The sorrow and horror in his eyes steals my breath, and a strangled sob lodges in my throat.

Will bites his bottom lip hard, and his face contorts into a pained grimace as he squeezes his eyes shut again. "Tori, I can't . . . not like this. It's too much, and I can't . . ." He trails off and drops his chin, folding in on himself and turning his head away from me.

I blink to let the tears fall so I can see him clearly, and run my fingers through his hair.

He scrunches up his face even more, but I continue until he relaxes a bit.

"It's all right, Will. I understand. I'm here for you, whatever you need, and I'm not going anywhere," I whisper as I lean down and kiss his cheek. "I'll see you tomorrow."

I leave quietly, hoping he's not going to break down the moment I'm out of earshot, but I really think he will. I curse myself for upsetting him even more, but I had to know if he'd let me give him comfort that way. I guess I should have known the answer.

And that's the way our days go for the entire week. When I arrive on Saturday, Will's feverish, and it's obvious he's had morphine, but if anything, it's made his mood even worse. He has completely shut down. I try to talk to him, tell him about my day, but he interrupts me and asks if I can just hold his hand. My heart feels like it's shattered in my chest, but I do as he asks.

Sunday is much the same, and I wonder about the morphine. I tell Jenny about his previous addiction, and she cuts him off when he asks for it on Monday, telling him he can't escape from reality that way, and he can only have it when he truly needs it. He's pissed, but he's so withdrawn that he doesn't even give me hell for ratting him out although I'm sure he knows I'm to blame.

By Monday, I can't deny Will has fallen into a deep depression. Now that he can't hide from his reality through morphine, he's decided sleep is the best way to escape. He drifts in and out of consciousness when I visit, not caring about the day or time. And everything seems harder for him. I didn't realize how much effort he was putting into being positive and ignoring his condition until he stopped completely. He's scratching more often, not caring if he breaks his skin, and he always looks exhausted. Pain is his constant companion. He lies with his arm perpetually curled over his belly, grunting at the slightest motion, sometimes even when he's perfectly still.

Jason calls me on Monday, frightened by the change in Will, so I explain to him what happened with the feeding tube the week before. Apparently, Will hasn't been too forthcoming with him. I reassure Jason—and myself—that Will *will* snap out of it, and I feel better knowing there are two of us in Will's corner for the long haul.

I sit with Will every day, watching and hoping he has the strength to come to terms with his fears and to realize he needs to make peace with his mother and to make the most of the time he has left. I miss him terribly. I hadn't realized how much I was depending on that brilliant smile, those shy glances and kind words. It's as if the beauty of his soul has already been extinguished even though he's still sitting right in front of me, and the thought of his living like this is actually worse than the thought of his dying.

I comfort him when he'll let me, holding his hand or stroking my fingers through his hair. I don't try to kiss him again. It's too much for him now, but I hope that when he snaps out of this, he'll realize he wants to kiss me again and as much as possible while there's still time, but I don't know. All I can do is wait and hope.

I wake up early on Friday morning after a poor night's sleep. I haven't been sleeping well all week, my worry for Will overwhelming pretty much everything, including my dreams. It's been a week since we talked about him confronting his fear, and every day, I've watched him slip deeper into depression. I've been there. I've supported him, and I've watched for any sign that he's coming to terms with what's going on in his head, but I've seen none.

This has gone on long enough.

He's dying, but he's not dead yet, and he can't stop time, so his only alternative is to move forward. What he's been doing for the past week is wallowing, and while I completely understand it, I can't let it continue.

I head to the fourth floor first, but I have no plans to wake him. He's been asleep every morning this week when I've come by, and I've only looked in on him briefly to make sure he was okay. He was feverish on Saturday and Sunday and then again on Wednesday, but other than that, his condition has remained the same. Thank God nothing new has happened this week—I don't think he could have handled anything more in his current state of mind.

I open his door enough to peer around it and find him sleeping. His face is turned toward me, which is a sight I haven't seen much of this past week. He's still self-conscious and upset about the feeding tube, so he hides it as much as possible by keeping his head turned to his right. That and he can't seem to look at me for very long without getting really upset. I understand though. What happened between us last week, while wonderful, has made everything harder for both of us and particularly for him.

I gaze at him for a few moments, drinking in the beauty of his peaceful face: long eyelashes resting on the dark smudges under his eyes and soft auburn hair trailing down across his forehead. He's just as beautiful as he ever was. I sigh and close the door softly, eager for the afternoon so I can see him awake and talk to him.

By the time it's four o'clock though, my eagerness has turned to uncertainty. What if he won't listen to me? What if my words have no effect on him, and he slides deeper into depression? What if he honestly doesn't care anymore, and there's nothing I can say to change that?

My fears threaten to overwhelm me as I head for his room, but I have to do this—for him and for us.

Will is staring at the far wall as I walk in. I make the door squeak on purpose, trying to draw his attention, but he doesn't acknowledge me.

He closes his eyes as I cross the room, already preparing to hide from me, but I'm undaunted. I take his hand between both of mine, thanking God he's not too warm today.

"Hello, Will. How are you?" I ask, trying to engage him in conversation. I've said almost nothing to him all week, respecting his wishes that I just be here, but today is most definitely going to be different.

Will ducks his chin, but he doesn't answer, so I reach out and caress his cheek a few times before grasping his chin and turning his face toward me.

He doesn't look up.

"I want to talk to you today. You don't have to talk back, but I want . . . I *need* you to listen."

He glances up at me, the pain and sorrow in his eyes piercing my soul. His face crumples as he squeezes his eyes shut, but he says nothing.

"We need to talk about what's been going on this last week."

Will flinches, pulling his chin away from me, and I see anger in his eyes. But I'll take it because it's the first active emotion I've seen from him in days.

"No," he says calmly but with conviction. "There's nothing to talk about."

"Yes, there is. I've sat here for a week and supported and comforted you, giving you time to work through your feelings about what's happening to you. I've watched and hoped you would come to terms with it, that you would move forward on your own, but you're not.

"Will, you're strong—stronger than anyone I've ever known. For almost two months now, I've watched you deal with the most difficult situation I've ever seen. And until you let me in, I watched you deal with it all on your own.

"I don't agree with the decision you made, but it took great strength to make it. And it took great strength to change that decision, to let Jason back into your life, and to let me get to know you.

"It also took great strength to try to wrest control of your situation away from the cancer by setting up your DNR so you could choose your own death instead of letting the cancer choose.

"I know you're scared. I know needing the feeding tube shocked you and made you realize you're really going to die and that you're not ready. But, Will, no one is ever truly ready. The most you can do is accept what's going to happen and the fear that comes with it, and move forward.

"But I've watched and waited, and you're not moving forward, and by doing that, you're letting the cancer win."

Will looks up at me, a mix of sorrow and confusion in his eyes.

"You've always said you don't want to let the cancer win all the battles, that you want to win the final battle by taking control. But this past week? You've been letting the cancer win the biggest battle of them all —the battle for your soul. This week, you've let it own you, and to me, that's a much bigger victory than just taking your life. If you allow it to break your spirit, then the cancer has won long before it actually kills you."

Will furrows his brow, and a spark of hope kindles in my chest.

"You can't let it do this to you. You can't just give up and sit here, waiting to die. You may not be able to stop it from killing you, but you certainly can stop it from killing you before it truly *is* time. You have control. You have control over what you do right now and every day until you have no more. I know I've said this to you before, but I don't think you were ready to listen then. I hope you're ready now.

"Will, this is all the time you have. Please, *please* don't waste it. Show the cancer that it can't break you, and do the things you want to do until you can't anymore. Call your mother and make peace with her. Spend time with Jason and me. Talk, laugh, *live*. Live every day as if it were your last because you know that day is coming. But every day you go to sleep happy is another day the cancer didn't win."

Will bites his lip and closes his eyes, and the spark in my chest ignites into a flame. It's not much of a response, but it could mean he's turning over my words in his mind, and they're working on him. I need to leave and let them do their job—I've done all I can; he has to do the rest.

"I'm going to go now because I think you need some time to think about what I've said. Please, *please* think about it, for me. I can't bear to see this break you, not when I know you have the strength to do so much more.

"I'll see you tomorrow," I tell him, leaning in to kiss his forehead softly.

He opens his eyes as I pull away, and I squeeze his hand before releasing it. He doesn't say anything, but he doesn't have to. He's thinking about what I said, and that's enough—for now. I walk out of his room feeling better than I have since our date. Because for the first day in all that time, I truly have hope.

Chapter 23

I sleep better on Friday night, encouraged by my last few minutes in Will's room. He really looked as if he was listening to me, and I hope and pray I'm right. I need him back as much as he needs to come back. This week without him has changed things somehow. They say you don't know what you've got until it's gone, and this week, the void in my soul where Will used to be has been a physical pain, tearing at my chest. The only thing that kept me from breaking down completely was knowing he could still come back, that if he could just get past his fear, he could come back to me.

I spend the morning wandering around my apartment, unable to focus on anything and watching the clock. I make myself a sandwich around noon, but I barely touch it, my anxiety level too high to allow me to eat.

By one-thirty, I can't take it anymore, and I head for the hospital. I honestly don't know what I'll do if my words didn't get through to him, and Will is the same as he's been all week.

Standing outside his door, I take a deep breath, trying to keep my hands from shaking. I want to see him smile again so badly I can taste it, and I want to see the determination return to his eyes more than I've ever wanted anything.

Bright green eyes meet mine the minute the door is open enough for me to see him, as if he's been waiting for me. He doesn't smile, but the engagement is unmistakable.

My shoulders sag with relief although I know we're not out of the woods yet. I cross the room and take his hand, smiling as convincingly as I can. His hand is warmer than it should be, but he seems quite focused despite the fever.

"Hello, Will," I say, my heart in my throat.

He squeezes my hand. "Hi, Tori."

The sound of him saying my name sends a familiar flutter through my chest, and I hold my breath, waiting, as he stares at me.

"I did what you asked. Since you left yesterday, I've done nothing but think about what you said."

He takes a deep breath. "You're absolutely right. All week I've been letting my fear and sadness control me, and that's letting the cancer win."

He glances away from me, and I notice the tendons in his neck moving. I realize he's trying to swallow, but it looks very difficult and painful. "Not being able to eat . . . was like I'd crossed some invisible line and lost too much of myself, and it really hit me that I'm . . . going to die. I panicked and fell apart.

"And you were right," he says, glancing up at me once more. "I did try to drown my sorrows in morphine. I'm glad you told Jenny about my past because the last thing I need is to become dependent again.

"I'm so sorry, Tori." He continues, reaching his hand up to cup my cheek. "I know I put you through a lot of pain this week, but I just couldn't see my way out of my own head. Your words yesterday snapped me out of it and made me see the truth.

"I'm still afraid. But I realize now that if I let that fear control me, the cancer has already won, and I decided a long time ago, I wasn't going to let that happen. Thank you for caring enough about me to remind me of that. It took courage to do what you did yesterday, knowing I might not respond at all or that I might push you away. I'm *so* sorry for what I did to you this week."

"Oh, Will," I say as tears roll down my cheeks. I need to be close to him, so I sit on the edge of the bed and put my arms around him, laying my head on his shoulder.

He winces despite my care, but he pulls me closer, holding me as my relief breaks me down. He buries his face in my hair as I cry, his hands gripping my arms tightly. "Can you forgive me? I don't feel like I deserve it, but I need you, Tori—more than I've ever needed anyone."

The words are out of my mouth before I even consciously think them. "I need you, too, Will."

He pushes me back so he can see my face. He looks happy but a bit surprised by my admission—almost as if he doesn't believe me.

"I do, sweetheart. I've missed you so much this week. You were here, but you weren't, and it was like the sun didn't shine."

I think I'm still in shock. Will needs me. He *needs* me. In all the time I've known him, he's never admitted he needed anything, and the first thing he admits he needs is me.

All this time, I've suspected he cared about me but was distancing himself to keep me from getting hurt. Even when we kissed two weeks ago, it didn't feel as if he'd let go of his self-sacrifice. It was more like he was going against his better judgment and couldn't help himself. But this? This is different. Admitting he needs me is doing something for himself, giving his own needs priority. Oh God, he's finally beginning to understand.

I run my fingers into his hair, and he leans into the touch, enjoying it for a moment before he squeezes the backs of my arms, pulling me closer so he can bring his lips to mine. The kiss is chaste, but after so long, it feels as good as any of the more passionate kisses we've shared, and I linger against his too-warm lips. I know he's probably not feeling up to more than this, so I reach up to cup his cheeks in my hands, lost in his brilliant green eyes.

He smiles at me, reflecting my own happiness, but it fades as he begins to speak.

"There's something else I want to do today if you're willing to help me."

"Of course, Will. Anything."

"I want to call my mother," he says, his voice quavering as he leans his head back and closes his eyes.

"Of course I'll help you, but is today really the best day to do it? I know you're not feeling very well—"

"Please?" he asks, opening his fever-bright eyes to plead with me. "It took me all week to get up the courage to do this; I'm afraid if I put it off, I might talk myself out of it again. I'm all right. I can focus enough to ... explain things. Will you stay with me?"

"Yes, of course I will," I tell him, taking his hand. "I understand why you want to do it today, and I'm proud of you. I know how hard this is, but I think you're making the right choice."

Will smiles, but there's trepidation in his eyes. This is bigger than letting Jason back into his life, bigger than admitting he needs me. This is changing a life decision that stood for four long years on a foundation of anger and hurt. This is breaking his mother's heart even more than his leaving did, but I'm more concerned about how he's going to handle her reaction.

"Do you have a way to contact her?"

"I hope so. I transferred her number over every time I got a new phone in case I ever needed it."

I walk around his bed and retrieve his phone from his bedside table. He looks at it briefly then drops his hand to the blanket, sighing.

Will sits for a few moments, eyes closed, gathering his resolve to make what is undoubtedly the hardest phone call of his life. I massage his hand, trying to channel strength to him through my fingers or at least the knowledge that I'm here for him.

Suddenly, he lifts the phone and scrolls for the number, hitting call and bringing the phone to his ear before he can change his mind.

Will holds the phone close to him, but since I'm sitting near enough to hold his hand, I can still hear every word.

"Hello?"

"Hi . . . Mom."

"Oh my God! Will? Is it really you?"

"Yeah, it's me. It's so . . . good . . . to hear your voice," he says, swallowing audibly and closing his eyes.

"Oh, honey, it's so good to hear yours too! I'm so glad you called! Where are you?"

"I'm still in Seattle, Mom. Is it okay I called?"

"Yes, of course! Will, is something wrong? You sound . . . different."

"Um . . ."

He bites his lip, holding back tears, and I rub my fingers over his.

"I have something to tell you, Mom. You might want to sit down."

Even I can hear the sharp intake of breath on the other end of the line.

"What is it, Will?"

"I'm sick, Mom. I have cancer."

His mother gives a choking sob, and Will squeezes his eyes shut tightly.

"Oh, honey, were you just diagnosed? What kind of cancer? Is it treatable?"

Will's breath is starting to come in pants, and he winces, freeing his hand from mine so he can curl his arm over his belly.

"No. I was diagnosed . . . two years ago."

"Two *years*? Then why . . . Oh! Please . . . oh, please don't tell me you're calling to . . . to—"

"I have non-Hodgkin's lymphoma, Mom. It's terminal."

"No . . . oh, no! My boy . . . my baby! Oh God, why? You're so young, and you have so much to live for! Oh, honey, why didn't you call me sooner?"

That's when Will loses it. The phone drops from his hand, and he curls in on himself, his body shaking with the force of his grief.

I pick his phone up and put it to my ear.

"Will? Will? Honey, are you okay?"

"Hello, Mrs. Everson. My name is Tori, and I'm . . . a friend of Will's. He can't talk anymore right now; he's a little upset. I think he's had all he can handle for today."

"I'm sorry! I . . . oh God, is he okay? I mean, I know he's not okay . . . Can I come and see him? I would come right now!"

"I think you'll need to talk to him about that, Mrs. Everson."

"Elizabeth, please. Are you . . . Is someone taking care of him?"

I don't even hesitate. "Yes, Elizabeth, I am. I'm sure he'll call you again soon. Right now he needs to rest."

"Okay. Please, can you tell him I love him, and I want to see him?"

"Of course."

"Thank you so much, Tori."

"You're welcome. I'm sure Will will be in touch."

I disconnect the call and turn to look at Will, still lost in his grief and wincing as sobs he can't control wreak havoc on his broken body. Crawling onto the bed as gently as I can, I put my arms around him. He hisses as I make contact with the swollen lymph nodes under his arms, but his hands cling to me. I pull his head down to my shoulder and hold him until his tears abate.

He's exhausted, and he falls asleep on my shoulder without a word. I sit there for a long time and hold him, thinking hard about what he did today and how all of it is such an important step toward his being ready to leave this world, and my own tears fall. I should be happy he did it, but the fact that now he's truly preparing himself to let go just tears my heart out. I don't want him to die. Somewhere in the process, I've gone past not wanting him to die alone and moved on to not wanting him to die at all. Emotion overwhelms me—stirring in my chest deeply and powerfully as I hold him there, spent from his grief.

As I look down on that unruly mop of copper hair, I know in my heart what I feel for him is more than need—it's love. It surges through me as if I've been struck by lightning, and I struggle not to shake with the force of it so I don't wake the angel in my arms. I love him. I love him, and I want to spend whatever life he has left loving him, no matter how much it hurts me in the end.

In a few short weeks, the man in my arms has wrapped himself around my heart, and suddenly, the weight of what might have been threatens to crush me. What if he weren't dying? What if I'd met him under different circumstances? What if he feels the same way about me? I've thought about this before, but now that I know I'm in love with him, the loss of what could have been cuts deeply.

I squeeze my eyes closed and try to block the possibilities from my mind; they're cruel thoughts that taunt and sting with their false promises. Will is going to die; all he has left is to decide how to spend the time that remains.

I hope he'll spend it with me. I hope admitting he needs me means he's going to let me stay with him to the end, no matter what happens, and that he'll allow himself to depend on me. I want to spend as much time with him as I can and do anything he'll let me until there's nothing left to do. His passing will surely destroy me, but I can't think about the consequences. Sometimes, the importance of the act outweighs the cost, and there's nothing in the world that's more important for me to do than this.

It's only late afternoon, but Will is still feverish, and I need to let him rest. It's been an incredibly intense day for both of us but even more so for him. I try to disentangle myself as gently as I can, but the sharp intake of breath and pained grunt let me know I've woken him.

His eyes meet mine, still red and swollen from the ordeal with his mother.

I caress his cheek with my fingers. "Go back to sleep, sweetheart. I'm going home now, but I'll come back tomorrow."

His eyes flutter closed as I pull the blanket up to his chest, and I lean over and plant a soft kiss on his forehead. I feel as if I should stay in case he wakes up and he's upset, but if I do, he'll probably stay awake when he really shouldn't. Pulling a post-it out of my purse, I scribble a note to him, telling him he can call or text me if he wants to talk. Then I drag myself away, my head swirling with the events of the day.

CHAPTER 24

I wake up on Sunday morning, and my first thought is to go to Will. Usually, I wouldn't go until later, but after everything that happened yesterday, it breaks my heart to think he'll wake up alone in that room, thinking about how upset his mother was along with all the other worries that were plaguing him.

And I need to see him. I *am* in love with him, and admitting that to myself has opened the floodgates that were holding back all my feelings—I want to spend every second I can with him.

My mind is made up before my feet hit the floor, and I grab a quick shower and some cereal, intent on being at his room by nine a.m.

I arrive at about ten after nine and slip into his room quietly. He's still sleeping, but he's restless and drenched in sweat.

Hoping to make him more comfortable, I pull off his afghan and fold down his blanket so it sits at his waist. With only the sheet covering it, I can see that his belly is distended even more than it was last week. It won't be long before he's having trouble breathing, and we hit another crisis. Will just seems to go from one crisis to another; it has to be wearing on him as much as it's wearing on me.

But I'm not dying.

That thought shakes me out of my self-pity and brings my focus back to Will. I'm going to be here for him today and not have another thought about myself. I take out my Kindle and settle in to read, hoping he'll be happy he's not going to wake up alone.

It's almost ten when I hear a grunt from the bed as Will shifts, and green eyes that are still fever-bright meet mine. He's confused, and for a moment, I wonder how high his fever is until his lips part in a smile.

"Hey, Tori. Isn't it a little early for you for a Sunday?"

"Yes, it is, but after everything that happened yesterday, I didn't want you to wake up alone," I tell him, reaching over and finally clasping the hand I've been yearning to hold for the last hour.

His eyes warm and soften, and his smile is brilliant, happiness radiating off him. "Thank you. You're too good to me."

"Nah," I say, blushing. *Will, life has been so unfair to you; there's no way anyone could be too good to you.* "How are you?"

Will takes a deep breath and sighs, letting his eyes fall closed. "Still feverish and a little out of it. Dammit, I hoped I'd be better today."

"Me too." I place my hand on his forehead to gauge his temperature, and my guess is 101 or 102, definitely higher than when I was here yesterday. My fingers find their way into his hair, and he leans into my hand.

"I'm sorry about yesterday," he says, his eyes still closed. "I didn't think it would upset me that much—"

"I did," I say, cutting him off before he can finish making his excuses. I slide my hand down to stroke his cheek, and he opens his eyes slowly. "Sweetheart, you reversed a big decision in your life yesterday, and I'm so proud of you. You have so much on your shoulders right now, and you handled it the best you could. It took a lot of courage to call her when you didn't know how she'd respond. You reached out, and I think you should be proud of what you did."

Will's lips curl in a gentle smile. "Thanks. You always manage to make me see things just a little differently, more clearly, maybe."

"That's what I'm here for," I tell him, squeezing his hand as I bask in the compliment.

Will looks down at his afghan, his fingers tracing the weave in his usual nervous tell. "Did you actually talk to my mom yesterday after I, um, lost it?"

"Yes, I did. I told her you were upset, and you needed to rest, but you'd call her again soon. She—"

"Did she say anything?"

I smile at him patiently. "Yes, she asked if someone was taking care of you, and I told her I was." Will smiles although he's still staring down at his afghan as his fingers continue to trace. "And she also told me to tell you she loves you, and she wants to come see you."

Will lifts his hand abruptly from the afghan, and his eyes snap to mine, the dull haze of fever cleared for a moment by confusion and panic.

"Sh-she . . . said she loved me? An-and she wants to come here?" Will gapes at me in shock as his breathing starts to accelerate.

"Yes, she did."

He lifts his hand to rub his forehead, wincing from the motion. The only sound in the room is his harsh breathing.

I give him a moment to collect himself, but he doesn't seem to be calming, so I reach up and capture the hand on his forehead between mine. "Hey, I thought this was what you wanted—to make peace with your mom."

Will's eyes remain closed as he swallows painfully. "Yes, I did, but I didn't expect . . . I didn't really think she'd want to talk to me, let alone see me! I figured I'd try, and she'd refuse to talk to me, or else I'd tell her, and then she'd hang up. I didn't expect she'd want to come to Seattle!"

He's almost hyperventilating now, and he grimaces as he uses the hand I'm not holding to clutch at his belly.

I reach one hand up to stroke his hair while I rub over the backs of his fingers with the other one. "Okay, just take a deep breath and calm down. She's only going to come if you tell her it's okay. You don't have to see her if you don't want to."

Will leans his head back, and it takes him a few painful minutes to slow his breathing. Finally, his weary green eyes meet mine.

"I'm sorry. This is harder than I thought it would be. I was so angry at her for so long; it's like even though I want to see her, I feel like it's conceding somehow to give in and let her come."

I stiffen at his words because I know this emotion well. Pride. I know much more than I would like to about letting pride stand in the way of doing things that should be done, and there's no way I'm going to let Will make that mistake.

"Will, I understand how you feel. A part of you still wants to be angry with her, and I'm not saying you shouldn't be because what she did was awful, but you can't let that stand in the way of trying to make peace with her. Just from what she said to you, I suspect she knows she made a horrible mistake four years ago. Give her the chance to try to correct that mistake and to make it up to you if she can."

Will sighs heavily. "You're probably right. But there's just so much . . . I don't know if I can handle this too."

I draw in a sharp breath. Will is finally reaching his limit, and his near-perfect control is beginning to slip. I'm starting to understand what's going on and what led him to admit he needs me.

"Sweetheart, you *can* handle this. And I'll help you through it if you let me. You're not alone. I'm staying right here," I tell him, lifting his hand to my lips so I can place a soft kiss there.

As my lips meet his fevered skin, I'm about to close my eyes, but a flash of green makes me pause. Will is staring at me, and his eyes hold such a mix of emotion that I can't even begin to sort it out. All I know is it's intense, and there's some kind of conflict raging inside him. I frown, but suddenly, the only thing I see in his eyes is need. Need for me to be closer. Need for me to somehow make this better for him. Need for me to be everything in this moment—everything he needs.

I scoot forward on his bed, taking his face between my hands as I bring my lips closer to his. A soft whimper escapes him as he realizes what I'm going to do, and his eyes flutter closed in anticipation. The kiss is chaste and gentle; the liquid fire that erupts in my chest is anything but. *I love you.* The words are on the tip of my tongue, but I don't say them because I know he can't handle it right now, not with all the emotion that contacting his mother has evoked.

His lips begin to move gently against mine, but I jump back as the door squeaks, and a nurse comes bustling in. If she's surprised by my presence, she doesn't let on. I back up and sit down in my chair, knowing she's about to assess him.

"Good morning, Will," she says brightly as she places a hand on his forehead then grasps his wrist to take his pulse.

Will looks disappointed, but he covers it quickly. He smiles back at her but doesn't say anything. This routine is well practiced.

The nurse nods, seemingly satisfied with his condition. "Is there anything you need this morning?"

"No, I'm okay," he replies, eyes closed.

"All right, then; I'll be back in a few minutes with your feeding," she says as she leaves the room, and Will's eyes snap open.

He swallows painfully, then looks over toward me, embarrassment and even a little fear in his eyes. "Tori, I . . . I'm—"

"Would you rather I not be here for your feeding?"

Will huffs out his breath. "I'm sorry. I'm still really uncomfortable with it. I know I shouldn't be embarrassed, but it makes me feel like I'm less than a person somehow. The stuff tastes awful, and the whole thing is unpleasant from start to finish."

"You can taste it? I thought since it goes straight into your stomach, you wouldn't taste anything."

"Strangely enough, you can. And I'd know anyway because I threw it back up the first few times until I got used to it," he admits sheepishly.

Yeesh. Will the fun never end for him?

"Don't worry about it, Will. I understand. I brought my book with me. Why don't I go grab a coffee, and I'll come back when the nurse is finished with you. And besides, you weren't expecting me this morning—"

"No, I'm thrilled you're here," he says, interrupting me, and warmth floods my chest.

"I am, too," I say, grabbing my Kindle as I stand. "Now have your breakfast and get cleaned up, and I'll be back in a bit."

Will smiles brightly, and I can't help but grin as I head for the door.

I spend the next hour reading and sipping hospital coffee while Will takes care of the necessities, and when I return to his room, he looks refreshed, having changed into a new nightshirt.

"Welcome back, Tori." He greets me, but I can tell he's not all there, and sweat is beading on his forehead.

I grin at him but detour into his bathroom, and when I return, his brow is furrowed as he looks at the washcloth in my hand. I place the cloth on his forehead, wiping away the sweat and pressing its coolness against his fevered skin, and he sighs in contentment. He lies there quietly while I cool his face and neck.

"That feels wonderful," he murmurs.

My fingers find their way to my favorite place, and Will sighs as I brush his hair back from his face. He's been feverish for more than twenty-four hours, and it's wearing him out, so I continue to stroke gently, hoping he'll fall asleep.

He's out in just a few minutes, but I continue to comfort him with my touch until he grows restless in his sleep. I'm staying for the day whether he's awake or not, so I get comfortable in my chair and read until a nurse comes to check on him around noon.

It's a different one than earlier this morning, and she pushes the door open roughly, either unaware or unconcerned about the squeak that could wake the dead. I groan and shoot a dirty look at her back as Will startles, his eyes opening slowly as the nurse takes his wrist to check his pulse.

She says nothing to either of us and leaves the room as quickly as she came. I make a note to myself to ask Jenny who she is because she's either new or she needs an attitude adjustment. But all thoughts of her leave my mind as Will looks toward me.

He stares at me for a full minute before speaking, and I wonder how much higher his fever is. That charming nurse didn't even take his temperature, so I put down my Kindle and perch on the side of his bed, running my hand across his forehead and down along his jaw. The heat is radiating off him in waves. He's definitely hotter than he was this morning.

"Tori," Will says dazedly, and I do my best to give him a warm smile.

"Hello, sweetheart. Are you all right?"

"Yeah, just . . . hot. God, I feel like shit today."

My fingers pause along his jaw.

"What?" he asks.

"Nothing. You just . . . I'm not used to your being so honest about how you're feeling. Your answer surprised me."

Will breathes heavily through his nose, almost a chuckle. "I don't make it easy, do I?"

"Well, no . . . but I understand why. I'm just happy you're letting me in a little more, that you trust me."

"I do," he says, reaching for my hand. "I don't deserve you, but who am I to argue when God sends me an angel?"

I chuckle and blush at his words because they remind me of the days when he's had morphine. He's clearly not thinking straight.

Will passes a hand over his forehead, and his expression becomes serious. "I need to call my mom back today. I know I'm really not in any shape to talk to her, but she's going to be worried about me. I at least need to call and tell her I'm okay."

"I don't think—"

"Please? I just don't want her to worry. I know my fever is high, and I'm not all here, but you can help me if I get confused. Every time I wake up today, I seem to be feeling worse, and I'm afraid if I don't do it now, I won't be able to later."

I swallow thickly at his words, but I can't deny them. If he slips into delirium, he surely won't be able to call her, and he's probably right that she's worried about him.

"Okay, sweetheart, of course I'll help you. But do you know what you're going to say to her? Are you going to tell her she can come and see you?"

"Yes," he replies, nodding slowly. "It's going to be difficult, but I need to see her. There are things I need to say."

I bite my lip hard, knowing that he's thinking this will be the last time he ever sees her.

"All right," I tell him as I walk around to his bedside table and pick up his phone. I notice his background picture is the one I sent him of Sebastian, and I can't help but grin. He adores that cat.

I find his mother's number and hit "call," placing the ringing phone up to his ear.

Will smiles at me as he reaches up and holds the phone in his warm, shaky hand just as his mother answers.

"Hello?"

"Hi, Mom."

"Oh, Will, I was hoping you'd call me again today! I was so worried! Are you all right?"

"I'm not having a good day, Mom, so I can't talk for long. But I wanted to tell you I was sorry for disappearing on you yesterday. I was upset."

"Oh, honey, don't worry about it. I know how hard it was for you to call after everything that's happened, but I'm so glad you did! I love you, Will, and I've missed you terribly."

"I've missed you too, Mom," Will says, his voice breaking on the word "Mom" as tears start to slide down his cheeks. My heart hammers in my chest as I watch him. Oh God, I would do anything to take away the pain he's feeling right now.

When Elizabeth speaks again, I can hear the tears in her voice as well. "There's so much I want to say to you—so many things I want to know."

"I know, Mom," Will says, disentangling his hand from mine and rubbing his forehead. "I just . . . I can't do this today. I have a high fever, and I can't think straight."

"Are you alone? Is Tori with you? I hope you're letting someone take care of you," Elizabeth says. I don't know what happened before, but at the moment, this woman is impressing me with her concern.

"Tori's here, but . . . I'm in the hospital, so the nurses take care of me." Will's reply is slow. He's struggling to keep up with the conversation.

"Oh, honey," Elizabeth says, and I can hear the anguish in her voice. "Can I come see you? Please, can I come and be with you so we can talk? I know I don't deserve it, but please, please let me come."

Will's eyes are closed, and I'm pretty sure he's barely hanging on. He had to do this today, but he really wasn't up to it. I hope he won't regret it tomorrow.

"Yeah, Mom, I'd like for you to come."

"Oh, thank you, sweetie! I have to go into work tomorrow to get things under control, but I can book a flight for Tuesday. Would that be okay?"

"Yeah . . ."

"Can you tell me what hospital you're in?"

"Hospital?" Will furrows his brow, and I know he's lost his battle with the here and now.

"Will? Let me talk to her, sweetheart. You've done great, but I'll take it from here."

Will hands me the phone, his gaze vacant as he stares at me. He runs his hand over his forehead again, mumbling "so hot" as he closes his eyes.

"Just rest. I'll try to help you cool off in a minute," I tell him, covering his phone with my hand.

Will rolls his head from side to side, but otherwise, he stays relatively still, so I take a deep breath and turn my attention to his mother.

"Hi, Elizabeth. This is Tori. Will's a bit out of it right now. I can tell you what you need to know so you can make arrangements to come on Tuesday."

"Oh, Tori, is he all right? He sounds so tired."

I pause for a moment while I consider what to tell her. At this point, she knows nothing about Will's condition, and she needs to be prepared so she's not shocked when she sees him. I'd like to say I'm doing this for her sake, but it's mainly for his because I don't want him to break down if his mother reacts badly to seeing him this way.

"I'm going to be honest with you. Will is very sick right now. He's been in the hospital for almost two months, and he's very weak. He's often feverish, like today, and his liver, spleen, and lymph nodes are painfully swollen. His cancer also causes an itchy rash and joint pain and swelling."

"Oh my God, this really is life and death, isn't it?" she asks, her voice trembling.

"I wish with all my heart I could tell you it isn't, but I can't. Hopefully, he'll recover from this, but his immune system is weak, and he's very susceptible to infection."

"That's what's going to kill him, isn't it? Not the cancer itself but some infection he can't fight off."

"Yes, that's likely," I tell her, trying to keep the quaver out of my voice and failing miserably.

Elizabeth tries to choke back a sob, and my heart aches for her. Regardless of whatever happened between them, it's obvious she cares about Will very much.

"Will and I didn't part on good terms, but I had convinced myself he would be okay without us—that he'd be better off without his father in his life. It killed me to stay away, but I really believed I was doing what was best for him. If I'd known he wasn't okay, I would have been there for him. I was a fool. I should never have let his father do this to us," she says angrily.

"He needs to hear that from you. He didn't think you'd want to talk to him, let alone that you'd want to come here. He needs you right now.

He needs all the support he can get to help him find a way to get through this."

"I can't even tell you how horrible, how heartbroken, I feel. If he'll let me, I'll do whatever I can to make it up to him and to support him. He's my baby, my only child." She sighs heavily. "I'm sorry, Tori. I'm sure you think I'm a horrible mother."

"Will hasn't told me the details of what happened between you; I only know he misses you, and he wishes things were different. I hope he gives you the chance to try to make things right between you because I can tell that you love him and want to make amends."

"I do. I've been given a second chance, and I'm not going to waste it. I'll be on a plane Tuesday morning. Can you give me the information that Will . . . couldn't?"

I give Elizabeth the details she needs to arrange her trip, and when I disconnect the call, I feel better about this whole idea than I ever have. Considering how strong her feelings seem to be about Will, I'm surprised her husband was able to convince her to sever ties with him. Did she sacrifice her relationship with Will just to keep his father out of his life? William Senior sounds like an asshole from what Will said, but if he's that bad, why would Elizabeth stay with him? It doesn't add up, and that makes me nervous.

As I close his phone, I glance over at Will. He was quiet the entire time I was talking to his mother, and he's sleeping now, but he's restless. I feel so helpless, watching him. He has so much he's dealing with emotionally right now, and then the damn cancer has to go and make things even worse for him.

I go to his bathroom and make another cold compress, wiping the sweat from his face, then pressing the coolness against his cheeks and neck. He leans into my touch, and his eyes flutter open, but they're unfocused. He stares for a moment, and then his gaze drifts to me and his lips curl upward.

"Tori," he whispers, blinking slowly and watching me through heavy-lidded eyes.

"Hiya, sweetheart. I'm just trying to cool you down," I tell him as I shift the compress to the other side of his neck.

"Thank you." His eyes fall closed, and that's the last I see of my favorite shade of green until early evening.

Will spends the afternoon in a fitful sleep while I read in the chair beside him, and I'm perversely grateful that he's exhausted instead of trying to get out of his bed while his fever is so high. Around six o'clock, I get one of the nurses to sit with him while I go grab a sandwich, and when I return, Will is agitated and mumbling in his sleep.

I lean forward to try to catch his words, but they're too slurred for me to understand. His restless motion continues until a sudden shift causes him to cry out in pain. I jump to my feet, but there's really nothing I can do. Maybe if I just touch him and talk to him, he'll settle.

As I move toward him, I plan to run my fingers through his hair, but the sheen of sweat glistening on his forehead reminds me it's been a while since I cooled him off. I detour to his bathroom and return with another cold compress and repeat the actions that are becoming so heartbreakingly familiar to me: across his forehead, refold the cloth, press gently on his neck one side at a time, then up to his cheeks.

I whisper to him as I work through my ministrations, and his eyes flutter open.

"Thirsty," he mumbles, running his tongue along his lips and swallowing painfully.

"Sweetheart, I can't give you water because you're having trouble swallowing, but I can give you some ice to wet your mouth, okay?"

"Yeah." Will can barely whisper the single word, and I scurry out of the room to get him a cup of chipped ice. I return as quickly as I can, and thankfully, it looks as if he hasn't moved in the time I was gone.

I perch on the side of his bed. "Will, I'm going to give you some ice to suck on, okay?"

He struggles to open his eyes, but they're unfocused and staring.

I pick up a piece of ice and press it against his lower lip. He startles at first, his eyes finding mine as he furrows his brow in confusion, but as I move the ice along his lip, he leans into the touch, poking his tongue out to gather the moisture I've deposited there.

I take a second chip and press it between his parted lips, and he takes it into his mouth eagerly. As warm as he is, the ice dissolves almost instantly, and he swallows again to let the liquid trickle down his throat.

"More," he croaks, and I take his hand in mine as I press another ice chip to his lips. We repeat the pattern until he turns his face away.

He starts to talk again, but this time, his words are clearer, his voice a little stronger. "N-need to call . . . worried . . ." He reaches out blindly as if he's trying to find his phone.

"Sweetheart, you called your mom this afternoon. You called her, and she's not worried now," I say, trying to reassure him.

"She can't . . . no . . ."

"You're safe. I won't let her hurt you," I tell him—anything to calm him down at this point.

"No!" he yells, and his eyes snap open, but they're still unfocused. "She's not the one . . . couldn't . . . protect me . . ."

His mother couldn't protect him? A shiver of fear runs down my spine, and I wonder if he's lost in memory or delirium. We've passed the point in our relationship where I don't press for answers. At this point, I'll take them any way I can get them.

"Your mother, Will? Is she the one who couldn't protect you?"

He nods, sweat rolling down the side of his face. "Couldn't . . . Didn't . . . know . . ."

"Sweetheart, what couldn't she protect you from?"

"Couldn't . . . no . . ."

Will falls into a fitful sleep, and I sit back down in my chair. *What did he need protecting from?* For the first time, I wonder if his mother's coming here is a good idea. She seems to want to make amends, and I know I was encouraging this, but I suddenly wonder if he can really handle it. He has so much else he's coping with, and I don't know how frightening the skeletons in his closet actually are.

Will's sleep is restless until about eleven o'clock when he becomes very still. When I notice the absence of sound from his movements, I quickly jump up to make sure he's still breathing. It's irrational, I know, but I'm too well trained at watching people die just to sit there when something changes.

His chest is still rising and falling as it should, and I step in to place a hand on his forehead. I breathe a sigh of relief—there's much less heat than there was before. I think the fever has finally broken, and he can get some more peaceful rest.

I sit back down for another half hour, but Will doesn't move in that time, and when I check his forehead again, it's cool and dry. It's been a very long day, so I stumble home and fall into bed as soon as I finish feeding Sebastian.

CHAPTER 25

Monday passes much as I expected it would. Will sleeps hard for pretty much the entire day, and although I look in on him in the morning and the afternoon, my favorite shade of green remains elusive.

I wake early on Tuesday morning and arrive at Will's room just before eight. I'm betting he's awake already since he slept so much yesterday, and I'm not disappointed as those gorgeous green eyes meet mine the minute I push the door open.

His smile is spectacular; my love for him bubbles up and overflows as I grin back happily. Thank God it looks like he's having a good day.

"Good morning, Tori," he says, his smile coloring his words with warmth and comfort.

"Hi, sweetheart." I greet him, taking his hand and kissing him chastely on the lips.

He looks surprised, but his smile widens. I absolutely hate that I have to destroy his good mood, but it's obvious he doesn't remember the plans that were made on Sunday, and I think he needs some time to prepare himself.

I take a deep breath and frown, which catches Will's attention immediately.

"What is it?"

"How are you feeling?"

"Oh, no," he says, shaking his head at me. "I'm fine today. I got plenty of sleep yesterday, and I'm not feverish, so there's nothing to talk about. I want to know what's bothering *you*."

"We need to talk about Sunday," I answer hesitantly.

His brow furrows. "Sunday? I'll admit I don't remember much of Sunday past the point when you came back to my room after I had my feeding and got cleaned up. Did I do something wrong?"

"No, sweetheart, you didn't do anything wrong. But you did convince me to let you call your mother so she wouldn't be worried about you."

"I did?" Will asks, looking confused and wary.

Argh. I opt for the "ripping the Band-Aid off" approach. "Yes, you did. And . . . you also told her it was okay for her to come for a visit. She'll be arriving later this afternoon."

"Today?" He gasps, shifting to sit up a little straighter and wincing.

"Yes." And suddenly I feel bad about letting Sunday happen. "I didn't tell you yesterday because I knew how much you needed to rest."

Will's eyes are unfocused, and he starts breathing faster as he curls an arm over his belly.

"Will?" He startles badly when I touch his arm, his eyes snapping to mine, tinged with fear. "Are you all right?"

"Oh God, Tori, I don't know if I'm ready for this. A few days ago I never thought I'd see her again, and now . . . she'll be here this afternoon."

"Hey," I say, caressing his cheek, "it's gonna be fine. Your mom is coming because she loves you, and she wants to see you."

"Yeah," Will whispers, looking down and away.

I glance at the clock over his door, and when I turn back, he's staring at me.

"You need to go. Do you have a nine o'clock today?"

"I can stay with you—"

"No. You . . . you need to keep your appointments. I'll be fine. I just need to get used to the idea, that's all."

I want to believe him, but he looks really anxious.

"Are you sure? Because I can—"

"Tori," he says, locking his eyes with mine. "I'll deal with it. Go. Do what you need to do."

I'm still not convinced, but if I stay despite what he's saying, it'll make him think I have no confidence in his ability to cope with this. "All right, but I've already put in for the afternoon off so I can sit with you until your mom gets here. I'll be back at noon, okay?"

"You didn't have to do that," Will says fretfully.

"No, I didn't, but I wanted to. It's my time off, and I can spend it how I like. And it so happens, I want to spend it with you."

Will grins as a blush creeps up his cheeks. "Well, I guess I can't argue with that."

"That's right; you can't." I sass back at him, but I'm still worried. Although he's joking with me, his breathing is still rapid, and his arm is still clutching his belly.

"Seriously, Tori, go. I need to have breakfast and get cleaned up—I'll be busy most of the morning anyway."

"Okay, if you're sure," I say, squeezing his hand.

Will nods, trying to look confident.

"All right, I'll see you at noon," I tell him, leaning over to brush my lips against his. He gives me a brief, chaste kiss because he's still breathing heavily.

I frown as I turn to leave, but I'll only be gone a few hours. Hopefully, he's still able to tap into that firm control he had over himself before he got his feeding tube because he really needs it today.

For the next two hours, I see patients, and I'm writing up session notes when my cell phone rings.

"Hi, Jenny. What's up?

"I think you need to come up here," she says, her tone firm and serious.

I freeze as panic shoots down my spine. "What is it? Did something happen with Will?"

"He's a mess! He's so worked up about his mom coming—I really think he needs to take something for his anxiety. I called psych because I know you can't authorize it, but they're backed up today."

Dammit! I knew he was snowing me this morning! I take a deep breath, feeling sick that I sat down here working all morning while he was obviously suffering. "I was already planning to take the afternoon off to sit with him until she got here, but I'll come up now. What's happened since I left?"

"He convinced me to skip his feeding because he was feeling really nauseated, and even so, he's been vomiting this morning. He begged me to send Jason away when he came—he was desperate not to have to see him this morning, so I took pity on him and did as he asked. He's shaky and on the verge of hyperventilation. I know he's causing himself pain, and he's going to be worn out by the time his mom gets here if he doesn't have a panic attack first."

I close my eyes tightly as Jenny's words wash over me, anger and frustration surging through me. "Oh shit, Jenny! Why didn't you call me sooner?"

"He begged me not to because he didn't want to disturb your work. I did as he asked, against my better judgment, but this has gone far enough. He needs medication. He can't deal with this on his own."

"I'll be there in five minutes, and I'll get Dr. Weaver to authorize some Ativan for him before I leave the floor."

"Thanks, Tori."

I hang up the phone, still squeezing it in my fist as I try to keep my breathing under control. God, I hope it wasn't a mistake to encourage him to contact his mother! I was so sure it was the right decision, but if it's upsetting him this much before she even gets here . . .

When I walk out of the elevator on the fourth floor, Jenny is already standing beside the nurses' station, syringe in hand.

She smiles at me sadly. "I'm sorry I didn't call you sooner. He kept telling me he'd be okay and that he didn't want to disturb you."

"It's all right. He convinced me to leave him this morning even though I felt like I shouldn't. It seems he's putting one over on everyone today," I say, shaking my head.

I eye the syringe warily. "Why don't you let me talk to him first? I'm worried if we both go in there ready to shoot him up with meds, he's going to freak out even more. I'll convince him he needs this, and then I'll call you, and you can come and give him the dose."

"Sounds like a good idea," Jenny says, squeezing my shoulder. "We'll get him through this."

"Yes, we will," I mutter to myself as I head down the hall.

Walking into his room, I freeze as my gaze falls on Will. His eyes are closed, and his harsh, rapid breaths sound loud in the silent room. Both of his arms are curled tightly over his belly, and they're shaking, sending tremors over the rest of his body as he grunts painfully. His copper hair is wild—sticking up in all directions as if he's been pulling at it. His face is ashen, and a sheen of sweat covers his forehead. There's a basin on the table in front of him, but thankfully, it's empty.

I go to him and run my fingers into his hair, hoping to comfort him, but he flinches away and yelps in surprise, his eyes wide with panic and fear.

"I'm sorry!" I exclaim. The tension in his arms lessens but doesn't go away entirely, and his breathing doesn't slow.

"Oh, sweetheart, why didn't you tell me you were this upset? I would have stayed with you!"

". . . thought I could handle it," he says between ragged breaths. "You had to work."

"You're more important than my work. When you need me, you have to tell me—I'm not a mind reader." I begin to scold him, but I know now's not the time. He needs medication and whatever else I can do to calm him. "You've worried yourself sick about this, and I'm afraid you're going to have a panic attack. You need to let Jenny give you some medication to help you calm down."

"No!" He snaps at me, his pained grunt morphing into a moan as he clutches his stomach. "I don't want to be doped up today!"

I keep my words calm and my touches soft. "I don't want you to be doped up either. I just want you to take some Ativan—it's an anti-anxiety med that'll help you relax. It won't knock you out; it'll just keep you from hyperventilating and reduce the shakiness. You're wearing yourself out, sweetheart, and you're hurting because of it. Please, let me help you."

Wild green eyes meet mine, the storm of emotion in them almost taking me under. "It'll really help?" he asks, his voice tinged with desperation.

"Yes, I promise. I would never let them give you anything that would hurt you," I tell him, caressing his cheek.

"O-okay." He stutters, still staring at me with wide, panicked eyes.

I reach over and hit the call button on his bed, then perch beside him on the mattress. "Sweetheart, can I hold you? I think it will help you feel better."

Will nods jerkily, but he doesn't move. He's so lost in his own head right now, I'm not even sure he understands me.

I slide an arm behind his back and one under his knees, and he cries out as I shimmy him over on the mattress. My heart breaks at the sound, but I know he needs this right now.

Will curls into me, resting his head on my shoulder as I wrap my arms around him. I hold him as tightly as I can without hurting him, whispering words of comfort as I stroke his hair.

Jenny comes in a minute later, syringe in hand, and I nod at her, letting her know Will has agreed to take the Ativan. She adds the medication to an IV port, then leaves silently so Will doesn't even know she was there.

We sit like that until Will's tremors begin to ease, and his breathing slows. His grip on his belly loosens, and he extends his arm, placing his hand on my thigh and rubbing gently, back and forth.

"Are you feeling any better?" I ask, brushing my lips against his forehead.

"Well, I can breathe more normally anyway. I feel kind of . . . weird. The things that were upsetting me are still there; I just can't get all worked up about them. Does that make any sense?"

"Yes, actually, it does. That's exactly what Ativan's supposed to do. At least you're not causing yourself pain now."

Will sighs but remains quiet.

"Sweetheart, will you talk to me? Please? Tell me what's going on in your head."

He exhales heavily. "I'm sorry, Tori. I didn't expect this to happen. I dealt with all of this a long time ago. But with her coming today, it's all coming back to me—all the pain, all the stupid shit I did, how fucked up I was back then . . ."

He raises his head, and the sea of green has calmed although now it's awash with sorrow. "I want to forgive her and let her into my life again, but I don't know if I can. I think her presence will always remind me of the things . . . I don't ever want to remember."

His words are ominous, and I wonder what it is he's referring to. The emotional abuse from his father? I still don't know when he attempted suicide. Is that wrapped up in this somehow too?

"I'm so sorry, Will. But I still think you're doing the right thing. Even if you're angry with your mom, you miss her, and I know she misses you. She wants the chance to make it up to you, and I hope you find you're able to give her that."

"How do you know?"

"Because I talked to her on Sunday when you were . . . unavailable, and she told me so."

"Really?" Will's eyes brighten, and the ghost of a smile plays on his lips.

"Yes, really. I think she regrets the choice she made, and she's very anxious to see you."

"I guess we'll soon find out," he says nervously, resting his head on my shoulder again.

We sit there for a few moments, and I listen to the sound of Will's even breathing.

"Sweetheart? Do you think you could sleep for a while? It's only one o'clock, and your mom won't be here until after three."

"I guess I could try." His eyes soften as he looks up at me. "Thank you. I know I wouldn't be able to make it through today without you."

He lifts his chin, puckering his lips and closing his eyes, expecting me to take it from there. I chuckle, and he can't keep his lips from turning up into a smile, but he tries his best to go back to puckering them, eyes still closed. *Could he be any more adorable?*

Warmth bubbles through me, and I bring my lips to his, kissing him tenderly. *I love you.* I say it with my soft touches, and I hope he hears it in the feel of my lips and fingers. I break away before the kiss becomes heated and caress the side of his face.

"You were going to take a nap." I remind him, smiling as he ducks his head and grins.

I slide off the bed, trying to ignore the sounds he makes as he shifts himself back to the center of the mattress. When he's finally comfortable, he lays his head back and closes his eyes.

"I don't know that I'll be able to sleep. I'm still pretty wound up about today."

"Close your eyes, and try not to think about it for now," I say soothingly. "If you fall asleep, I'll wake you up in plenty of time before she gets here."

"All right," he whispers. He shifts around a bit, but he's sleeping within five minutes, and I'm glad he's able to relax his mind enough to do it or that he's exhausted enough to.

I stay with him because I don't know when he's going to wake, and I don't want him to be alone and stressing.

At three o'clock he's still out, but his mom should be here about three thirty, and I know he needs some time to get himself together.

"Will. Sweetheart, wake up." I coax him as I stroke his hair.

He breathes in deeply, and a smile plays at his lips, but I can see the exact second he remembers what's happening today. His eyes snap open, and the smile fades.

"What time is it?"

"It's three. Your mom should be here in about a half hour, and I thought you'd want a few minutes to wake up a bit and put yourself together."

"Thanks, Tori," Will replies, and now he does smile at me although it's strained.

I get him what he needs to brush his teeth, and I comb his hair for him since he spent the morning tugging at it. When I finish, I smile at him, sliding my hand along his jaw. It looks like he shaved with a straight razor this morning because his skin is smooth and baby soft. I don't think I've ever seen him without a fine dusting of stubble on his face. He looks . . . beautiful.

"You look very handsome today," I tell him, because I know beautiful isn't a "manly" word. I watch as the color rises in his cheeks.

"Thanks," he says again, but suddenly, he looks like he's going to be sick.

"Sweetheart, do you need more Ativan? I know how hard this is going to be for you, and another dose will make it easier."

"No . . . I-I'm okay," he answers shakily.

"Are you sure? I think you should. You were in really bad shape this morning, and I don't want you to have to go through that again."

"No, I can handle it, Tori. Really. It's the anticipation that's the worst— she'll be here soon, and then I'll be fine."

He sounds as if he's trying to convince both of us, and I sure hope he's right. I nod and take his hand, holding it firmly to quell the tremors I feel there.

"Will you stay if I decide I want you to? I don't really know what I want yet . . ."

"Of course I will. I'll stay for the rest of the day if you want me to, or if you want some time alone with her, I'll disappear. It's whatever you're comfortable with, sweetheart. You're in control here, and nothing is going to happen unless you want it to."

Will's breathing accelerates, and he swallows painfully. "Can we talk about something . . . not related to today? I really need some distraction." His vivid green eyes are barely holding on to their calm, and they focus on me pleadingly.

"Of course," I tell him as I squeeze his hand. "So, we haven't had a movie weekend in almost three weeks. Do you wanna have a date on Saturday?"

Despite his anxiety, he finds it within himself to smile. "Yeah, I'd love to have a date on Saturday."

We chat about what movies we might want to watch, and Will relaxes a little more. He's still anxious, but his breathing is almost normal, and his hands have stopped shaking. We keep up our easy conversation until there's a tentative knock at the door.

Will tenses and gasps, his eyes snapping to mine in panic.

"She loves you. It's going to be fine," I whisper, squeezing his clammy hand as I hear the door squeak.

A middle-aged woman with brown hair and familiar, bright green eyes stands hesitantly in the doorway, and Will's gaze turns soft and warm as a small smile touches his lips.

I'm about to let go of his hand when he suddenly goes absolutely rigid. The smile freezes on his face, and for just a second, I see pure terror in his eyes. *Oh . . . my . . . God.* He covers it quickly as his gaze turns hard, but I know what I saw. I can almost feel him curling in on himself. I turn back to the door to see an enormous man standing behind his mother.

William Everson Senior is tall—six-foot-five, at least. His hair is unruly and brown with auburn tints like Will's, and his jaw is sharply defined, but the resemblance ends there. His eyes are a deep brown—almost black—and hard, and he's built like a linebacker. Will never said, but I'm guessing he *was* a linebacker. He dwarfs the woman in front of him, almost looming over her, and even I can feel the tension this man brings simply by stepping into the room.

Will grips my hand tighter, stress and tension radiating off him, and he whispers a word meant only for me. "Stay."

He doesn't have to ask me twice. He doesn't even have to ask me once. Unless he orders me to go, there's not a chance in hell I'm leaving this room. Why the fuck would Elizabeth bring Will's father with her?

The air is thick and crackling as Will and his father glare at each other. His mother breaks the silence.

"Oh, Will!" she exclaims as she crosses the room, stopping awkwardly in front of where I stand, holding his hand.

He tears his eyes away from his father, and they soften as he gazes at her. "Hi, Mom." He greets her, his voice deep and unsteady with emotion.

"You must be Tori," Elizabeth says, taking my other hand. "I'm so pleased to meet you."

"It's nice to meet you, Elizabeth." I look to Will, and although he's watching our exchange, his breathing is uneven, and he looks like he's going to be sick. I have no idea how to calm him since I don't know what the dynamic is here.

His father has slid into the room, but he's standing against the back wall with his arms crossed. His expression is frozen and stony, but his eyes move, watching his wife and son like some sort of predator. He has yet to acknowledge me, but I'm sure he gave me the once-over when I was looking at Will.

"Here," I say as I put Elizabeth's hand in Will's and back away a few steps. Will shoots a wary glance my way, but he doesn't have to worry.

I'm not going anywhere. I position myself in the middle of the room so I can observe everything and step in if I need to.

Elizabeth lifts Will's hand to hold it between both of hers, and he winces.

"Oh, honey," she says brokenly, tears streaming down her face.

"It's okay, Mom. I'm all right. I'm so glad you could come."

Will's eyes never leave his mother, and I realize I'm watching a dynamic between mother and son that's played out many times before. They're acting as if his father isn't even there, presumably because it's the only way to have a pleasant conversation. They're trying their best for something normal, but the malice that is William Senior is oppressive.

"Are they taking good care of you? Is there anything I can do?" Elizabeth asks him.

"Yes, they are. The staff is wonderful, and Tori's been here with me. It's been a rough couple of weeks, but I'm hanging in there."

A derisive snort echoes from the back of the room, and I whip my head around to see William Senior shaking his head and smirking.

I turn back to Will, and he closes his eyes and swallows thickly. When he opens them again, he glares at his father.

Elizabeth squeezes his hand, but Will shakes his head slowly.

"Why are you here?" He demands an answer from his father, his voice quiet but strong.

"I came to see if you were telling the truth." His father sneers, and his tone is patronizing.

"Why the *hell* would I lie about this?"

"I guess you wouldn't, but I can see nothing has changed. You're still the whiny, little brat you always were."

I see mother and son flinch from the sting of the words, but I'm grinding my teeth together. I'm on the verge of saying something when Will continues.

"You haven't changed either. You've seen me now, and you know I'm telling the truth. If you have nothing more to say to me, then leave."

His father laughs in a way that makes my stomach turn. "You couldn't stand up to me even when you were healthy and strong"—he chuckles —"and you think you're going to do it now when you're a weakling in a bed?" He steps away from the wall, and the implied threat sends a shiver down my spine.

This has gone far enough—too far, in fact. I step forward so I'm standing in William Senior's line of sight, between him and his wife and son. I hear Will whisper my name warningly, but there's not a chance I'm letting this continue.

"It's time for you to leave, Mr. Everson," I say firmly, and for the first time, he meets my eyes. He gaze is meant to be burning and paralyzing, and I hear a gasp behind me from either Elizabeth or Will, but I'm not afraid of him. He has no power over me as he does over the two people behind me.

I hear Will's breathing pick up, and I break eye contact with this bastard to glance over my shoulder.

"Who the hell do you think you are, telling me what to do!" His father roars at me, but I hardly notice because I'm focused on the look of anguish on Will's face. There's no way this man is getting away with making Will look like that. I don't care who he is.

I round on him again and take a step in his direction. I don't even try to veil the threat in my words. "It doesn't matter who I am. What matters is that Will told you to leave, and he's the one who's in charge here. Now you can either respect his wishes, or I'll call security to escort you out, but either way, *sir*, you're going to leave this room!"

He stares at me, dumbfounded. I don't think anyone's ever spoken to him that way in his life and certainly not a woman who doesn't even come up to his shoulders. I hold my ground, waiting for him to make his decision.

"Tori," Will calls, but I raise a hand to silence him.

"Make your decision, sir, or I'll make it for you," I tell him, crossing my arms in front of me.

He looks as if he wants to call my bluff, but if he does, he's about to find out exactly how serious I am. I stare him down for a full minute, and as soon as I start moving toward the door, he makes his choice.

He huffs out a breath, and with one last glare at Will, he stalks from the room.

I release the breath I've been holding, but I stay where I am for a moment until I can get my anger under control.

"Honey, are you okay?" Elizabeth says, her words laced with alarm.

I whirl around to see Will's head bowed, his face scrunched up, and an arm curled over his belly. *Damn.* He was barely handling the thought of seeing his mother, let alone this clusterfuck that just happened.

He grunts in pain, and I go around to his other side. "It's okay, sweetheart. He's gone now."

"Tori, I can't . . . breathe." And suddenly, he's gasping for air.

Oh, *shit*! I knew seeing his father would upset him, but I didn't think it would escalate into a full-blown panic attack! I should have been paying more attention, but I was so focused on his father that I didn't see the signs.

"Dammit!" I swear at myself under my breath, trying to keep my own composure so I can help him.

"Will, you're having a panic attack. Breathe, sweetheart. Focus on breathing in through your nose and out through your mouth as slowly as you can. You're safe. Nothing bad is going to happen to you. I'm here, and I'm going to take care of you, okay? Stay with me. Just breathe, and look right here," I say, gently lifting his chin to meet my eyes. He looks like a frightened animal—terror etched on every feature as he looks at me. I don't even know if he truly sees me. He's shaking badly, and for a second, it almost launches me into my own panic, but I hold on, reminding myself how much he needs me right now.

"Remember our movie weekend three weeks ago? I had such a good time watching *The Matrix* with you. You were so funny when I tried to take away the bag with your chocolate in it—I'll never forget the look of utter exasperation on your face."

I continue to talk to him, holding his hand and running my fingers through his hair. After a few minutes, his breathing begins to slow, and the terror starts to fade from his eyes.

"Are you all right, Will? How are you feeling now?"

He raises a hand to his forehead, rubbing distractedly. "I'm . . . I don't know. What the hell just happened?"

I raise my eyebrows, but then I realize he might not have been able to focus when I told him what was going on. "You had a panic attack, but everything's okay now. You just need some time to calm down.

"What—" I start to ask him what the hell his father did to him, but the words die in my throat as I watch Will's panic escalate again. He shakes his head furiously at me, wincing and panting, his wild eyes begging me not to ask the question—at least, not now. Whatever his father did, Elizabeth must not know about it, and he's desperate for her not to find out.

Anger surges through me, and I try not to direct it at him because the person I'm really furious with is his bastard of a father.

"You're going to take some more Ativan," I tell him, leaving no room for argument.

He just nods, still breathing heavily. Then he lies back against his pillow and closes his eyes.

My anger is instantly replaced by pity and fear. He's not even going to argue with me about the Ativan. As I look more closely at him, I realize he's barely holding it together.

"Hang on, sweetheart. I'm going to get you what you need."

I turn to leave and nearly jump out of my skin as I almost run into his mother. Elizabeth is standing frozen a few feet behind me, staring at the two of us.

"Are you all right, Elizabeth?"

"Yes, I'm fine, I . . . How did you know what to do?" she asks, still staring at me.

"I'm a psychologist. I'm used to dealing with things like this with my patients," I tell her simply.

She raises her eyebrows as if she's impressed, but her gaze shifts back to Will. "Is he going to be all right?"

"Yes, but he needs more medication. I'll be right back."

I dart down the hall and catch Jenny coming out of another patient's room, and she frowns when she sees me.

"What happened?"

"Will's father showed up, and Will had a panic attack. He really needs more Ativan," I tell her, trying to keep my voice even.

"Shit! What the hell did his father—"

"I don't know, but I'm going to find out as soon as possible." My teeth are clenched so tightly, my words are little more than a growl, and Jenny takes a step back. I need to get a grip on myself. I'm shifting so fast between anger at his father and pity for what Will's going through, it's making my head spin.

Jenny puts a hand on my arm. "You look like you could use something too."

"Yeah, a Valium so I don't go find his dad and shove him down a stairwell," I tell her, trying to take deep breaths. "I think Will needs to be medicated for a few days until he stabilizes. I'll get Dr. Weaver to approve it, but if you can give him another dose now to help him get ahold of himself..."

"Of course, I'll bring it right down," Jenny says, turning on her heel.

I stop outside Will's room and take a few more deep breaths, hoping things have gotten better and not worse on the other side of the door.

Will is still lying with his eyes closed, his breathing rapid and shallow, arms clutched over his distended belly. Elizabeth stands a few feet away, heartbreak etched across her face.

I give her a small smile as I move to stand beside her, and we both wait in silence until Jenny comes and gives Will more Ativan.

After about five minutes, his breathing starts to slow. He uncurls his arms from his belly and glances over at me, and I'm relieved to see calm reflected in his gaze.

"There you are. You left me for a little while; I was worried."

A ghost of a smile crosses his face. "I'm back now. I didn't mean to scare you."

"I'm fine. How are *you* doing?"

"Better." He looks past me to his mother and smiles at her.

"Hi, Mom. I'm sorry about that. I didn't expect Dad to be with you."

"Will, I'm so sorry!" Elizabeth exclaims, taking a few steps forward. "Your father insisted on coming with me. There was nothing I could do!"

"It's all right, Mom. I know how he is." Will drops his head wearily, and when he looks at me, his eyes are sad and watery. "I'm sorry you had to see that, Tori."

"There's nothing for you to be sorry for. *I'm* sorry he upset you that way."

"I could tell. You were quite . . . adamant with him."

I smirk. "I never did get around to telling you the tale of 'Tenacious Tori.' The story goes an awful lot like this afternoon."

"Why does that not surprise me?" Will says with a smile.

Thinking about what happened starts to make me angry all over again, so I try to push it from my head for another time. "Is your belly okay?"

"Yeah, I was just breathing too hard. It's better now."

"Good," I say, smiling at him. "Do you need some time to rest?"

Will's gaze is vacant for a moment, but when he comes back, he looks a little more stable.

"No, I'm okay. I think I need to talk to my mom."

"Okay, do you want me to leave for a bit?"

"Will you come back later?"

"Of course. Call me when you're ready, okay?"

"I will," he says as I lean in and kiss him on the forehead.

"Thank you," Elizabeth says, and I know those two words cover a lot of ground—for giving her time with her son, for standing up to her husband, and for taking care of Will when he was alone.

"You're welcome," I answer, smiling at both of them as I turn and leave the room.

For the next two hours, I hang out at the nurses' station with Jenny because I have no idea where Will's father went, and there's not a chance in hell I'm going to let him back into Will's room today—or ever, if I have anything to say about it.

I don't know what that man is guilty of, but my gut tells me his abuse of Will wasn't only emotional. Fear of harsh words doesn't evoke the kind of terror I saw in Will's eyes this afternoon. That only comes from . . . I shudder, trying to push the thought away, but I know in my heart it's true.

Jesus, no wonder he didn't want to talk about his past and his family. He went through so much in his life already—abuse, addiction, attempted suicide. And his cancer is relentless—every time he's fought back, he's relapsed, each time worse than the last. For the first time, I have a crystal clear picture of why Will's not fighting for his life, why he's just waiting to choose the moment when he wants to die.

I gasp as tears of hopelessness roll down my face. His past doesn't offer him any reasons to go on, and his mother's visit isn't going to change that. My only hope is to spend whatever time he has left with him until he decides it's time to let go.

I jump as Jenny touches my arm, pulling me out of my thoughts.

"What is it?" she asks, and I realize it's been a few weeks since we've really talked. The position she's in between Will and me has put a strain on our relationship, but she's still my best friend, and I need her right now.

I sigh as I let the heartache wash through me. "I'm in love with him, Jenny. I've tried to deny it, but I can't anymore, and it's tearing me apart."

"Oh, sweetie," Jenny says, wrapping her arms around me. "I knew it. I was hoping you'd realize it before it was too late."

"I guess I've known it for a while now, too. I just wasn't willing to face it. I was so done with relationships after Peter. I wasn't looking for anyone else, but Will's so perfect. It's cruel that we should meet now when there's no hope."

Jenny pulls back and looks into my eyes. "I think this is exactly when you were supposed to meet because this is exactly what he needs and what you need after Peter. Tori, you need to tell him how you feel about him."

"How can I? If he doesn't feel the same way, he's going to push me away, and I'm going to lose the time I have with him, and if by some miracle he does feel the same, it's only going to make things worse for him. He's more worried about other people's pain than his own, and when he finds out I love him, and I'm planning to be with him and watch him die . . . I can't do that to him. I just can't."

"He needs to know. Do you really intend to let him die not knowing how much you care for him . . . not knowing he's loved?"

"Fuck, Jenny, I don't know! I want to tell him, but I'm so afraid of losing him."

Jenny grips my arms, and I glance down at her hands. I don't think she realizes her fingernails are digging into me. "Do you trust me?"

I look up at her in confusion. "Of course I do—"

"Then *please* tell him. I'm sure you won't regret it."

I stare at her, wondering how she's so sure about this and why she thinks it's so vitally important. "I'll think about it. I can't tell him yet though. He can't handle anything more with his mother here and the talk I'm planning to have with him about his father. He's so unstable right now, I need to support him and not add any complications."

"Fair enough. But please think about telling him as soon as this blows over. It's important, Tori."

I cock my head at her, but I'm distracted by the sight of Will's mother approaching. She smiles tentatively, looking like she's afraid I'm going to bite her head off. I guess I did come on a bit strong with her husband.

"Will's pretty tired, but I think he's going to—"

My cell phone starts ringing, and I smile as I see that it's Will calling. I raise a finger and put the phone to my ear.

"Hi, sweetheart."

"Hey, Tori. My mom just left. Are you still at the hospital?"

"Yes, I'm still here."

"Could you . . . come by for a bit?" He sounds exhausted, but I'm happy he still wants to see me.

"Of course. I'll be there in a few minutes, okay?"

"Thanks. I'll see you soon."

I disconnect the call and notice that Elizabeth is smiling at me.

"I'm going to come see him again tomorrow," she tells me.

"Alone?" I ask, raising my eyebrows at her.

"Yes. I don't think my husband will want to come, and if he does, then I'm not coming either. I won't have Will upset like that again. I'm truly sorry for what happened today. If I could have prevented it, I would have."

I think she knows how angry I still am, and I have to give her credit for owning up and addressing it. I nod, not precisely telling her it's okay but acknowledging her apology.

"Can I give you my number? I have to fly back on Thursday because of my job, but I'm going to try to take some time off and come back soon— if Will lets me. He can call me anytime he wants, but if something should happen, and he can't call me . . ."

"Of course, Elizabeth. I can call you if the need arises," I tell her, trying to talk past the lump in my throat.

"Thank you. And thank you for watching over him. I can tell he cares very deeply for you, and I'm so glad he's not alone."

I blush and swallow uncomfortably. How can she tell how he feels about me? I'm sure they had more important things to talk about. And little does she know how hard he tried to be alone in all this. If I hadn't come along, I believe he would have succeeded.

"I better get going," I tell her, pointing down the hall toward Will's room.

She smiles knowingly. "Yes. Don't keep him waiting."

I'm still not sure what to make of her, and my decision will depend a lot on what Will has to say about their visit. I wave at her and move toward Will's door, catching sight of Jenny's smile as I turn.

Will is nearly asleep when I enter his room, but the minute he sees me, his eyes open wide, and he smiles brilliantly.

"Hi, Tori. I've missed you," he says sweetly, entwining his fingers with mine as I take his hand. He looks dreadfully tired, but his eyes are like a calm sea, reflective and clear.

"Hi, sweetheart. Are you feeling all right? How was your visit with your mom?"

"It was good. We talked about a lot of things. You were right. She apologized to me for . . . what happened, and I'm trying my best to forgive her. It's a start, and I'm so glad she came."

Relief washes through me, and my shoulders sag as if a weight I didn't even know I was carrying is suddenly lifted. "I'm glad. After what happened earlier, I was so worried this had been a mistake."

He blinks slowly, fighting exhaustion. "No. You were right. I needed to do this—for me *and* for her. Thank you for helping me see that."

He squeezes my hand, holding me with his gaze. "I know there are some things I need to tell you, but I'm beat, and I can't take any more today."

My eyes widen in shock. I thought it was going to be an uphill battle to get him to tell me what happened with his father, but somehow, he thinks he owes me an explanation? "Oh, sweetheart, I wasn't going to ask—not today, anyway. You've had an incredibly difficult day, and I'm so proud of you. You should sleep now, and we'll talk tomorrow if you're up to it."

As an afterthought, I add, "I had an order put in to keep you on Ativan for a few days. I want to make sure you don't have another panic attack."

"Thanks, Tori," Will says, his gaze warm and soft. "That scared the hell out of me, and I'm sure it did the same to you. I've never lost control like that before."

"You're under an incredible amount of stress right now. It's not surprising at all that you reached your breaking point. I think it'll get easier as you sort things out with your mom. And I'm here for you, for anything you need, okay?"

"I know," he says, and I feel the familiar flutter in my chest.

"But right now, I think you need to rest," I tell him, seating myself on the side of his bed. "Why don't you close your eyes, and I'll sit here with you until you fall asleep."

He smiles as his eyes fall closed, and exhaustion finally overwhelms him. I sit there for a long time, stroking his hair and trying not to think about anything but the love I feel for him. I hope tomorrow will take care of itself.

CHAPTER 26

I make my usual morning stop to see Will, but he's still sleeping. I have no idea how he slept last night, and his mother isn't coming until late morning, so I ask Jenny to make sure he's awake in enough time to get ready and to tell him I came by.

Four o'clock finally arrives, and I hurry up to the fourth floor, but I stop outside his door as I often find myself doing lately. My heart starts beating faster. I'm beyond eager to see him, but I'm also nervous about how his day went and afraid of what he's going to tell me about his father.

I take a deep breath and force myself to push the door open, and relief washes over me when I see he's awake and smiling. He's calm. His breathing is normal, and his eyes are clear and a brilliant, tranquil green.

I smile as warmth and happiness spill out of that place deep in my chest, and it's like I can breathe again after a day spent worried and stressed.

"Hello, Tori," he says in that velvet voice of his, and I'm just as affected by it as the very first time I heard it—even more so now that I know I'm in love with him.

"Hiya, sweetheart. You look like you've had a good day."

"It's been intense and pretty tiring, but I think 'good' will work," he says, grinning at me.

I make my way over to him, taking his hand, but I also lean in to brush my lips against his. He responds by burying his hand in my hair and cupping the back of my neck, deepening the kiss with eager lips and an insatiable tongue.

Fire explodes in my chest because we haven't really kissed like this in more than two weeks, and I run my own fingers into his hair, threading them through his soft, copper locks as my tongue dances with his. He moans softly, and the heat between us intensifies. I know things can't continue this way, so I channel all my passion into the way my mouth moves on his—the only means I have to express the love that is all but overwhelming me.

We kiss hungrily, the flames spreading to lick through every part of my body as I breathe faster, trying to get enough air without breaking away from him. His hand leaves the back of my head, and I tense in anticipation, wondering if he's about to touch me—somewhere, anywhere— but I don't feel anything, so I peek with one eye. I watch in fascination as his hand disappears below his belly. He moves as if he's adjusting himself, and he groans against my mouth.

I freeze, and suddenly, he does too, drawing back and following the glance I can't help but cast toward his hand now that our kiss is broken. The blush that races up from his chest and over his neck and cheeks is fierce, and he drops his head against my shoulder in obvious embarrassment. I don't want to make him feel worse, but I can't help the chuckle that escapes me.

We're both still panting, and I bring my hand around from the back of his neck to grip his chin, forcing his eyes to meet mine. He looks at me sheepishly, a small smirk curling his lips despite his embarrassment. *I love you.* The words are on the tip of my tongue, but I don't say them. Instead, I bring my lips to his again, running my tongue along his lower lip before I whisper playfully, "So you're happy to see me?"

He tries to duck his head, but I still have a hold of his chin, and an adorable grin spreads across his face as the blush roars back at full strength. "Yeah," he answers shyly, and it's all I can do not to throw myself at him.

I bring my lips back to his. "I'm glad," I whisper as I grab his lower lip gently between my teeth. He groans, and the sound shoots right between my legs. "Will you . . . touch me?" I breathe against his lips, and he freezes again, pulling back with wide, eager eyes.

"Where do you want me to touch you, Tori?" he asks, his voice low and husky as his heated gaze rakes up and down my body.

"Anywhere." I almost moan, my eyes falling closed.

I draw in a rapid breath as the backs of his fingers pass feather-light across my cheek, his index finger brushing my nose, then passing down over my lips. He stops there, his finger gently tracing them, first upper, then lower, leaving tingling heat in his wake.

I let out a whimper, opening my mouth to suck the tip of his finger in, and his groan of pleasure sets me on fire.

"Jesus, Tori," he murmurs, letting me explore his finger with my tongue before withdrawing it slowly, moving down to trace my collarbone before laying his hand flat against my chest, laid bare by the V-neck t-shirt I'm wearing.

His breath comes faster as he slides his hand below the line of my shirt, slipping his fingers under my bra to cup my breast in his hand. My heart is hammering under his fingers, and I wonder if he can feel it too.

Will pulls his hand back so the tips of his fingers brush over my nipple, and I moan when it peaks to a firm bud. He winces as his lips crash into mine, voracious and seeking as his tongue thrusts out along the heated line of my lips.

I welcome him in eagerly, nipping at his tongue before we're entwined again, warmth and wetness, whimpers and moans. He massages my breast and pinches at my nipple as we make out like teenagers, our breath coming fast and hard as my hand tangles in the hair at the back of his neck.

The rumble in his chest sounds like a growl as his other hand comes up to slide along my neck. I kiss him with everything I have, but suddenly, he pulls back, grunting sharply. *Oh fuck, this is hurting him!* He leans his forehead against mine, biting his lip as he slips his hand out of my shirt and lays it protectively over his belly.

"Will—"

"Just give me a minute."

"Sweetheart, you're hurting," I say, cupping his cheek in my hand.

"Yes, but for once, I'm happy about the reason for it," he retorts, raising his eyes to mine as his breathing slows. His vivid green eyes are pleading. "Please, ignore it, Tori. It hurts me pretty much anytime I move, so if I'm going to be hurting, I'd rather it be from enjoying my time with you."

"But—"

"No buts," Will says firmly. "I can't just lie here and do nothing. You've been telling me I should do things for me. Well, this is what I want. I want you. I want to be with you, and I want to be able to kiss you and touch you like . . . like a normal guy would."

My heart squeezes painfully. "You are so much more than 'normal,' Will, but in the way you mean, you *are* a normal guy to me, and I want to let you do whatever you want with me. But I don't think we need to go so far that you're gasping in pain like you just were. Let's go a little slower, okay?"

He looks down, unhappy with my answer.

"Sweetheart, we'll be as 'normal' as we can, all right? I'll still let you try to kiss my face off, but maybe not for quite as long, okay?" I tell him, ducking my head and trying to meet his eyes.

He chuckles, but it turns into a groan as he bites his lip again. "All right. I'm sorry. I just—"

"I know," I say, stroking his cheek. "Don't worry about it."

"So . . . we can do that again?" he asks, smirking as his eyes dart to mine.

"Yes."

"And you'll let me touch you?"

"Will, I've been wanting you to touch me for weeks now. As long as we're not hurting you, you can touch me anywhere you want."

His eyes widen, his face lighting up with wonder, then with mischief.

"But not now," I say, raising my hands in front of me. "So, you were telling me that your day was good?"

Will smiles at my smooth change of subject, but he sighs and furrows his brow. He knew there were going to be some difficult things to discuss today, and suddenly, I wonder if his ardor just now was an attempt to delay or escape them. Maybe it's not a conscious attempt, but he seems to be clinging to me when he's stressed lately.

He looks down as he starts speaking. "Yeah, it was good. Today, my mom and I talked about me and everything that's happened since she last saw me. She asked lots of questions about my cancer and my current condition."

I know they shouldn't, but his words sting. Will hasn't told me any details about how the treatment for his infection is going—the only indirect information I've gotten was when I overheard him tell Jason he can't shake the infection, and that was almost three weeks ago.

"What did you tell her?" I ask, staring down at my hands.

Will reaches for me, and I take his outstretched hand, but I don't look up.

"You're thinking she knows more than you do now, aren't you?"

I nod as a tear slips down my cheek.

"I'm sorry, Tori. It's . . . After everything that's happened, it's very hard for me to let anyone in. I can't just open up, even if I want to. It has to happen a piece at a time. I wish things were different, but I can't change them now."

I glance up at him, and his gaze is full of sincerity and longing. He's fighting so hard against his instincts when it comes to me, and I love him that much more for trying.

"You know all about my diagnosis and relapses and how I ended up here. I've had this blood infection for more than two months now. They were able to lower the bacterial count in my blood, but they haven't been able to eradicate it, so after they'd given me the standard treatment for four weeks, they started changing the cocktail of antibiotics to see if they could come up with a combination that would kill even more of the bacteria. The first new combination they tried didn't work any better, but they started me on a second one last week, and the bacterial counts are getting lower. Dr. Evans is hoping this one will wipe out the infection completely."

The seed of hope I hear in his voice warms my heart, and I squeeze his hand. "That's fantastic! If the infection is gone, will Dr. Evans discharge you?"

"Yes," Will answers, but he suddenly looks uncomfortable. "But . . . I can't go home because I won't be able to take care of myself. Jenny is supposed to get me some information about an in-patient hospice center in the area that I could go to until I get stronger or . . . I end up back here."

I stroke my fingers over his hand, and as I look at him, I realize I don't want him to do that. I want him to come home with me so I can take care of him and be with him every minute. It would be hard on both of us but no harder than my having to watch him go to an in-patient facility and have strangers continue to care for him. I roll the idea around in my mind, already working the logistics of time off and finances.

"Tori?"

"Hmm?"

"I, um, asked you a question," he says, looking shy and unsure.

"I'm sorry; I got lost in my own head for a minute. What did you ask me?"

Will looks as if he's not sure he should believe me, but he takes a deep breath and says, "I asked you if you'd still come and visit me if I wasn't here at the hospital."

Oh damn, what a question to miss! He's thinking I didn't answer right away because I didn't know what to say, that I was hesitating. I want to blurt out that I want him to come and live with me, but that's probably not a good idea until we're sure he's going to be discharged, and I can give more thought to the details. "Of course I'll come and see you wherever you are. Every day if I can."

I love you.

"You're very special to me, Will, and I'll always be here for you, no matter what."

His smile is brilliant and contagious, and I grin at him as he raises my hand to his lips, kissing it softly.

"You're very special to me, too, Tori," he says, staring into my eyes. The warmth flutters in my chest as I think I hear the words he's not saying, the words he might not ever say, but I think he means them anyway, just as I do.

"Thank you for sharing all this with me. Will you tell me what the doctor says from now on? I really feel better knowing what's going on."

"Of course. It was hard to talk about this for the first time, but I'm sure it'll get easier for me."

Speaking of hard to talk about, I think it's time I bring up the elephant in the room—the issue I really want him to tell me about today.

"Will . . ." I begin, but I meet his eyes and become lost in their green depths. I can't bear to go any further. But I have to. "Will you tell me about your dad? About what he did to you?"

He huffs out a breath followed by the usual painful wince. "I knew you'd know the minute he walked in yesterday, and I couldn't stop myself from reacting. I knew you'd see it for what it was."

"You're right. I did," I say, trying to talk around the lump in my throat. "And now I need to know how he hurt you. Please."

He swallows audibly. "I've never told anyone this. Not Jason. Not even my mother."

"You don't have to tell me, but I think it might help you to talk about it. Things get big when you keep them in your head. They take on a life of their own. Bringing them out into the open and talking about them can make them seem smaller."

Will casts a glance at me, acknowledging the wisdom of my words. He bows his head and takes a deep breath, letting it out slowly.

"It started when I was thirteen. We used to horse around when I was that age, and then one day it turned really rough. He left bruises on my chest. He told me he was sorry, but he said he needed to 'toughen me up.' So he kept doing it—always when my mother wasn't around —and he never left marks where they could be seen. I actually believed he was doing it for my own good until the first time he smiled while he did it. Then I knew he was doing it because he enjoyed it."

I reach for his hand, and he grabs mine between both of his, holding on tightly to keep their shaking at bay. "Did it ever . . . escalate?"

"Yeah, it was worse when I did something wrong. The worst was the first and only time I decided to borrow the car without permission. He broke two ribs and my wrist. I had to tell my mom I fell down the stairs to cover it up."

Jesus Christ, I should have killed that man when I had the chance! How the hell do you do that to your own child? And how did Elizabeth not notice this going on right under her very nose? "Your mom never suspected?"

"No, I don't think so. Obviously, he has a temper, and he yelled a lot at both of us, but I don't think she ever thought it was more than that."

"So you don't think he—"

"No, I don't think he's ever laid a hand on her like that," Will says, shaking his head. "At least, not that I ever saw. He's an emotionally abusive asshole, but I think he does actually love her, as twisted as that sounds."

"Did it ever get better?"

"No, I . . . escaped to college. He got his hands on me a few times when I came home that first summer, so I made sure never to give him the opportunity again. I stayed away as much as possible until Jason and I got back from Europe. I had hoped once I was out on my own and somewhat successful, he'd accept me for who I am. But I was wrong."

Suddenly, it hits me like a lightning bolt. I pull my hand out from between his and turn his right one over so the scar on his wrist is visible. "Was this because of what your dad—"

"Yes. When I told you I came to Seattle after Europe, that wasn't entirely true. Jason and I went back to San Francisco for a while and tried to make a go of it there. I, um, did this,"—he runs his thumb over the scar—"a few weeks after I overdosed."

"What made you do it?"

He closes his eyes and sits quietly for a moment. Then he slowly begins to speak.

"It was really bad when I got out of the hospital after the overdose. I don't remember a lot of that time. I just wanted to escape, so . . . I spent a few months drunk and high. But it wasn't enough.

"Um, after all those years of my father telling me I was worthless, I actually started to believe it. He forbade my mother to see me, but at the time, I was so pissed at her for just *standing* there when he told me I disgusted him, I didn't want to see her anyway. My work wasn't selling in San Francisco, and I was hitting rock bottom, realizing I was dependent on pot and Ecstasy, and I *couldn't* stop, and I just . . . decided I didn't have anything to live for."

I honestly believe my heart has stopped; my chest hurts so much as I imagine the pain and heartache he must have been feeling. "What did you do?" I whisper.

"Jason found me. We shared an apartment, and one day, he came home and found me passed out on the bathroom floor, bleeding. I was lucky he happened to come home early that day, or I surely would have succeeded."

"Oh, Will," I say, gripping his hand tighter. I can't believe how close he actually came to killing himself.

"What happened then?"

"Holy Christ, was Jason pissed when I woke up in the hospital, but . . . I got the help I needed, and a few months later, we left for Seattle. I needed a fresh start, and Seattle offered a whole new type of landscape for him to paint. Things were better here for both of us. I continued therapy and figured out how to paint again without the 'inspiration' of pot and Ecstasy. And then, my work really began to sell well. It took me almost two years to put everything back together."

He swallows hard, then raises his eyes to me. He chuckles and tries to smile, but it's more of a sour grimace. His eyes are frozen bitterness and sorrow. "Ironically, I finally felt like I had everything back together about six months before I was diagnosed. I must have done something awful in a former life to end up with that kind of karma."

I perch on the side of his bed so I can wipe away the tear that's sliding down his cheek. "Will, I'm so sorry."

He shrugs, wincing and closing his eyes, causing a few more tears to escape. "It doesn't matter. Some people just get the short end of the stick, I guess. Sometimes, I wish I hadn't worked so damn hard to escape the addiction though. This would be a hell of a lot easier if I were high. And none of this would have even happened if Jason hadn't found me."

"No, Will," I say, shaking my head.

"It's true," he says, his eyes red-rimmed when he finally raises them to mine.

"If you'd succeeded or stayed addicted, then I never would have met you, and I can't live with any reality where that never happened," I tell him, looking deeply into his eyes.

Will snorts. "Yeah, lucky you; you get to sit here and watch me die."

"No, sweetheart. I get to share part of your life with you, and nothing will ever be the same."

I love you.

He bites his lip and raises his eyes to mine, and I can see the storm raging there. Conflict and sorrow and regret for things he can't change, things that were never his fault in the first place. Tears well up in the corners of his eyes . . . and suddenly, the storm breaks.

His face crumples as a sob tears from his chest, and I'm in his arms before the echo of the sound dies out, pulling his head to my shoulder. His tears are bitter and anguished, and I cry right along with him for all the horrible things that have happened to him and what is yet to come. I hold him and stroke his hair long after his tears are spent, and even with the medication, his breathing is still labored and uneven. Two weeks ago tonight, he was telling me he couldn't eat anymore and that he wasn't going to let the doctors help him. Since then, he's gone through a severe depression, confronted his fears about his death, made peace with his mother, encountered his father, and told me his whole painful history in the process. The amount of stress and anxiety he's endured has been incredible, on top of being terminally ill. He truly is the strongest person I've ever known.

I hold him tighter as waves of longing wash over me. I want to wipe away all his memories of everything that has hurt him. I want to protect him from the disease that's stalking him. But most of all, I want to tell him I love him with all my heart. But I'm afraid. I'm afraid after everything else he's had to deal with, my love for him will throw him right over the edge. But I do want him to know that he's loved, that in the past two months, he's become my whole world—the person I'm living for. I *will* tell him, I just have to give him a little time to rest between storms.

"Are you all right?" I whisper when it seems as if his breathing is finally back to normal.

"Yeah. I just feel . . . empty."

"I know, sweetheart. You needed this after all the stress of the past few weeks."

"I'm tired," he mumbles.

"Go to sleep, then. It's been another long, tough day for you, but tomorrow you can relax."

I slowly lower him back to the mattress, and although he grunts from the pain, he doesn't open his eyes. My fingers find their way to their favorite place as sleep consumes him.

CHAPTER 27

"Oh . . . Will . . ." I pant as his fingers circle my nipples, raising them to tight little peaks. I can feel his smile against my lips, and a thrill of happiness spikes through me. The past four days have been amazing.

Will woke on Thursday, feeling better after his breakdown, and things continued to improve from there. The antibiotic treatment they're giving him now appears to be working. His bacterial counts are steadily dropping, and he hasn't been feverish since last weekend. His level of pain is the same, and that still worries the hell out of me, but the lack of fever has allowed him to regain some energy, and he seems to be channeling it all straight to any place I'll let him touch.

And when he's not doing that, he's drawing. Almost every time I've come to his room, including some of the mornings, he's had his sketchbook propped against his chest, working diligently. It's always the black sketchbook, and he slaps it closed the minute he knows I'm there. My curiosity about that book is starting to get to me—I need to ask him to show me that one.

He seems . . . hopeful. Jenny spoke with the hospice center for him, and they don't have any immediate beds available, but he's at the top of the list. That means when the doctors clear him, which is likely to be early this week, he can leave the hospital as soon as they have a bed for him. I'm still nursing my desire to take him home with me, but I haven't said anything about it yet. I want to talk to Jenny first to get her opinion, and I haven't gotten the chance to do it. She was pretty busy on Thursday and Friday, and quite frankly, I'd had my hands full with a horny and feisty Will.

I'm brought back to the present with a gasp as I feel Will's tongue swirl around my nipple. *How the hell . . . ?* While I was lost in thought, he's managed to kiss his way down my neck and chest, and although he's bent over, and I can see a bit of a grimace on his face, he has my nipple in his mouth and is rolling it between his teeth.

I moan shamelessly, and he echoes the sound in a way that makes my thighs clench tighter. We've been making out like teenagers for four days now, and although I can't do much in the way of touching him, he's exploring my body as if it's an undiscovered country. Groping is now standard fare, and yesterday he got bold and slid his hand into my panties. He has yet to try it today, but he's heading that way fast.

He still has my nipple in his mouth, and I throw my head back, panting and groaning his name as he peppers my chest with eager kisses. "That feels . . . so good." I whimper, and then he's kissing his way up my neck to smash his lips against mine.

"I wish you could touch me," he says, his words but a whispered breath.

His hand is down below his belly, and he groans as he touches himself. I can't just reach a hand down there because of his tender areas, and he's too uncomfortable to let me see where I'm going, so this is where we've ended up. What we're doing has driven him crazy to the point that he can't help but stroke himself.

"I wish I could touch you, too." I purr at him, pulling his lower lip into my mouth. We kiss passionately, our lips trying to compensate for what we can't do with other parts. The fire in my belly is molten and pooling quickly toward my center. My clit is throbbing as I tangle with Will's tongue, and I'm about to put my own hand down my pants when he suddenly pulls back, gripping his belly as he grunts in pain.

It takes him a minute to get his breath back, but when he does, he grins at me like the cat that ate the canary.

"We should have stopped." I scold him, but it does nothing to wipe the grin off his face.

"Didn't want to," he says, running his hand down my cheek as his green eyes dance.

I'm mesmerized by the look on his face. He's so damn happy right now! The response of his infection to treatment has done wonders for him, both inside and out. His smile is contagious, and I can't help but chuckle as I lean in to brush his lips again.

"Are you all right?"

"Yeah," he says, but he winces again, and I frown at him.

"Is the pain getting worse?"

"Um . . . maybe a little bit. But I feel so much better now that the infection is clearing up. I'll gladly take a little more pain if I don't have to be exhausted and feverish all the time."

I glance worriedly at his swollen belly, but he puts a hand under my chin and draws my eyes to his.

"Hey, it's fine. Dr. Evans is going to drain the fluid as soon as my blood work comes back clear, so I won't have to worry about that for a while. Then the pain will decrease to almost nothing, just like it did last time." He grins at me, and I can't help but grin back. His mood is infectious. I can't even believe the change that's come over him.

He glances down, running his finger over his afghan. "Maybe . . . once the infection clears and I'm at the hospice center, I'll be able to do some PT and get back on my feet again. I've been so weak from the infection, but maybe once it's gone, I'll get strong enough that things could almost go back to what they were."

"I hope so, sweetheart," I tell him, running my fingers down his jaw. "I'll keep my fingers crossed for you and help out in any way I can."

"I'm counting on it," Will says, winking suggestively at me and pulling me in for another kiss.

"Oh, I forgot to ask. Did you talk to your mom today?"

"Yeah. She's so excited that I'm doing better, and she's planning to come up for a week or two once I'm settled at the hospice center. She can stay at my place while she's here. That way she'll get to see some of my work."

"That's a great idea. I know she's going to adore your work, and you'll get to spend a lot of time with her."

Will looks down again, and I see those long fingers start tracing squares. After a moment, he looks back up at me, a serious expression on his face.

"Thank you, again, for what you did last week. I'm so glad my mom and I had the chance to reconnect even though it was difficult. I don't know that I ever would have done it if it weren't for your encouragement and support. It means a lot to me that you were willing to do that."

In that moment, I feel as if one of the broken pieces inside me has just been mended. I wonder if there will ever be a time when everything will be healed, but for now, small steps will have to do. "You're welcome, sweetheart. I was happy to help."

I glance at the clock. It's almost six, and like clockwork, Jenny comes bustling in with Will's feeding. Now that he's been eating this way for almost three weeks, he's gotten used to it enough that he lets me stay. I think the true motivator, though, is that his feedings take an hour, and if he lets me stay during that time, he gets to see me for that much longer.

"Hi, Jenny," he says brightly, and she and I exchange a smile. She's as pleased with Will's progress as I am.

"Hello, Will," she answers as she begins setting up. "So, are you going to be ready to give her up in an hour? Tori and I have dinner plans when I get off."

"That's right! I forgot," Will says. He looks me up and down. "I guess I can let her out of my sight for a little while."

I swing at him playfully but don't make contact. "I would usually be going home not long after that anyway, sweetheart, so I don't see how your blessing is required."

"Hmph." Will grumbles, crossing his arms over his chest and pouting adorably.

"Okay, okay, maybe your blessing *is* required. If I ask for it, will you put that pouty lip away? You're putting puppies to shame with that thing!"

He laughs, but his arm is around his middle immediately, and he holds his breath through the spasm.

I glance over at Jenny, and she's frowning.

"I can't wait until Dr. Evans drains the fluid again," Will says. "The pain really is getting sharper." He shakes his head and goes right back to where we were. "Yes, you have my permission to have dinner with Jenny tonight, and I'll put the pouty lip away."

I reach up and flick his bottom lip, and it disappears as he smiles. "Good, because you're not going to always get everything you want, so you better save that for special occasions."

Will looks into my eyes adoringly. "I have most of what I want, and what I don't have, a pouty lip won't get me anyway."

I blush, bringing his hand up to my mouth to place a soft kiss on the back.

"I have what I want too," I tell him, and we sit quietly for a few moments, just enjoying each other's company.

We chat until seven o'clock when Jenny comes and stops Will's feeding. These past few days, I've been staying until around seven thirty each night because Will needs to remain upright for a while after he "eats." We've passed the time watching *Jeopardy*.

"I guess I'm the only one who gets to see if red-sweater-glasses dude from last night can stomp on another two challengers," he says, looking forlorn and disappointed.

"I'm sure you'll tell me all about it tomorrow," I answer, putting my hand on his shoulder. "I've been promising Jenny a night out for weeks now."

"Go," Will says, waving a hand in my general direction. "Have a good time, but tomorrow night, you're mine for the continuing saga of red-sweater-glasses dude in his quest to be the ultimate *Jeopardy* champion."

"Whatever you say, sweetheart," I tell him as I sit on the side of his bed and lean in for a kiss. Our lips meet, and it's the same as always—the comfort of softness and the thrill of heat as what I can only describe as joy erupts in my chest.

"Have a good night," I say, blowing him a kiss as Jenny drags me from the room.

We head to our favorite pizza place uptown, chatting and laughing the whole way. It's light and relaxing, and neither one of us brings up Will until we're seated across from each other in our favorite booth.

"So," Jenny says, gawking at me and grinning.

"So . . . what?" *Did that sound innocent at all?*

"You and Will, that's what! He's been so happy since Thursday that I'm not even sure it's really him, and almost every time I've walked in on the two of you, you've been in a hot lip-lock."

I can feel the heat creeping up my neck, but I ignore it. "Well, he's feeling better now that the treatment is working, and since I know all his secrets, he's a lot freer with me."

Jenny frowns for a second, but it disappears so quickly, I wonder if I really saw it. "I'm so happy for you. He's a truly wonderful guy, Tori, however much time you get to spend with him."

"I know. And, um, speaking of time I get to spend with him, I've been thinking."

"Uh oh." Jenny deadpans, and I reach over and swat her shoulder.

"Now this is serious! I've been thinking about asking Will to let me take him home when he's discharged instead of going to the hospice center."

"To your apartment?"

"Yeah."

"That's very generous of you, but are you sure you're ready to handle that?"

"I don't know. That's kind of why I'm asking you about it. I want to be with him as much as I can, and I figure my learning to take care of him would have to be more comfortable for him than letting a new group of strangers do it. I'm sure we could have a nurse come in during the day to help out. And I also think it might be easier for him to avoid infection if he isn't in such a hospital-like setting."

"But what about you? Your job?"

"Well, I can take a leave of absence without too much trouble, and I have my savings that I can dip into for a while—"

"You really have thought this through, haven't you?" Jenny asks, covering my hand with hers.

"Yes. I want him to be comfortable and happy, and I'll do whatever I can to make that happen. And maybe he'll get to the point that he'll be able to take care of himself again . . ." My words die in my throat as I see the look on Jenny's face.

"Jenny? He's been doing so well, and he's so hopeful . . ."

"I know," Jenny says, shaking her head. "But I think he might be a little too hopeful."

"Do you think, or do you know?"

"Oh, Tori, I know! He's getting over this infection, and that's fantastic, but his cancer is advanced. The swelling in his lymph nodes isn't going to go down so he can eat again, and the problems with his liver and spleen aren't going to go away. He has no immune system to speak of. After he leaves the hospital, it's not going to be long before something else overwhelms him."

I feel as if I'm falling, so I reach out, grasping at what I can. "But it doesn't have to be that way. It could be a long time until he gets another infection."

Jenny sighs. "It could, but the numbers aren't on his side. His counts of non-malignant T cells are really low—too low to fight off an infection if his system is challenged. It'll probably all come down to what he's exposed to."

"Oh," I say, covering my mouth with my hand. I swallow thickly as pain and loss well up and try to choke me. I had allowed myself to hope, too. "How long? How long do you think it'll be before he ends up back in the hospital?"

"I don't know . . ." Jenny sputters, unable to meet my eyes.

"Just tell me, Jenny. Now's not the time to start sugarcoating things."

I can tell she's extremely uncomfortable, but she looks me right in the eye. "I really don't know how long he'll last—it could be months, like you said, but . . . I think he'll be back with another infection within a month, six weeks on the outside."

A month. Six weeks. "Well, that makes it even more important for him to come home with me."

Jenny cocks her head to the side. "I don't know, Tori. Between the feeding tube and the constant pain meds, it would be a lot for you to handle at home. He might be better off at the hospice center because they can more easily monitor all that. Unless he's really wanting it to end now with no more chance of intervention, then I would say take him home."

"I don't think that's his plan." His plan is to get much better, and my heart aches as I realize someone needs to prepare him for what's likely going to happen.

"I think you should ask him to go home with you anyway," Jenny says. "He may say no, and the hospice center may be the best place for him right now, but at least he'd know you want to take him home.

"Tori, tell him how you feel. Tell him you love him, and you want to spend the rest of his life with him. He needs to know. It's so important that he know."

I stare at her. There it is again. There's something more here than just her thinking he needs to know he's loved, but I have no idea what it is.

I also know that if she could tell me, she would have by now. "Well, telling him I love him does kind of supply the rationale for why I want to take him home with me."

Jenny nods encouragingly.

"But I'm still afraid he's going to freak out if I go into any of this."

"He might, but that's no reason not to tell him. Even if he's upset at first, I think he'll come to his senses and realize that your loving each other was meant to be."

"Do you really believe that?" I ask her, searching her face.

"Yes, I do," she says with conviction. "I think you're both the best thing to ever happen to the other, and everything is going to work out as it should."

"I hope you're right."

"Me too," she says, squeezing my hand, but she doesn't remain quiet for long. "So, have you talked to Jason lately?"

"No, why? Should I have?"

"No, I guess not . . ."

"Have *you* talked to Jason lately?" I watch her cheeks bloom crimson as she looks away from me.

"Well . . . yeah," she replies, suddenly finding the tablecloth incredibly interesting. *Well, well, well. What have we here?*

"And?

"And what? He's a nice guy. I like talking to him."

"Uh huh," I say, crossing my arms. "I seem to remember saying similar things about Will. Do you remember what you said to me?"

"Yes, but this is different. He's just . . . a nice guy."

"We've established that," I reply, unable to hide my smirk.

Jenny throws her hands in the air. "All right, all right, maybe I do like him, but I can't really tell if he's interested. He talks to me, but he's here to visit his friend who's dying, so I try not to eye-fuck him or come on to him."

I flinch as I realize the dying friend she's talking about is Will. Something about the way she said it makes my heart ache a little more. *Fuck.*

I shake my head to clear my morose thoughts. "Well, he seems like a nice guy," I say, and we both erupt into laughter.

"I'm glad we've established we both can spot a nice guy from a mile away," Jenny says, still chuckling.

"Yes, and neither of them is bad-looking either."

"You can say that again," Jenny answers, grinning.

"But seriously, Jenny, Jason has been there for Will through thick and thin, and I have a lot of respect for him because of it. If he's that true a friend, I can't imagine how loyal and affectionate he'd be as a boyfriend."

"Argh, stop! As if I don't spend enough time thinking about what he'd be like as a boyfriend!"

"Well, maybe Will and I can help you out. If Will goes to the hospice center or home with me, maybe you and Jason can come and visit him together. That would get you out of the hospital, and it wouldn't be inappropriate to talk to him about whatever you want to in that situation."

"That's true, and I do plan to visit Will anyway. He and I have developed quite a rapport over the past two months, and I really do care about what happens to him . . . and not only because my best friend is in love with him."

I smirk as heat flares on my cheeks. I never wanted to be in love with anyone again, so it's both thrilling and terrifying at the same time.

We chat and goof off the way girlfriends do, but in the back of my mind, I keep thinking about Will and bringing him home with me. I want this. I want it more than I've ever wanted anything. Well, that's not true. I want him healthy and cured more than I've ever wanted anything, but having him home with me is something that could actually happen. But even if he decides the hospice center is better for him, I want him to know this is what I want. And I want him to know I love him.

I laugh a little louder and smile a little wider as I hang out with Jenny, knowing that for better or worse, after tomorrow, nothing between Will and me is going to be the same.

CHAPTER 28

I sleep fitfully on Monday night, too excited and nervous about the conversation I'm going to have with Will the next day. I wake up early, so I might as well go and see him. I'm not going to bring up his coming home with me until the afternoon, but maybe some time with him this morning will help calm me down.

When I open Will's door, I hear him before I see him. His breathing is loud—coming in uneven pants that are punctuated by desperate-sounding grunts. Adrenaline rockets through me, and I shove the door open, causing it to squeak hideously.

I'm across the room in a flash, already taking in Will's situation. Both of his arms are wrapped tightly around his belly, and he's curled inward as much as is possible for him. He's shaking. Every muscle and tendon in his body is stretched taut, and his jawline is sharp from clenching his teeth. His face is scrunched into a terrible grimace, and sweat is beading on his forehead and dripping down the sides of his face.

"Will, what is it?" I reach my hands out to touch him, but I stop in mid-air, helpless. No touch of mine is going to make this any better.

"I need . . . morphine." He pants in between the awful noises of pain he's making.

"Did you call Jenny?"

"Just . . . now."

"I'll be right back," I tell him as I whirl around and dash out the door.

I tear down to the desk, but no one's there. I glance frantically up and down the hall and spy Jenny as she's stepping out of another patient's room. "Jenny! Will needs morphine!"

Her eyes widen as I approach, but she's in motion instantly. "Shit! How much pain is he having?"

"Oh, Jenny, this is the worst I've ever seen him! He's shaking and drenched in sweat." I try to keep the panic out of my voice but fail miserably.

"Okay. Let me get what I need, and I'll be there as soon as I can. Go be with him until I get there, all right?"

I nod and sprint back up the hall. My hands are shaking so badly, I fumble with the handle when I reach Will's door, and when I finally get it open, I race to his side.

"Will, Jenny is coming right now. She went to get the morphine, and she'll be here in just a minute."

"Thanks," he mutters, clutching his belly even tighter. "Ahh . . . *fuck!*"

I feel like my insides have turned to jelly, and I'm one big bundle of adrenaline and panic as I watch him. I don't even try to touch him. He's so focused on the agony he's in that I doubt he would even acknowledge my touch, and if he did notice, it would only annoy him. I try to soothe him with my words instead.

"Jenny is almost here. She's going to give you morphine right away, and then the pain will stop. It's going to be okay; I promise. Everything is going to be fine."

Jenny comes bustling into the room, and her eyes go wide as they fall on Will.

"Oh, Will, I'm so sorry!" She hurries to his side, and with each step she takes, I can see her rein in her emotions and put on her professional bedside manner. "Let's get you fixed up, okay? Tell me, where does it hurt?"

"M-my belly."

"Anywhere else?"

"N-no. Well, no more . . . than usual."

"Are you having any trouble breathing?"

"N-no."

"How bad is the pain—on a scale of one to ten?"

"T-ten. M-more than ten."

"The worst pain you've ever had?"

"Y-yes. It's never . . . been this . . . bad. It's taking . . . all I have . . . not to scream."

"Okay, let's get you some relief, then. I'm going to give you a pretty high dose of morphine because we don't want to have to increase it. This should start working within five to ten minutes. I'm sorry; there's nothing I can give you that's faster. Then I'm going to call your doctor so we can try to figure out what's causing this."

"O-okay."

Jenny hangs the IV bag and begins to adjust the dials on the infuser, but I keep my eyes on Will. He's still shaking and gasping, and I'm still afraid to touch him. *Holy hell, what's causing this now?* The ups and downs of his condition are beginning to wear on me. I don't know anymore whether I'm going to be greeted by my smiling, sleepy boy or by something like this. The adrenaline is still coursing through my veins, and I'm shaking right along with Will. I take a few deep breaths to try to get myself under control.

Jenny finishes her adjustments and addresses Will again. "Okay, I'm going to call Dr. Evans now, and we'll get to the bottom of this. I'll be back in a few minutes."

Will doesn't respond, and Jenny frowns at me as she leaves the room.

Even though I can't do anything, I'm drawn to Will. I stand as close as I can without touching him and speak softly. "Just hang on for a few more minutes, okay? Then it'll get better. Is there anything I can do for you right now?"

"T-talk to me."

I'm struck dumb for a moment by his request, but I quickly realize it doesn't matter what I say; he just wants to hear my voice. I'm a mess and my wits are scattered, but I need to do this to help him. "Well, I've got a busy day ahead . . ." As I begin, I croak out the words, but my voice gets stronger as I focus on the task.

I tell him about the patients I need to see and the emergency psychology staff meeting that was called for this afternoon, and as I do, Will's breathing begins to slow, and his shaking turns to spasms of shivers. His shoulders begin to relax, and he uncurls himself so he's lying on his back again. He rests his head back on the pillow and takes a full, deep breath. The shivers are gone, and his arms finally loosen their grip on his mid-section.

But as he's calming down, I seem to be ramping up.

I can't take this anymore! How the hell am I going to sit here and watch him go through this when my heart shatters every time I see him in pain? He was fine yesterday. Fine! *I thought we'd have at least a few weeks before another crisis. Christ, hasn't he suffered enough? This is so fucking unfair! Why? Why!*

"Goddammit!" I swear, unable to contain myself.

Will jumps at my outburst, struggling to open his eyes. "Mmm'okay," he slurs, reaching his hand out for me.

"No, Will, you're *not* okay! You're so far from okay, I can't stand it! What the hell else is going to go wrong? I can't just *sit* here and not be able to do anything to help you! I can't—"

I glance up at Will, and he's looking at me blearily, his brow furrowed. I don't know if he followed all that since he's so drugged up, but he clearly knows I'm upset.

"Tori," he whispers, again reaching out for me, but I can't take it. I just can't *be* here right now.

"Will, I—" I turn on my heel and run from the room before I can say anything I'll regret.

I make it as far as the empty waiting room at the end of the hall where I collapse into a chair, my head between my knees and my hands buried in my hair. My mind goes blank, drowning in a sea of pain and frustration, and inside it feels like I'm screaming on an endless loop.

I jump as I feel a hand on my back, but I stay where I am, unable to stop my tears as the hand rubs circles there. I cry until my eyes are sore and my throat feels raw, and then suddenly, my brain kicks back into gear, and the words come spilling out.

"I can't do this! I've watched patients in pain so many times, but with Will, it just tears my heart out! I love him so much; it's as if it's me who's in pain every time he's suffering. And I can't lose it like this! He needs me! I have to be strong; I can't freak out every time—"

"Hey," Jenny says, gathering me into her arms. "You can't be strong all the time. This morning was really scary, and it got to you. It happens. How many times have you helped patients and their loved ones get through things like this?"

"I know," I say, shaking my head in frustration. "And I know all the things I usually tell people, but dammit, sometimes, they don't work! Sometimes, you just lose it to take some of the pressure off, and—"

"And you know that too."

I scowl. Of course, she's right. The way I'm reacting is perfectly normal; it's just making me crazy because it's me and not someone I'm trying to help.

"Yeah, I guess I do. Dammit! You were right though! He's not really going to get better at all, is he? He's going to come down with some new infection, and we'll be right back where we were, or worse!"

"Now, now," Jenny says, soothing me as she pats my arm. "We don't know what's going on with him. It could just be that it's time to drain the fluid in his belly, and if so, that's easily done. Don't freak out until we get some answers. Dr. Evans is going to be up here soon, and I'm sure he's going to order blood work and who knows what else to try to figure it out."

"I just don't want to let him down. I know how hard it is for him to watch me be upset because of what's happening to him, and it's only going to get worse the closer he and I get and the closer we get to . . . the end."

"Honey, you won't let him down. He's going to see how much you love him, and it'll carry him through the hard parts. He knew this was going to affect you when he made the choice to let you in. But he made it anyway because he needs you. And you need him too."

"Yes, I do," I say, wiping away my tears.

"Now, you better go back down there and tell him you're okay because even though he's high, he knew you were upset, and he called me and asked me to come find you."

"Shit," I mumble, still wiping at my eyes.

"He's pretty out of it. I'm sure he won't remember whatever you said to him. Just reassure him that everything's okay."

"Thanks, Jenny," I say as I stand up on shaky legs.

"Anytime. I only reminded you of what you already knew."

As I turn to leave the room, I smile at her, and she winks back.

I feel horrible as I walk back down the hall. I know I needed to blow off some steam, but I can't run out on Will like that, not when he needs me so much to help him get through this.

His eyes are closed when I go back in. All the lines of pain are gone from his face, but my chest tightens as I remind myself it's an illusion; the morphine is masking what he would be feeling.

I reach up and run my fingers into his hair, and he sighs contentedly. *Wow! It really is amazing what a little morphine can do.* He lies there quietly, and I'm reluctant to disturb him, so I continue stroking his hair and watching him. His breathing is so even that I'm starting to wonder if he's asleep, but then he opens his eyes lazily.

"Tori," he whispers in his breathy "I'm drugged up and exhausted" voice.

"Hey, sweetheart," I say, taking his hand.

His brow furrows. "You were . . . upset . . ."

"I'm fine. I just needed some air," I tell him as a few tears slip down my cheeks.

"Are you sure?" he asks, bringing a hand to his forehead.

"Yes, I'm sure; everything is just fine."

"F-f-fuck, how much m-morphine did Jenny give me?" Will slurs, barely able to keep his eyes open.

"A lot, sweetheart. That was some serious pain you were in." I try hard not to cringe at the memory of the last hour.

"'m not feelin' any pain now," he says slowly, struggling to form the words. "Which is . . . kinda weird 'cause somethin' always hurts."

My heart clenches at his words. "I know. But morphine takes it all away, and that's good."

"Yeah. But I'm . . . definitely high. 'm tired."

"Well, you can sleep all day until I come back at four. But it *is* better without all the pain, isn't it?"

"Yeah, it's better . . . and worse," he says, suddenly more alert. I watch as he wraps an arm around his belly and scrunches up his nose. "Dammit." He swears, swallowing loudly.

Then his eyes widen in what almost looks like panic. "Tori, can you hand me that basin on the table, and then . . . go?"

"What?"

"I'm about to pay the price for my pain relief," he replies as a small moan escapes him.

What the . . . Oh! Dammit, can't he catch a break? As I look more closely at him, I see he's gone as white as a sheet, and a sheen of sweat is visible on his forehead.

"Will, don't worry about—"

"*Please?*"

He swallows again, and I hurriedly hand him the basin. "Okay, okay, I'll go, but I'll be back at four," I tell him as I start to back away.

"Thanks. I'll be better . . . by then," he answers as he holds the basin under his chin.

I scurry from the room, pulling the door closed as I hear him begin to retch. Jesus Christ, why does it have to be so hard for him? Tears of frustration slide down my cheeks as I head down the hall to find Jenny.

She's at the nurses' station, and as soon as she sees me, she's up and has her arms around me.

"How is he?"

I sniffle and swipe at my eyes. "The morphine is working, but you'd better go check on him. He chased me out of the room because he didn't want me to see him throw up."

Jenny shakes her head and sighs. "Dammit, I hate that morphine makes him so sick. We figured out that changing the dose is what made him continuously nauseated, so now we're just giving him a constant dose, but there's nothing I can do about the nausea when he first starts taking it. I'll go take care of him. Are *you* all right?"

"Yeah, I'm fine. You were right; he didn't remember what I'd said, and I was able to convince him everything was all right."

"I told you you'd be able to smooth it over! Now, I better get down there and see to him. He hates vomiting."

"Who doesn't?" I ask as I watch her scurry down the hall.

I go about my day, but my head is in room 412, and I call Jenny twice for updates on Will's condition. She reports that he's stopped vomiting, and he's resting comfortably, thanks to the morphine. I'm sure that's stretching it as far as what she's allowed to tell me, but I'm grateful.

Argh. I can't tell him I love him and ask him to come home with me today. He's high from the morphine, and until the doctors figure out what's going on with him, he might not be going anywhere, and I don't want to upset him by forcing a discussion about it. I'll wait until his blood work comes back, and then once we know where things stand, I'll ask him.

He's watching TV this afternoon when I arrive, staring listlessly at the screen, his eyes only half-open.

He looks over when the door squeaks. "Hi, Tori," he whispers as his eyes fall closed, and he opens them again slowly.

"Hi, Will. How are you feeling? Still high as a kite?"

He chuckles, and for once, it's not followed by the usual wince. I'm happy and sad at the same time.

"It's not as bad as this morning. It's gotten easier to form words and to focus, but . . . I'm still feeling pretty good."

He pauses and his eyes go unfocused for a moment as he scratches at his arm. I'm about to call him back to me when he starts talking again.

"I'm sorry about this morning. Not the 'good morning' you were expecting, was it?"

"No, certainly not, although I'm guessing it wasn't the morning you were expecting either."

He frowns, licking his lips. "No. I don't know what the hell that was. All of a sudden, I was awake and in terrible pain."

"Did they figure out why? Did Dr. Evans come by to see you this morning?"

"Yeah," Will responds, and I realize he's not really going to elaborate unless I can do something to help keep him focused. I take his hand and bring it up to my face, rubbing his fingers over my cheekbone.

"Are they going to drain the fluid again?"

"Actually, that's not the problem. They did—what's that thing Jenny was holding when they drained the fluid the first time, that lets you see inside?"

"An ultrasound?"

"Right! They did an ultrasound. My liver and spleen have gotten even larger, and that's what's causing the pain. They think the fluid has been acting like a cushion, which is why they're not going to drain it . . . at least for now."

A chill runs down my spine. *Shit.* Whatever is causing his liver and spleen to get bigger can't be a good thing. "Did the doctor have any idea why this is happening?"

"No, but they took a ton of blood this morning to try to figure it out."

Will shifts his hips and still winces despite all the pain medication he's on. "Dr. Evans said I'll probably need morphine until they can figure out how to reverse this . . . *if* they can figure out how to reverse this." He's looking down and away now, trying to get his emotions under control. "I don't know if they'll still discharge me even if my blood work is clear. Evans said maybe, but he's worried about what could be causing this."

I reach over and put my hand on his cheek, coaxing until watery green eyes meet mine. "Hey, it's gonna be okay."

He closes his eyes and a lone tear escapes. "You know, one of these times it isn't going to be okay," he says quietly. "I thought I was ready for that, but I don't know anymore."

My chest tightens. I know this needs to happen. He was in denial before, and now he's confronting his fears, but watching him go from calm and sure to uncertain and afraid is killing me slowly.

"You're not alone, Will. You have me and Jason, and your mom will be coming back soon. You can talk to me about this. You know that, right? If you tell me what you're thinking, then you're not alone anymore. And I don't want you to be alone—not at all."

He smiles, but it quickly fades. His eyes shift down to his afghan, telling me I'm about to get the truth.

"I don't know what I'm thinking. I'm . . . scared. I want to believe I'm still going to get out of here, but nothing ever seems to go my way. I want to go back to yesterday when I was happy and just waiting for confirmation that I was better."

I sit on the bed next to him, but before I can touch him, he shifts over with the tiniest of grunts. He pats the mattress next to him then raises his arm. "We can really cuddle now. The only thing I can feel in the way of pain are some twinges in my belly—everything else is numb."

"Are you sure?"

"Yeah. I'll let you know if you hurt anything, but I don't really think it's possible right now," he says, grinning at me drunkenly.

I turn and scoot back into the space beside him, resting my head on his shoulder, not quite in the crook of his arm. With the fabric of his night-shirt stretched tight, I can see the lump on the inside of his torso under his arm. His eyes follow my gaze.

"It was really tender before, but I can't feel anything now, I promise. I hate the side effects of the morphine, but it's actually kind of nice to be able to move without flinching all the time. I'd forgotten what it was like not to feel pain every time I move. I could get used to this."

It's not funny, but my lips turn up in a grin at his attempt to make it that way. I reach my hand up, and he nods at me. "You can touch it. That way you'll know you're not hurting me."

My grin grows a little wider—that's exactly why I wanted to touch it. I brush the lump tentatively with the tip of my finger, and Will doesn't even respond. I'm so used to the wince and the flinch that I pull my fingers back immediately, and he chuckles and shakes his head. I glance up at him and reach forward again, using two fingers this time. I had thought it would feel like the lymph nodes in your neck do when you're sick—soft and kind of squishy, but the one under his arm is hard.

"The cancerous blood cells accumulate there. That's why it's hard. It's almost like a tumor," he tells me.

I shudder, and he pulls me closer. "Enough about that. I'd rather spend some quality time with you since I'm feeling pretty good. Will you still kiss me even though I'm high? I promise I won't throw up on you."

I giggle and reach my hand up to cup his cheek. "Of course I will. I've been wondering when you were going to ask me."

He angles toward me, wincing a little, but then his lips are on mine, and everything else fades away. His kiss is soft and tentative at first, chaste and playful. Our lips move together slowly, the heat rising with every gentle taste and sweet nip. I can feel the warmth building in my chest and traveling down between my legs. I whimper, and Will moans in response, pulling me closer and thrusting his tongue into my mouth.

He holds nothing back today because he can move without pain. His arms encircle me, and his hands tangle in the back of my hair, our moans making me throb as his lips devour me. I get lost in what he's doing to me, forgetting myself completely and sliding my hands down his sides. He groans against my mouth, the sound borne of lust and not pain, pulling me even closer to him as his tongue dances with mine. We kiss until I'm breathless and lightheaded, and I pull back, gasping.

Will leans his head back against his pillow, panting just as hard as I am, but he's grinning blissfully. He opens his eyes, rolling his head to the side to look at me. "That was the very first time we've stopped kissing because of you and not me. Yup, I definitely like morphine. If I weren't so itchy and spaced-out, it'd be damn near perfect," he says, reaching up to scratch absently at his chest.

I chuckle and he winks at me, making me laugh out loud.

"God, I love that sound. It's the most beautiful sound in the world. I need to figure out how to make you do that more often, because . . ." He trails off as a blush spreads across his cheeks.

"Because why, Will?" I prompt him, caressing his cheek with my fingers. I probably shouldn't press since he's not himself today, but I can't resist the honesty and lack of filter that's a by-product of the combination of Will and morphine.

He smirks at me, and I'm pretty sure he knows what I'm doing, but he's going to let me do it anyway. "Because that sound does things to me. Right here," he says, placing his hand over his chest.

Heat blooms in my own chest almost every time those impossibly green eyes of his meet mine, and my insides flutter giddily at the sound of his velvet-smooth voice. And oh God, my heart clenches when he smiles at me, and I'm guessing that's what he feels when he hears me laugh. "I would ask you what kind of things, but I think I already know," I say, leaning in to capture his lips again.

But he's not done. He brushes my lips, then pulls back to gaze into my eyes. "That's not the only thing I love," he says softly, and I hold my breath, wondering if he's about to tell me what I've been so eager to tell him for days now.

His stare pierces me for a long moment, but he doesn't say the words. He's saying them with his eyes, though, and the morphine is clouding his judgment; otherwise, I don't think he'd be doing this. I believe he loves me, but somehow, he's not ready yet.

"I love your eyes," he whispers. "They remind me of Hershey's Kisses, and you know how I feel about those."

I clap my hand over my mouth to try and stifle my laugh, but I'm too late, and some of it escapes. So I just give up and laugh out loud, and even though his brow furrows, he smiles at the sound.

"That wasn't very smooth, was it?"

I laugh again because I can't help it, pulling him close and kissing him. He responds immediately, burying his hands in my hair and making love to me with his lips until I pull away gasping.

"Well," he says between panting breaths, "if that's what I get for half-assed compliments, I wonder what you'll give me when I have my head on straight and I can really dazzle you!"

I chuckle, shaking my head at him. "That's what you get for being completely adorable, not for your half-assed compliments."

"Either way, I'm doing *something* right," he says, grinning at me drunkenly. "But, seriously, Tori. I can't tell you how glad I am that you're here. I . . . I need you here, more than I ever thought I would."

"Why do you need me here, Will?" I ask, still smirking from our previous exchange.

"Because you're . . . my angel. I swear to God, that's exactly what I thought you were the day we met. It was as if you walked right out of one of my dreams. I don't need to worry about heaven because I have an angel right here with me. I can't imagine there's anyone up there who's better than you."

Oh, Jesus. Well, that wasn't half-assed. "Oh, Will," I stammer, struck dumb by the honesty and sweetness of his words.

"You don't have to say anything," he says, looking nervous. "I know it's not the same for you."

"What do you mean?"

"Well . . ." He stalls, his gaze shooting down to the afghan. "I know we've been fooling around, but—"

"No, Will." I interrupt because I can't even bear to let him say the words, much less entertain that they're true. "You are the sweetest, most amazing man I've ever met." *I love you.*

"I want to spend with you whatever time you'll let me. It's exactly the same for me."

"Yeah?" he asks, grinning at me.

"Yeah." I grin right back.

It's as if my words somehow flipped a switch because suddenly, he smashes his lips to mine, his tongue demanding entry as he runs it along my lower lip. I welcome him in, cocking my head to the side and pulling him closer, our tongues tangling and caressing as I moan against him.

The sound spurs him on, and he angles further onto his side, bringing his hands to my chest to cup my breasts and tease my nipples through my bra until they harden and peak behind the satiny material.

"Will, what if someone—"

"They won't," he answers quickly, blushing. "The only one who ever comes in around this time is Jenny, and I . . . kind of told her I wanted some alone time with you. She said she'd make sure we weren't disturbed."

I raise an eyebrow at him. "Had this all planned out, did you?"

"Well . . . I'm always in pain, and I feel so much better with the morphine–"

Putting a finger to his lips, I sit forward and unclasp my bra with one hand. Before I even manage to lean back, Will has my shirt and bra lifted up and out of his way, and I gasp as I feel his tongue swirl over my nipple. I bury my fingers in his hair, groaning as he nips and sucks, the heat building between my legs with every pass of his talented tongue.

"Oh, Will," I moan, and he hums gutturally at the sound.

He kisses his way up my chest, laying a line of wetness and heat on my collarbone, but then his lips are gone, and my eyes fly open, startled at the loss of contact.

His eyes are closed, and he shakes his head before opening them, pulling his head back in surprise at my stare.

"What's the matter?"

"Nothing. I'm just lightheaded from the morphine. I got a little dizzy there for a second. I'm fine though."

I frown at him. "Maybe we should stop . . ."

He stares at me incredulously. "Are you kidding me? When I can finally show you how I feel about you without it hurting me?"

A shiver runs through me. He's so honest and direct when he's medicated, and the depth of his feelings for me is so obvious. I smile as my chest expands, brimming with love and just plain happiness. "All right, sweetheart, if you're sure."

"I'm more than sure," Will answers, and I get lost in a sea of green as he moves closer, until we both close our eyes and our lips meet.

The kiss starts out soft and gentle, but I can feel the hunger building as Will's lips move against mine. My belly twinges as he runs his tongue along my lower lip, and I let him in, reaching up to lace my fingers into his soft auburn hair as we explore each other.

His hand creeps up to my breast again, his index finger circling slowly as my nipple hardens beneath his touch. I gasp as he pinches it gently, groaning against my mouth in a way that makes my thighs clench.

I slide my hands over his shoulders and down to just above his elbows, splaying my fingers on his chest as I plunder his mouth hungrily. Oh my God, what I want to do to him! I want to touch him so badly, I can taste it, but I restrain myself. I don't want him to think about anything other than us right now.

"Oh God," Will groans. "Do you have any idea what you're doing to me? How much I want to . . . I can't, but I want you to know. I want you to know I'd touch every inch of you. I would worship you with my body and make you feel better than anyone's ever made you feel before . . . if I could."

My mouth drops open, shocked and completely aroused. I tend to think of Will as sweet and a bit innocent, but he's making me rethink the innocent.

Suddenly, he pitches forward and grips his belly with a sharp gasp, and our bubble of happiness freezes solid and shatters.

"What is it?" My heart is pounding as I touch his arm. This is our reality. What just happened was a fantasy from a life we cannot have.

He doesn't answer; he's holding his breath between grunts, tension radiating off him as he curls inward.

I move to get up, ready to fly from the room to get Jenny, but he grabs my arm and holds me in place. A minute or two passes, but it feels like years as I watch him struggle. Finally, he collapses back against the bed, breathing harshly.

"Will, what happened?"

"Breakthrough . . . pain," he pants, still trying to calm himself. "Been happening . . . off and on . . . all day."

Fuck. I lay my head on his shoulder and stroke his chest as we cuddle silently, but it's not a happy silence because little shivers are running through him, and the air is heavy around us. Suddenly, he pulls my chin up and crushes his lips to mine, kissing me desperately. I start to respond, but this is all wrong—

"Hey, *hey*," I say, gripping his arm.

He pulls away, angling his head to the side and down, trying to hide his reaction.

"I want to kiss you, but I also want you to tell me what you're feeling. Don't use what's between us to hide from things."

He sinks his teeth into his bottom lip but doesn't look up. "I'm sorry. I let myself forget about things for a while—the morphine makes it easy —but it all came rushing back as soon as the pain hit."

He lifts his eyes to mine, watery and sorrowful, and it's enough to make my heart stop. "I'm scared, Tori. I'm so afraid and confused. I don't know what to do. I thought I had everything figured out, but now . . . I don't want to die."

His words confuse me, and I wonder if he's really thinking clearly or if the morphine is affecting him more than I thought. *What can he do, after all? Is he talking about his DNR?* But this is the first time he's actually voiced that he doesn't want to die. *Oh, Will.*

"Hey, we don't know anything yet. Let's wait until your blood work comes back, and then we'll figure it out."

He lies back against the pillow, eyes closed, silent. He slowly rolls his head toward me, looking at me from under heavy eyelids.

"You're exhausted."

"It's the m-morphine," he says, slurring his words a little. "All of a sudden, I can't keep my eyes open."

"You should rest, then. You've had a busy day."

"Yeah. Somehow it managed to be the best and the worst day all at the same time. This morning I was in the worst pain I've ever felt, and then tonight, you made me feel ... incredible."

"You made me feel incredible too," I say, smiling and blushing fiercely, but his eyes are already closed.

"Sleep well, sweetheart," I tell him, kissing the top of his head before I slide quietly off his bed.

CHAPTER **29**

I stop by to see Will in the morning, but he's still asleep, and there's no way I'm going to wake him. He's worried about what the doctor might tell him today, so I'm guessing he didn't sleep well, but right now, he's out like a light.

As I'm leaving, I stop by the nurses' station where Jenny is typing away. I lean on the desk until she finishes her thought.

"Was he awake?"

"No, he's still sleeping. I'm guessing his night might not have been good, so I didn't want to wake him."

"Hmm," Jenny says, tapping her chin. "The night nurses didn't mention anything, so maybe he did better than you think. Morphine usually knocks him out, so that might have kept him from staying awake and worrying."

"I hope so." I put my hand on top of hers. "I know you can't tell me anything he might find out today, but . . . can you call me if he gets news from Dr. Evans, and he needs support? I don't know if he'd want me with him or not, but I'm worried about him getting bad news all by himself. He was so ready to get out of here, I'm afraid if it's something bad, he's really going to be upset."

"Of course I can. Evans is doing rounds on the floor this morning, but Will's blood work won't be back until mid-afternoon sometime, so I'm thinking he'll see Will this afternoon, close to when you usually come by. I'll tell Will you were here this morning, and if anything happens sooner, I'll call you."

"Thanks." I round the desk and give her a hug.

She holds me close. "Be strong, Tori."

Her words send a shiver of fear down my spine, and as I pull back, I see tears in her eyes. My own eyes widen. I know she doesn't know anything for sure, but . . . *Fuck, we're not even going to get a month, are we?*

"It'll be all right. We'll help him get through it," she says, wiping a stray tear from her cheek.

"You're scaring me, Jenny."

"I'm sorry. I'm worried about him too. I thought he was finally going to catch a break, but—"

"But your liver and spleen don't swell to the point of causing intense pain for no reason," I say.

Jenny nods. "Maybe it won't be that bad though. If his blood work comes back clear, Evans will probably just watch him for a few days, and maybe the swelling will go back down. You never know. Let's keep our fingers crossed."

I look in her eyes; she doesn't really believe what she's saying, but there's no point talking about it until we know for sure. "Thanks, Jenny," I say, giving her another hug. "I better go, but I'll be back at four or sooner if he needs me."

"I'll keep an eye on him."

My day passes slowly, and my thoughts are never far from Will. I don't hear from Jenny all day, so I guess either Will was okay with whatever he found out, or he hasn't found out anything yet.

As I'm walking from the elevators, I freeze as I see Dr. Evans leaving Will's room. I watch him come up the hall, eyes on the floor, and as he passes me, he sighs and shakes his head.

My stomach drops, and I feel queasy. I quicken my steps, the adrenaline already starting to speed up my heart. I can hear muffled sound as I approach the door, and although I'm terrified, I make myself push it open. My heart shatters at the sight before me.

Will is hunched over, face buried in the crook of his elbow as he sobs. His body shakes with the force of his anguish, and my knees go weak from the sound of his pain. I've seen Will break down a few times, but this is beyond anything I've ever witnessed.

I rush over to him, putting my arm around his back, trying to soothe him, but he thrusts out his elbow, hitting me in the shoulder and pushing me away.

He sobs pitifully, and suddenly, he's yelling. "I'm never going to leave here! I'm going to die in this room! *Fuck*! I actually let myself hope! I am *so fucking* stupid! Oh God, I can't do this anymore! I just wanna go home! I can't stay here! I need . . . to go—" While he's shouting, he reaches up his sleeve and yanks on his IV, crying out in surprise and pain because it's not an ordinary IV line; it's a PICC line with a catheter threaded through his vein almost all the way to his heart.

I lurch forward, pushing his hand out of the way and gripping his arm over the insertion point to try to stop the bleeding. With my other hand, I find the call button, managing to hit it more than once before Will really begins to fight me.

"No, let me go! I can't stay here! I have to leave!" he screams, his eyes wild as he thrashes in the bed, trying to push me away. But my grip on his arm is solid, and he doesn't have the strength he once did. I'm able to hold him down but just barely.

Jenny's voice comes over the intercom. "What do you need, Will?"

"Jenny! Bring a sedative!" I yell as Will continues to struggle against me.

"Let me go! I have to go!" he cries, tears still streaming down his cheeks.

"Will, please!" I beg him, trying not to hurt him as he fights against my grip. Each second feels like an hour, and pain surges through me with every frantic beat of my heart until Jenny finally comes flying through the door.

She takes in the scene for half a second then swears when she sees the blood all over the right side of the bed. "Is the catheter still in his arm?"

"Yes." I grate the word out, still trying to hold down a fighting Will.

Jenny rushes to the far side of the bed and injects whatever she's got into the IV port on the PICC line. It takes about a minute, but Will's movements become more feeble until he finally passes out underneath me.

"Holy shit! What happened in here?" Jenny exclaims, but I can't answer her yet. I'm gasping as if I just ran a marathon while I still hold on tightly to Will, unable to let go.

"Tori. Tori, you can let his arm go. I need to see how much damage he did to his line."

Jenny gently uncurls my fingers from Will's bicep, and I stare at the blood that covers them. Will's blood, that's all but useless to him because it can no longer help him fight off infection. What's coating my fingers is the reason he's dying, the reason I won't get to spend my life with the man I love.

My stomach turns, and I stumble to Will's bathroom, landing on my knees and heaving up my lunch as I grip the bowl with my still-bloody fingers. I lean my forehead against the wall, panting, as Jenny pulls my hair back over my shoulders.

"Is he all right?" I whisper, trying to get ahold of myself.

"He's out cold, and he probably will be for a few more hours. He got his PICC line halfway out, but on the bright side, he didn't pull it all the way out. I stopped the bleeding for now, but I'm going to have to rethread the catheter, and his arm is gonna be pretty damn sore for a few days.

"Are *you* all right? Blood doesn't usually upset you . . ." Jenny trails off, rubbing my back.

I squeeze my eyes shut, fighting back the tears that threaten to escape. "It wasn't the sight of blood. I started thinking about how *his* blood is the reason he's dying, and—"

"Oh, honey, don't think like that. Let's get you cleaned up, okay?"

Jenny helps me up from the cold, hard tile and leads me over to the sink where she turns on the water. She pulls my hands under the stream, washing away Will's blood while I turn my head away.

"What the hell happened?"

I take a deep breath and find that some of my composure has returned although my heart is still aching and tears sting my eyes. "I don't know. I saw Dr. Evans leaving the room as I came down the hall. He didn't look too happy, so I walked faster. By the time I got here, Will was already hysterical. I don't know what Evans told him, but it must have been bad."

"Dammit, I *told* Evans to find me before he talked to Will! He's an excellent oncologist, but sometimes, he focuses too much on the patient's physical condition without taking their mental state into account. If he'd told me, at least I could have been here with Will even if I didn't have time to call you."

"He was only alone for a minute or two. It probably would have happened even if you or I had been here. Whatever Evans told him must have destroyed all the hope he had—" I break off as a sob tears from my chest, and Jenny pulls me into her arms. I cry, but the sound is just tired and broken. I'm mourning the loss of my own hope even though I don't yet know the reason.

All of a sudden, I need to see him. I push away from Jenny and approach his bed with unsteady steps. I flinch at the sight of the blood that's spattered on his nightshirt and blankets—including his afghan—and I focus instead on his face. His chin rests almost on his shoulder, and he's completely still—more so than he ever is when he's asleep. It scares me because he doesn't breathe any deeper or sigh as he usually does. All signs of pain are gone from his angelic face, and as his anguished cries echo through my head, for the very first time, I wonder if he wouldn't be better off if all the pain were over.

I take his hand between mine, and the tears flow down my cheeks freely. I can't bear the thought of losing him, but watching him suffer like this is even worse. I can't imagine the world without him in it. He's become such a big part of my life over the last few weeks—the gaping hole that will be left when he leaves will consume me.

But it's not about me.

It's about what's best for him, but right now, I don't know what that is. He needs . . . peace. And the emotional ups and downs of the past few weeks are wrecking him to the point where he completely lost his shit today. I've seen patients in his position become hysterical before, but I never thought Will could become unhinged quite that much. I was wrong.

I don't know what the right answer is, but I know I have to be with him. I need to take care of him—in any way I can—to ensure this doesn't happen again.

"I'm going to get Weaver to authorize more Ativan for him until things get better . . . or worse. And I want to stay with him tonight. I don't want him to wake up alone."

"I think that's a very good idea," Jenny says, putting her hand on my shoulder. "Why don't you go feed Sebastian and grab some dinner? Will is going to be out for at least three or four more hours, and I need to reposition his PICC line and get him cleaned up. I'll let the night nurse know you're going to stay if you're not back by seven."

I'm reluctant to leave him, but she's right. If I want to sleep here, I need to take care of some things first, and while Will is unconscious is the best time to do them.

Saying goodbye to Jenny, I hurry home, moving through my tasks as quickly as possible so I can get back to the hospital. I go to my craft closet and pull out another afghan so I can replace Will's green one while I clean off the bloodstains. This one is also a basket weave, but it's cornflower-colored. It won't match his eyes, but hopefully he'll like it almost as much. I change into track pants and a t-shirt and pack a small bag of necessities plus my work clothes for tomorrow.

Will is still deeply asleep when I return. He looks . . . peaceful. All the blood has been cleaned up, his PICC line has been fixed, and he's wearing a fresh nightshirt. Dropping my bag beside his bed, I caress his cheek with my fingers. I think for a moment about pulling out my Kindle, but the truth is, even though it's barely nine o'clock, I'm exhausted. I have no idea when Will is going to wake and if he's going to need me to stay up with him when he does, so it's probably a good idea to get some sleep now while I can.

I glance at the couch under the window, but it's too far from him to provide the comfort I want to give him, and what if he wakes up and doesn't notice I'm here? No, I'm going to sleep on his bed with him, so I'm awake the moment he is.

I shift him gently into his usual spot for weekend movie watching, brushing the hair from his forehead and making sure he seems comfortable before crawling onto the mattress beside him.

Someone is running their fingers through my hair. It feels nice, so I lie still and enjoy it, floating on the edge of consciousness. And then I remember I live alone with Will's cat for company, and suddenly I'm wide awake.

It takes me a second to realize where I am, but the semi-darkness and the bright green eyes watching me catapult my mind into the present, and everything that happened today flashes through my head.

Will looks calm, his eyes heavy-lidded as he watches me. I don't think the effects of the sedative have completely worn off yet, but something must have woken him.

"Hey, sweetheart," I say, bringing my hand up to stroke the side of his face.

Will manages a weak smile, but his eyes fall closed. "Wha happen'd?"

"You had a bad day, but you're okay now. I'll tell you all about it in the morning, okay?"

"'kay," Will answers, and he's silent for so long that I wonder if he's fallen back to sleep. Suddenly, he opens his eyes again, his lips drawing up into a smirk. "This isn't the way I wanted to sleep with you, you know," he says drunkenly, raising an eyebrow at me.

Warmth floods my chest, and I giggle like a schoolgirl. It just feels so good to see him being playful, and his adorableness goes up exponentially when he's been drugged.

"But . . . I got you in my bed anyway." He tells me this as he runs his finger down my nose.

"Yes, you certainly did. And I'm going to stay until the morning if it's okay with you."

"'course. We should have done this s-sooner," he says, shifting to lay his head on my shoulder.

I put my arm around him, and he snuggles into my side, wincing as his distended belly comes into contact with my hip. "Are you all right?"

"'m perfect," he whispers, sighing as he cuddles closer.

"Go to sleep, sweetheart." I place a soft kiss on his forehead.

He's out almost instantly, and I rest my chin on the top of his head, burying my nose in his soft auburn locks. I fall asleep thinking about what kissing Will feels like, not allowing myself to think about what happened today.

I wake much as I did in the middle of the night, except this time, soft fingers are running over my forehead and down to my temple. I'm smiling before I'm even truly aware.

He pauses then resumes as I open my eyes to brilliant green. The look on his face floors me. He's looking at me with so much, oh God, it has to be love, that I pull in a sharp breath. I can feel it, radiating off him in waves as I lose myself in his eyes. And in that moment, I know. Even if he doesn't yet know it himself, I know he loves me. Will is in love with me.

"So beautiful," he whispers, his fingers tickling my cheek as they slide down and come to rest on my lips.

Suddenly, his gaze clouds with desperation and pain I can't even put a name to, and I have to bite my lip and close my own eyes to keep from losing it. *I love you.* God, I just want to say it. I want the whole world to know I'm in love with the sweetest, most wonderful man there ever was, but he's so fragile right now. The last thing I want to do is make him push me away at a time when he needs my support so much. He's not ready yet. I can only hope he gets there before we're out of time.

When I open my eyes again, he's looking down, but I reach out and lift his chin, a shiver rolling through me as I'm once again caught in a sea of green. I smile softly. "Good morning, sweetheart. How are you feeling?"

"You spent the night," he says, ignoring my question.

"Yes, I did. I was worried about you, and I didn't want you to be alone, even for a minute."

Will sighs. "I'm so sorry, Tori. I know I put you through hell yesterday. I just completely lost it when . . . when I found out . . ." He's breathing heavily, and as I watch, his eyes lose focus.

I cup his cheek, massaging in gentle circles. "Breathe, Will. I'm right here with you. We'll get through this. What did Dr. Evans tell you exactly?"

"You don't already know?"

"No. Jenny isn't supposed to tell me, and when I got here yesterday, all that mattered to me was taking care of you—getting you calm and stable again."

He frowns and looks down at his afghan, eyebrows drawn together in confusion. "This is . . . different, isn't it?"

The fact that he's not sure concerns me, but he's had so many meds through his system in the last twenty-four hours that I'm going to chalk it up to that. "Yes. You got blood on your green one, so I brought you another one until I can get that one clean."

His eyes soften, and a hint of a smile touches his lips. "I'm sorry I did that. I honestly don't know what came over me. I felt so desperate; I had this overwhelming need to escape. I was aware of what I was doing, but I couldn't control it. It was like instinct or something, and I didn't know how to calm down again."

"It's all right, sweetheart. I'm just glad I was coming down the hall when Dr. Evans left your room. You might have really hurt yourself if you'd been all alone. And it might not have really been you," I tell him, running my fingers into his hair. "Morphine can cause mood swings, and you're on a truckload of it right now. I'd be willing to bet that's why you couldn't get control of your emotions. Are you still feeling like you're high?"

"Yes," Will answers, closing his eyes and resting his head back against his pillow. "It's better than yesterday—Evans told me the side effects would lessen the longer I'm on it—but I still feel like I just took a big hit of something. I'm trying my best not to enjoy it," he says, smirking at me.

"It'll get better. I promise. You're already a lot better than you were yesterday—even I can tell."

"Yesterday." Will sighs, shaking his head. "Jenny had to sedate me, didn't she?"

"Yes, she did. You weren't calming down, and you'd pulled your PICC line halfway out. I was barely able to hold on to you, and I was so afraid I was hurting you—"

Will takes my face in his hands and presses his lips gently to mine. "You didn't hurt me. I'm still on morphine; I can barely feel any pain right now. I'm so fucking sorry you had to do that."

He bows his head, squeezing his eyes shut, his hands shaking as they still cup my cheeks.

I raise my own hand and wipe away the tear that escapes, then lift his chin and press my lips to his—an echo of the comfort he just gave me. "It wasn't your fault. Everything's okay now."

"Weaver put me back on Ativan, too, didn't he?" Will asks, not opening his eyes. "I can tell because I'm upset, but it's . . . muted."

"Sweetheart, I think you need it."

"Is it normal for people in my . . . position to need anxiety medication?" he asks, peering up at me from under his eyelashes.

"It can be, yes."

"So . . . no." He shakes his head in frustration.

"Will, you have to remember, most of the people I've helped before were much older than you. They'd had long lives and done what they wanted to, or at least they'd had the opportunity.

"And no one I've ever befriended was alone by choice then reversed that decision and allowed loved ones back into their life after a long separation. Not to mention the shock of your father showing up here. You've been under a tremendous amount of stress, and I think that's also a big part of what has you off-balance. And it doesn't matter what anyone else felt or didn't feel. You're doing the best you can, and if you need a little help to keep yourself calm, then that's okay."

"Fuck!" Will swears. "Nothing's okay!"

"Will, what did Dr. Evans tell you?"

He huffs out a frustrated breath and stares down at the new afghan, but there's no tracing today. His fingers press into the weave over his thigh, depressing the skin. "Well, the blood infection is completely gone, but they can't discharge me. They're . . . watching me."

"Why?"

Will sighs again, his voice quavering as he speaks. "Because my white blood cell count has shot through the roof. The cancer elevates it to begin with, but something has made it go really high, really fast, and that, along with the increase in swelling in my liver and spleen, makes Evans think something really bad is happening. We just don't know what it is yet."

I do my best not to react, but it takes me a minute to regain my composure. "How do you feel?"

"About the same as I have for the last few days. I might be a little more tired, but I figured that was the morphine. I haven't noticed anything else." He bites his lip, closing his eyes tightly. "The odds are pretty good that it's another infection, that I'm going to get really sick again."

As I watch him, I also hear what he doesn't say—that this might be the last time he gets sick, that if he keeps his DNR in place, he could die this time.

I close my eyes and breathe deeply, trying to get control of myself. I knew it had to be something like this, but hearing him say it, hearing the desolation in his voice is breaking me. But I can't break. He broke last night; I broke the day before, and it's just not an option. I have to stay strong for him so I can help him find the strength within himself.

"I'm so sorry, Will," I say, pulling him close to me. He lays his head on my shoulder, but there are no tears this morning, no hysterics. He's resigned, as if he's already accepted that he's not going to get to leave here. Pain flares in my chest as I hold him, and we both grip each other a little tighter. We don't know how many hugs we have left.

And from that moment on, something changes in Will. Some part of him shuts down, and I can feel the distance start to grow between us again. I don't want to leave him, but he convinces me to go to work, telling me he's tired and needs to rest. How can I argue with that? But I can see the change, and it's certainly not for the better.

And he's suffering. He's anxious all the time, and the Ativan is the only thing keeping him from having full-blown panic attacks. I know part of it is because he's facing his death, but something is . . . off. I've been through this and seen enough variations to know that the way he's feeling isn't normal. Some sort of conflict is raging inside him, but for the life of me, I can't figure out what it is.

We don't have to wait very long to figure out what's going on with Will —by Friday morning, he's developed a cough. It started out dry and raspy, but it's quickly become wet and heavy, and there's fear in his eyes every time he does it. Pneumonia is a leading killer of lymphoma patients. Dr. Evans takes a sample from Will's lungs immediately, but it'll take a few days to culture whatever is causing the infection and get a diagnosis.

Will's relationship with Jenny has also deteriorated over the past few days. They're very cool with each other all of a sudden, and several times, I've caught them breaking off their conversation as I enter the room. They seem to be extremely frustrated with each other. I know

Will isn't going to tell me what's going on, and Jenny would have told me by now if she could, so I try to rein in my curiosity.

I spend all day Saturday and Sunday with him, but it's nothing like our previous weekends. He's quiet and preoccupied, and by Sunday evening, he's running a low-grade fever. This new development is obviously frightening him, but he doesn't say anything. He just holds my hand, squeezing it a bit tighter every time he coughs. He hasn't kissed me since Thursday, but I chalk it up to him not feeling well. I'm not doing a good job of fooling myself.

He's been dozing through our movie, and I know I should go and let him rest, but I can't bring myself to leave his side. I feel as if he's starting to slip away from me. I know he's getting sick, and I should probably just blame it on that, but there's something . . . more. I reach over and brush the damp hair from his forehead, and he opens weary eyes to stare at me.

"I should go, sweetheart. I think you need your sleep."

"I don't wanna sleep," he mumbles, squeezing my hand a little tighter and watching me, his gaze calm but sad and so deeply thoughtful. I want to ask him what he does want, but I swear I can almost see all the things he can't have swirling in his eyes.

"Okay, then I'll stay a while longer." I continue stroking my fingers through his hair, and we watch each other silently—both of us too afraid to voice our fears and too worried to voice our hopes or feelings.

"I'm so glad you're here, Tori," he whispers as his eyes fall closed, unable to resist his exhaustion any longer.

"I am, too," I answer, leaning in to place a soft kiss on his forehead before finally mustering the will to leave him for the night.

CHAPTER 30

On Monday morning, I arrive at Will's room around eight o'clock, as usual. As I near the door, I hear raised voices, but with it closed all the way, I can't make out who else is talking or what's being said. I knock, which is something I haven't done for weeks, and immediately, I hear Will call for me to come in.

As I enter, I see Jenny standing with her arms crossed, glaring angrily at him, while Will glares right back, his expression stony.

"Ask her."

"That's enough, Jenny!" Will yells at her, his fever-bright eyes flashing.

"Ask me what?"

Will takes a deep breath as he lowers his head. When he raises his eyes to me, I can tell he's trying to be relaxed, but his anger is bubbling right under the surface.

"It's nothing, Tori," he says, smiling, but the warmth of it is forced. "Jenny was just leaving."

His stare is cold as he watches Jenny make her way across the room, but she turns in the doorway and stares right back at him.

"Think hard about this, Will."

I swear I've never seen him look so angry as Jenny turns without another word, pulling the door shut quietly behind her.

Will is seething, huffing out frustrated breaths as he covers his face with his hand.

"What the hell was that about?"

"Fucking Jenny! She needs to learn . . . to mind her own . . . goddamn business!"

"Will!" I admonish him, shocked by his harshness. "I'm sure she's only trying to help you—"

"No one can help me," he says bitterly, curling an arm over his belly and wincing. I haven't seen that very much in the last few days, and I certainly didn't miss it.

"You're in pain."

Will nods, wincing again. "They had to . . . cut back my morphine."

He loosens his grip on his middle, and I take his hand. It's warm, but thankfully no warmer than yesterday. "Why?"

"Because I'm having trouble breathing . . . and the morphine . . . makes it worse."

My eyes roam over him. The circles under his eyes are dark today; I wonder how much rest he actually got last night. The hand I'm not holding is clutching at the center of his nightshirt over his chest, and his breathing is labored and uneven.

"Does your chest hurt?" I ask as I squeeze his hand, but I'm pretty sure I already know the answer.

He closes his eyes and nods. "More than anything else, and that's . . . saying something. It's so tight. And it's definitely . . . harder to breathe."

He raises his eyes to me, and the sorrow and fear there is paralyzing. "I think this is going . . . to be really bad."

He's been keeping me at a distance, but I can't handle the weight of his words without comfort, and I know he's suffering without our closeness, too, even if he's unwilling to admit it. I get up and perch on the side of his bed, wrapping my arms around him and resting my head on his chest.

He immediately starts coughing, and I lift my head as he scrambles for a tissue, covering his mouth as the spasms shake him. He sounds absolutely horrible. His cough is deep and wet, and it sounds as if there's a ton of mucus in his chest that he should be coughing up, but he can't. And the effort is causing him terrible pain—I can see it on his face and in the iron grip of his arm over his belly, every muscle tensed. It goes on for what feels like an eternity, but I imagine it's only a minute or two before he collapses back against the mattress, exhausted.

"Oh, sweetheart." I lean in to hug him again but I'm careful not to put any weight on his chest.

"I'm gonna get . . . you sick," he whispers.

"I have a fully functional immune system. I'll take my chances."

He leans his cheek against my forehead, and I smile a little because it's the first real show of affection he's given me since Thursday. I want to just lie here and enjoy it, but my curiosity about what he and Jenny were arguing over is too great.

"Does what Jenny wants you to ask me have anything to do with what's been bothering you these last few days?" I lift my head so I can see the truth in his eyes.

He doesn't disappoint because his eyes widen and then narrow, giving me the answer before he even opens his mouth.

"Tori," he says warningly.

"Sweetheart, I don't want to upset you, but I know something's on your mind. Something more than whether or not you have pneumonia. I'm not going to press you, but I want you to know I'm here when you're ready to talk about it."

Will says nothing, but he nuzzles his face into my hair, and I hold him a little tighter. He again convinces me to go to work even though my mind is completely focused on him at this point. I wander through my day seeing patients, barely able to concentrate enough to do my job because my head is filled with thoughts of whether or not Will is coming down with pneumonia and what might be bothering him that has him so withdrawn.

By three o'clock, I give up and head back to his room. I open the door quietly and find him staring down at his afghan, his face a mask of sorrow. *Uh oh.*

I cross the room and take his hand, but he closes his eyes and turns his face away from me. He's having even more trouble breathing than he was this morning—his respiration is shallow, and he seems to be fighting to pull in each breath.

"What happened, sweetheart? Did you see Dr. Evans this afternoon?"

Will nods slowly but doesn't volunteer any other information.

I take a deep breath and vow not to get aggravated. Will needs to come first despite the fact that this uncertainty is driving me insane too. "What did he say? Do you have pneumonia?"

Again, Will nods, but this time I don't have to pull the details out of him. "Bacterial . . . I forget . . . the exact name. He got the results . . . this morning."

"It'll be okay. We'll get you through this," I tell him, trying to offer comfort over the pounding of my heart. This is better than not knowing. At least now we know what we're dealing with, and the doctors will know how to treat it.

But Will doesn't look comforted at all. In fact, he looks even more upset.

"Sweetheart, what is it? What else did he tell you?"

Will drops his head, staring down at the afghan and looking more defeated than I've ever seen him. He whispers so quietly, I have to lean forward to hear him.

"Evans asked me . . . if I want them . . . to give me drugs . . . to make me comfortable."

I inhale sharply, and I swear my heart stops. *No!* "D-does that mean . . . does he think . . ." I'm barely able to form the words. I take a deep breath and force them out, and each one pierces me as it passes my lips. "Does that mean he thinks you're not going to make it through this?"

"Not without . . . respiratory support. And if I keep my DNR . . . they can't give it to me."

"But if you just let them help you, you can get through this, and you'll get better again. You could still live for a long time yet—"

"Yes, but how?" he says, cutting me off. "In the hospital, unable to eat . . . or do anything for myself? Too sick to hold you? To kiss you? To do anything . . . I still want to do?"

I become still as I realize what side of this argument he's on. I don't know if he's trying to convince himself or me, but his words tell me what decision he's leaning toward.

"W-what . . . what are you going to do?"

"I don't know," he whispers, his eyes watery from unshed tears. "It would be so easy . . . to say yes. I'm in so . . . much pain.

"Tori, I'm so fucking tired. I'm tired . . . of doctors and hospitals. I'm tired . . . of fevers and pain . . . and I'm tired of seeing . . . the pity on the faces . . . of everyone who . . . walks through that door. But most of all, I'm tired of being . . . so weak and sick . . . that all I can do . . . is lie here and wait . . . for it to end."

I close my eyes, trying to take in what he's said, but it's too much for me. I squeeze my eyes shut as I try not to sob. The pain in my chest, my head, is almost unbearable. But I know it's nothing compared to his. I shiver and pull the strength from somewhere in myself to utter the hardest words I've ever had to say.

"Will, if you need to say yes, then do it. You've fought so long and so hard—if you think it's time, then let go. I'll be here for you, no matter what."

He says nothing, but he pulls me toward him, and I help him move over through gasps and moans so I can lie beside him on his bed. He curls into me, his shallow breaths harsh as he fights through the pain of moving so he can get close to me. When he finally stills, it takes him at least five minutes to stop shaking and to slow his breathing to something near what it was when I came in.

He's going to give in.

He hasn't said it, but I can tell from the way he's lying against me. He's defeated, and he's only looking for comfort, for reassurance that I'll still be here for him. He might not know he's made up his mind yet, but I do. All I can do is wait for him to come to a conscious decision, then tell me.

I want to argue with him. I want to tell him whatever it will take to convince him to hang on; to convince him to hope that things could get better and to fight until his last breath; to fight for himself; to fight for me. To fight for *us*. But I know how incredibly selfish that is even if I want it for him, too. I can't ask him to continue to endure this. I *can't*.

So I do the only thing I *can* do. I hold him as tenderly as I can, running my fingers through his hair as tears flow freely down my face.

But there are no tears from Will. He's already moved beyond that point.

The silence is only broken when Will coughs, and I instinctively hold him tighter to try to lessen his pain. I think he dozes off a few times between spells, but I can't be sure.

Inside my head, I'm screaming. It's taking everything I have to keep from shaking, to keep from letting him see the raw pain that's coursing through me. *This can't be the way it ends! Not after what we've found with each other, not after I've discovered what an amazing, beautiful soul Will is. No! God can't take him from me. He can't take Will from this world where he creates such beauty and has such passion—where I'm in love with him, and I'm going to die too when he leaves me.*

My selfish thoughts rage on and on, and I let them. I let myself work it through in my head until finally, my thoughts come back to him, to how long and hard he's fought this; to how much pain he's in and how sick he's likely to become. My words to him were brave earlier, much braver than I actually am because I haven't yet found a way to let him go. I *need* to find a way to let him go.

My thoughts are interrupted as Will begins to cough, and it's a powerful and long spell that leaves him gasping in pain. I hold him tightly, trying to channel my strength and my love through my touch and to keep my own pain hidden inside.

When he's able to breathe again, he pulls his head back from me but looks down at the afghan. He fidgets for a moment even though it's painful for him. I tense involuntarily, and I hope he can't feel it.

"I have to ask you something. I need to know, before . . ." He swallows painfully, and his hands begin to shake.

The fact that he's asking and not telling me something sends relief through my stiffened muscles. "Anything, sweetheart. What do you need to know?"

Suddenly, his eyes meet mine, intense and desperate. "What would have happened . . . if we'd met . . . and I wasn't sick?"

My eyes widen. I don't know what I expected him to ask, but that certainly wasn't it. Why does he want to torture himself with what might have been? I've been sitting here for almost two hours struggling not to contemplate that in any detail, and *that's* what he wants to talk about? Won't knowing I would have fallen for him and that I want to spend my life with him just make what he's going through now that much worse?

Should I tell him I love him? Is that what he needs to know? Will that help him make the decision he's struggling with? I look at him appraisingly, and what I see in his eyes is . . . fear. And I know, without a doubt, the source of that fear. He's afraid I'm in love with him. He doesn't want me to suffer that much when he dies, and he doesn't want to acknowledge what we could have had. So I decide not to go that far, but I can't lie to him. I can't deny what we could have been. What we *would* have been.

I look him directly in the eyes, and I know my gaze says what my words don't. I can't help it—I can't look at him any other way. "I would have been attracted to you. I would have wanted you to ask me out on a date. Things would have been as they are now, except we would have had time for them to go further. And I would have hoped they would go much further."

He closes his eyes and drops his chin to his chest. I don't know what I've done, but I break out in goosebumps as I watch the change sweep over him. His hands begin to shake again, and when he finally raises his eyes to mine, I gasp.

His eyes are alive again, and the sea of green is whipped up into a hurricane of emotions, too many for me to even name. There is so much conflict and pain and sorrow, I don't know how he can contain it. Maybe he can't.

"I need . . . to be alone now." His voice quavers with emotion as he pants out the words.

"Will! Oh God, what did I do?" I beg as the panic spreads down my spine and flairs at the base.

"Tori, I can't . . . Please go!" he cries, his voice breaking as he bites into his lip.

"I can't leave you like this! Not when I know you're going to break down the minute I close the door! Please, let me help you. What can I do to help you?"

He stares down at his afghan, breathing heavily, and by some miracle, he manages to get himself almost under control. "Tori, please. I need some time . . . to think about this, and I need to do it . . . by myself. I'll be all right, I promise. I'll text you . . . in a little while. I just need time."

I'm not convinced. At all. But how can I insist that I stay when he's begging me to go? How can I deny him anything? "You promise you'll text me? I'll come back later tonight if you want me to—"

"I promise. Please, Tori. Do this . . . for me." He's pleading, staring into my eyes.

I'm fighting to hold back my own tears, but I nod. "All right. Call or text me if you need anything. I'll be back first thing tomorrow morning."

"I will. I'm going to sit here for a while . . . and then I'm going to try . . . to get some sleep."

I slide off the bed, trying to convince my feet to carry me from the room, but it's just not working. I know I shouldn't be leaving him, not like this, but I can't force him to let me stay.

"Goodnight, Tori," he says, and somehow his words convince my reluctant feet to obey him. I desperately want to lean in and kiss him, at least on the forehead, but I know instinctively that doing so will unleash the storm, and I can't do that to him, not when I said I would go. So I turn and stumble from the room, forcing myself not to look back as I close the door.

I move away quickly because I know if I hear any sound at all from behind that door, I won't be able to stop myself from running back to him.

"Tori?"

Jenny is standing at the nurses' station, and her eyes widen as I look up at her. "What happened? Is he okay?"

"He's . . . No, he's far from okay," I say as she winds an arm around me. "He not going to lift his DNR, and he's going to let you give him drugs to make him comfortable."

Jenny gasps. "He told you that?"

"No, but I think he *will* tell me tomorrow. I'm not sure he's consciously made the decision yet, but I know. I could tell by the way he was acting today."

"It's early," Jenny says, looking up at the clock on the wall. "Why are you leaving so soon? Did something happen?"

"Yes, and I don't understand it. He asked me what would have happened if we'd met and he wasn't sick, and I told him that things would have gone as they have and even further."

"Oh *fuck*! I honestly didn't think he'd ask you. Did you tell him you love him?"

"No, because I knew it would be too much for him. Somehow, what little I did say was too much anyway because he got really upset and told me he needed some time alone."

"Oh goddammit," Jenny says, covering her mouth with her hand.

"Why, Jenny? Why did he ask me that? Is that what you were insisting he ask me when I walked in this morning? How does knowing that have any effect on what's going on right now?"

Jenny stares at me, and I suddenly realize what I see in her eyes. It's pity. "Tori, you know I can't. I want to more than I've ever wanted anything, but I can't do it. He has to tell you himself. Just know I'm doing everything I can to help you both."

She stares at me more intensely. "I still think you need to tell him you love him. Even though your instinct says not to . . . Even though he reacted the way he did today, he needs to know because I think he's in denial about it, and he needs to see the truth. He *has to* see the truth. It could make all the difference in the world."

I don't understand, but I'm too tired and confused to try to figure it out. So, I place my trust in Jenny. "I'll tell him. I'll tell him tomorrow."

"Good," Jenny says, looking relieved. "Now, go home. I'll make sure the night nurses keep a close eye on him."

Because he's going to get sicker. I'm honestly afraid to go home, but short of sleeping in the waiting room, I see no other choice.

Jenny must sense my reluctance. "I'll tell them to call you if things get bad or if he needs anything, okay?"

"All right." I force a small smile. "He promised me he would text me later, too."

"Good. Now go home and get some rest. You look exhausted. In fact, it's nearly seven, so I'll walk you out."

Jenny shepherds me from the building and to my car and gives me a hug as we stand beside the door. "Hang on, honey," she tells me, squeezing me tight. "You're doing the right thing. No matter what happens, being with him is the right thing, and I know you'll never regret it."

"No, I won't," I answer, because right now, that's the only thing I *am* sure of.

CHAPTER 31

It's eight a.m., and I'm on my way to the hospital. Will texted me around nine o'clock last night—just a short message saying he was all right, and he was going to bed—and I texted back that I hoped he slept well.

I didn't sleep well though. I spent the night wishing the morning wouldn't come because although I'm anxious to see him, I don't want time to move forward. The roller coaster we're on feels like it's almost reached its peak, and we're about to plunge into the abyss from which there's no escape. A feeling of dread has been growing in the pit of my stomach since yesterday when I figured out Will was going to give in.

I had to drag myself out of bed this morning; the only thing keeping me moving was the thought of seeing him and holding him again. I'm not going to work today. I'm going to sit with him all day if he'll let me because my need to be close to him right now is overwhelming. *Please, God, don't let him try to push me away!*

Jenny greets me with a big hug as I walk down the fourth floor hallway, nearly knocking me over. "How are you this morning? Did you sleep?"

"A little. Did *he* sleep last night?"

"Not much, but he's sleeping now. The night nurses told me that around four o'clock, he finally asked for something to help him.

Between the pain and the shortness of breath, he couldn't settle down enough on his own."

"I'm going to stay today. I just can't stand to be away from him right now."

Jenny shakes her head, and there's pity in her eyes. "I'm so sorry, Tori. I know how hard this is. But I think you should consider going to work, at least for the morning. They gave him Ambien at four, so he's going to be out at least until lunchtime, maybe longer, given his condition. I think you need to keep yourself occupied right now—sitting at Will's bedside while he sleeps is going to drive you crazy."

Despite my desire to stay, I know she's right. If I go in there and stare at him for the next four hours, I'm going to be a weepy mess by the time he wakes up, and that's not going to do either of us any good.

"I'll call you the minute he wakes up."

Dammit, how am I going to keep my mind occupied for the next few hours when all I can think about is him? I trudge down to my office and decide to keep my morning appointments. Maybe focusing on someone else's problems will help me forget about my own.

Lunchtime rolls around, and I haven't heard from Jenny, so I call up to the fourth floor to see what's going on. Jenny is with another patient, but Heidi, one of the other nurses, tells me Will is still sleeping.

By three o'clock, I can't take it anymore, and I find myself standing outside his room.

I'm afraid.

He's getting sicker, and his difficulty breathing is scaring me. I'm also terrified he's going to tell me he's giving up. What the hell am I going to do if that's his decision? I know I told him to let go if he needed to, but I think a part of me believes he won't do it, that he can't give up on life— and on us. I don't know how I'll react if he says he's going to give in and die without a fight.

I mentally give myself a good shake. Will is waiting for me on the other side of that door, and here I stand, worried about my own feelings.

As I turn the handle, the sound of his labored, wheezing breaths assaults me. *Oh God, it's worse than yesterday. Much worse.*

His eyes are closed, but the tension in his muscles tells me he's not sleeping. And he's in motion—he rolls his head restlessly, and there are beads of sweat on his forehead.

I'm across the room and holding his hand before I even realize I've cleared the doorway, and he angles his head toward me, his brilliant green eyes sparkling with fever.

He tenses the moment he realizes it's me, and his gaze is sad and . . . distant.

And suddenly, I feel it. It's almost a physical sensation, as if the floor between us has fractured, creating a void I can't cross. He's begun to move in a direction I can't. He's seeing things I can't see, feeling things I can't feel—it's the difference in mindset between the living and the dying that always comes, and it's beginning for Will. It's happened to every patient I've ever helped as they've gotten closer to death—they start to see things in a different way—to understand. Normally, I find it peaceful to watch, but as I look at Will, I can't breathe. *No!* He can't let go! *I* can't let him go! I'm not ready! I don't know if I'll ever be ready, but oh God, I'm not ready now!

He's looking down at his afghan, so he doesn't see that I'm nearly hyperventilating. "I told him yes," he whispers, and he closes his eyes, his face scrunching up in sorrow. "Too much pain. I couldn't . . . no more. So they gave . . . me enough morphine . . . but now it's really hard . . . to breathe."

No.

No. No! *No!*

My chest constricts as my heart breaks into pieces, and I have to cover my mouth to keep the cry of anguish from escaping. I want to be happy that the pain will be over for him, and he'll be at peace. I try to force myself to think only of him, but I can't manage it because I'm the one that will be left. He'll be gone, and I'll be left to suffer with the loss of the only person I've ever truly loved.

I can't do it.

"No. Oh God, Will, no." The words come tumbling out of my mouth, and he reacts as if I've slapped him.

"I'm sorry, Tori. I can't tell you . . . how sorry I am. For both of us." He closes his eyes, and my heart breaks a little more as his hands begin to shake.

"I shouldn't even . . . be talking to you. I've had so much morphine . . . and my fever is climbing . . . from the pneumonia."

"Why, Will? Why does that mean you shouldn't talk to me?"

"Because I know . . . I'm going to tell you . . . things I shouldn't! Goddammit!" He swears, pounding his fist on the mattress as he struggles for breath. "I shouldn't do this to you, but I can't let go . . . without you knowing. Without you understanding . . . what you've done to me," he says, closing his eyes as tears roll down his cheeks. "I was ready to die, and now . . ."

I hold my breath, knowing this is the turning point of it all, the moment everything has been building to since I first walked into this room two months ago.

"And now I want something. More than I've ever wanted . . . anything before . . . but it's too late . . . and I can't have it."

"What do you want, Will?"

"Oh God, Tori . . . I want you. I love you. I think I fell . . . in love with you . . . the moment I laid eyes on you . . . but I couldn't let myself . . . feel it because I'd already . . . made my choice. There was nothing for me . . . but now . . . there's so much I want to do, so much I want to give to you."

Suddenly, the fire in his eyes freezes solid and turns flinty and cold. "But I can't. I should never have let you in . . . because now I've made it . . . worse for myself . . . and God knows . . . what I've done to you. I can't do this to either of us . . . anymore. I can't watch you watch me . . . get worse. God help me, I just . . . can't do it."

He's almost hyperventilating, but somehow, he manages to maintain his control. He bites his lip—hard—but he raises his eyes to me, wild and tormented. "Tori, I want you to go . . . and I don't want you . . . to come back tomorrow."

I flinch back as if he's slapped me. "No . . ."

"Yes," he pants, squeezing his eyes shut. He coughs, and the sound is deeper and wetter than I've ever heard it before. It takes him several minutes to stop as I watch helplessly. When the spasms finally end, he lies there with his eyes closed, trying to get his breath back. I touch the straw from his cup to his cracked lips, and he takes a small sip, but only enough to wet his mouth. When he opens his eyes, they are wells of sorrow. "This is it, Tori. When it gets to the point . . . that I can't breathe . . . on my own . . . they won't do anything."

"No . . ." I'm full on panicking now, and I can't seem to get the words out to tell him that he can't just let go; he has to fight because I'm in love with him too. If he truly loves me, then there's a world of difference between choosing death and fighting for life and losing, and I need to make him see that. "Will—"

"I can't . . . let you see that. I can't let you . . . watch me die. I want you . . . to remember me . . . kissing you and smiling, not gasping for air. Not begging . . . for the end. Please don't let . . . the anguish in your eyes . . . be the last thing I see."

His desperation shatters what's left of my heart. Oh my God, he's really going to do it this time. He's really going to give in. I have to change his mind, but my brain feels like molasses, and I can't gather my scattered wits. I shake my head to try to clear it, and as I look up and meet his eyes, I'm overwhelmed by how much I love him. I *have to* tell him I'm in love with him! "Will, I—"

"Tori, please." Fresh tears roll down his cheeks as he looks at me. "Do this last thing for me. Don't make . . . me beg."

I stare at him in horror. How can I go against his wishes at a time like this? Telling him I love him will just make it worse for him; I know it will. That's why he doesn't want to let me speak. I make some sort of gasping, choking sound, and I can't move. I'm drowning. *I'm* the one who's dying. I'm stuck, and I can't seem to make time move forward again. And I don't want it to. Because when it does, I'm going to have to do as he asks and leave this room, and I swear the world will end. When he dies, I'll die too.

"Kiss me," he whispers, and I move forward because these are words I can understand and something that I'm aching for. I want desperately to kiss him on the lips, but I can't bring myself to cause us both that extra ounce of misery, so I lean in to kiss his forehead.

As I'm just about there, he lifts his chin and pulls my face toward him with both hands, his fever-warm lips brushing mine with painful gentleness. I close my eyes, and we remain frozen there until I think I'm going to break from the joy and pain of it.

He drops his hands, and I open my eyes, but his are still closed.

"Had to . . . just once more," he murmurs. He rests his head back on his pillow, eyes still closed, and I know he can't bear to look at me. I won't get to see those beautiful green eyes again, and it's enough to make me sob.

"Please . . . go," he whispers, and as I watch his chin quiver, I know he's barely holding himself together, but he's not going to back down.

I slowly back toward the door, my eyes drinking in every detail of him. This can't be happening. This just *can't* be happening!

I stumble out of the room and fall to my knees in the hallway. I can't move. I can't breathe. I am a mass of uncontainable anguish.

And suddenly, I'm home. I don't know how I got here because I didn't think my feet were ever going to carry me anywhere again, but somehow, I'm sitting on my couch with my head between my knees. I still can't take it in. *Did that really happen?* Did I go see Will, and did he tell me he was going to let himself die, and I couldn't be with him?

I was having enough trouble trying to accept that he was going to die before my very eyes, but this? Oh *Jesus*, this? To deny me the chance to hold and comfort him, to face it all alone? He did this to try to save both of us pain—there's no way he could know this would hurt me more than anything!

There's no way he could know because I never told him. Jesus Christ, I never told him *anything*! I never let him in, never told him that the only thing worse than me watching him die would be me *not* watching him and knowing he died alone!

Oh God, he's all alone! He's lying in that hospital room all alone, gasping for breath with no one to hold him. No one to run their fingers through his hair and cuddle up with him. No touch to comfort him. At all.

I'm up off the couch and grabbing my keys, and make it as far as the front door before I stop. He asked me—no, he *begged* me—to do this one last thing for him. He begged me not to let my pain be the last thing he sees. How can I go against his final wish? It's bad enough, what I'm suffering and what I'm going to suffer when he's gone. I can't destroy the little bit of peace he thinks he has because in his mind, it *is* better this way, but that's only because he doesn't know the truth. He doesn't know he's done the worst thing to me that anyone could ever do.

I sink to the floor where I am, and the pain is so intense, I swipe my hand out in front of me, trying to push it away. I can't breathe. My chest is so tight I start to hyperventilate, and the tips of my fingers begin to tingle. I know what's happening, but I can't stop it, so I curl in a ball as the panic tears through me. I gasp for breath, and the thought that this is just what Will's doing drives me further into panic. I lose touch with reality for a while until my heart rate slowly starts to come back down, and I can pull in enough air to stop my head from spinning.

And then I cry. I lie on the floor weeping until I swear I have no tears left.

But it's a lie. There will be more tears as soon as I can recover enough to cry them.

I lose track of time, and the cycle repeats itself. I go to the door a dozen times—twice I even make it out to the car, but recalling the look on Will's face and the raw pain and pleading in his eyes drive me back inside every time. But I'm slowly wearing down.

I'm on the floor in the hallway outside my bedroom. I don't know how I got here. I'm a sweaty mess, and I'm panting, but I'm suddenly aware of myself again.

I can't do this. I can't live with him dying all alone, and I can't live with him dying without knowing I love him. I've tried to respect his wishes —I've *tried*, but when it comes down to it, he'll be gone, and I'll be left to live the rest of my life with the guilt and regret he doesn't even know will exist. He'd *never* do this to me if he understood, so I have to make him understand. I have to tell him why I can't let him die alone just as I should have done long ago.

He never would have made this choice if he knew *my* secrets, but there was never a good time to tell him—never a moment when he wasn't already bearing too much pain and sorrow. He would never hurt me on purpose if he could avoid it, and this is destroying me. And I think it will be better for him to know he's loved, that he's made such a differ-ence in my life. When it comes right down to it, I think he'll need my comfort even if he doesn't know it yet. I *have to* make him understand.

Once I finally make my decision, a fraction of the weight falls away from my shoulders. It's six a.m. I want to jump in the car and fly to the hospital right now, but I'm a mess, so I stumble to the shower.

As I'm stepping out, I hear my phone ringing, and my heart lodges in my throat. *Oh God, please let him still be alive . . .* "Jenny!"

"Will asked me to call you. He wants you to come see him."

I let out the breath I've been holding as relief washes over me. *Thank God he's come to his senses!*

"I was actually getting ready to come see him."

"Tori, I think you should hurry. He's going to go into respiratory arrest soon, and he still has his DNR. I don't know how much longer he's going to last."

"O-okay, I'll be r-right there," I stammer. I throw some clothes on and bolt out the door, my hair still dripping.

I make it to the hospital in record time, and I'm dashing toward the first floor elevators.

"Code blue, code blue, room four-twelve. Code blue, code blue, room four-twelve."

Everything stops. My breathing, the world turning, the sun rising. It all stands still, and the next thing I know Jenny is holding on to me. But I'm fighting her—I have to get to Will. He can't die! It can't end like this, not without his knowing how much I love him! *No!*

"Tori!" Jenny yells as she shakes me—hard!

I focus on her, and her voice cuts through my haze of panic.

"They're helping him, Tori! Will lifted his DNR. He's letting them help him to breathe."

I sag against her as her words sink in. Will isn't going to die today. He's fighting to live.

CHAPTER 32

"What happened, Jenny? Tell me *everything*."

We're sitting in the waiting area down the hall from Will's room. After Jenny finally got through to me that they were helping Will, I went into a bit of a daze, and she brought me here to compose myself. I'm gripping the bottle of water she's given me, but I feel . . . lighter. Despite the fact that Will's very sick, I feel hope.

"Well, I switched shifts yesterday because I was afraid this was going to get bad for him, and I wanted to be with him in case you didn't stay. He was up all night because he was having an extremely hard time breathing. I asked him where you were, and he told me what he did. We talked about it through the night, and I tried to convince him this wasn't the right choice, until he got so mad at me that he told me to leave."

Jenny glances downward, looking extremely guilty. "I . . . I told him you were in love with him."

I draw in a sharp breath. "Jenny!" Anger flares in my chest, and she must see it on my face because she raises her hands in self-defense.

"Please, don't be mad! I was running out of time, and I needed him to see exactly what he had to fight for. I think, in his heart, he already knew anyway—he just needed someone to say it out loud."

"Wh-what did he say when you told him?"

"Well, he looked surprised—I don't know if that was because you love him or because I was the one telling him. That was when he got so mad, and he asked me to leave."

Making an effort to calm my breathing, I stop for a moment and think about it. If her telling him helped convince him to lift his DNR . . .

"It's okay, Jenny. I think you're right, and he did know; he was just afraid to hear me say it. After he asked me to leave last night, he wouldn't let me say anything to him, and I think it's because he knew I was going to tell him I loved him. I wanted him to hear it from me, but if it helped him decide to fight, then I'm glad you did it."

Jenny breathes out heavily. "I was so worried you were going to be angry. I just couldn't stand there and watch him choose to die without knowing how you feel about him."

"I couldn't either. That's why I was on my way to the hospital when you called me this morning."

Jenny puts her hand on my shoulder and squeezes.

"What happened next?"

"Well, I left him alone for a little while, but before too long, he called me to his room and asked me to call you to ask you to come, so I did. I went back to tell him you were on your way, but at that point, I could tell he didn't have very long. I told him you were coming, but I didn't know if he'd still be breathing when you got here, and that's when he lifted his DNR. I don't think he realized he was that close to death if he didn't let us intervene.

"As soon as Will said the words, I called Dr. Evans to come and intubate him. I waited with him for you and for Evans to get there, and"—she pulls Will's black sketchbook from the table beside her—"he asked me to give you this. He could barely speak at that point, but he also asked me to tell you he loves you."

I take the sketchbook from her and hug it to my chest, bowing my head as I hold on to a piece of Will's soul. Jenny smiles tearfully at me.

"It was a good thing I called Evans when I did because about ten minutes later, Will's lung collapsed. He went into respiratory arrest, but Evans was right there to help him immediately. Right now, they're inserting a chest tube to drain the air and fluid around his lungs, which will allow the collapsed one to re-inflate. They're also planning to drain his abdomen again. It should help, but he still has the pneumonia to contend with. He shouldn't have waited this long to let us help him."

I loosen my grip on the sketchbook, and Jenny moves to get up, but I still her with a hand on her arm.

"Stay. Please?" *I don't want to be alone right now.*

"Of course," she says, sitting back down and putting her hand on mine.

Setting Will's sketchbook on my knees, I steel myself, then flip open the cover. I pull in a long, slow breath as I stare at the picture before me. Will has captured me in charcoal. The image is a perfect likeness, my head cocked slightly to the side, staring off into the distance. It's stunning. When I can breathe again, I begin to leaf through the book, and I'm confronted by image after image of . . . me. My hands, my eyes, my lips—Will's artist's eye captured every detail of me as I talked to him, and he etched them onto every page with painstaking precision and accuracy. And with love. Love pours from every drawing I discover, and I can just see him in my mind's eye, sketching as he waited for me to come every afternoon.

As I get toward the end of the book, I come across an image of me that's wistful and sensual. I'm looking to the left, my hair down over my shoulder, wearing a tank top, but the details of my arms and shoulders are unfinished. It occurs to me that he's never really seen my shoulders bare, so he must be waiting until he does to finish the sketch.

The last picture in the book freezes my heart and soul. This one is of both of us, our foreheads pressed together, eyes closed, our lips mere inches apart as we move toward an inevitable kiss. The image is so vibrant that I find myself staring at it, waiting for the image of myself to move in and capture his lips. It's the most beautiful thing I've ever seen.

Oh my God, he really is in love with me.

A sob tears from my chest, and I put my fist over my heart as a biting, bitter ache consumes it. I love him so much I can barely contain it, and the proof he feels the same is almost more than I can bear.

"Oh God, Jenny," I whisper, and she pulls my head down onto her shoulder as my tears fall. I didn't think I had any tears left.

I shouldn't do what I'm about to do, but I have to know. Will has decided to fight for his life, and I have to know if there's any hope it can be more than just a battle he can't win.

"Jenny, is there any hope for him? If he recovers from the pneumonia, does he have *any* options at all for treatment?"

She bites her lip and closes her eyes.

"Fuck." She swears, but then she squares her shoulders and looks me right in the eyes. "He made me promise, and I could lose my job over this, but dammit, I'll take that over having his death and your broken heart on my conscience. Yes, he has options, Tori. He's had options all along and one in particular that could even be a cure."

"Oh my God," I mutter, reaching out to the chair arm for support as a tiny spark of hope flares in my chest. Maybe I don't have to help him to die; maybe I can help him to live. "Jenny, what is it?"

"He can have another round of chemotherapy followed by a stem cell transplant. The regular chemo alone obviously isn't working for him since the cancer came back twice, but the combination of high-dose chemo with a stem cell transplant has a half-decent rate of success."

"You mean, he was not only choosing not to fight, but he was *choosing* to die?"

"I guess, in the strictest sense, yes. But he's already relapsed twice, and chemo is no picnic. I thought since he didn't have family and friends to support him, he decided he just couldn't do it again. He didn't have a reason to do it again. But now . . .

"I think that's why he lifted his DNR. He loves you, and he's decided to fight—maybe even to go into treatment again. Because he wants to be with you."

Oh, Will.

"When, Jenny? When did he make you promise not to tell me he had treatment options?"

"It was on a Sunday—that first week you visited him, I think. He was still worried you were there to figure out if he was crazy, but he somehow knew you hadn't seen his chart. I'm guessing you told him you hadn't seen it? He told me explicitly that he didn't want you to know anything about his prognosis, and he threatened to report me if I told you."

"Goddammit! All this time I was with him, and he was still going to choose to die!" I yell, my anger overwhelming every other emotion.

"But he didn't," Jenny says softly. "He fell in love with you and decided he needed to fight, and I think he's going to choose to try to live, too."

"B-but—" I stammer, my head spinning.

"Tori, you have to understand. Will has already been through chemo twice. It's horrible. And he did it without a lot of support the second time, from what it sounds like. And after all that, he relapsed a third time. He didn't feel he had any reason to keep on trying. Until he met you.

"Jesus Christ, do you know how hard it's been for me to keep my mouth shut about this?" Jenny asks, gripping her hair tightly. "Why I wanted you to take him as a patient? Why I begged you to tell him you loved him? All this time, I've been trying to get him to see that now he has something to fight for—something *worth* fighting for. I swear to God, the two of you were enough to make me want to pull my hair out!"

"Oh, Jenny," I say, as it all suddenly clicks into place. She's been working to get us together all along, working to convince Will to take one more shot at living. Holy *shit*.

"That's why he's been mad at me all week. I was pushing him to ask you what things would have been like if you'd met and he hadn't been sick, so he'd know he had a reason to try again. He knew you cared about him, but he couldn't see it had changed you as much as it had him. He's been wrestling with his decision for a while now, but once he found out he was getting sick again, his struggle kicked into overdrive.

"He's scared, Tori. He's so terrified to try again and fail and to take Jason, his mother, and now you through it with him. He agonized over it last night, but in the end, his love for you won."

I'm . . . stunned. Christ, I had no idea all this was going on! I knew something was off, and Will seemed to be struggling with something, but I had no clue that it was whether or not to try to live! I cover my eyes with my hand as I feel the tears start again, and Jenny pulls me into her arms.

"Tori, you need to be there for him and help him fight this. When he recovers from the pneumonia, I'm sure you can talk it out. But he needs you right now. If you're feeling angry—or betrayed—remember that he loves you, and in the end, he chose you."

"I'm not angry with him. I just wish I could have known what he was going through so I could have comforted him. Oh, Jenny, thank you!" I exclaim, throwing my arms around her. "Thank you for trying so hard to save him!"

Jenny shrugs her shoulders, grinning. "I liked him from the very beginning, which is why I got you involved, but then, when you both started falling for each other . . . I knew it was meant to be. Some things are, you know, so I'm sure this is going to work out."

We just hold on to each other for a few minutes. I truly do have the very best friend in the world. "I owe you—a lot," I whisper, and she just squeezes me tighter.

"You don't owe me anything, and there's still a long way to go. First, he has to survive the pneumonia before we can get to trying to cure him."

She's right, of course, but all I can feel right now is hope. He chose me. He's choosing life, and he chose *me*. Somehow, the feeling of betrayal was washed away as Jenny painted the picture of Will's suffering this week, and it was replaced by so many others: pity, pride, sympathy, understanding, and most of all, love. Choosing to not give in, for me, is the single greatest gift Will could give me, and it's more than most people have to give or ever could give.

We have a long, hard road ahead—a road I didn't even know existed. Will took the first steps alone last night, but he won't be alone anymore —now that I know everything he was fighting against, we'll take the rest of the steps together.

ACKNOWLEDGMENTS

There are so many people to thank for helping me get to this moment, I don't even know where to start! I suppose that means I should just start at the beginning. Thank you, Mom and Dad, for instilling in me the belief that I can do anything I set my mind to and for supporting all of my choices. (It's not sci fi, Dad, but maybe someday!)

To my wonderful husband, Jared, for his support, input, incredible artistic talent, and for putting up with me through two fandoms and several mountains of angst while I searched for my place as a writer and my courage to take this step. I'm so happy you're by my side, whatever tomorrow brings.

To Noah and Tori, for their unwavering conviction (Of *course*, you're a writer, Mom!) and acceptance of this second life of mine.

Not unlike a child, it also takes a village to raise a novel, and *Come Back Tomorrow* is no exception. I wrote the first words of this story as fanfiction in January of 2014. I worked on it for a year before I could muster up the courage to put any of it online despite the fact that it wasn't my first story. This one was important, and I'd put so much of myself into it that it truly did feel like raising a child—and still does. (This is why I chose to release this book on my son's due date—he chose not to be born then, but I figured something in my life should be!) So many people have had a hand in getting this novel and me to this point—I hope you know, whether mentioned by name or not, how important you are and how grateful I am to have you in my life.

Thank you to Domie, Shell, Shelli, and Bethany—you were the first ones to read my words and encourage me to believe they were worthwhile.

Belynda, you have always been there, and I know that you will always be there if I need you. Thank you for all those moments you believed in me when I didn't believe in myself. I know I wouldn't be here without you.

Beth, you have always encouraged and inspired me. It was you who convinced me that I needed to share this story with the world when I did, and the ride since then has truly been amazing. Thank you for your example of how to successfully publish, but more importantly, your example of how to always find the silver lining and be grateful for it.

Sally, my words still shine with your polish after all these years, and I can see your fingerprints in so many places. Thank you for your support, your encouragement, and your efforts in trying to teach this hopeless case how to properly use commas. (I still haven't learned—ask Sue!)

Sue, I can't tell you how much I've enjoyed our partnership. You've helped me raise my work to a whole new level and taught me how to write more clearly and with more emotion. You've made editing a joy, and our "back and forth" never fails to teach me new and important things. Your support and encouragement mean more than I can say, and the fact that you offered to take me on when I know who else you work with boosted my confidence in ways I can't even begin to explain. I hope our partnership lives long and prospers.

Savage, thank you for sharing your knowledge and wisdom so freely and for reminding a panicked, first-time author to take a deep breath, rinse, and repeat. Your success and your generosity are an inspiration—I hope someday I can move the hearts of my readers the way you do.

To the Jennifers, you both support me in such similar ways, it's amazing that you don't even know each other! Thank you for your unwavering support and your willingness to read and give an opinion on whatever I send you. It's so comforting to know you're always there when I need you.

Jada, thank you for the fantastic cover design and for patiently accommodating a newbie who asked for so many little "revisions."

Thank you to everyone who read, reviewed, and discussed this story in its first incarnation, both in my group and elsewhere on the web. And to those who shared their own stories with me along the way—I hold your loved ones in my heart. I wish more than anything that I could give them a happily ever after.

And to you, dear reader, thank you for taking this journey with me. I hope my words have and will continue to live up to your expectations and your hopes.

ABOUT THE AUTHOR

Amy Argent is the author of the *Embrace Tomorrow* Duet: *Come Back Tomorrow* and its sequel, *Whatever Tomorrow Brings*. Amy can honestly say she writes day and night—clinical trial documents as a medical writer by day and contemporary romance as a novelist by night . . . and possibly into the wee hours of the morning. She has a PhD in Genetics that she agonized entirely too much over, but it did  result in a fascinating day job—the details of which tend to creep into her fiction.

Amy can be found in Raleigh, North Carolina, with her husband, two teenagers, and two hedgehogs, where she's most likely planning her next departure from reality—destination: Dragon Con, the closest Renaissance Faire, or the nearest book.

COMING OCTOBER 2021
FROM TURNING TREE PRESS

**WHATEVER
TOMORROW BRINGS**
Book 2 of the Embrace Tomorrow Duet

AVAILABLE FOR PRE-ORDER NOW!
(Through your favorite eBook retailer or get a signed paperback
through amyargent.com

Can't wait? Read on for the Prologue of Whatever Tomorrow Brings!

Prologue

"Will you stay? At least for a few minutes? You're the first visitor I've had."

Intense green eyes, so warm and yet distant. So alone and vulnerable, yet so resilient and strong.

"Can I come back tomorrow?"

So many days spent with him, gaining his trust by giving him my own. Telling him my stories. Holding his hand through pain and fear. Falling in love with him a day at a time. A smile at a time.

"I'm scared, Tori. Jesus, I'm fucking terrified. This is really going to happen, and I don't have any control . . . I don't know how to deal with this. I feel like I'm falling apart, and there's nothing left to hold on to."

"Hold on to me, sweetheart."

Depression and then resolve. To make peace with the demons from a past full of heartache.

"It's okay, Mom. I'm all right. I'm so glad you could come."

Hope and then disaster.

"Do you have pneumonia?"

"Bacterial . . . I forget . . . the exact name. Evans asked me . . . if I want them . . . to give me drugs . . . to make me comfortable.

"I told him yes. Too much pain. I couldn't . . . no more."

And then . . . oh God, and then . . .

"Tori . . . I love you. There was nothing for me . . . but now . . . there's so much I want to do . . . so much I want to give to you."

"Tori, I want you to go . . . and I don't want you . . . to come back tomorrow."

And I left.

"Code blue, code blue, room four-twelve. Code blue, code blue, room four-twelve."

And he nearly left this world before I could get back to him. Before he could see the truth of what was between us.

"They're helping him, Tori! Will lifted his DNR. He's letting them help him to breathe."

And now he's fighting for his life against pneumonia. But that's just a consequence of the bigger monster—the cancer that has destroyed his immune system and continues to ruthlessly try to take his life.

"Jenny, is there any hope for him? If he recovers from the pneumonia, does he have any options at all for treatment?"

"Yes, he has options, Tori. He's had options all along, and one in particular that could even be a cure.

He can have another round of chemotherapy followed by a stem cell transplant. The regular chemo alone obviously isn't working for him, since the cancer came back twice, but the combination of high-dose chemo with a stem cell transplant has a half-decent rate of success."

He didn't tell me he had options. I was too afraid of his reaction to tell him I loved him. We're quite the pair, aren't we? But now he knows I love him, and now I know the decision he'd been struggling with since he came down with pneumonia. Hell, probably since long before that.

"I think that's why he lifted his DNR. He loves you, and he's decided to fight —maybe even to go into treatment again. Because he wants to be with you."

"Tori, you need to be there for him and help him fight this. When he recovers from the pneumonia, I'm sure you can talk it out. But he needs you right now. If you're feeling angry—or betrayed—remember that he loves you, and in the end, he chose you."

He chose me.

Will chose me, and he's fighting for me. He's fighting for *us*. And I'm going to help him fight, with everything I have.

Manufactured by Amazon.ca
Bolton, ON